UNVEILED

A NOVEL

UNCOVERING THE VEIL OF THE FACADE

CELSI-LEIGH

First paperback edition May 2021

Written by Celsi-Leigh Garrick
Edited by Celsi-Leigh Garrick and Johanna Petronella Leigh
Cover design by César Pardo
Interior design and layout by Susan Gerber

ISBN 978-0-578-92101-3 (paperback)

Published By:
Celsi-Leigh Publishing
authoresscelsileigh@gmail.com

To everyone that ever felt that their life was not enough, the work of this novel is to show that there is no such thing as a perfect life. Everyone has their own story, life journey, and unique life experiences. Walk in your truth and show the world who you are, it's never crowded in your lane.

To the only person that I ever had in my corner, you carried me into this world and you held my hand through every step of the way. The tough love paid off, thank you for never giving up on me. Thank you for being a mother and a father. Thank you for working so hard to create a better life. Thank you, mom! ~ C.S.G

To the person who saw me for me when no one else did and pushed me to be better, thank you for being you! We cannot possess people, thank you for being a part of my life experience. Thank you! ~ R.R.J.

PART I

CHAPTER ONE

*"A Little Dialogue about Some Real Sh*t . . ."*

PRESENT DAY—2020

"Which breakfast option would you like to go with, Mrs. Malika? We have cereal, waffles, eggs, sausages, fruit, and a list of other options already prepared this morning, ma'am," Harrold, my personal server offered.

I stared onward, lost in deep thought.

"Ma'am?" Harrold questioned, observing my distance.

"Cereal, I want cereal," I answered, looking up at him.

Harrold nodded and made his exit out of the dining area.

"Your estate is lovely. I have never had anyone read me the options for breakfast at their home. Now to get started, I am not sure where you would like to begin but I am ready! The fans are dying to know what the novel is all about. You started with nothing; does this really tell us all the truth about how you came this far? You have a breakfast menu inside of your home. Malika, it is safe to say that you have come a long way. We need all of the juicy details," Celsi Leigh, the journalist, complemented.

She wants to know how I ended up with a breakfast menu inside of my home, huh. Shit, I want to know too, breakfast used to be the worst part of my day, I thought before a traumatizing memory came back to me.

MARCH 1988
BRONX, NEW YORK

"Hmmmmm!" I croaked, rolling over in the bed.

The bright sunlight coming through the small window right above my bed always did the trick at waking me up. I did not need an alarm clock because my body knew the routine. I looked up at the clock that sat on the wall. It was six-thirty-two in the morning. I had approximately sixty minutes to get up, get dressed, and get to school. I could not be late because that would result in a call home, and that call home would result in a beating. It was only Wednesday, and I had already received seven beatings this week for a variety of reasons. It was safe to say that I could not afford any more ass whoopings.

The cold wooden floor felt like ice blocks hitting my feet as I stepped down from the mattress. A mattress and a baseboard that was it—no box spring or fancy bedroom set. Slowly, I stood, tiptoeing towards the room door. My father, Trevor Tanners, was somewhere in the house passed out from yesterday's alcohol binge. I had to move silently, in an effort to not wake him. Waking him would cause yet another ass whooping.

Hurriedly, I exited the small room and made my way to the bathroom. I pulled the string hanging next to the light bulb to turn the light on. The bright pink tiles that lined the bathroom walls mixed with the bright light created a blinding concoction. There was an imaginary timer inside of my head, I had thirty minutes to wash, get dressed, and fix my hair. There would only be about ten minutes to grab breakfast and my school was only a few blocks away so the remainder of the time should do. I had to move quickly.

The rusty faucet squealed as I turned the water on. There was only one temperature, cold, so there was no need to wait for the water to warm up. The water heater was currently not working because, in true Trevor Tanners fashion, he spent the gas money on rum at the bar. Brown water ejected from the shower as I stood waiting for the color to change. Per routine, it took a few seconds for the water to become clear.

Standing, waiting for the water to change colors, a small tingle brought my attention downwards. The feeling of roaches crawling on my skin was all too familiar to me. I rolled my eyes upwards, shaking my head in disgust.

"Eww!" I grunted under my breath, shaking my leg to get the roach off of my foot.

This house was crawling with roaches, I could never seem to escape them. I looked back up just in time to see that the water was now clear. Quickly, I got out of my night clothes and rushed into the shower. My teeth shattered uncontrollably as the cold water came crashing down onto my light brown skin. I allowed the icy water to run down my face, the cold water always woke me all the way up. I grabbed my toothbrush from the ledge, removed the foil wrap and began brushing my teeth inside of the shower. This was my routine; I did not feel clean unless I did everything inside of the shower. Next, it was time to wash my body. In an attempt to warm myself, I hopped around, bouncing from leg to leg, lathering my washcloth. There was only a small amount of the dry soap bar left so I was careful not to overdo it. Five minutes later and I was finished. I hopped out and grabbed my towel that was previously placed inside of the sink.

After exiting the shower, I dried myself and hurried back to my room. My school clothes sat folded on the disheveled dresser. Quickly, I moisturized and applied deodorant before throwing my clothes on. I pulled my hair into two ponytails before rushing down the stairs and into the kitchen.

Zzzzzzzz! Trevor's loud snores echoed throughout the dark living room.

Trevor laid sprawled out, fully clothed down to the shoe, hanging off of the dingy brown couch. His mouth hung open, spit draining out the side onto the couch cushion. The pungent stench of rum and sweat created a nasty odor that clung to the inside of my nostrils. I held my breath, tiptoeing past him towards the small kitchen. Thankfully, Trevor was in a deep drunken slumber so there was no chance of me waking him.

Secretly, as I entered the kitchen, I hoped that Trevor did not leave the cereal box open on accident. He was known for coming in drunk and making a mess in the kitchen, often wasting the little food that we did have. The cereal was not out sitting on the counter so that was a good sign that Trevor did not eat it all. I stood in front of the brown cabinet that had no cabinet door, jumping to reach the box of Sugar Flakes. Lucky for me, Trevor did not leave the cereal box open. Cereal was the only thing we had left at the moment and if that box was opened then it would be crawling with roaches.

I placed the box on the counter before heading to the fridge. Milk, I needed milk. I opened the fridge to find that there was nothing there, a droplet of milk sat in the carton. There was not even enough left to wet my cereal. I looked up at the clock that sat on the wall. I still had about five minutes before I had to walk to school. I grabbed the cereal bag from inside of the box and stuffed it into my book bag. I also grabbed a plastic spoon and a cup.

My father's sister lived in the home next door. She always left her door open; it was rather early so with any luck I could sneak inside and get some milk before walking to school. Quickly and quietly, I exited the kitchen and crept out of the house.

I walked up the steps of the neighboring row home. As I approached, I prayed that the door would be unlocked. Slowly, I turned the knob and the door opened. Yes! I thought, creeping inside. I looked around the living room to find that no one was there. I unzipped my bookbag and pulled the small cup from inside. Get in, pour some milk inside the cup, and get out. That was the plan. I hurried to the kitchen, rushing before I woke anyone. I knew that I was not allowed inside of her home but on necessary occasions, I crept inside.

My eyes bulged when I saw Deena, my father's sister, sitting around the dining table inside of the kitchen. A cup of hot tea sat before her. Shit! I'm busted, I thought. No lights were on inside of the home, so I assumed that everyone was still asleep.

Deena looked up at me, turning her nose up before she spoke.

"What the fuck you doing in my house? Didn't I tell you not to come here?" she questioned, scrunching her eyes at me.

"Yes, I, I, I . . ." I began before she cut me off.

"What the fuck are you slow? Speak!" she barked.

"I needed some milk; we didn't have anything to eat before I went to school," I confessed, sorrow reflecting in my eyes.

She was silent, never taking her eyes off of me as she brought the teacup to her lips. She sipped her tea before placing the cup back onto the table. Slowly, she stood from her seat and walked over to the fridge. She removed a small carton of milk from the refrigerator before walking over to me. Standing in front of me, she opened the box of milk. I held out my cup, waiting for her to pour the milk inside. What she did instead, I would have never seen coming.

Looking me directly in my eyes, Deena brought the milk carton to her lips and spit a glob of saliva directly into it. She then closed the carton and shook it up before placing it back inside of the fridge.

"Tell your black ass, drunk ass daddy to buy you some fucking milk. Don't bring your ass back here! Get the fuck out!" she barked.

Bolting, I dropped the cup and rushed to the door. Fuck food! I did not need anything to eat!

PRESENT DAY—2020

"Ma'am?" Harrold asked.

Harrold's voice snapped me out of my thoughts and back to reality. I looked up at him just in time to catch the concern written all over his face.

"I'm so sorry, Harrold, were you speaking to me? I did not hear anything you said," I stated, coming back to reality and out of my trance.

I looked up at Harrold, confusion sprawled all over my face.

"Oh, no worries. I was just asking 'Would you like me to pour the milk over your cereal?'" he asked once again.

"Oh yes, please. Thank you," I replied.

Harrold poured the milk over the Frosted Flakes that sat in the Versace bowl before me. In true Malika fashion, I did everything elite; fine China and designer household items were my forte.

"Now, I will be recording. So, you can feel free to simply talk and I will work my magic in bringing this article to life! Tell us, Malika, what can we expect in this novel?" Celsi questioned.

I nodded my head in understanding, chuckling slightly.

"Get ready, this is one hell of a story. I want them to know the good, bad, and the ugly. I'm done with secrets, I'm done pretending. The fans can expect raw and unfiltered honesty, all that glitters is never gold," I announced before bringing the darkness to light.

Let's have a conversation, a little dialogue about some real shit. Everybody's out there pretending, faking it until they make it, let's take a moment to get candid because what is real anymore? Have you ever wondered who you were? Who your spirit was? What's your purpose, or do we even have a purpose? Who you would be without a bunch of lost motherfuckers running around following trends instead of being original? Who would you be in a world that is not tainted by systematic racism, classism, and limitations that history has placed on the Kings and Queens that are within us? I wonder who I would be. That is the place that I am at right now, trying to find myself. In times where authenticity no longer exists, people are desperate for the lifestyle, selling their souls for attention, instant gratification is at an all-time high, self-respect is at an all-time low, love is conditional, and people will do anything to appear as if they live a luxury life . . . can you say that you really know yourself?

We are going to spend one fucking moment being honest with ourselves. Repress your societal obligations of what it means to be popular or family obligations of upholding how you were raised. The obligations that influence how we think, act, or how we think we should act to fit in or be accepted.

After all of that is taken away, who are you? Don't know? Neither do I. Not many are honest about who they are, most are too busy trying to keep up with who they aren't. Half of the world is too busy keeping up with a bullshit façade to compete with everyone else. How many people can really be their true fucking selves without fear or judgment of other people's opinions? Truth is, most of us are lost, trying to find ourselves and our own path in a very complex world.

On the outside looking in, it would appear as though I have it all. I have become really good at pretending, appearing! Pretending to have it figured out as I search to find my way. A beautiful successful woman, the IT girl, that's me! Yeah right, maybe having it all is the illusion that I want everyone to see. The image that I fight to maintain because millions of people are watching me and not for one minute can I get a fucking break. I keep up appearances because I have to; the public doesn't view me as a regular person going through regular shit that everyone goes through. People think that they know my life because I'm in the public eye. People think that I don't go through regular shit, but I do because I am human. Tuh! I make it look good but it ain't all good! The façade of my life is wrapped in expensive vacations, illustrious shopping sprees, high-profile events, and my rich husband that I have been with for the last ten years. The key word is facade.

The truth is right before everyone, but they never seem to notice the emptiness that lingers in the soul of my eyes. The bruises that lie underneath my flawless makeup. Would they believe me if I say that I am not okay? I wonder if they could see past who I have become and find that young girl that scammed and robbed people to pay my way through college? The same young girl that lost so many healthy babies that I lost count or the girl with no family that had to lie and steal to make a way. Would they ever think that I was the same woman that stayed with a woman beating, cheating, having a baby by another bitch while beating healthy babies out of me . . . bitch ass husband? Would they see the ghosts of the people that I murdered haunting me? Tuh! Yea right, everyone sees what they want to see. I have millions of comments on my posts of people telling me how I should live my life but what would all of these people do in my situation? Does anyone actually take a minute to look, to pay attention, to read body language or energy? My guess is no—actually, I am stamping it as no. I do not think that we would have so many people walking around pretending that they are okay, battling mental illnesses and doing so much despicable shit to keep up with society. I guess that is why everyone acts as if they are shocked when shit hits the fan, huh? Truth is, everyone is fucking selfish and lost; they see what they want to see for their own benefit. A bunch of lost motherfuckers following other lost motherfuckers; the blind leading the blind. Attention has become the new drug and as a society, we are overdosing.

My bad, where are my manners? I have not even taken the time to formally introduce myself, yet here I am telling you my problems, got you all up in my shit. You know I can't give it to y'all dry like that! Let me run it back, we have to start over at the very beginning. Welcome to my crazy life story. Now, be prepared to cry, laugh, scream, yell, text your partner and tell them you love them or hate them because this is a lot. Whew!

The memories! I guess I should start with my name and all that get to know me first shit, huh?

Malika, Malika Sasha Samuels, that is my name. I would start here, but to get to know me we have to start at the very beginning of my life. This crazy, interesting life that I would not trade for the world because it is my story. The story about Malika Tanners, Lil LiLi, LiLi, Lika, or Sash if I really fuck with you.

CHAPTER TWO

"I'm Original, It's Only One LiLi . . ."

APRIL 25, 1988
KINGSTON (STANDPIPE), JAMAICA

While people were lining up to see *Coming to America*, N.W.A's *Straight Outta Compton* was hitting the charts, and Hurricane Gilbert was ravaging the small island of Jamaic, my life was just beginning.

Aunt Dedra often said to me, "I told your mother not to have a baby by the fucking devil himself and yet she had you."

In some sick twisted way, it would appear that I am the spawn of Satan, also known as Trevor Tanners.

My mother, Mallory Hines, died moments after I was born like so many other black women. I was raised in a single father household with my father who wished that I had died alongside my mother. Mallory was gorgeous and strong-willed. She had to be strong-willed, in order to put up with my father. Trevor was such a fucked-up individual that it was inevitable that he would fuck my life up or traumatize me in some way. Mallory suffered from high blood pressure and word on the street was that Trevor's heavy hand contributed to her untimely death.

I was the curse that killed my own fucking mother. A murderer.

Trevor often called me "a murdering evil bitch that should have died instead."

Shit, he was not the only one who called me that. There were a few of my mother's family members who also felt that way.

"One likkle evil pickney!" They would say in Patois, the traditional Jamaican dialect.

I received all of this for being alive, all for breathing. I hadn't asked for any of this, yet they treated me like I had control over it all. I never understood why, I never asked to be brought into this world. I guess that is why I blamed myself on so many occasions when I was being physically abused by an alcoholic son of a bitch. I reasoned that I deserved to be abused because of the murderer that I was.

My life in Jamaica was short-lived as I was only raised there for a short period of time; until I was four years old to be exact. Trevor Tanners and I moved to the Bronx, New York City in 1992. Growing up with Trevor was traumatizing; the type of shit that leaves you with post-traumatic stress disorder and all types of daddy issues that result in years of needed therapy. The problems that members in the black community like to pretend do not exist but currently are ruining so much of our youth. I can show you better than I can tell you.

JUNE 19, 2001
THE BRONX, NEW YORK CITY

"Lika, come here!" Trevor yelled, slurring his words through his heavy Jamaican accent.

"Yes, Dad," I responded, exhaling as I hopped down from my twin bed.

At the young age of thirteen years old I had the attitude of a teenager and the responsible mindset of a young woman that was in her twenties. I did not have the luxury of having a childhood, my life circumstances required me to grow up quickly.

I sashayed down the stairs and into the kitchen to see what Trevor could possibly want from me because he always wanted something. Trevor seemed to think that I was much more of a maid to him and his whores than his daughter. The high ponytail that I wore complimented my round face, large beautiful green doe eyes, caramel complexion, full lips, perfectly arched eyebrows, dimples, and long eyelashes.

Trevor sat before the round wooden table, in a dining room chair that was covered in plastic with green upholstery. The kitchen was painted forest green with brown wooden cabinets and green marble granite counter tops. I hated everything about this home, especially the kitchen that I spent way too much time in.

Trevor sat looking how he usually did, drunk out of his mind. A blue dad cap sat lopsided atop his bald head. His oversized white wife beater was dingy with brown food stains and a large hole, accompanied by ill-fitted baggy light denim jeans. A roach sat, relaxing, on his shoulder.

My green eyes rolled to the ceiling in disgust. I shook my head as I walked into the kitchen; I was instantly repulsed every time that I saw Trevor's face. He was a slim dark-skinned man with a salt and pepper untamed beard and bad acne, the kind that left craters in his face. Thank God for Mallory's beauty because Trevor was a hideous man, at least he was nowadays. Old photos told me that he was once quite attractive. Years of not taking care of himself had finally caught up to Trevor.

Trevor sat slumped in the chair, trying to formulate his slurred words. A bottle of clear Jamaican rum sat rested on the table, in between his tight grip.

"Yuh nuh, see wah time it is?" he questioned, slurring his words.

In true Trevor fashion, everything was a question where the magical answer would somehow result in an ass whooping for me.

Of course, he had his rum for breakfast, I thought, walking past him and over to the fridge. It was now time for breakfast and instead of Trevor, the father, making me, the daughter, something to eat, it was my responsibility to feed him. Since nine years old I had been making my own meals and his too. There were rare occasions when Trevor was sober enough to act like a parent. Sometimes, one of his concubines that were desperate for a man would come around and cook but those days never lasted too long because soon enough they realized they were not that fucking desperate after all, they'd rather be single.

"Likkle murdering bitch, yuh nuh hear me a chat to yuh!" Trevor barked, spit flying from his mouth as he pointed his finger at me.

Trevor stumbled to get out of his seat, falling back into it as soon as he lifted himself from the chair.

Here we go, I thought, emerging from the white refrigerator with four eggs and six sausages.

"Aye, bring your ass over here! Look so much like your fucking mother why she neva tek yuh wid her!" Trevor continued; his cruel words were routine.

I had heard the words so many times that they no longer hurt my feelings. My childhood was a prison sentence, and I was counting down the days until I could be free.

Suddenly, as I was placing the eggs and sausages on the counter, like lightning Trevor flew from his seat. He snuck up on me from behind, grabbed me by the neck and lifted me in the air directly in front of the countertop, choking me with his right hand.

Crack! The egg that I had in my hand hit the ground as my little fingers clawed at his hands.

"I should kill you! You disrespectful likkle light-skinned

bitch!" Trevor threatened, spit particles raining down onto my face.

Gasping for air, I clawed at his hands, mentally begging him to release me. My eyes bulged in my head. *Nine . . . Ten . . . Eleven . . . Twelve,* I thought, counting down the seconds that I had been choked in my head. Trevor choking me was not new to me, I knew that I had about fifteen seconds before I passed out. Panicking, I dug my nails into his flesh. I prayed that Trevor would release me and that today would not be the unlucky day that this sick fuck killed me.

Unexpectedly, he released me before rushing out of the kitchen, causing my body to come crashing down onto the white tile. With both of my hands, I grabbed my neck and breathed frantically. Air rushed to my lungs as I tried to breathe. My frail young body laid on the cold tile, shivering as I came to. Tears flowed from my eyes so heavily that I was unable to see beyond the flood puddles that were forming. I was so young and innocent, yet my life was burdened with so much trauma. As I attempted to gather myself from the floor Trevor stalked back into the kitchen, staggering and stumbling.

"Aye! Get up and mek mi food before mi kill yuh bloodclaat in here!" Trevor commanded, barreling over top of me.

Somehow, I found the strength to pick myself up off the floor. I wiped the heavy tears from my eyes. I was tired of my life. Actually, tired was an understatement. I was exasperated, exhausted, fatigued, weary, drained, burned out, all of the above for one thousand Alex! I was everything that a thirteen-year-old girl should not be.

Trevor sat back down in his seat while I stood at the counter, staring down at the eggs and sausages. *I wish I would have died with my mom,* I thought.

Dazed, Trevor stirred me out of my thoughts with a smack so hard that I could have physically flown backwards in time. I grabbed the side of my cheek with my hand as a burning sensation ragged through my cheek. Welcome to my life living with Trevor—for no reason at all, nothing to provoke him, he found pleasure in getting drunk and emotionally and physically abusing his only daughter.

Suddenly, I grabbed the knife from the counter and acted before I could think twice.

"Ahhhhhhhhhh!" Trevor cried as I plunged the knife into the side of his neck.

I shoved the knife as deep as it would go before using all my strength to turn it so that it would go deeper. I bolted, running out of the kitchen in an attempt to get out of his reach as quickly as possible. I ran through the kitchen doors and upstairs.

"Aye Gyal! Come here! Ahhhhhhhhhh!" Trevor shrieked from the kitchen floor.

Looking down at my blood-covered hands, my face contorted in horror as I rushed into the bathroom to wash the blood off of them. The seconds felt like minutes as I scrubbed Trevor's blood off of my trembling hands. I was not sure of what my next move was, but I knew that I had to be out of the house as fast as possible, either he would come and find me or if I was lucky, I killed him. Either way, I had to get out of the house as quickly as possible!

Hurriedly, I ran to my room, grabbed a large suitcase from the closet and threw all the items that I could fit into the luggage. I did not have that much stuff, but I made sure to leave nothing behind. The only items that I cared about were the things I had left from my mom: a gold necklace with a heart-shaped pendant and the only picture that I had of her. I ran into my father's room and rushed to the closet. I looked through all of the shoeboxes on the floor until I found his stash of money that he had buried in a shoebox buried inside of the closet. I was responsible for cleaning the entire house, so I knew the exact location of where most things were hidden. I opened the shoebox that was originally for his black Air Force Ones.

Shockingly, there was more money inside of the box than I anticipated. I always assumed that alcoholic Trevor was running low on funds but all I saw was fifty-dollar and one-hundred-dollar bills wrapped in knots.

Drunk ass always crying broke, pretending like he doesn't have any money, I thought, shaking my head.

I grabbed all of the money from inside of the box and threw it into the book bag that I used for school before rushing out of the room, down the stairs, and out of the house. I had no intention of ever returning to that house or seeing Trevor again. I did not want to know nor cared to know if he was dead or alive.

I hope he is dead; he deserves to die. I hope he's dead; I hope I killed him. The thought buzzed around in my head like a bee.

I wanted him dead . . . and could anyone blame me? To think that a thirteen-year-old young girl had withstood more beatings, bruises, and emotional abuse than anyone should in an entire lifetime. I had enough and it was either his life or mine. I planned on taking this secret with me to my grave. They say that death is the beginning; whether Trevor was dead or not he was dead to me. That day was the rebirth of my new life, even if I had no idea where I would end up, anything had to be better than life with Trevor. I would be better off, anything had to be better than experiencing the hell I went through in this home.

Trevor did not die from his stab wound. He was very much alive and very much still a drunk. I never went back to that house, but a few days later social services came looking for me at school. Trevor elected to not inform the authorities about how he got his injuries but did inform them that he no longer wanted any parental rights. Thankfully, Trevor was too ashamed to announce publicly what really happened to him, but the entire neighborhood knew the truth. The authorities suspected that I was the person responsible for Trevor's injuries but without hard evidence or a statement from Trevor there was no proof. My teachers, who had suspected that I was being abused for years informed the social services of my suspected abuse. I was placed in a foster home close to where my father's house was. I was able to stay in the same school and stay close to the neighborhood that I knew.

I was placed with a foster family that did not give a fuck about me or any of the other four children that were at the house. I hated everything about that foster home and all of the raggedy kids that were there. I fought damn near every day because they were jealous and clicked up. I kept to myself, barely speaking and only when I needed to. The other girls could not stand that I had no interest in being friends with them. The items that were valuable to me, I kept at school in my locker. I did the best I could to make the money I took from my father's closet stretch but, in a few months, it started to run out. I began stealing any and everything that I could. I stole clothes, food, toiletries, hair products—everything you could think of I stole it. I became one of the best boosters around my way. Everyone knew if you needed something come and find me. The local hustlers and bad bitches would pay me to steal. I got their designer pieces for the free and sold it back to them for the low. Shit, I even got my pieces for the free. I kept myself up so well that if you did not know me you would never know I was a foster child in the system living in a dirty project apartment with too many occupants. I spent the next year and a half of my life in survival mode, doing any and everything to get myself through.

AUGUST 2002

THE BRONX, NEW YORK CITY

The crisp morning air awakened me as I dragged myself down the block to the bus stop at the corner of Two-Eighteen and White Plains Road. It was a Saturday morning and the energy of outside matched the mood that I was in, grey and foggy with no sun in sight. It was the end of the summer and it was humid and foggy outside. Each step that I took felt heavy like I was walking with weights wrapped around my ankles. As I hauled myself down the street, a year 2002 black Mercedes S500 blasting "Jigga My Nigga" by Jay-Z cruised down the block.

A light brown-skinned guy wearing an oversized black Moschino tee shirt, freshly done corn row braids, gold diamond chains, and a diamond earring rolled down his tinted windows and flashed his smile at me.

"The best way to describe me in a word, insane, I dick down chicks all emerged in my fame, Jigga been dope since Slick Rick's first chain."

The words to Jay-Z's song blasted through the speakers of the Mercedes-Benz. I looked over at the car and rolled my eyes, today was not the day. I was not in the mood to entertain any bullshit. At fourteen, I had the body of a girl that was in her late teens. My shape was immaculate, the perfect coke bottle figure. My breasts bloomed early, causing them to sit up just right and perky; not too big and not too small either. The angelic face that I was graced with is not even worth being mentioned; I was gorgeous and there was nothing else to it. I had it whether I wanted it or not, with a body and a face like the one I was blessed with it was only right that I would grow up to become a problem.

"You want to tell me your name or you're gonna make me get out the car?" The guy asked, flashing his smile.

I rolled my eyes at him and continued walking down the street. I was not in the mood for company.

"Alright, I see how we got to play this," he stated before abruptly stopping the car and hopping out.

His baggy dark denim Rocawear jeans sagged as he walked over to me. He stood directly in front of me, blocking my path.

"Excuse you," I said, attempting to sidestep him.

Swiftly, he stepped to the other side, blocking my path once more.

“You can’t take a hint! Mo . . .” I began but my attention was diverted when I saw the bus pulling to the corner.

Fuck! I thought. That was the earliest bus this morning and I needed to be on it to make it to midtown before noon. I had been paid up front to get a few items for a few hustlers from around my way. Annoyed, I diverted my irritation to the man before me.

“See, fucking with you I missed my bus!” I scoffed, rolling my eyes and folding my arms over my chest.

“No ma, fucking with me you don’t take the bus. It’s going to take more than a hint to get rid of me, I don’t hear no too often, I usually get what I want. Where you got to go, I’ll take you?” he offered, looking down at me.

Hmmmm, I don’t take the bus, huh, I thought, scrunching my eyes at him. I had been so not in the mood that I did not even take the time out to look at the man in front of me. He was kind of fine if I do say so myself, ok, fuck it, who was I kidding. He was fine as fuck, not kind of anything, and extremely tall. I was only five feet, so anyone was taller than I was, he stood looking down at me at about six foot four inches.

“Midtown,” I replied, dryly.

My attitude still remained but was slowly dying down.

“You look at me when you talking to me but come on. I’ll take you,” he asserted, pinching my chin between his thumb and pointer finger, turning my head so I could face him.

His brown eyes were intense, captivating even like they were attempting to stare into my soul. I was always so caught up in my shitty home life that I never really took the time to pay attention to boys, matter of fact, who was I kidding, I did not have time to think about boys. This guy in front of me, however, was a man, nothing like the little boys that I saw at school or around the neighborhood.

“I’ll give you one last time to rethink this, you might be

missing out on a once-in-a-lifetime opportunity," he said, staring down at me.

I was silent for a minute as I pondered the opportunity. In all honesty, I would never make it to midtown in time on public transportation.

The handsome stranger did not say anything. After a few moments, he began shaking his head right before turning to walk back to his car.

Rashan Hawkins, known to the streets as Shan or Skinny was a youngster from Brooklyn who was heavy in the streets. He was only seventeen, but he had been in the streets hustling since the age of thirteen and had come a long way. He made a name for himself at first as the wild one, the loose cannon; the one who shot first and asked questions later. He garnered a lot of respect in the streets; he was a hustler and a damn good one at that. Not to mention that he surrounded himself with some solid old heads that helped him to learn the game. He was used to getting his way with any young girl or even some older women that he set his sights on, but I was different.

"Wait!" I said as he opened his car door.

He looked up at me, attempting to hide the smirk spreading across his face.

"Come on then, Ma," he said in a sultry voice with a thick New York accent.

The smile on his face said *I knew she would get with it.*

"Don't Ma me. I'm not one of your groupies," I said, rolling my eyes while walking over to the car.

He walked over and opened the passenger door for me to get in.

"You got a lot of mouth to somebody that's just trying to help your mean ass," he challenged while shutting the car door.

"Well, you don't have to try to help me do a damn thing since I'm so fucking mean," I shot, looking out of the window.

I was not the nicest, friendliest, or very social; I usually kept to myself.

"You know being mad at the world ain't going to fix whatever you're going through, right? You got a nasty attitude on you," he stated as we drove down White Plains Road.

"Never said it would," I responded dryly.

"What's your name, shorty?" he questioned.

"Lika, you?"

"Shan."

"How old are you? And where are we going, midtown is the other way?" I questioned.

"Seventeen baby and looking at you, you a little young. You look like you might be trouble for a nigga. How young is young?" he asked.

I turned my head from the window and looked over at him before answering the question.

"Seventeen and you rolling like this? Mhmm," I responded as I turned the knob on his stereo, turning the music down.

"Yea, age ain't shit. I've been out here on my own for a while. You still ain't answer what I asked you," he stated, taking his eyes off the road to look over at me.

"Fourteen, but age ain't shit, huh," I answered, smiling slightly.

"Oh, you a baby, well you can be my baby if you act right," he said smoothly.

"Whatever! You kick that line to every girl you pick up?" I scoffed.

"I barely know your name, much less you. Why're you worried about what I say to other girls? Worry about yourself," he said with a light chuckle.

"Well, I'm original, it's only one LiLi so anything you say to me make sure it's original," I replied with an attitude and a roll of the neck.

"Well, excuse me then Lil LiLi, I'm an original nigga so you don't have to worry about that," he shot back.

I scoffed and folded my arms as I stared at him intensely.

"Where are we even going?" I asked, eyeing him.

"I figured Lil LiLi could use something to eat before we get to midtown. You got a little time to kill now that we driving," he informed, leaning back and gripping the steering wheel with one hand.

Who is he? How did he know just when to show up? I thought, eyeing him suspiciously.

CHAPTER THREE

"And the Award Goes Too . . ."

JUNE 16, 2003

NEW YORK, CITY

"You bowlegged as shit, you know that?" Rashan asked as I exited the bathroom after taking a shower.

Rashan stood in front of the kitchen counter, changing the CD in his CD player. I fastened the towel that I had wrapped around my body and looked down at my feet. My feet were turned inward, facing each other. I was indeed "bowlegged as shit."

I had been staying at Rashan's apartment in Brooklyn for the past few months. Occasionally, I went to my foster home, but my foster parents did not give a fuck about my whereabouts. As long as they still received their monthly check for having me in their care, they could care less where I was or what I was doing.

"Yea, yea. I know," I replied, chuckling.

"You can fix it if you want, I fixed mine. All you have to do is turn your feet the other way as you walk," he coached.

"I don't know how to do that," I protested.

"Let me show you," he stated before coming off of the counter.

He stalked over to me, standing in front of me to coach me.

"Like this," he instructed, demonstrating how he wanted me to turn my feet.

I looked down, following along to his instructions. This was the dynamic of our relationship, he led, and I followed. In true Rashan fashion, he had the answers to everything. He was a fixer, always thinking of ways to improve and make things better. He consistently had great advice, taking from his previous life experiences to help others.

Rashan and I had been inseparable since the day that the two of us met. It started out as a friendship, something innocent, with us getting to know each other. He looked out for me, genuinely trying to help me because he saw something special in me. Our relationship was not really sexual, I was young, and he was older than I was, so we chose to take it slow, extremely slow.

Rashan was a hustler, but he also dipped and dappled into a few other activities. He was known throughout the boroughs as a stick-up kid that robbed major players throughout the city. Rashan was a lone soldier, he had one friend that he hung with, Tay. Tay had been Rashan's best friend since they were kids. Rashan did not believe in hanging in groups. He was independent and believed that a group could do nothing but, potentially, bring you down. Accomplices were potential witnesses in a criminal investigation. Rashan was grimy to other niggas in the streets. He was unable to trust people. He knew what he was capable of, so he believed that others were capable of the same things. He was unable to trust himself; how could he trust another? Somehow, I was able to break past Rashan's barrier of distrust. The connection that we shared was effortless.

Rashan and I were so much alike that it was sometimes hard to believe that we did not know each other our entire lives. We understood each other. Rashan was from Brooklyn, he never knew either of his birth parents. His mother was a drug addict battling a crack addiction that no one could help her shake. The last he heard from or saw of his mother was when he was twelve. He never knew his father; he wasn't even sure if his mother knew who his father was or might be. He was raised by his no-good aunt Kiesha that only took him in so that she could receive extra money from the state. Kiesha was too busy with a different man every other day of the week to take care of Rashan, so he raised himself. He filled the voids that he felt from not receiving love at home with his hustle. He started out as a lookout for a local drug dealer. Rashan's life changed the day that he robbed the drug dealer he worked for at gunpoint and then beat the shit out of him inside of the dealers' stash houses.

Our relationship came to fruition over time. In the beginning, he wasn't sure if he wanted anything deeper than a friendship. We fell hard and fast for each other despite our hesitation. It was that young love that you could not get enough of. Love so potent like Whitney Houston and Bobby Brown. We had no parents to offer us direction. We both loved each other more than we could fully comprehend. We were each other's family, truly all that each other had since the day that we met.

JUNE 19, 2003

"Did you figure out what you tryna wear for my birthday, Sash?" Rashan asked as we drove down Eighth Ave.

Rashan's birthday was quickly approaching, June twenty-eighth to be exact.

"I was thinking maybe some fly shit! I saw this Gucci purse, and this Moschino dress. I'll be the hottest young chick out!" I replied, hyped up.

I sat up in my seat and turned to him, enthusiastically.

"Here you go talking that fly shit." He chuckled, turning his head to look at me.

"Well, you not the only one out here that's tryna be on some shit. Besides, if I'm going to be next to you, I have to look the part." I winked before turning my head to look out the window.

"You already look the part, Lil Li," he assured, pulling in front of Polo Grounds projects on Eighth Ave and One-Fifty-Fifth.

Rashan spotted the person he was looking for, Tay, his close friend, standing in front of the building talking to a few known hustlers.

"Let me go talk to my man for a minute, lock up," Rashan instructed, opening the car door.

I nodded in understanding as Rashan exited the car.

"Aight so boom, let me get this straight he's not going to be in the spot? That ain't how we usually do this," I reasoned trying to understand the plan in its entirety.

We always stuck to the same routine every time we committed a robbery. The routine was simple; we waited in a location before the target arrived then we went in. Entering while the person was not in the location was throwing everything off and brought more attention to me than I needed. I could not understand why we were switching shit up so close to the execution. Everything felt rushed.

Rashan protested against my involvement in his criminal activities. He encouraged me to go to school, he did not want me in the street life that he was in. Rashan understood the risks and dangers of the game and he did not want me to fall victim to the dangers of the life he was in, he saw so much more for me. I, however, was persistent. I was already boosting and selling to locals. I wanted to earn my own money. I did not want to feel as if I ever needed him or anyone. I never had anyone genuinely care about me and want to help me. I had a wall up. I threatened to run off and do my own thing if he did not cut me in, so he did. He figured he was better off with me on his team, and if I was going to force my way into the game anyways, at least he could protect me. My role in his affairs never really sat well with him, it went against everything that he believed in, but he understood my way of thinking and wanted me to do it right if I was going to do it at all. I went to school every day then came home, got my work done, and somehow still was able to find time to be an accomplice to Rashan's crimes. He learned fast how mature I was for my age in some ways and together we made the perfect team. I helped him to distract his victims during the robberies and occasionally, I committed the robberies with him.

"Sash, we've been over this. He's a paranoid nigga, follow the directions man! Not to mention, if he doesn't take the bait like we anticipate you'll need to say something to him. That will never work if he thinks it's a set up. This is all just a part of the plan; it'll make all this shit go smoother," Rashan replied, using his hands as he spoke for extra emphasis.

"I get that, but I don't feel good about switching this plan up. I'm telling you this doesn't feel right to me. Y'all niggas buggin and if some shit go down, I'm the one that's gotta be in that nigga face," I confessed.

I just could not get with it, the idea felt too rushed, and I did not like random changes. *How are we changing shit up but rushing to get this done?* I thought.

"How many times are you going to say the same shit? You with the shit or not? You wanted to do this shit, I'm more than happy putting one of them hungry bitches on. I don't even want you in this, but you insist so what you want to do?" Rashan questioned, irritation dancing on his lips.

"Whatever. I'm doing this shit. You stay tryna cut me out.

Pull up near the spot before he gets here," I sashed, rolling my eyes and folding my arms over my chest in true Malika fashion.

Rashan never listened to me, he called the shots and what he said was law. He was smart but he was arrogant. I feared at times that arrogance would be our downfall.

"Love you too," Rashan stated, pulling the car in front of Sunny's.

"Yea, love you more," I replied, hopping out of Rashan's Mercedes.

The walk from the car to Sunny's was only a few steps down the block but each step felt heavy. I sucked up my nerves and walked in to give an Oscar-winning performance. Walking towards Sunny's *and the award goes to*, replayed over and over in my head.

Butterflies filled my stomach, and a wave of nausea came over me as I walked through the door. I always got a nervous feeling right before a job. It was show time at the Apollo, and I was center stage with all of the lights pointed at me or so I felt. It was as if all eyes were on me and everyone could see that I was acting. I felt like exactly what I was, too damn grown and too damn young to be living this life. I was only fifteen years old. I could think of a list of shit that fifteen-year-old girls should have been doing yet aiding, and abetting armed burglaries were not on that list but there I was. I sashayed into Sunny's, attempting to keep my composure. I looked young and innocent, like Boots' perverted ass liked them.

Just chill, you got this! I thought, approaching a stool three seats away from the seat that Boots always sat in. For a man that was so heavy in the streets, his moves were way too predictable. I sat idly in the stool, awaiting Boots' arrival. It was ten-nineteen in the morning. Boots would be entering Sunny's any minute, he always arrived between ten and ten-twenty and ten-thirty, but always by ten-thirty. I picked up a menu and began scrolling to see what I would order. I needed to look and act natural, like a real customer.

"Can I get you anything?" the waitress asked, approaching me from behind the counter.

"Yes. Can I have orange juice and you can come back later. I'm not sure what I want yet," I stated.

Ding! The bell attached to the door rang, echoing throughout the small diner.

"Ok. I'll be back," the waitress replied, walking over to the stool that was frequented by Boots.

Boots was a short and stocky dark-skinned man. He was kind of handsome and surprisingly enough, not the type to be flashy. As much money as he was holding, I expected to see diamond chains, necklaces, and designer clothing, but he was a simple man. He strolled in, wearing a grey FUBU sweatsuit with white Nike Air Force One sneakers.

"I just put your food in Boots, should be ready for you any minute. I'll bring your tea right out," the waitress greeted, as Boots sat down in the stool.

"You keep a G together, Shonda," Boots replied.

I tried desperately not to look over at Boots, but I could see him staring at me through the corner of my eyes. This entire play felt so wrong that I did not know what to do. I reached into my purse and pulled out a clear gloss. All else fails, apply some lip gloss . . . *Just chill!* I thought, attempting to keep my poker face.

"Whatever she got, put it on my tab," I heard a deep baritone voice say to the approaching waitress.

I diverted my attention from the lip gloss that I was twiddling in my hands to look around the room, hoping that it was Boots that offered to pay for my meal. Boots was smiling at me, his gold tooth glistening. He stood from his stool and walked over to where I was sitting. The plan worked like clockwork just as Rashan said that it would. Boots' fetish for young girls was something serious.

Got him! I thought, excitedly.

I sat up in my stool, ready.

"Byron," Boots introduced, extending his hand for me to shake it.

"Tanya," I replied, shaking his hand.

I used a different alias for every job. In the event that I ever ran into any of these licks again or if our victims began conversing with each other, I provided a fake name as an extra precaution. I was Tanya on that day. Tanya sounded like a good girl. A girl that I can say is in school and has goals or something. A good girl with parents and shit. Tanya did not sound like Malika, the girl that was currently setting up a man to rob him blind.

Boots took my hand, bringing it to his chapped lips and placing a soft kiss on my knuckle.

"So, Tanya, can I get to know you?" Boots asked.

Ok! If I am being honest, Boots was corny as hell. The old man game was killing me, but I chuckled and pretended like I was with it.

"It's nice to meet you, Boots, what about you like to know about me?" I flirted, still trying to remain modest.

Impatiently, the waitress stood in front of me with her hand on her hip, tapping her foot on the floor as she waited for me to order the rest of my food. I sensed a tad bit of jealousy that was not present before. It was most likely because I was speaking to Boots.

"Come on, baby I have other customers to take care of," she sassed.

"She'll order when she's ready. Oh, and wrap my shit up, I got to run," Boots scolded, his eyes never leaving me.

The thick Dominican woman put her hands up in surrender before turning to walk away.

“Ok, papi.” The waitress flirted.

“Wait! No, I’ll have shrimp and grits. I have to go; I don’t have time to be here too long.” I ordered before the waitress walked away.

The waitress did not respond, she only nodded her head as she made her way to the back. I was not sure what the two of them had going on, but she was upset. I had Boots’ attention so there was no point in pretending that I did not know what I wanted to eat.

“Listen, I have to run but if you give me your number, you got a cell phone, can I call you? Matter of fact, how about you let me take you out tonight, Ma?” he said before dipping into his pocket and retrieving a large wad of cash.

He peeled off ten hundred-dollar bills.

“Get yourself something nice to wear tonight,” he stated, placing the money on the counter before me.

“Oh no, I can’t accept that,” I protested, pretending to be modest.

I would take that and every other dollar that he had to his name if the opportunity presented itself.

“Listen, that ain’t nothing, it’s yours, baby-girl. Now what’s up with that number gorgeous?” he asked.

Hearing the word baby-girl come from his lips made my skin crawl. I could feel the pedophilia drip from his tongue as his perverted ass said it. I cannot lie Boots was holding and I knew messing with him I would have been able to get a few dollars out of him, but he was too old. Boots was thirty-eight and I was fifteen, he was a bit too much for me at this age.

I took a napkin and wrote down the number to the phone that Rashan and I bought, specifically, for this mission. Tay and Rashan had provided me with the details of how Boots pulled the young girls. He was a trick, nothing more, nothing less. He lured them in with money and the promise of giving them the world. He was simple in appearance; he was not a flashy man, but he knew how to spend a little more to get what he wanted, when he wanted it. I handed Boots the napkin with the number to my cell phone and flashed a smile in his direction.

"I usually don't do this, but you're persistent," I stated, lying.

"Yea, I'll see you at 8:30 tonight," he said while licking his chapped lips before turning away and walking out the door.

His sick ass was genuinely excited thinking that he had a chance at pleasure with an under-aged young girl. Unlucky for Boots, he was about to get fucked and not in the way that brought him pleasure.

8:50 P.M.
MIDTOWN, NEW YORK CITY

Boots outdid himself with planning our outing, everything was perfect. The high-end five-star restaurant Tony's Steakhouse was beautiful, and the ambiance was amazing. The fanciest restaurant that I had ever been to was the buffet near Co-op City. This was grown man taste.

Boot and I had only been inside of the restaurant for a short period of time, but I had to find a way to alert Rashan that he could enter the house. The plan was simple, at the beginning of dinner I would let Rashan know we were here, and he would hit me back once they made it in and out of the house.

"Excuse me, I have to use the bathroom," I informed Boots before standing and exiting my seat.

As I got up to walk downstairs to the restroom, Boots looked me up and down, taking in my beauty. I looked amazing, if I do say so myself, fifteen where? In the Dolce and Gabbana black bodycon, much too high heels, and flawless makeup I could have easily passed for twenty. We had gone the extra step of having Trina, Tay's sister, give me a makeover for the evening. I needed to not only act the part but to look the part.

Once I was out of Boots' view, I damn near ran to the

bathroom. I checked all of the stalls to make sure that no one else was using the restroom. I had to be certain that I was alone before making the phone call. The stakes were high and one wrong move could cost me everything.

My fingers moved at the speed of lightning over the keypad as I typed the numbers to Rashan's phone. I was in such a panic that I had to say the numbers out loud to make sure that I was dialing the correct digits.

"Five. Five. Five. Zero. One. Three. One," I murmured, typing on the keypad. The phone only rang twice but those two seconds felt like two minutes.

"Yo," Rashan answered, calmly.

"I ordered for both of us," I said before hanging up.

There it was that was the signal. Now all I had to do was wait for his signal that they pulled it off . . .

9:55 P.M.
MIDTOWN, NEW YORK CITY

I sat at the dinner table across from Boots waiting to hear from Rashan. I was sweating bullets. Literally, I could feel the droplets of sweat underneath my dress and my body was extremely hot. Usually, I was not this nervous, but the stakes were higher than they had ever been. Boots was a heavy player in the streets and this score could change everything. Boots was known in the streets for being ruthless. I was playing with fire and I knew it. Boots was a cold-blooded murderer, and he would not hesitate to kill me if he suspected that I had anything to do with this robbery. The seconds felt like minutes and the minutes felt like hours as I anxiously awaited a call from Rashan.

"You ok? You're kind of quiet over there," Boots questioned.

His words jolted me from my thoughts and brought me back into reality. I looked up to find Boots eyeing me suspiciously as he cut hit steak.

"Yes, I'm kind of nervous, this is new to me," I said sheepishly, trying to form a smile.

My age came in handy after all, I played the role of the naïve teenager, using it to my advantage. I had to play it cool.

"Oh baby, no need to be nervous, get used to the life! You can have it all if you with me, I take care of what's mine," Boots said, licking his lips.

I shifted in my seat, uncomfortably. Nervously, I pushed my hair behind my ear.

Bzzzzz! The vibrating of the Nokia that sat in my lap caused me to look down. R displayed on the screen, causing me to breathe a huge sigh of relief. I stayed seated not wanting to be obvious, I needed to call and confirm that everything went as planned. Suddenly, I was much more social and wanted to converse. To pass the time, I began making small talk with Boots.

"How did you like the food?" Boots inquired.

I placed my fork down on the dinner table before responding.

"It was good, some of the best I ever had," I answered, honestly.

"Good, now you'll think of me anytime you come here. That's what it's like with me baby, everything is the best you ever had," Boots replied, smiling.

I could have thrown my food up. *Bitch please,* I thought, fake chuckling.

"Oh, really?" I replied.

"I'm serious, this shit is nothing to me," Boots boasted.

"Hmm, well, I do like how that sounds," I stated, blushing.

Boots was a simple mark, his reputation for young girls was true and accurate. I was surprised that his perversion did not lead to him falling victim to this plot prior to this day, he was a sucker for the under-aged and pretty. If I was older, he would have been a great trick. I am talking bags, shoes, cars, money, diamonds, anything that a girl could ever ask for. I had bigger and better things in mind, however. I did not want the small change, I already had someone to take care of me. I wanted more money than a man like Boots would be willing to provide and that was exactly what I was playing for.

I was ready to go, but due to the fact that I knew this was a setup, I did not want to pressure leaving right after the mission had been completed. I waited patiently until Boots decided that it was time to leave. I continued making small talk to help pass the time. Boots was not completely intolerable, but I was extremely uncomfortable. Everything about this entire endeavor felt off, like I did not belong there yet there I was.

Bzzzzzzz! Bzzzzzzzz! Bzzzzzz! The vibrations of a phone ringing from across the table captured my attention. Boots stared down at his flip phone before answering.

"Hold up for a minute," he said before getting up from the table and walking towards the front of the restaurant.

Sitting at the table idly, I decided to call Rashan to make sure that the burglary was successful. Quickly, I dialed Rashan, all the while keeping my eyes on the front of the restaurant in case Boots returned. Rashan answered on the first ring.

"How's dinner?" Rashan answered.

There it was that was the signal. I pressed the button to end the call. I smiled to myself, breathing a sigh of relief. Mission accomplished. Boots' sudden absence right after the invasion made me nervous. Something was not right. Maybe I was paranoid but, in my gut, something felt off.

CHAPTER FOUR

"Fake Love . . ."

JANUARY 14, 2004

Following the burglary, the entire city wanted to know who robbed Boots. Rashan's reputation in the streets as a stick-up only added to everyone's growing suspicion that he was behind it but there was no proof. Rashan, however, was smart and wanted the heat off of him. He laid low and got his money without being loud or flashy, never wanting too much attention. He purchased a luxury condo for the two of us in Jersey City and we stayed out the way. I enrolled in a private high school and I kept myself out of the streets. There was no longer a need to hit licks or steal from department stores, we were up. Rashan provided everything that I needed. He kept up with my grades and made sure that I continued my education. I had everything a city girl could want; Dior, Gucci, Moschino, Louis Vuitton, Chanel, Prada, Cartier—if it was designer, I had it. I was that bitch if I do say so myself and the streets knew it. The bitches hated me, young and old. To make matters worse, Rashan copped me a brand-new 2004 red BMW 328i, fully loaded. I was pushing that new thing and it was safe to say, I was under these bitch's skin.

We were young moving fast, too fast to see what was coming our way. After the lick we hit with Boots we had not done another robbery. Instead, Rashan and Tay started flooding the streets with products. The drugs that they found during the robbery allowed them to begin taking over sections in a few boroughs. They had a few projects on lock. Rashan's name was now mentioned with the players that were making real money in the city. He was the boss of their operation, but he maintained a low profile. Only making appearances when absolutely necessary.

Tay, on the other hand, was the total opposite of Rashan. He was flashy and cocky. Tay was caught up in the hype of the streets, indulging in women, jewelry, and flashy cars. The money fed Tay's ego. Rashan, in contrast, was trying to keep the cash flowing in without drawing any unwanted attention. The love was real, but the hate was even more real. Fake love was at an all-time high.

JANUARY 14, 2004—12:19 A.M.

The cold wall gave me chills as I leaned my bare body against it. I was only wearing an oversized tee shirt and the condo was chilly, despite the heater being on. I pushed a stray hair out of my face, the messy bun that sat atop of my head was wild and untamed.

"Mir, what are you still doing out here? Come to bed," I whined, pouting.

My fingers tugging at the ends of the oversized tee shirt that I wore as I gave Rashan my puppy dog eyes. I hated falling asleep without him next to me.

"Go to sleep Sash, I'm waiting on Tay to come through," he replied, taking his attention from the TV to look up at me.

"Tay?" I questioned, raising an eyebrow.

After the take, Rashan and Tay's relationship had taken a drastic turn for the worse. Rashan felt that Tay was moving recklessly. Tay, on the other hand, wanted love and attention, even if it was fake love. It was Tay's time to shine and Rashan was standing in his way. Rashan knew that the streets did not love anyone, so he was cautious. Tay despised Rashan's way of leading but Tay was not a leader. He was incapable of thinking logically. Tay felt that Rashan looked down at him. That Rashan thought he was better than him. Jealousy was the true beef. Tensions became high between two men that were once brothers. Both Rashan and Tay had their reservations about the other; despite this fact Rashan still loved Tay. Rashan felt that the love they once shared as brothers was mutual. Rashan neglected to realize the most important thing; money was the root of all evil.

"Yea, that nigga called me, so I told him I'd hear him out. I'm not trying to beef with my brother so hopefully, we can resolve this situation," Rashan informed me.

"Hmm, well, hopefully, this conversation helps. I'm going to sleep," I stated, sashaying back inside of the bedroom.

JANUARY 14, 2004—1:39 A.M.

It had been over an hour since I initially inquired about Rashan coming to bed yet there was still no sign of Tay. I was irritated because I knew I would not be able to sleep properly until he was in the bed with me. Frustrated, I tossed the oversized black comforter off of me. Slowly, I began climbing out of the bed.

Hopefully, I can convince him to come and lay down, I thought. Suddenly, as I prepared to make my way out of the bedroom, I was halted by a knock at the front door.

Knock! Knock! Knock! A light knock erupted from the front door.

Yes! Finally, that's got to be Tay! Nigga took forever! I thought, laying back down in the bed. As I closed my eyes and began to get comfortable, Tay's words jolted me out of bed.

“I’m sorry bro, I ain’t have no choice. It was you or me!” Tay’s voice boomed throughout the apartment.

It was you or me?! Did I just hear that shit correctly? Oh nah, what the fuck is going on?! I thought, panicking. Instantly, I jumped from the bed, rushing to the bedroom door. I placed my ear on the other end of the door. I needed to have some idea of what the fuck was happening before I opened it. Heavy footsteps paraded on the other side of the door. I was not sure what was happening, but it was not just Tay and Rashan, I could hear the men in the living room.

Fuck! Fuck! Fuck! Oh my god, Rashan! I thought, spinning around in circles. I did not know what to do. I was stuck but I needed to think and move fast. I needed to see what the fuck was happening. Slowly and quietly, I cracked the bedroom door and peeped through the crack, not wanting to alert the men of my presence in the room.

“You pussy ass niggas wanna take from me! On my muva you niggas dying tonight!” Boots barked, forcing his way into the condo.

Boom! The sound of the gun connecting with the side of Tay’s face echoed throughout the room.

Boots pistol-whipped Tay across the left side of his face. Blood rushed from both Tay’s mouth and the side of his head as he cried out in agony.

“Ahhhhhhhhhh!” Tay cried.

“Come on, man! I told you what you wanted to know, don’t do this shit man. That’s the nigga right there!” Tay pleaded like a bitch.

Rashan stood stuck on the other side of the room. He looked around in disbelief, like everything was happening in slow motion. I knew him well enough to know that he was processing, thinking, plotting his next move. The men were all so distracted with Tay that it gave Rashan the perfect opportunity. Quickly, he looked back at the bedroom and our eyes connected. He looked at me with sorrow-filled eyes. A look that said I love you so much. Then, it all happened so fast! His eyes went dark and cold.

Rashan reached into his waist, retrieving his pistol. Boots and the other men were distracted, so focused on Tay that they did not see Rashan coming.

Bang! Bang! The sound of gunshots reverberated throughout the condo.

Rashan sent hollow tips through the back of one of the gunmen's heads and through the side of Boots' shoulder. The gunman dropped to the ground instantly, dying on impact.

"Fuck!" Boots bellowed, clawing at his shoulder with his remaining good hand.

The other two gunmen with Boots followed up, sending bullet after bullet in Rashan's direction.

I jumped every time the henchman squeezed the trigger, holding my breath.

Bang! Bang! Bullets were sent flying throughout the condo.

Rashan kept firing as Boots' remaining soldier shot at him. Bullets were flying everywhere. In the midst of the madness, Tay attempted to get up from the floor.

Bang! Bang! Two shots from Rashan sent him crashing back down.

"Fuck you think you going!" Rashan barked, his ego now taking over.

Rashan knew that the chances of him making it out alive was slim to none but he was a shooter, and, in this moment, he did what he knew how to do, shoot. He would die shooting before he just allowed anyone to play with him.

Swiftly, Boots came back from the shoulder shot evading the other bullets that Rashan sent his way and began firing back, hitting Rashan in his chest.

Bang! Bang! Bang! Gunshots riddled Rashan's body.

"Shit! Fuck!" Rashan yelled.

Rashan never stopped shooting but he was outnumbered. The other two men were shooting at Rashan as well, but he was not letting up.

Bang! Bang! Bang! Bang! Bang! Bang! Bullet after bullet tore through Rashan's chest, six in total.

My hands flew to my mouth in an attempt to muffle my screams. The uncontrollable tears came on instinct, I did not know what to do. Suddenly, I had a life-altering thought!

Gun! Get the fucking gun! The thought went off in my head like an alarm. Hurriedly, I ran to retrieve a pistol from the nightstand. I grabbed the 9mm and flew to the door. All I could think of were the memories of Rashan showing me how to shoot if I ever needed to. With shaky hands, I opened the bedroom door and aimed at one of the shooter's heads. Rashan was a great teacher and all of the practicing with him paid off, with utter shock I hit my target.

Bang! Bang! The bullet struck one of the gunmen between his eyes and on the side of his head.

Instantly, his body dropped to the floor. Both Rashan and Boots looked over at me at the same time. Rashan's eyes locked and the pain that I saw in them brought me to my knees. I could see life leaving his body as he mouthed the words: *I love you now run.*

Watching him go lifeless, sucked the air out of me. Rage, that was all I could feel. I started shooting recklessly. Just aiming and shooting. Boots was injured and it was difficult for him to keep going but he tried, relentlessly.

"You little bitch! You dead, bitch!" Boots screamed at the top of his lungs, hobbling in my direction.

Bang! Bang! Bang! He continued, sending bullet after bullet my way.

One of the bullets that I shot struck Boots in the same shoulder that he previously got shot in. I had been hit too, running off of so much adrenaline that I did not feel the shot. I did not feel any physical pain, the emotional pain of what I had witnessed was all too much for me. I rushed into the bedroom, locking the door before hiding in the corner of the room.

The blood was coming from a wound to my calf, I had been grazed by one of the bullets.

Bang! Bang! Bang! Boots and the other remaining gunman fired bullet after bullet through the door.

They were not letting up. I was scared shitless but somehow fearless, watching Rashan die I knew that I had no one and nothing left. I was ready to die with him, I expected to. I sat stoically in the corner waiting for them to break the door or run out of ammunition. I counted the shots like Rashan taught me so that I would know if they ran out.

One, two, three, then the bullets stopped coming as the only remaining gunman began to kick the door in. I ran to the closet, locking myself inside. Sitting on the closet floor, I ejected the magazine from the gun to check the remaining number of bullets.

"Shit!" I cursed under my breath, seeing that there were no bullets left.

I then slid the hammer back to check inside of the chamber, there was only one bullet left. There were two skilled killers and only little ole me with one bullet. The odds were not in my favor.

Boom! The sound of the door crashing down as the gunman burst into the room.

I peeked through the corner of the door to see Boots following close behind, bleeding profusely. He was panting, moving slower than he was before. His injuries weighed him down. He would not be able to go on like this for much longer. The men proceeded to search the room, looking for me.

"Tanya, huh? Little ass girl, think she's slick! Bitch, you can't hide, come the fuck out," Boots yelled from outside the closet.

Boots' voice seemed to be getting louder and louder. Realizing that he was getting close to where I was, panic swept over, paralyzing me to the ground. Abruptly, Boots snatched the closet door open. A sinister smirk spread across his face as he barreled over top of me.

"Get up!" Boots barked, spit particles raining down on me.

Roughly, Boots reached down and yanked me up by my neck, before placing the barrel of the gun to the side of my head. He gripped me by my elbow and pulled me over to the bed, all the while still holding the gun to my head. I only had one bullet remaining so it would make no sense to waste it, it was two against one. Like he was reading my mind, Boots looked down and finally noticed the gun that I was holding.

"Grab that!" he instructed the soldier, referring to the 9mm in my hand.

"Step out. I need to teach this little bitch a lesson," Boots instructed; his eyes fixed on me.

The henchman did as he was instructed.

A lesson! I thought, my eyes popping out of my head. *What the fuck was that supposed to mean!* I thought, fearful.

"Lay down!" Boots snarled at me, throwing me onto the bed.

Petrified, I did not move. I sat there, staring up at him with tears streaming down my face shaking my head from side to side.

"Lay the fuck down!" Boots ordered, getting louder.

"No! No! No!" I whimpered, scooting away from him.

Slappppp! Boots smacked me so hard that my head spun to the other side.

He raised his gun to my forehead before continuing.

"Lay the fuck down! Don't make me repeat myself again! Fuck you don't understand English!" he instructed, holding the gun to my head.

Trembling, I did as I was instructed, and leaned back. Must, sweat, and blood infiltrated my nostrils as he climbed on top of me. I was repulsed. My stomach turned as the contents of the day's meals threatened to come back up. A nasty concoction of blood and sweat dripped from his body onto me.

Violently, he yanked at my panties, ripping them off of me. My body stiffened at his touch. I felt like bugs were crawling up my skin, I was disgusted. My insides turned as I pinned my eyes shut.

"Please, don't do this," I whispered.

Boots looked down at me, smiling devilishly.

"You want to play grown woman games, huh! Tanya, right! Well, take this grown dick, Tanya!" he snarled atop of me.

The cries that erupted from me came from the depths of my soul. I was crying so hard that I could not breathe. I wanted to run but how could I, there was nowhere to go, no way up. Boots yanked up my oversized tee shirt, exposing my breasts. Roughly, he moved his hands over my breasts, pinching my nipples. My breath caught in my throat as I began to picture happy times and good memories with Rashan. I wanted to die; anything was better than this hell. I had never been violated like this in my life.

Holding the gun to my chin, Boots began to fiddle with his sweatpants. I wanted to run, kick, scream, shit anything but the gun to my chin gave me pause. One wrong move and everything would be over, but was death better than this? *Is my life really worth going through this? Am I better off moving and letting him kill me?* Thoughts ran rampant throughout my mind as I contemplated my options.

Looking down at me with lust-filled eyes, Boots pulled his small four-inch erect penis from his pants and began stroking himself. I was not a virgin anymore nor was I innocent, but he robbed me of my innocence. He robbed me of my body.

"No! No! No!" I screamed as he entered me. Something in me changed right then, so many pieces of me died as he forced himself inside of me. I zoned out, mentally detaching myself.

I felt that I was in a different universe. Physically, I was there but the spirit inside of me was so far removed. I laid there, lifeless, as he panted on top of me. Every thrust inside of me was like a knife going into my chest. Uncontrollable tears escaped my closed eyes. I was mourning the loss of a childhood that I never got to have. The loss of something that I could not comprehend, I felt naked, exposed.

Suddenly, Tay's yelling brought me back to reality. Everyone was so concerned with me once I started shooting that they forgot all about Tay, shit I forgot about him.

"The fuck he in there doing to her?" Tay screamed.

"Sit the fuck down nigga! Before you next, getting fucked in your ass!" the gunman responded.

"I didn't agree to no fucking rape! This shit is over!" Tay yelled before the gun shots rang out.

Bang! Bang! Bang! Gunshots echoed throughout.

"What the fu . . . !" Boots began but was silenced by a bullet to the head.

"Ahhhhhhhhhh!" I screamed.

My screams mixed with the gunshots as Boots' dead bloody body croaked over on top of me, his penis still inside of me. Instantly, Tay rolled Boots off of me, he found me trembling and covered in blood beneath Boots. My naked body was exposed as I cried hysterically.

"Fuck! Towel, where is a towel, a shirt, something?!" Tay asked, searching frantically.

I was in no shape to talk so I pointed towards the bathroom. Tay was barely able to stand from the shots to his torso that Rashan sent his way earlier, but he was still moving. Tay hobbled to the bathroom and returned moments later with a towel.

"Clean yourself up, we have to go. The police are on the way!" he said, handing me the towel before hobbling out of the room.

I wrapped the towel around myself as he exited the room.

A wave of anger swept over me. Everything that I had been through tonight was karma for us robbing Boots, but most importantly it was because of Tay. He had to go, there was nothing else to it. Without a second thought, I grabbed the 9mm that the gunman sat on the edge of the bed. I walked into the living room to find Tay bent over Rashan's dead body, sobbing.

"I'm sorry, bro! I didn't have any other options. I'm sorry, man! Imma take care of Lika, I promise."

Slowly, I crept behind Tay and raised my gun to the back of Tay's head.

"Li . . ." he began.

Bang! I pulled the trigger, Tay's lifeless body flopped to the floor.

"Tell him when you get up there," I stated, calmly before sinking to the floor.

Life had left my body. I had nothing left. I could hear the sirens ringing off in the distance, but I was tired of running. I had been running since the day that I stabbed my father. Rashan's dead body beneath me brought uncontrollable sobs. I laid there. Crying, I clung to his bloody body until I passed out from fatigue and blood loss.

When the police arrived, I told them that Rashan was my cousin who I stayed with from time to time because the conditions at the foster home were unbearable. I told them that the men came in to rob him and they ended up raping me. The rape helped me evade criminal charges for killing Tay. I was only fifteen going on sixteen years old, still under-aged but I was eligible to be charged as an adult if they found that I was guilty. The police chalked it up to just another black-on-black crime. The prosecutors decided not to charge me, I evaded charges on self-defense due to my rape and the situation. I was removed from the old foster home and placed in a group home for a short period of time until they found another home. I could not understand why or how I made it out alive. Everyone was murdered except for me. I was raped, almost shot, and traumatized yet I made it.

I found a way to keep all of the things that Rashan bought for me. I still had my car that I managed to sneak around and keep. I kept my nice things in the trunk of my car. I still had the money that Rashan kept in a stashed location in the unfortunate event that anything ever happened to him. He knew that he was playing with fire and that ending up dead or in jail was a real-life possibility for the outcome of his life, so he stayed prepared as a precautionary measure. I had ninety thousand in cash along with thousands of dollars' worth of jewelry and high-end designer items. The money and valuables would prove to be enough to keep me going until I was able to solidify another income. I was not sure what I would do, I was done with the streets. I just had to make it through to my eighteenth birthday in foster care.

It turns out that Tay did not take heed to the warnings that Rashan provided. Rashan requested that Tay lay low. Instead, Tay did everything that he was told not to do. He flaunted and flashed his jewels and newfound success all over the city. It was not difficult for Boots to catch up to Tay and once he did, Tay sold Rashan out at the drop of a dime. Tay told Boots everything, including my role in it to assist in setting Boots up. Tay was a snake. There was no loyalty within him. As the saying goes; there is no honor amongst thieves. Unfortunately for Tay, he had sold out one of his only true friends to die anyway because there was no way that I was allowing him to walk out alive. Tay planned on double-crossing Rashan but failed to see the opportunity for a triple cross, also known as Malika.

CHAPTER FIVE

"Blood Could Not Have Made Us Any Closer . . ."

APRIL 25, 2006

The two years following Rashan's passing seemed to fly by. In the beginning, it was extremely difficult for me. I was raw and alone battling a loss and a traumatizing rape, unable to grieve because I did not know how to. They do not teach kids growing up in poverty about Post Traumatic Stress Disorder and depression. I did everything to escape my reality. I experienced every negative emotion that a person could experience. I was living in darkness, smoking blunt after blunt, sleeping all day, refusing to eat, running away from reality; until I had enough of myself. I became tired of wallowing in my self-pity.

I changed my outlook on the passing of Rashan and allowed the time I spent with him to serve as life lessons. Rashan was the first male to show me kindness without an ulterior motive. The connection that we shared was genuine and he wanted to make me a better person, a greater version of myself. A part of me died the day that he was murdered but that death was a rebirth for the woman I would become. He lit a fire inside of my soul to reach the potential that he saw in me even when I did not.

Rashan would say, “You aren’t like these people out here; they all see life inside of the box.”

He showed me that good men existed in the world. Men that had the ability to see more in you than you saw in yourself, uplifting, supporting, and pushing you to greatness. I grew up experiencing emotional and physical abuse by the man that was supposed to be my protector and caregiver. I thought that abuse was the reality of life, something normal to experience. I believed all men were abusive until I met Rashan. Once you experience the essence of a real one, there is no turning back because anything else will not do. Boots raping me added insult to injury for what I already felt, I could not trust a man. I thought every guy had the potential to harm me, so I stayed away. I was too scared to risk being hurt any more than I had already been.

My emotions served as motivation to create the future that I wanted for myself. I wanted what it was that Rashan saw in me. The streets were not for me, the risks outweigh the reward. On the days that I could not find my own motivation, his words played over and over inside of my head.

Rashan used to say, “You are not working hard enough. You need to be up early every morning getting the things done that you need to, not in here with me. It takes hard work, patience, and dedication. I feel like I should be a millionaire but obviously, I am not working hard enough, there is something more that I could be doing to get there.”

His voice played in the back of my mind as I studied for exams, took exams, made presentations, prepared for my college entrance exam, and planned out my future. I was all that I had and could depend on, so I showed up every time for myself. I hoped that he joined my army of angels with my mother, that they were there together pushing me forward, shaking their heads at some of my choices, and proud of me for my accomplishments.

The money that he had stashed away, from the setups and

robberies, paid for my private school education for the remainder of high school. I applied to twenty-two universities and got accepted into nineteen and received full scholarship offers to eleven. Your girl had options! All high-ranking universities, the types of institutions that little Black children coming from a single-family home were not expected to attend. I did it and I was proud of myself, the first generation of my family to attend a university.

The universe worked in mysterious ways. It seemed every time I left or lost one family, I gained another. I gained a mother, Ms. Sheema and two sisters, Ava Day and Noelle Reynolds also known as A and Noe-Noe. My foster mother, Ms. Sheema was placed in my life at the perfect time. The home she provided for me gave me a sense of family. Ms. Sheema provided guidance and love, a mother's love, the love I never had. She taught me how to cook like a real chef, plan for my future, and not to let my problems consume me. She showed me how to be kind, even when kindness was not shown to me, to have faith and believe that life would get better, even when everything was going wrong.

Ms. Sheema was a thick dark-skinned woman grounded in her black roots. She showed me how to be a woman, a kind, gentle, and Black woman. I learned about my body as a young woman; the art of sexuality and seduction and gained priceless wisdom. The lady was wise but stuck in her ways. She was also kind, the type to give you the shirt off of her back and try to help you even at the expense of herself. She was tough and a firm believer in discipline, staying on top of me to be the best I could in school, and treating her foster kids as if we were her real kids. As nice as Ms. Sheema was, she was not to be played with because that lady was crazy as hell and had her shit with her. Her mouth was a force to be reckoned with, she was always yelling and somehow knew exactly what to say to get a rise out of everyone. Ms. Sheema was always loud for no reason, she did everything loud, all of the time.

The four of us became a real family, blood could not have made us any closer. A and Noe-Noe became my sisters and two of my best friends. I understood them and they understood me, we understood each other. Those two ladies were crazy as hell, but they filled a void in my life that I never knew I had until then, a sisterhood.

APRIL 25, 2006—12:01 A.M.

"Happy birthday, bitch!" Noe shrieked before bum-rushing me with a hug.

I cringed at her touch; affection was uncomfortable for me. Your girl was officially legal, and it was time to get lit.

Noe was screaming per usual. I am not sure if it was the Tequila that caused her to be loud because my sis was a little drunk. Honestly, who the fuck am I kidding? Noe was loud all of the damn time. She was a big ball of personality, sass, and humor wrapped in a ball. Noe was short, brown-skinned, and thick in all the right places. She had an oval-shaped face, light brown eyes, long eyelashes, and full lips.

I was the quiet one, but Noe was the center of attention, always. Sometimes the extra-ness of her personality got on my damn nerves but that was my girl. You either hated or loved Noe-Noe, there was no in-between. When I first moved into the foster home, I did not like Noelle. Actually, I could not stand her, but she grew on me. She was loud, blunt, moody, and had a smart-ass mouth equipped with a comeback for every line. She was sassy honey and for no damn reason.

If asked: "What's the weather?" Noe would reply: "Do I look like the bitch on the news at ten, how the fuck you expect me to know?"

Noelle was an asshole, but she had a good heart and did not take any shit from anyone no matter who you were. She was as real as they came, the cloth that she was cut from rare and no longer being manufactured. Noe was a go-getter, always thinking of her next move and new ways to make money. Hustler of the year, every other day Noelle had a new hustle.

"Yes! Happy birthday to my good sis! You are legal mamas!" Ava followed up.

Ava, the laid-back gangster stuck in a female body, was similar yet different in comparison to Noelle. She was tall, skinny, and light-skinned. Ava had thick eyebrows, dimples, and long hair that she changed frequently. Ava was a free spirit. She was into crystals, horoscopes, and a list of other spiritual shit. Ava was the chill one, with a genuine spirit. As chill as she was, do not be fooled, she was a firecracker waiting to explode. The popular saying "I do not argue, I fight" was made for Ava. Who knew so much aggression could fit into such a lady; oh, and the mouth, please do not get me started! My sis was the epitome of a smart mouth and was sensitive as hell but would never admit it.

Ava was very protective of the people in her life. She rode for you no matter what, she swung before you even got a chance to. There was no such thing as a fair one when Ava Day was around. A was the one you called and always knew she would be there, even when she did not want to or you two were not on good terms. She always came through because that is who she was. Dealing with Noe and A, I was not sure if I wanted to argue, fight, gossip, or laugh.

"Thanks, y'all!" I said, excitedly.

"Noelle, I just know that couldn't have been you cussing in my damn house." Ms. Sheema fussed, emerging from the bathroom in our cramped apartment.

"Pooh, it's her birthday! We having fun, my bad," Noelle stated, turning to roll her eyes.

“I’m not your Pooh, we are not girlfriends. Now, ya’ll stand together let me get a picture!” Ms. Sheema commanded, holding up a disposable camera.

Ms. Sheema loved pictures and memories; she was a hoarder of anything reminiscent. The three of us gathered to pose for a photo. Noelle stood to the left, placing her hand on her hip and holding up her other arm as if a pocketbook was hanging on her wrist. She was wearing a black *Tommy Hilfiger* crop top revealing her flat stomach, pink diamond heart belly ring, and the tattoo right above her large ass. She paired the crop top with fitted low-rise dark denim *Apple Bottom* jeans. Her long box braids were pulled up into a ponytail and large gold bamboo hoop earrings complemented her bone structure.

Ava stood to my right, opting for a simpler pose than Noelle. She stood, hand on her hip leaning to the side, she resembled the recording artist Ciara on the red carpet. A paired a white bandeau top that hugged her small boobs and showed off her flat stomach with low-rise light denim jeans. Ava’s red hair sat in a high bun. Diamond stud earrings and gold bangles were her choice of accessories.

I stood in the middle of the girls, posing like Beyonce on the cover for the Destiny’s Child single “Soldier.” It was officially my birthday, and I was now legal according to the law. I was finally grown, and it felt good that I no longer had to worry about dealing with the state. I was lucky enough to have a foster mother who treated me like family so I did not worry about where I would go now that I was eighteen. I made sure I was dressed to impress for my birthday, your girl looked good. My pink halter dress hugged my curves and showed off my C-cup twins. I paired the dress with *Gucci* wedges, a *Louis Vuitton* clutch, diamond hoop earrings and a silver necklace with an M pendant. In true LiLi fashion, my hair was pressed straight in a fresh Dominican blowout hanging long down my back.

“Now Ava, turn to the side a little more, and Noelle, pull

your damn jeans up a little. Everyone suck in!" Ms. Sheema directed.

Ms. Sheema was a perfectionist, she always had something to say about what someone was wearing or what they looked like. She snapped the photo and placed the camera down on the end table.

"Ok, I got it. Ya'll look good. Enjoy the night out! Malika, happy birthday and be safe girls!" Ms. Sheema stated.

"Bye, Ma, we be back later," Noelle said before we all headed out the door.

"Ok, so what's the move, y'all? Malik is having a party tonight at Epic. You know that shit is going to be crazy!" Noe yelled enthusiastically from the passenger seat, while simultaneously applying clear gloss to her lips.

"Girl, no! That's a dub! It's mad ghetto at Epic, all the dirty ass hood niggas from Lincoln projects be there! Listen, I got y'all, I already set this up," Ava revealed, scowling.

"Set what up?" I asked, raising my eyebrows at Ava through the rearview mirror.

I did not like crowds of people and parties in New York City did not do it for me. Ava knew that so it was no surprise when she followed through with the perfect plan.

"Girl, don't eye me, now you know I know what you like! I had Tamir throw a kickback at his house in Queens. We got bottles, weed, edibles, and the vibes!" Ava boasted.

"Ohhhhh, bitch! You do know what I like! I'm with that!" I beamed.

"Y'all bitches love to chill," Noe shot, rolling her eyes.

"Yea, and chill on me," Ava sassed.

This was an example of the verbal boxing matches that they constantly fought. Noe wanted to be out on the town, matter of fact, Noe wanted to be around one of her players, Malik.

Malik was a hustler from the Bronx. He was known as a young nigga that was having it his way. He had money, jewels, foreign cars, designer clothes, and the city loved him. Noe was one of the many women that Malik was dating. Noe wanted to have a good time. Noe did not seem to care what Malik did with other women as long as he was cashing her out, she was okay with whatever position she played in his life. Additionally, Noe was entangled in a complicated situationship with, not one but two different guys, Rich and Tamir. Noelle was a rolling stone, she had a different dude for every need, love, money, connections, and sexual pleasure!

"Girl, you can see Malik any day! Today is about me!" I said, cutting my eyes at her.

"Alright, y'all, don't start that shit tonight! Now, y'all ready?" Ava interjected.

Ava reached forward and grabbed the bottle of Tequila out of the cupholder.

"Yes, let's go." I pulled out of the parking spot.

Noe turned the car radio up higher, *Me and You* by Cassie played on Hot 97.

"Girl! This. Is. My. Song!" Noe hollered.

"Baby, tell me if you like it (Tell me if you like it.) It's me and you, now, Uh, I've been waiting, Think I wanna make that move, now, Baby, tell me how you like it," Noe wailed.

Noe could not sing, she sounded like a wounded animal.

The drive to Tamir's house was filled with music, laughter, gossip, and most importantly, drinking.

We arrived at the kickback just in time. The house was a small row home on the southside of Queens. Tamir did not come from a wealthy family, but he had a hard-working father and a loving mother who provided for him, stayed on him about basketball, and made sure that he got good grades. Tamir attended our private high school on merit, receiving a full basketball scholarship. He was the star basketball player for high school, and with that came a lot of attention and love from everyone.

Despite the fact that Tamir loved basketball, he was a nerd. Yup! You heard me, a nerd. While most basketball players from similar upbringings as Tamir only got by with their schoolwork or had others do their work for them, Tamir loved school, especially the subject of biology. He expressed that basketball was his second love, a talent that he loved because he knew he had a gift. Tamir planned to use his gift as the way out of the city. He could go on and pursue his dreams of becoming a doctor, but his logic was why work that hard when he was a guaranteed prospect for professional basketball.

Tamir's house was packed, and the party was in full effect. "It's Goin Down" by Yung Joc blared through the speakers as we entered. The aroma of marijuana lingered, blunts were being passed in a rotation, and everyone had a red cup in hand.

"Yo!" Tamir choked out, coughing on the blunt that he was smoking.

Tamir stood from the couch he was sitting in next to the door and passed the blunt to the next person in the rotation before walking over.

"Wassup!" Ava greeted.

"Hey," Noelle remarked.

"Wassup, ya'll," Tamir welcomed.

"Hey bro!" I greeted, excitedly.

"Li, happy birthday! Damn, happy birthday, sis. You legal now! How you feeling, you good?" Tamir questioned, his thick New York City accent coming through.

Tamir extended his arm to me, offering a side hug. I returned the hug, embracing him.

"Thank you, thank you! Shit, everything is everything, I'm just happy to be here. Thanks for throwing this for me, this was dope!" I beamed.

Tamir was tall, six foot four, and skinny with a muscular

build. He had a cool dark chocolate skin complexion that resembled that of a Hershey kiss. He was a solid young man with a bright future ahead of him. Tamir played basketball and received full scholarships to multiple division one universities.

"Heard you! We got everything you need, let's get you right," Tamir replied, enthusiastically.

"Oh, so Malika is the only person you can speak to today?" Noe quizzed.

Noelle rolled her eyes, folded her arms under her breasts and cocked her head to the side, glaring at Tamir.

"Nah, now this. Shit, Noelle, don't start that shit today. Everything ain't about you, damn. It's her fucking birthday," Tamir responded.

Tamir scowled and shook his head, walking away.

Noe and Tamir had a weird relationship. I opted to mind my business and not insert myself into their drama because the two were so hot and cold, there was no telling what was going on with the two of them.

Before Noelle could respond, I cut her off to avoid the argument that was brewing between her and Tamir.

"I know you got a bottle for me!" I piped up.

The statement was much more of an assertion than a question.

"Sis, come on now, you know me. I got the Champ for you and the Henny! Not to mention a blunt just for you. Matter of fact, hold up, I got you," Tamir bragged, tapping me on the shoulder with the back of his hand.

Tamir walked away, headed to the center of the smoke cypher, leaving the three of us standing idle. The kickback had a good vibe and good energy. There was the right mix of girls and guys, only a few people from around the way and a few who attended Tamir and I's private high school. The music was on point, the blunts were going around, and of course, the alcohol made everything better.

Tamir returned with a blunt hanging from his lips. In his hand, he held a large sandwich bag filled with an ounce of weed, an empty sandwich bag, and a tobacco leaf. He tossed the bags and the leaf to me then proceeded to pass me the blunt.

"Take what you want out there," he offered.

"Good look, bro." I thanked him and accepted the blunt.

I took three puffs and passed it to Ava, who also indulged in smoking weed. I proceeded to fill the sandwich bag with the desired amount before passing it back to him, that was for later.

"Y'all good though? Go help y'all selves to something to drink." Tamir nodded towards the kitchen.

"Nah, we want that bottle that you were talking about," Ava chimed in, passing the blunt back to Tamir.

Noelle did not smoke so Ava knew not to pass it to her.

"Aight, come on, I'll walk y'all in the kitchen." He volunteered before leading the way into the kitchen.

Tamir led Noelle, Ava, and me into the kitchen. The atmosphere of the gathering was nice, it was a great feeling to be with my girls and local friends. I had always been a loner, growing up I had few acquaintances and even fewer friends. Sadness came over me on the walk to the kitchen. *Damn! I'm going to miss this,* I thought, walking into the kitchen. College was approaching, and although I was not sure where I would be attending, I had no intention of staying local.

Tamir's kitchen was packed to capacity. Everyone was standing around drinking and talking. Tamir handed me an unopened bottle of Hennessy.

"No chasers, that's not what we on tonight! It's your birthday, sis, we on that shit tonight!" Tamir pressured, staring down at me.

He was hyped up and in rare form.

"Yea, you bugging if you think I'm drinking this shit! Nigga said we on that shit tonight, yea, you must have had too much already, you know better!" I argued, pursing my lips to express my disapproval.

"Man! I am not trying to hear that shit, all these people here to celebrate you and you being pussy!" He dared, applying the peer pressure quite thick.

"Bro, the Henny though? That's OD. Niggas wildin!" I hesitated, opening the bottle.

Tamir stared at me with his head cocked to the side, I could feel the unspoken what are you going to do question lingering.

"Scary ass," he said, turning to grab the cranberry juice.

He knew I would have no excuse once he gave me a chaser. Suddenly, Noe grabbed the bottle from my hand.

"Yea, let me get this because you being boring!" she shot.

Unexpectedly, Noe took the bottle straight to the head. I looked over at Ava who was laughing and shaking her head.

"Here this bitch go!" Ava joked.

"No bitch, here you go!" Noe said, swiftly bringing the bottle to Ava's mouth.

Ava's eyes popped in surprise but did not protest, she opened her mouth and allowed Noe to pour cognac down her throat. In true Noe fashion, she overdid it and almost spilled some of the liquor onto Ava as a result of her pouring too much too fast. Ava brought her hand up, halting Noe from pouring any more.

"Yea, A! That's how you do it!" Tamir hyped her up, turning back around with the cranberry juice.

He got distracted talking to one of the thirsty girls from our high school in front of him. I lightly tapped Tamir on the shoulder, indicating that Noelle was watching.

"Fuck off!" Ava gargled, gulping down the rest of the drink, pursing her lips to express her disdain for the harsh taste.

Tamir handed the cranberry juice to me. I reached for a cup only to be blocked by Noelle.

"No! Girl, open up! Shots! Shots! Shots!" Noelle chanted over the music.

"No cup! Drink that shit then chase it down," she said, raising the bottle to my mouth.

I rolled my eyes before I opened up. She poured the drink, from the bottle, directly into my mouth. I swallowed with urgency and quickly followed up with cranberry juice. My face was screwed up in agony. *Ewww!* I thought as the liquor burned its way down my throat. I hated the taste of dark liquor. As I went to put the can of cranberry juice down, I was met with Noe and the Hennesy bottle once again.

"Bitch! It's your Lika Day! Not to mention you leaving us soon, so it's only right that we get you lit tonight! You're taking three!" she yelled, pouring another shot into my mouth.

Some of the Hennessy spilled out of the corner of my lips, causing me to wipe my mouth with the tips of my fingers.

Again, Noelle returned with the bottle, following up with another pour. She was relentless.

"Alright, y'all, we lit now!" Tamir announced before heading out of the kitchen.

"Hmmm! Girl, Tamir looking a little good tonight, I might have to go and get some of that again," Noe exclaimed; lust laced in her tone.

That was the last thing I remembered from that night. The shots of *Hennessy* mixed with the marijuana I was smoking completely erased my memory for the remainder of that night. All I remembered was that was one of the last nights that I spent with my friends before going away to college. To be honest, I would not even say remember because much of the night was very vague after those moments spent in the kitchen. It was one of those nights I would cherish forever, some memories are worth more than gold. A night with good vibes and good energy when everything felt easy.

CHAPTER SIX

"Draft Day . . ."

AUGUST 22, 2006—3:22 P.M.

My back ached as I stretched in my twin bed inside of Syracuse University's Flint Hall.

"Uhhhhh!" I groaned, tossing and turning in the uncomfortable bed.

The incoming sunlight burned my eyes as I forced them open. I had only been there for twenty-four hours, but I could not get comfortable sleeping on the hard mattress. I threw the white floral duvet off of me before sitting up in the bed. I was up for most of the night, per usual, unable to rest. Needless to say, I was tired and cranky. I looked around the cluttered room trying to decide if I should lay back down or finish unpacking, hopefully before my roommate arrived. I arrived the night before so that I could get a head start at setting up. I was nervous and anxious about the beginning of this journey, hoping that I made the right decision.

Slowly, I climbed down from what felt like a steel cot. There was still so much to do considering I still had suitcases of clothes to unpack. I only had, approximately, two hundred square feet to pack away an entire wardrobe. I looked around admiring my decorating skills. I loved decor, actually, I loved anything creative, but I rarely took the time to tap into my creative talents and passions. My side of the room was done in teal, pink, and white. Lights hung above my bed, a white mirror decorated the door, a lamp stood next to my bed, and Beyonce and Aaliyah posters hung above my white floral bedspread. You could not tell me that both Beyonce and Aaliyah were not my sisters, I loved them.

I enjoyed my alone time inside of the room but that was short-lived. A rattling of the doorknob pulled my attention to the front of the room. Suddenly, the door swung open. A five-foot-seven, slim light-skinned girl with full pink lips, and chinky eyes stepped inside. Her hair was done in a side part with long curls that hung down her back. Her round face was pulled into an unpleasant scowl as she wrestled to take her key out of the door. Startled, her bulging eyes looked up at me.

"I didn't know you were already here!" she hollered.

Unexpectedly, a bright smile spread across her face and she dropped her large Michael Kors tote bag by the door before rushing over to me. Well, that bag for sure looked more like Fichael Kors but that's none of my business.

"Hey! I'm Tayana but everyone calls me Taya! Nice to meet you!" she shrieked.

I rarely met anyone that was this enthusiastic with a complete stranger. New York girls were known for a lot of things but being friendly was not one of them. I was not a fan of girls that I did not know but I was willing to give it a try since I would be living with her. Most girls that I encountered these days were jealous of me. I intimidated them for whatever reason. The shit was beyond me because I was really chill if you got to know me, but I rarely let anyone get past my wall to actually know me. Shit, I had my own insecurities to deal with; there was really no need to be intimidated.

I side-eyed her before extending my hand for her to shake it, she was too animated for my taste.

"Hi, I'm Malika. Nice to meet you," I said, greeting her with a Karen smile.

The smile that Caucasians often offer at the grocery store when you two accidentally make eye contact.

To my surprise, she disregarded my hand and pulled me in for a hug. Eagerly I pulled away from her embrace, I was uncomfortable, to say the least. Something about her overly friendly nature rubbed me the wrong way. Well shit, everything about her rubbed me the wrong way. Why the fuck was this random girl touching me.

"Nice to meet you, sis! You are so cute! We are here, at college! I cannot believe this! Where are you from? What's your major? Tell me about yourself, I want to know everything! I'm from Philly, and I am majoring in Communications!" she rambled.

This girl needs a damn Xanax, I thought. Now, do not get me wrong, I was used to Noelle's hyper personality, but you had to get to know Noelle to know that side of her. This bitch right here was just too damn friendly, the type of friendly that I did not trust.

"Thanks. I'm from the Bronx and I'm majoring in Business Management for now," I responded, casually.

"Well, sis! I love your side of the room! Let me start getting unpacked, maybe we can go out! I heard it's some cookouts and some of the frats were having a kickback! You know what that means! Niggas, upperclassmen!" she shrilled.

By this point, I was beginning to understand that was just her personality. Taya was loud, hyper, and too damn friendly.

"Yea, I'm actually going out with my bro later tonight to one of the cookouts, I'll let you know if you can come through with us," I offered.

I was not sure about this girl or if I even liked her, but I was making an effort to be open to new people.

AUGUST 22, 2006—7:43 P.M.

The aroma of burnt hot dogs, barbequed chicken, and hamburgers flooded my nostrils as Taya and I approached Slocum Drive on South campus.

"Lean wit' it, rock wit' it, Lean wit' it, rock wit' it, Lean wit' it, rock wit' it, Lean wit' it, rock wit' it, Lean wit' it, rock wit' it," blasted through the speakers.

Taya and I walked towards the large crowd that was gathered in front of building two-twenty-one.

It had only been twenty-four hours since I was an official college student and already shit was rolling. Instantly, I understood why Syracuse University was among the country's top Universities and ranked the number one party school.

Death stares found their way to me as I strutted through. A white *Baby Phat* crop top with a diamond *Baby Phat* logo on the front, low-rise fitted light denim *Baby Phat* jeans that cuffed my round ass perfectly, white *Chanel* sandals, and a silver *Gucci* monogram tote killed the competition for the day. My hair was pressed to perfection in a fresh Dominican blowout that I made sure to get before I left the city, and my lip gloss was poppin, to say the least. I accessorized with large silver hoop earrings that said Lika on the inside, a diamond *Michelle* watch, and oversized *Gucci* glasses. To say that I was the flyest at the cookout was an understatement, not being cocky but these girls could not stand it with me. I was that freshman, actually I was that girl, period, no matter the class and my attitude carried it as such. The upperclassman females all stared and snickered, but I did not give a fuck, the hate always meant that I was doing something right.

Taya looked cute and simple. She wore a *Von Dutch* jeans

skirt, a pink bandeau top, silver sandals, and a pink and blue *Von Dutch* purse with *Von Dutch* written on the front of it. Taya's braids were pulled up into a high ponytail, she had diamond stud earrings from the hair store, and a silver necklace with her name Tayana.

I made my way over to Tamir, who was huddled with Syracuse University's elite division one basketball team. The boys were surrounded by a crowd of thirsty females, everyone trying to get the attention of one of the players. I walked past all of the desperate females and straight over to Tamir. Tamir committed and accepted a full ride to Syracuse a little before I decided that I would be attending. It was comforting knowing that I had a close friend that was here with me, a piece of home, someone to look out for me.

Tamir stood in the middle of the crowd, wearing an oversized grey Sean John sweatsuit. White Nike Air Force Ones blessed his feet, those sneakers were the gospel to hood niggas. Niggalations verse one: Thou hood nigga shall have a fresh pair of Air Force Ones, also known as Uptowns and Fazos.

Abruptly, Taya grabbed my elbow. I stopped and turned to look at her with a death stare that read *girl get the hell off of me.*

"What?!" I snapped.

Taya released my elbow, holding up her hands in defense.

"Girl, do you know who that is? Why are we walking over there to them?" she asked, like a true groupie.

"Yea, duh dummy, I brought us here," I shot.

Quickly I turned back around so that I did not have to continue seeing the dumb-ass look on Taya's face. She stood there starstruck over Tamir. *When will these girls learn he is just regular?* I thought.

Tamir looked up as I approached. He leaned down and whispered something to one of the girls around him. Instantly, the girls that were blocking my path moved out of the way.

"Sis! What's good, Lika!" Tamir beamed.

He reached down, pulling me in for a one-handed hug.

Tamir was treated like a celebrity everywhere that he went. He was anticipated to go to the league. The previous power forward was drafted to the Denver Nuggets, giving Tamir the opportunity to be the only starting freshman that season. Having been there since June, he had already begun making a name for himself at the University. As an athlete, he was required to start school ahead of the fall semester, beginning in early summer to train, work out, and take courses ahead of the up-and-coming basketball season.

"Mir!" I greeted, leaning in to reciprocate his hug.

"Damn, this is really the first time in three years that I have not seen your ass in months!" I recalled.

Tamir was one of my only friends from my private high school. There were not that many black students that I clicked with from my high school, so I cherished the few friends that I had.

"I know, sis. I missed your crazy ass. Come on, get a drink, what y'all want?" he asked in true Tamir fashion, he was always ready to get somebody lit.

Suddenly, when he said y'all I recalled that Taya was with me.

"Oh, my bad. I'm being rude. Mir, this is Taya. Taya, this is Tamir," I introduced, nodding my head towards Taya.

Tamir looked Taya up and down, taking in her appearance.

"What's good?" he greeted, nodding his head.

Taya looked on, attempting to conceal her nervousness. Needless to say, she was not doing a good job at that. I was not sure how she would act but I was happy that she was keeping her cool.

"Nice to meet you!" Taya beamed.

Tamir smirked. I rolled my eyes because I already knew what that smirk meant. Tamir was a rolling stone, that smirk meant that he was plotting on her because he knew she was open for him. Tamir turned to me, speaking in a low tone.

"Easy," he said before turning to get us some punch.

I shook my head because I knew exactly what that meant.

The remainder of the cookout was lit, I had a ball. That was my first taste of the crazy parties I would experience in college. My four years of undergrad flew by quickly. Reflecting on my college experience, I wish I appreciated my time there a bit more. I was too caught up in my real life, partying, and scamming to enjoy the experience.

JUNE 24, 2010

MADISON SQUARE GARDEN: NEW YORK CITY

It's so damn hot in here, I thought, exhaling sharply.

The palms of my clammy hands provided faint relief as I aggressively fanned myself. The sweat forming underneath my makeup caused me to retrieve a napkin from the table sitting before me. Next, I located my MAC setting powder in my purse and applied it to my face. After all, this was Draft Day for the professional basketball league. A lot of big names and potential stars were in the building so I could not be caught slipping.

Anxiously, my right leg jerked up and down. Patience was not a virtue that I possessed and after sitting inside of Madison Square Garden for over an hour I was uneasy. To make matters worse, it seemed to get hotter after every minute that passed. The draft did not officially begin yet, but we were all in attendance, ready and waiting to hear the name Tamir Rawlins called. Yes, you heard me correctly! Tamir was going to the league! My best friend was going to the league. Tamir and I grew extremely close through my years at college, he was my slice of home, my brother. We made it through those years together.

Tamir sat across the table looking suave. He was swagged out in an all-black velvet *Tom Ford* suit and black Gucci loafers. He looked like money, if I do say so myself, a gold Presidential Rolex graced his wrist and the waves in his freshly lined haircut complemented his face. Shit, Tamir had no choice but to look like money, after all of the hours Noelle and I spent putting together his outfit for the night.

Tamir was calm, in control, and unfazed, I could not read his reaction, but he carried a certain confidence that I had never seen in him before tonight. Through our countless conversations, he revealed how nervous he was about this night so the confidence he displayed tonight came as a surprise.

After Tamir's first year at Syracuse, he was offered prospective contracts with various teams. However, school was important to him and unlike most athletes with the talent that he possessed, he valued the importance of finishing school. He did not want to rush into a professional basketball deal, so he waited. He was aware of the possibility of injury for professional athletes and wanted something solid to fall back on. Tamir waited until he earned his bachelor's degree before deciding to enter the draft. His decision to wait was extremely risky but it worked out for the best. Tamir earned Syracuse two championship rings, which boost his stock more than he ever imagined. His time playing in a Division one basketball league allowed him to master his talent before entering the draft. Now, the amount of money they were offering my brother was unreal. He was getting that bag!

Noelle sat to the left of Tamir, looking gorgeous, as the girlfriend and baby mother of a soon-to-be NBA player she represented him well. Yes, you heard me! The mother of Tamir's child! Those two crazy asses were made for each other! Noelle always secured the bag and Tamir had the bag.

It was not about the money for Noelle though, she loved

him. Their connection was genuine, and their personalities were similar. Noelle came up to Syracuse to visit Syracuse one weekend and then ended up rekindling with her on-again-off-again boo.

The two had been inseparable ever since then. Tamir often joked about trapping Noelle and not wanting to risk her ending up with anyone else. If you ask me, I think he got her pregnant on purpose. Noe looked flawless as expected. Her long hair was styled into a high ponytail and gold diamond chandelier earrings framed her perfectly made-up face. She wore a strapless black bodycon Herve Leger dress that she paired with strappy gold Christian Louboutin sandals. Noe wore her own matching version to Tamir's gold Presidential Rolex. Tamir copped them matching his and her luxury watches. He was still in college at the time of the purchase, but endorsement deals, and other shady business ventures kept his money coming in.

Tamir's sister, Tamia, and his parents, Ramon and Leanne, were also in attendance and looked elegant. Tamia was the female version of Tamir. Tamir with a wig was the best description I could find for Tamia. It was kind of scary that they were not twins because they looked exactly alike. Tamia was seven years younger than Tamir, way off from being his twin. She was dark-skinned, thin and model tall, five foot ten. She looked stylish in a white pants suit, complemented by a jet-black center part wavy bob and a diamond necklace.

Tamir's mother and father brought the class and elegance. Ramon was tall, dark-skinned and shared the same features as his children. Tamir and Tamia were the splitting image of Ramon, Leanne bore no resemblance to the children she carried for nine months. Ramon was bald with a goatee, wearing a grey suit and a silver watch. The beautiful Leanne had long dark hair, and a cool dark-skinned complexion, that of a dark-skinned Indian woman. Leanne wore a black chiffon blouse tucked into a mid-length black skirt. Her tresses were curled and hung down her back. I looked around at the table observing the people that had become an extension of my family; they all filled me with so much joy.

He did it! We are really sitting at the damn NBA draft what the fuck! I thought, shaking my head.

Suddenly, the lights inside of the arena dimmed and a spotlight was shining on the stage. Holding a mic in his hand, a tall bald white man began to approach the stage. My stomach clenched and butterflies began to flutter inside of my stomach. This is it, the start of what we were all waiting for.

"Good evening and welcome to the draft for the National Basketball Association . . ." the league commissioner began.

Damn! Can we just get to the part where they say Tamir already! I don't even know what the fuck he is talking about. Just say his name, I cannot take this, I thought. The host continued to make his announcements for the opening of the draft, but my rambling thoughts caused me to zone out. I was so anxious that I could not focus on anything that he was saying. The unexpected brought me out of my trance and back to reality.

"The Miami Heat first-round draft pick is Tamir Rawlins, power forward from Syracuse University!" the commissioner announced.

My head whipped to the side to look at Tamir. Disbelief filled me as an uncontrollable flood of tears erupted from my eyes. The crowd erupted in applause and loud cheer; the most anticipated draft pick had officially been picked. Everyone at the table, except for Tamir, jumped out of their seats, reveling in the amazing news. Tamir sat in shock, glued to his seat. He heard the news but was unable to process what was happening. Roughly, Noelle tugged on his arm attempting to pull him out of his seat.

"Baby Daddy!" Noelle wailed with tear-filled eyes.

Tamir looked up at her and their eyes connected.

The expression on his face read: *did he say my name, is this shit real?* Noelle nodded her head at him compulsively.

"Yes, baby! You! They called you!" she reassured him.

Slowly, Tamir rose from his seat. Instantly, Noelle jumped on him, wrapping her legs around his waist and her arms around his neck, pulling his body into hers. Unable to contain her excitement, she kissed him repeatedly and passionately.

"I love you! I love you! I love you so much! I knew you could do it!" Noelle shrilled as Tamir placed her on her feet.

I could not hear what Tamir was saying over the commotion, but I read his lips as he spoke.

"I love you more my love," he responded to Noelle.

Tamir began walking around the table, giving out hugs to everyone before he went to the stage.

The first stop was Leanne. He towered over his mother as she wrapped her arms around him in a warm embrace. Leanne's facial reaction spoke volumes. Her smile was proud, and her eyes looked on with so much admiration as she placed the palm of her hand on the side of his cheek.

Tamir then swaggered over Ramon. Ramon wrapped his arms around his son patting Tamir's back and burying Tamir's head in his chest. Ramon whispered something in Tamir's ear. The exchange was that of a proud father and his thankful son. Third was Tamia, she looked up at him in admiration once he arrived before her. The two hugged and Tamia made a comment that caused Tamir to burst into laughter. It was beautiful to watch the exchange between Tamir and his family, the admiration and love that they shared for each other was inspiring.

Last but not least on the list was me, Tamir stood before me looking down in silence. The look in his eyes was one that I had never seen before that day. A look that reflected gratitude and appreciation. The emotion of the silent moment was too heavy, causing me to swell in emotion as my tears came once. I had never been prouder of anyone in my life. I witnessed the hard work that Tamir put in to get to this moment and finally, it was his time. He reached down and extended his arms out to me. I lagged for a moment, but I matched his embrace.

"Thank you, I'm not sure that I could not have made it here without you in college with me. My sister, my best friend, you kept me levelheaded. Thank you for being a real friend, LiLi," he acknowledged, squeezing me tightly.

"I love you more T. I'm so proud of you! You worked so hard for this! You deserve everything that's coming to you and more!" I whimpered, pouting my lips to hold my cry in.

Tamir released me and smiled. He whipped his head to the right then left, looking around at all of us then around at the remainder of the stadium. He took a moment to take in everything before walking towards the stage. Too excited to sit back down, we all stood in front of our seats awaiting his acceptance speech. By the time he reached the stage, Tamir was smiling from ear to ear; his pearly whites shining brightly.

"Wooooooooo!" The crowd applauded as he greeted the commissioner.

Tamir accepted his Miami Heat team hat and leaned in to hug the commissioner before his eloquent acceptance speech.

"Miami! I'm speechless! Thank you to the team and the commissioner for this opportunity! I want to give a shout-out to the special people in my life, my mother for giving me life and being the most loving and supportive woman I have ever known. My father for pushing me and showing me the importance of hard work. My sister for being my baby nugget, I love you. Noelle, the mother of my baby girl, thank you for being you, my other half, and for giving me Armani! Last but not least my best friend, Malika, for being with me through my entire college journey. Literally, shooting in the gym with me on the days I had no motivation. You stayed on top of me, never letting me slack! Y'all are my village and I love you all so much! I can't wait to play with the Heat this season!" Tamir concluded.

Following Tamir's speech, a series of applause and loud cheer erupted. The night concluded with the remainder of the draft and then to an after-party. Tamir was offered a five million five hundred-thousand-dollar contract to play for the Miami Heat for two years. Tamir getting drafted introduced us all to a different world, the world of the rich and elite.

CHAPTER SEVEN

"A Little Louder, I Can't Hear You . . ."

OCTOBER 29, 2010

AMERICAN AIRLINES ARENA: MIAMI FLORIDA

The opening game for Tamir's first season as a professional athlete came quickly. There was no way in hell I was going to miss this game, not only for Tamir but the boys were out. We were playing in the big leagues now with first-class access to some of the most desired men in the industry. Ava, Noelle, Taya and I sat courtside, bad bitches per usual.

Ava looked model-esq, emulating a tall glass of milk, she wore a white silk halter blouse that clung to her cleavage, fitted white pants that gave her little booty a nice plump, and silver Christian Louboutin platform heels. Ava's big curly red hair was pulled into a high ponytail and silver diamond hoop earrings highlighted her face.

My girl Noelle came to shut shit down! Noelle gave the people, my man is officially a professional athlete, and I could care less if he is a rookie; she carried as if Tamir was the franchise player. Noelle wore a gold sequin strapless Gucci dress that hugged her body in all the right places, and black thigh-high Chanel boots with a six-inch heel. Her makeup was flawless, the red matte lips and a light gold shimmer on her eyelids brought out the blonde highlights in her long curly tresses. She accessorized with a gold Rolex with diamonds on the face and a red Hermes Birkin bag. This was Noe's opening game too.

Taya was simple yet pretty. Her hair was straight with a side part bang. Taya wore a simple black dress with black platform heels, diamond stud earrings and a black and brown Fendi monogram clutch.

Then there was the Don, Malika, or should I say, myself. My hair was long, straight and black, straight bangs graced my forehead. I wore a pink bodycon skirt that hugged my hips and ass perfectly, and a white blazer with a white lace bralette underneath. The girls—my DD-cup boobs—sat up perfectly and the gold *Chanel* pin that graced the front of my blazer was the perfect accessory. I wore nude platform Christian Louboutin heels paired with a classic nude Chanel bag with gold accessories. I layered my David Yurman bracelets to complement my gold Rolex and in true Malika fashion had diamond rings on most of the fingers on my left hand. We all served something different yet beautiful, catching the attention of everyone in the building, even some of the fine ass players. There was one player that I had my eye on that night, shit, everyone had their eyes on him. He was the star player and unbeknownst to me, he had his eyes on me as well.

We had great seats thanks to Tamir. Noelle would not settle for anything but the very best, and the very best was courtside. In true Noe fashion, she was a diva and since Tamir got drafted she had become the head diva. Humility was not a virtue that Noe possessed, everyone, everywhere that she went was going to know that she had money. I looked around the stadium in awe, the feeling was surreal. The three of us, except for Taya, were foster kids from the Bronx, how the hell did we get here?

"Ahhhhhhhhhhhhhhhhhhhh!" the crowd erupted in excitement.

Christian Samuels, the star player and starting shooting guard, made an outstanding three-point shot with one second left on the shot clock.

It was the end of the second half officially bringing the Heat to a two-point lead and winning the game one-hundred-and-one to ninety-nine. Everyone jumped from their seats, unable to believe that Christian made the impressive shot! Christian had a hand, the shot would have been unattainable for most but for someone that possessed the skill that Christian did, the shot was effortless. The energy in the arena was amazing; it felt as if we were all on a game high!

"Girl! Tonight is gonna be on ten!" Taya declared, turning to look at the crowd behind us.

"Bitch! I am ready, ok!" Noe agreed.

Surprisingly, Taya had become a good friend of mine and was cordial with my sisters. As I turned to respond to Noe I was hit in the face by the unexpected.

Christian Samuels stood at six-foot-seven inches hovering over me. Sweat dripped from his glistening tattoo-covered caramel brown skin.

"Oh. Sorry," I uttered, shocked.

I was taken aback, trying to find words but nothing came. I did not understand why he was right in front of me or what was happening. *Could he feel my intense stare the entire night?* I thought. He stood silent, staring down, his light brown eyes piercing into mine like daggers. The look in his eyes was intense, dangerous yet alluring and they pulled me in. I attempted to look away from my eyes held still, a lump forming in the back of my throat. *This man was so damn fine, God damn he took my breath away.* Something told me danger was present but a part of me wanted danger, I could not help myself.

"Christian, and you?" he asserted.

The tone of his voice was so sexy. Immediately, I could feel the flow of my juices between my legs. Unbeknownst to him, he turned on the faucet to my kitty with just the sound of his voice. I could feel the stares as we stood there. This was a bold move for him, he knew that all of the attention was on him. I was sure that this encounter would become one for a sleazy gossip blog. I heard him speaking to me but somehow no words came out of my mouth. Suddenly, Noe's elbow brought me out of my trance.

"Malika, nice to meet you," I replied, attempting not to blush.

I was not doing a good job at hiding my blushing, thank God for makeup because I was sure my cheeks were turning bright red underneath my MAC cosmetics. Christian smiled before responding, his perfectly straight white teeth shining.

"Malika, you coming out with me tonight. I'll have my people come back out and grab you," he stated.

He ran his pointer finger across my cheek before walking away. His touch left the side of my face tingling. His energy lingered in the spot that he stood after he departed. I was calm, not wanting to appear too excited in public knowing that there were so many eyes watching. Inside, I was screaming *What the fuck just happened!*

JUNE 24, 2010

MADISON SQUARE GARDEN: NEW YORK CITY

"Bitch!" Noe hollered under her breath.

"Girl, do you know who the fuck that was?!" Taya yelled a little too loud.

"Girl, chill out! We in public, you OD right now!" Ava scolded, rolling her eyes.

Ava was cool with Taya on the strength of me, but she did not care too much for her. Ava found Taya to be annoying and a little fake and phony. Ava did not trust her, but she was unable to pinpoint the reason why.

"Nah, but sis, that was the one! Not one of the ones, but the one! That man has a sixty-five-million-dollar contract! Girl! Do you know how women line up for him!" Noe exclaimed.

Noe was a gold digger and not afraid to show or tell it to anyone, she was about the money. She was loyal but she did not do broke or regular men. Tamir knew exactly who he was with and he respected her more for it. It was the standard that she set for herself, how could a person not respect it.

"I am so lost right now, I'm confused," I responded, dazed.

"Bitch, what is it to be lost and confused about? He liked what he saw so he made it known," Ava stated.

"Well. Like. I was going out with y'all tonight, what do I do? Should I make him wait, like what should I do?" I questioned.

"Girl, make him wait? Huh? Yea, you buggin sis, buggin the fuck out!" Noe responded, her eyes bulging.

"Yes, mamas go have a good time. I will not be mad at you if you let him touch the kitty, shit I would," Taya joked; her face scrunched into a nasty scowl.

"Honey, you won't be mad at her if she let anyone touch the kitty, let's be serious," Ava shot, giggling.

Noe followed up in laughter, cosigning.

"Right!" Noe laughed.

Annoyed, Taya rolled her eyes. The two would sometimes tag team Taya making side comments and jokes.

"Yea, whatever," Taya said with a slight attitude.

Taya was quick to get in her feelings.

"No seriously, y'all! I guess I'm going." I hesitated.

"Look mamas, just go, this could be a once-in-a-lifetime experience, do not mess this up!" Taya responded.

On cue, a man in an all-black suit appeared behind me, tapping me on the shoulder.

"Malika?" the man questioned as I turned to face him.

"Yes," I quizzed.

"Mr. Samuels has instructed me to escort you to his vehicle, right this way," he stated, stepping to the side to allow me to exit.

I looked over at my girls nervously.

"Go!" Noe insisted.

"And have fun!" Ava called out behind her.

Nervously, I picked up my Chanel bag from my seat and followed the man. He led me to the back of the arena where the players' locker rooms were located and outside to where the players entered the arena. A shiny black Rolls Royce Phantom sat at the entrance. The engine was running, and a driver stood in front of the back passenger door.

"Good evening, Ma'am," the driver greeted in a thick Latino accent as he opened the door and nodded his head.

The door opened revealing a smiling Christian Samuels seated in the backseat of the Phantom.

This must be a damn dream. No man should be this fine, some shit was just not right. Emulating a GQ model, Christian wore all black, a black blazer with a black Louis Vuitton shirt underneath, dark denim jeans and black Louis Vuitton sneakers. He kept it simple, wearing only a plain silver Patek Philippe watch. He looked scrumptious.

Slowly yet seductively, I entered the luxury vehicle. The foreign leather felt like butter melting into my soft skin. I thought BMW and Mercedes-Benz cars were luxury, but this was wealth, not luxury. The diamonds sparkling from the car ceiling amplified the ambiance of wealth. This was the type of shit that I could get used to. A bottle of 1982 Dom Perignon Brut sat in the center console with two champagne glasses and a tray of assorted fruits.

"For you to only have met me a few minutes ago you set this up pretty quickly," I commented, tilting my head to the side.

Secretly, I sunk my fingers into the leather seats.

"I knew what I wanted when I spotted you mid-game," he said smugly, a smirk playing on the corners of his lips.

"Oh, and you just knew I was going to come with you, huh? What if I had other plans?" I questioned, sarcastically.

"That was a chance I was willing to take, if you wanted to go with your other plans instead then you would have missed out on a once-in-a-lifetime opportunity." He flirted while taking his attention off of me to look forward.

He was cocky but not too much, he knew exactly who he was and the power he possessed.

"Oh, really? You sound really sure of that," I contested, smirking while side-eying him.

"I'm a confident man, I know what I bring to the table," he stated, lifting the champagne glasses.

He handed me a glass and proceeded to pick up the expensive bottle. He opened the bottle and reached over the console to pour me some champagne.

"Help yourself," he offered, nodding towards the fruit tray.

I took the glass of *Dom Perignon* to my lips and pulled in. The taste was magnificent, the aged champagne was smooth. Unexpectedly, he reached over and picked up a strawberry, bringing it to my full moist lips. He placed the strawberry in my mouth, his fingers sweeping past my lips. *Whew child, what is this man trying to do,* I thought before bringing my hand to my lips.

"It's something about you," he revealed, glaring at me as we pulled up to a red light.

I had been so lost in his essence that I did not notice when the car originally pulled off.

"What about me?" I blushed.

"I don't know. You pull me to you; I can usually have anyone that I want but I never really find myself wanting anybody like this. I don't even entertain the women that come to my games," he said, staring at me intensely.

"Well, I don't know what to tell you, I am something special. You might have hit the lottery." I flirted.

“Mhhhh, yea, maybe I did,” he affirmed.

Suddenly, the thought hit me, *where the hell was this man taking me*. I looked out the window to see that we were cruising down Ocean Drive.

“Where—” I began but he beat me to it.

“I figured you might be hungry; I know I am after playing,” he responded as a matter of fact.

He must have been reading my mind because I never turned down food.

We pulled up in front of Prime 112, a high-end restaurant where all of the athletes and celebrities frequented. I reached for the door and he placed his hand on my thigh, halting me.

“You mine now, and anything that belongs to me receives the very best. The best does not open her own doors,” he stated, intensity lived in his eyes.

The driver opened his door first.

“Thanks, my G.” He thanked the driver, climbing out of the car.

Next, the driver opened my door. Christian stood waiting for me, extending his hand as I exited the car. Paparazzi stood out front snapping photos of the two of us while we were escorted inside of the restaurant.

“Aye Christian, over here!” someone said as Christian held his hand up over his face to block the cameras.

“Amazing shot tonight brother!” Another called out while we walked inside of the restaurant.

Never in my life had I seen so many flashing cameras being pointed at me. I could not believe that I was out with Christian Samuels much less that he had me out for everyone to see. I did not know if he had a significant other, but I assumed that any man this bold had to be single.

“Good evening, Mr. Samuels, would you like your usual table?” The waitress greeted me.

“Yes,” Christian answered.

"Oh, you have a guest this evening. Please give us a moment to prepare for the additional party," she stated, looking me up and down before walking away.

Yea, he has a guest tonight, sis. Move along, I thought. Christian and I stood, awaiting her return.

He squeezed my hand reassuringly, to say do not pay her any attention. The lady returned moments later.

"Right this way," she said, leading us to a table in the restaurant's most discreet section.

Heads turned as we walked to the table. All eyes were on Christian and, by default, on me. I caught some nasty stares and envious glances from the women inside of the restaurant. This feeling was surreal. *Was this really happening to me at this moment? Yes, it was happening. This shit was real. I was really in a restaurant with one of the most famous athletes in the country. What the fuck!* I thought in awe.

The table was placed way in the back, allowing us some privacy. The security guard sat a few feet away from us, and no one was seated beyond his table except for Christian and I. Christian pulled my chair out, motioning for me to take a seat. Nervously, I sat down, butterflies tingling on the inside of my stomach. Christian sat across from me and reached across the table to hold my hand.

"You come here a lot, huh?" I stated, alerting him that I made note of the waitress's earlier comments.

"After almost every single home game. I usually come here alone or with some teammates," he responded.

"So, correct me if I am wrong but why are you single?" I asked.

I felt the need to get to the bottom of this.

He smiled before responding.

"I'm not single," he said as a matter of fact.

"Oh oops, so who told you that I would be ok with being

a side chick? And for someone who is not single, you sure are bold having me out here like this. I want no issues," I said, rolling my eyes.

Instantly, I was turned off. Who the hell does this nigga think he is? Yea, had me fucked up! I snatched my hand from his and folded my arms across my large breasts.

Christian laughed.

"This shit is not funny; this is very ghetto to put me in this situation. Matter of fact, take me home," I shot.

"For one, watch your mouth, you're a lady, don't curse at me. Two, it is funny because I told you in the car your mine and somehow you seem to think I'm playing. I'm not single anymore because you are mine and that's it," he declared, smirking.

Instantly, I began to feel hot. I wanted to protest because who was he talking to, but he was so damn sexy. Shit, I liked the idea of being his. I could get down with being the girl of a rich and famous athlete or whatever this was exactly. The remainder of the dinner seemed to fly by. Christian was charming, assertive, and alluring. He made me feel like I was floating on a cloud the entire night. He was so intrigued with me. He wanted to know everything about me. I was attracted to his assertive confident demeanor. I had no idea what all I was in for beginning with that night.

OCTOBER 29, 2010—12:15 A.M.

I sat in the back of the Phantom on cloud nine after our date. We closed the restaurant, the remaining staff members left once Christian and I were finished. It was safe to say that I was more than a little drunk from all of the glasses of champagne and the shots of Louis XIII. Christian raised the partition, separating the driver in the front from us in the back, before reaching over and pulling me into him. Staring deeply into his eyes, he placed his finger under my chin, pulling my face to his. I gazed into his dark and mysterious eyes.

"You are beautiful, you know that?" he asked, causing me to blush.

Everything that followed happened so quickly that I was unable to catch myself. Honestly, I did not want to catch myself. Passionately, he kissed me, burying his tongue inside of my mouth.

"Mhmmmm . . ." I moaned.

Still kissing me, he reached one hand inside of my blazer and behind my back. Slowly, he unhooked my lace bralette, freeing my breasts. He paused for a moment, pulling away from me to look me in my eyes. *Whew!* I thought, breaking away from the intensity of his stare. My juices flowed uncontrollably, overflowing between my legs and drenching my G-string thong. Your girl was in heat and ready for whatever he was trying to do.

"Take that off," he commanded, tugging at my blazer.

On command, I began removing my blazer. Christian assisted me by removing my bralette. My nipples hardened, stiffly coming to attention at his touch. He looked down at them, then licked his lips before he reached down and took my breasts in his mouth one at a time. He was gentle yet firm as he licked and sucked on my breast, lightly biting on my nipple. Moaning a little louder than I intended, my head fell to the side in pleasure.

"Mhhmmmmm . . ." I moaned.

He continued, twirling his tongue over my nipple as he moved one of his hands to my neck. Softly, he choked me with one hand and used the other to creep between my legs. My breath caught in my throat. I could climax at just his touch. When he reached my treat, he was taken aback by the moisture that rained on his fingers. He removed his mouth from my nipples and smiled before trailing kisses up my neck and on my ear. The ear, oh my God, the ear was too much. Loudly, I gasped, unable to contain my pleasure. My ear was my spot!

"You soaking like this for me, baby?" he whispered, biting my ear.

I said nothing and he began to play a torturous game. Unexpectedly, he inserted two fingers inside of me.

"Answer me when I'm talking to you," he whispered, biting down on my ear even harder and choking me.

I bit down hard on my bottom lip; the rough shit turned me on.

My head fell back as I tried to find the words, but nothing came out. When he did not receive an answer, he began to stroke me with his fingers.

"What I say," he whispered, slipping a third finger inside of me.

"Yes," I whimpered, panting I was barely audible.

"A little louder, I can't hear you," he commanded.

"Yes, baby," I moaned.

Smiling, he pulled his fingers out of me. He brought his sticky fingers to my lips and placed them inside of my mouth for me. Without protest, I licked them. Secretly, I was a freak and tasting myself aroused me.

He watched me like a hawk as I sucked his fingers, not leaving one drop of my wetness behind. He unbuckled his pants and removed his girth from his boxers. What I saw when I looked down blew me away. A thick dark brown ten-inch penis stood up in the air. I was taken aback. I was wet before, but I was now overflowing. He pulled a gold-wrapped condom from his jacket pocket and slid it down his erection.

"Come get on your dick, baby girl," he stated, pulling my body onto him.

Submissively, I obliged. I wanted that dick and I wanted it

right at that moment. He leaned the seat back as I climbed on top of him. Did this man just recline his back seat? Oh, this was some rich shit. Slowly, I slid down his shaft, taking in every inch that I could. He fit inside of me perfectly, it was like my pussy walls were suctioned to his dick. Slowly, I rode him. He sent me to the land of sexual euphoria as the pain mixed with the pleasure. The sex was so good.

"And it's tight!" he whispered in my ear as he wrapped one hand behind my neck, placed one of my breasts inside of his mouth and used his other hand to firmly grip my ass.

He lifted me up and down, matching my rhythm with his own stroke.

"Mhhmmmmmmmm . . ." I moaned, repeatedly.

We were not the only ones inside of the car, but I did not give a fuck. We did not care about anyone or anything else.

"Come for me," he grunted, increasing his speed.

"This my pussy now, you hear me! You mine! This shit mines!" he declared as I rode him, speeding up to match his new pace.

"Fuck. Shit!" I yelled, coming to my first orgasm of the night.

He matched my rhythm perfectly. Sexually, we were in sync with each other. I had never experienced anything of this magnitude. Our sexual chemistry was out of this world. Our escapades continued until we arrived at his estate. No one exited the car until we both climaxed for the second time. That dick was every bit of amazing. I mean, sex so good that you start going crazy just at the thought of him giving that shit to anyone else. The shit that would make you slap a bitch just for looking at him while he wore grey sweatpants. We were both on a sexual high. That night we had passionate sex, over and over, until the morning. Then we woke up and did it all again, multiple times, all over the manor of his twenty-million-dollar estate. We had sex in the bed, shower, movie theatre, closet, and the kitchen while we made breakfast. Literally, we had sex everywhere that we went the next day. We could not get enough of each other. I did not know that it was possible to have that much sex but whew! We tore the house and my pussy down! I'm talking ice baby, I needed to ice my kitty because he put her out of commission. After that night my life changed—forever.

CHAPTER EIGHT

"Floating on a Cloud . . ."

AUGUST 10, 2012
CALABASAS, CALIFORNIA

Christian and I fell hard for one another; together we created a dangerous concoction of love and lust. In the beginning stages of our relationship, Christian was picture perfect, he did everything right. He was thoughtful, loving, and caring. He paid attention to my wants and needs. He bought me gifts, listened to me, provided a monthly allowance of fine hundred thousand dollars, the dick was bomb, and last but not least, he was fine! I felt like I was in a dream, a dream too perfect to be true.

Christian was rich, rich as fuck. His most recent contract with the Los Angeles Lakers amounted to ninety-two million dollars. He also had multiple major endorsement deals, owned businesses, and real estate. Christian was paid and very generous with his funds. He introduced me to a life of luxury, riding in the finest cars, eating the finest cuisine, traveling to the most exotic locations, shopping sprees with an unlimited budget, and living in the most luxurious homes. It was new to me, but I adapted well. Quickly and with ease I adjusted to the life of the elite. I lived the life of a rich bitch and I loved it. I was not only the girlfriend of Christian Samuels, but I became an overnight socialite and business owner. With the help of Christian and my social media followers, I launched a successful business as a sports agent, entertainment manager, and influencer. Christian made me his agent which brought in a lot of great clientele. My life was amazing, and I would never trade those good times for anything. I was floating on a cloud of happiness; ignorance is bliss, and I was living life blissfully.

I laid in the living room, on the grey velvet sectional, watching old episodes of the TV sitcom *Martin*. I was up early to prepare breakfast for the both of us. I decided to stay in the living room because Christian was still asleep after coming in from his early morning workouts and I did not want to wake him. It was the off-season which allowed us to spend a great deal of time together.

Christian walked into our living room. A GQ model he was, his six-pack abs glistened, he had a fresh haircut, and he wore Versace boxers that provided a nice view . . . if you catch my drift. The print of his thick penis was so damn alluring on this morning. *Mhhhmmmmm. Mmmhhhhhhhh. Mmmhhhhhhhh, he looks so damn good I might have to get some this morning,* I thought, admiring my man. How could one man look so damn good?

"Good morning, baby," I greeted him as he entered the room.

Christian bent over and placed a kiss on my forehead.

"Morning, sexy." He flirted while lifting my feet from the cushion so that he could sit down.

He placed my feet in his lap and began to massage them.

"Your plate is in the microwave; do you want me to get it?" I asked.

"Not yet, what did you make?" he questioned.

"Fried chicken and waffles, a fruit salad, and fresh orange juice," I replied.

"Yea, in a minute. You know exactly what I like," he spoke.

Slappppp! The sound of Christian aggressively smacking my ass echoed throughout the room.

"Owww!" I cried out.

It was much more a cry of pleasure than that of pain because I liked that rough shit. He loved doing it as well, he probably would do that all day if he could.

"Shut up, you like that shit . . . I was thinking, this weekend we could go to the Amalfi Coast in Italy. We have a new team owner, and the organization wants to get everyone acquainted. This will be a good look for us, especially because I am new to the team. A few of the star players, Jovan, Terell, and I, along with the new owner, the old owner, and some other higher-up folks in the league were invited on a yacht trip to network and discuss some business opportunities. Everyone is bringing their wives and girlfriends. I think it will be a great opportunity for you to network and get more information about your business out there, especially as my agent and my woman," Christian informed.

This news was major, and a great opportunity for me to meet some people in higher positions.

My eyes widened as I looked at him in complete shock. He must be losing his mind; this was way too rushed. I needed more time to prepare.

"It's Wednesday, you said this weekend as if in three days, how do you expect me to be ready to go to the Amalfi Coast in three days?!" I stressed, tilting my head to the side.

"Take my black card and go shopping later. Stop acting like you can't just make a phone call and have somebody do everything for you. When are you gonna realize you're rich now?" he pointed out.

Christian and I had been having the same argument for almost the entire two years that we had been together. I had a difficult time accepting the fact that what was his was mine. I did not want to get too used to the luxurious life without securing it for myself or at least being legally married. We were not married yet; he did not even propose for that matter. I was very aware that at any moment he could walk away, and I would be left with nothing. As a result of my monthly allowance, I had a large sum of money saved up. Not to mention I had my salary as his agent, money made from social media postings, and some income from real estate that he helped me acquire. The life that Christian's wealth provided us was much more than what I could provide with what I had saved, much more than I could have provided for myself.

My delay in answering his question caused him to continue his speech.

"I'm serious, Lik. I do so much to let you know that all I provide in this life is yours and that I am not going anywhere. Why is it so hard to accept that fact?" he pressed further.

Once Christian got started on a topic, he was determined to talk about it, even if the other person did not want to.

"It's not that I cannot accept it, but I've had the life I knew taken from me once before. Until I solidify my own finances for myself, I can't be naive enough to think that this is permanent," I answered, honestly.

"I get that but at this point, I do everything I can to make sure that you have your own money and that you continue to make your own money so I don't really know what else there is that I can do. What do you want? More properties? Another business? I need my lady to be comfortable accepting my wealth so whatever we have to do to get you there that's what we're going to do," he stated while looking me directly in my eyes.

"No baby, I do think I want more clients for my sports agency though. We can do that for now, that will give me more income of my own and expand my business," I said, matching the intensity of his stare.

"Ok, this weekend is perfect for you to meet some important people, team owners, things of that nature. We can go from there and see what happens . . . Oh, and you can get my food now," he instructed.

I could have seen that coming. That man could eat so it was only a matter of time before he asked for his breakfast, no matter how much he claimed that he was not hungry. I began to get up from the sectional only to get pulled back down onto his lap. Instantly, I felt his motivation for pulling me back down onto his lap; his penis was rock hard.

"On second thought, I just got an appetite for something else," he whispered while nibbling on my ear lobe.

Christian knew exactly what he was doing, my ear was my secret spot. I began to giggle and fake whine as if I did not want it. He would see right through my bullshit. I wanted sex the moment that he appeared in the living room.

"Come on, let me get the food first, freak," I protested, attempting to pull away from him.

"Ok, let me just taste it real fast," he begged.

Christian knew exactly what to say and do to get me hot and bothered. He was pulling my card because he knew that I rarely said no to oral sex. Before I could respond, Christian lifted me in the air and playfully threw me down onto the couch.

"Christian!" I giggled.

"No!" I continued to protest.

He threw my legs back over my head and before I could protest any further his tongue was inside of me and he was sucking on my clitoris. Due to the fact that I was not wearing any panties, he had easy access to my womanhood. I looked down at him, taking in the beautiful sight before me. He was staring up at me looking me directly in my eyes as he continued to suck and lick on my pussy. The intensity of his stare mixed with the sight before me was making the moment even more pleasurable. I was unable to contain my loud screams of pleasure. He buried his face inside of my sweet box while, simultaneously, placing two fingers inside of me.

"Ahhhhhhhhhh!" I screamed in ecstasy because God damn!

What the fuck! I thought as I tried to express my pleasure in moans. My moans did no justice in comparison to how good he made my body feel.

"Still don't want it?" he quizzed, briefly coming up for air before burying his face again.

Christian was so damn nasty, and I loved every minute of it. His tongue was buried inside of me like he was digging for gold. *Why the fuck does this man do my body like this, damn!* I could not get enough but at the same time, I could not take anymore. How did this man know my body this well? How was it possible that he could eat pussy this damn good! I felt my climax building as he continued to probe my clitoris with his tongue and moist mouth. Like a peach, he sucked and devoured my box.

"Baby, I'm coming!" I cried.

"Mhhhhmmmmmmm!" he groaned from between my legs.

The feeling was building but approaching slowly. Something about Christian knowing I was about to orgasm always caused him to put in overtime. He immediately took his tongue game from a ten to a one hundred. There were two seconds left on the shot clock and my pussy was the basket, he slam dunked in that shit!

"Fuckkkkkkkkk!" I wailed as the sensational feeling took over my entire being.

AUGUST 2012

AMALFI COAST, ITALY

I stood in our luxury suite admiring my appearance in front of the full-body mirror. I looked so damn good; it should be a sin to look this damn good. I was dressed in all black. I aimed to be a little sexy but still classy. After all, we were accompanying the wealthy. These people at this dinner had the power to make or break both Christian and I's careers. My jet-black hair was styled in a center part blunt cut bob, and my makeup was simple with a matte red lip to compliment my all-black attire. I had on fitted black pants, a black chiffon Vera Wang blouse, a black Givenchy blazer, a black Hermes belt with a silver buckle, and black Christian Louboutin So Kates graced my feet. I accessorized with a silver Audemars Piguet with a diamond face and a black crocodile skin Hermes Birkin bag. Christian approached me from behind, wrapping his hands around my waist and pulling my body into his. He smelled so good that I could bathe in his cologne.

"You look beautiful, as always," he said, resting his chin on the top of my head.

"Thank you, baby, and as usual you look as handsome as ever," I replied, admiring his appearance.

He wore all black as well to compliment my outfit. He wore a fitted black Balmain suit, black Tom Ford dress shoes, and a diamond iced out Rolex. I loved to admire him whenever he was dressed up. We emulated a true power couple, he looked like money and so did I.

"You ready to go out?" he asked.

"Yes," I answered.

Christian and I were on a massive-sized yacht somewhere in the middle of the Gulf of Naples and the Tyrrhenian Sea. Everything was so unbelievably beautiful that it felt like a dream. The yacht was incredibly beautiful; equipped with five floors, a rooftop pool, private suites, a special dining area, and so much more. It was our first night on the yacht. I did not know a majority of the other guests that were in attendance, specifically because Christian was new to the team.

The new team owner planned a dinner to get everyone acquainted and to introduce himself to the players that were expected to carry the team to the NBA finals. Christian and I held hands as he led me into the main dining area. The main dining area was located on the roof of the yacht with glass walls on all four sides. The view was impeccable, and the night sky made everything so much more visually appealing. The water was blue, and the scenery was indescribable. Christian and I sat at our designated seats in the middle of the table. To no surprise, we were the last couple to enter. I was sure to be late to my own funeral because I was always late. Everyone looked gorgeous sitting around the table in their suits and formal wear.

The team owner stood at the head of the table. He was a tall light brown-skinned man with a perfectly lined haircut and a full beard. He was fine, if I do say so myself, and to my surprise, he was much younger than I would have ever imagined him to be. I was expecting to see an old white man. It was rare to find a younger black man as the owner of a major sports team. What I saw, instead of an old white man, was a fairly young black man who did not look a day over forty. He wore a fitted suit; the jacket was dark grey with black lining and the pants were black. He paired it with a silver plain-faced Audemars Piguet watch that I knew to be worth at least sixty thousand dollars. I had no business admiring the man the way that I was but something about him attracted me. His demeanor revealed that there was more to him than meets the eye, his energy was alluring, that of a boss. He was pulling my energy to him without actually speaking to me or touching me. Something about him, his energy, his spirit, was so familiar to me yet we had never met before.

The team owner stood with his glass raised ready to make a toast but before he began, he took a minute to familiarize himself with the faces of everyone in attendance. He stilled when his eyes landed on me, our eyes connected, and his stare lingered for a moment but not too long to raise the attention of others. His stare was intense, the connection was magnetic, a connection that I had only had the pleasure of experiencing once before—with Rashan. The saying goes that the eyes are the windows to the soul; he was staring directly into my soul. The intensity of the moment caused me to shift uncomfortably in my seat, and suddenly I was extremely hot. I raised my hand and began fanning myself. *Girl! You cannot look at that man like that. Get the thought out of your head, that is inappropriate,* I thought. Using my other hand, I gripped Christian's hand under the table. I needed to remind myself of the reason that I was there. *You have a good man, do not even think a thought that could ruin that,* I thought.

"I want to formally introduce myself to you all, my name is Ethan Jacobs," the owner began before slightly pausing.

Ethan huh? I thought.

"I am the new owner of the Los Angeles Lakers. I will be taking over operations this up-and-coming season. This is the first basketball team that I have purchased. I currently own four soccer teams, two baseball teams, and one professional hockey team. I am very passionate about sports, but especially basketball. Outside of sports, I have other business ventures. I own a major tech company that I started at a very young age and made a lot of money from, which I have invested wisely. I am proud to be one of the only black men that owns professional sports teams, though I hope to change that in the future. I hope to make this transition easy for the entire team but especially you all, the star players. We can go around the table, everyone can introduce themselves and we can go from there. But first, if everyone could raise their glasses in a toast to success and to becoming NBA Finals Champions of twenty thirteen," he announced.

Following the commencement of the speech, Ethan Jacobs proceeded to raise his glass. The guests at the table followed his lead in raising their glasses. What Ethan happened to leave out, that I would find out later on, was that he was from a wealthy family, actually correction, he was from—the—wealthy family.

His family owned oil wells all over the middle east. They were billionaires, and had generational wealth stemming back for over a century.

"I never met a black man that owned an NBA team, that's major," Christian congratulated.

We all stood with our glasses raised, the other guests nodding their heads in agreement.

"Yes!" the wife of another player chimed in, agreeing with Christian.

"To becoming NBA Finals Champions in twenty thirteen!" another player hollered as we all clanked our glasses in celebration.

The black excellence among us was radiant. The champagne in my glass was immaculate, better than any other champagne I had ever had before. While taking in the delectable flavor of the drink, I made a mental note to find out the name of the bottle that they served us. The guests in attendance began introducing themselves to Ethan. The waiter served a seafood cocktail, featuring shrimp, lobster, crabs, and fresh oysters. As a pescatarian, I was more than happy with the appetizer options that were offered. The dinner continued with everyone introducing themselves. Christian and I were closer to the end of the table, so it took a while before it was our turn to speak. Christian stood to speak, just as everyone else did when it was their time.

"Hi, Ethan, nice to meet you. I'm Christian Samuels and this is my lady, Malika. I might have to add the Samuels to her last name soon, I don't know," he said, pausing to look down at me.

He smiled down as I chuckled.

"I know everyone here except for you Ethan, some a little deeper than others. I'm here this year to help bring a championship to Los Angeles. I've been training with these guys sitting at this table for the last few months and I feel pretty confident in what we can do this season. To Roger Wilks, the previous owner, thank you for bringing me into the team at the time you did. It was an honor to be able to become acquainted with you. I plan to show you why you worked so hard to sign me to this team. To Ethan Jacobs! I'm excited to play for a team that is owned by a Black man. This is major, not only for you, but for the culture. You always hear of Black men making it out of the hood to play for the league but never actually owning it. This is an exciting time, and I am happy I got to not only witness it, but also, to be a part of it," Christian continued.

"Thank you!" Ethan replied from his seat at the head of the table, nodding his head.

"I'll allow my lady to introduce herself," Christian stated, sitting back down in his seat.

"Hi, everyone," I greeted, rising from my chair.

"My name is Malika Tanners. I am the lady of Christian Samuels, maybe soon to be wife, fingers crossed," I said looking down at Christian as everyone at the table began to chuckle.

Suddenly, I felt a strong energy coming in my direction. It was as if this energy was burning right through me, connecting directly with my soul. My smile faded and I looked up to continue my speech. Ethan's stare was penetrating my being. A stare that I felt before I looked up from Christian. While everyone else found the soon-to-be wife comment to be cute and funny, Ethan was unmoved. His body language said something that I was unable to read. Was it anger? It may have been anger. No one else at the table seemed to notice but something in his eyes told me that he was uneasy about something; I did not understand. I resumed my introduction, making an attempt to keep my composure. I did not want to alarm any of the guests at the table, especially Christian. *Maybe it's nothing and I am tripping,* I thought.

"Aside from being Christian's lady, I am also his agent. I represent a small subset of clients outside of Christian. I have my Bachelor of Science in Business Management from Syracuse University. I am currently looking to expand my firm, sign a few new clients, and also hire additional staff. I am excited for you all this season and I am looking forward to seeing my baby bring home another championship!" I exclaimed, forcing myself to smile.

I could feel Ethan staring at me throughout my entire speech. No matter how hard I attempted to focus, eye contact between the two of us seemed to be inevitable. I observed that when I mentioned Christian Ethan became tense. *Maybe this nigga is crazy or some shit, he doesn't even know me,* I thought. I hoped no one else in attendance was able to pick up on the weird vibe between the two of us.

Unexpectedly, as I was lowering into my dining chair Ethan spoke directly to me.

"I may have a few players from some of my other teams that are interested in signing to a new agent. I can put out some feelers to see who might be interested and set up some meetings so you can connect with them," Ethan volunteered.

I was caught off guard and left fumbling to find words to formulate a sentence or some sort of response. The intensity of his stare was already too much for me but when he spoke directly to me the energy between us was set ablaze, magnetic even, almost pulling me to him. The awkward silence that lingered as everyone awaited my reply caused Christian to respond for me.

"Yes, that would be great. We would really appreciate it," he offered, reaching for my hand.

"Yes, thank you! That would be amazing," I thanked, finally finding my words.

"I'll have my assistant reach out to you once everything is done. No thank you needed," he responded.

I knew he was more so speaking to me as opposed to

Christian. I sat in my chair hoping that no one else noticed the energy between the two of us. Christian responded to Ethan; he was speaking to Ethan even if Ethan was not speaking to him.

"Yea, we appreciate it either way," Christian replied, lifting my hand to his lips.

Christian was being territorial, making it clear who I was with and whose woman I was. Ethan, in an attempt to smooth over the tense moment, smiled and made a corny joke at the head of the table. I blew out a sigh of relief hoping that no one else picked up on the moment that occurred between the three of us. The remainder of the dinner was beautiful, filled with laughs, smiles, dancing, drinking, and men talking business. There was money in the air, the atmosphere felt different being around such wealth. Ethan and I kept our distance for the remainder of the evening. At times, we found ourselves staring into each other's eyes. I could not understand for the life of me the intense feeling that was between this man and me, but it was overwhelming. *Yea, I have to stay away from him. What is this? Why do I feel like I know him?* Those thoughts ran rampant through my mind all night.

CHAPTER NINE

"Only the Beginning . . ."

AUGUST 2012

AMALFI COAST, ITALY

Slam! The sound of Christian slamming the door to our suite echoed throughout the room.

Startled, I swiftly spun around in the direction of the door.

"Why did you just slam the . . ." I began but was cut off by a raging Christian.

"What was that shit about with you and the team owner nigga?!" he pressed.

He began pacing the small space, walking back and forth between the door and the king bed. I stood still, confused and unsure of what to say.

"You hear me fucking talking to you!" Christian shot.

"Huh? What shit?" I questioned; my forehead bent in confusion.

I had hoped that Christian did not notice the weird exchange between Ethan and me, but that hope seemed to have gone in vain. Christian stopped pacing and looked up at me.

The look in his eyes was one that I had never seen before, I had seen Christian angry . . . but this was different.

"Don't play fucking stupid, Malika. You know what the fuck I'm talking about," he continued, raising his voice.

My eyes widened in astonishment, because who the fuck was he talking to? Christian and I rarely had arguments or disagreements, so his extreme aggression caught me by surprise.

"First of all, lower your tone . . ." I instructed, attempting to defuse the situation.

Christian cut me off before I was able to finish the remainder of my response.

"Malika, stop fucking playing with me. You think I ain't see that shit between you and that nigga? What you star struck over some money? He owns the team, so you want to hop on his dick now, huh? One rich nigga ain't enough for you bitch, you want more!" he screamed.

His words hit me in the face like a grenade. Who was this person?! Where did this extreme aggression come from?! I had never seen this man before this day!

"Bitch! Who the fuck do you think you're talking to?! Bitch! Your fucking mother is a bitch! Your mother, your grandmother, your fucking aunties, they all bitches!" I yelled, angrily.

The words that came out of his mouth disrespected me beyond measure. He was not only disrespectful, but he deeply hurt my feelings. A bitch, yea, he lost his fucking mind. When they go low, I go lower.

Unexpectedly, Christian flew from where he was standing over to me. He was so close that I could smell the alcohol on his breath. Spit particles rained down on me as he rambled.

"Your fucking mother is a bit—" He paused, realizing the gravity of the words that had just escaped his mouth.

I stood there holding my breath, stuck in a state of shock as the words hit me like an eighteen-wheel tractor-trailer. He mentioned my dead mother. The hurt resonated throughout my entire body like a water wave. My eyes burned as I fought the tears that wanted so desperately to fall, I could not let him know how much he affected me.

“Malika, I’m trying really hard to hold my composure! Stop fucking trying me! Where do you know that nigga from?!” he barked, pinching the bridge of his nose.

I scoffed, rolling my eyes. I pushed him, attempting to walk past him but he grabbed my arm and pushed me backwards towards the wall, pinning me down. I turned my head to the left, jerking my arm in an attempt to get him to release his tight grip.

“Get the fuck off of me,” I protested, fighting against his grip.

“No, answer me! I’m sorry I mentioned your mother,” he stated, his tone was lower.

“Tuh!” I scoffed.

“Yea, ok,” I stated, dryly.

I kept my head turned to the side, refusing to look at him. Everything about this man, my man, disgusted me in this moment.

“Where do you know that nigga from?!” he quizzed once again, lifting my wrist and slamming it back down on the wall.

“Get the fuck off of me. You’re not sorry and you fucking disrespected me! Aside from my dead mother bitch to say is one rich nigga not enough! Nigga, are you fucking slow?! I never asked you for none of this shit! You did this! And for the fucking record, I don’t know that man! I never met him before today, you son of a bitch! I can’t believe this shit! Fuck you! Get the fuck off of me!” I argued, fighting against his grip once more.

To my surprise, he released me, stepping back to give me a little room. I shoved Christian out of my face and hurriedly moved off of the wall.

"Malika," he said softly, reaching for me.

I pushed his hand away and looked at him in disgust as tears escaped from my eyes. Unwilling to let him see me cry, I rushed towards the door, bolting. I was caught off guard by the hysterical cries that erupted from within me. His words cut deep. I had to deal with everybody else in the world consistently making comments about me. Everyone assumed that I was with Christian for his money. To hear those same accusations come from the man that I consistently expressed my feelings and reservations about his finances to cut deep. Not to mention, my mother! Of all things, my dead mother! Christian knew the deep burden I carried with me my entire life feeling like I killed my mother. I always felt that I was better off not being born because then she would have had an opportunity at life. The heaviness I felt was a bit too much for me, I needed to get away. Was this who Christian was all along? Was he just angry? Who is this man that I have never seen before?

"Malika!" he screamed after me, but I did not look back.

I ignored his calls and instead, ran out of the room. I needed a minute. I needed to think, to get away from him. I was so hurt by his words and him calling me out of my name was simply unacceptable. I never let any man I dealt with disrespect me and I was not about to start now. He brought me back to my days as a child, dealing with my father. Hurriedly, I rushed up the steps and out the doors where the suites were located. I ran until there was nowhere else to run, all the way to the rooftop where I was able to see into the night sky and the Tyrrhenian Sea. The tears became uncontrollable, flooding my vision. A part of me traveled back to the place where I was a little girl, reliving my trauma with my father. Something about the coldness in Christian's eyes reminded me of Trevor Tanners. Another part of me felt guilty and as the saying goes, the guilt was making me tilt. I knew exactly what Christian was referring to when he asked about the connection between Ethan and me, but I would never admit it.

I bent over the rail, hanging over the ocean I gasped for air. I was crying so hard that I could barely catch my breath. Suddenly, the feeling came over me that I was not alone. I felt Ethan before I saw him. He was standing to my left, looking off into the water. He looked up at me and our eyes connected, seizing my crying. He seemingly hit an imaginary switch and something inside of me felt better. Suddenly, Christian's words did not hurt or matter as much. Christian just did not matter to me at all. I was lost in Ethan's eyes before he spoke.

"Out of respect I will keep my distance from you, but did he hurt you?" he questioned in a low tone.

I could have easily told him that this was none of his business but everything in me told me that this was his business; I was his business.

"Not physically," I responded, sincerely.

There was a flash of an emotion that I could not read, then a sudden flash of anger.

"Did he hurt you, Malika?" he asked again, more assertively this time.

My name should not be allowed to come out of his mouth. He said Malika with so much care like he already knew me. Who was this man and why was I so drawn to him?

"No, just a disagreement. I needed a moment to myself that's why I came out here," I replied.

My response was more out of fear of what he may do to Christian if the answer was yes. He looked at me passionately. I felt naked under his stare, like he could see right through me. He squinted before turning his head to the other side. He was thinking, contemplating something.

"Ok. I'll leave you to yourself then." He paused before continuing.

"I know I'm overstepping but you feel so familiar to me," he added.

He placed a cloth napkin on the ledge before turning and disappearing. *Wow. He felt it too,* I thought. Suddenly, thinking of his admission of feeling that we knew each other before today, a wave of guilt swept over me. I knew that I was wrong but that did not excuse Christian's disrespect. I took a few moments to gather myself before walking to where Ethan once was. I retrieved the napkin that, I assumed, he left there for me. The inside of the napkin was embroidered with E.J. and it held his scent. Secretly, I wanted to keep it and hold onto a piece of this mystery man, but the thought alone made me feel even more guilty than I already did. I cleaned my face and placed the napkin back on the ledge before walking away.

Christian sat on the corner of the bed still wearing his suit from dinner. I had only been gone for about forty minutes yet worry was etched all over his face. I closed the door and walked towards the bathroom, attempting to avoid his stare. Once I was close enough to him, he grabbed my arm, pulling me to him.

"I'm sorry. I don't know what that was about. I don't want to see you cry. I didn't mean what I said about your mother, I was wrong for that. I don't want to hurt you," he whispered while holding me tightly.

I was quiet for a moment, thinking of a response. I wanted to be angry at him, but I could not get Ethan out of my head. Guilt washed over me like the plague. Submitting to his embrace, I clung to him, hoping that the yearning inside of me for Ethan would disappear. The feeling that I had for Ethan did not dissipate instantly and it caused me to cling to Christian even more.

"I'm sorry too, baby. Sorry for calling Ms. Arlene out of her name and Ms. Netta. I'm sorry if anything I did at dinner was disrespectful to you. There is nothing to worry about. I love you," I whispered.

In reality, I was apologizing due to my guilt, apologizing that another man could make me feel the way that Ethan did. Ethan made me feel something that I thought died the day that Rashan did. I wanted to believe that Christian had nothing to worry about but deep down inside he had everything to worry about. I loved Christian, I did, but the feeling that Ethan and Rashan provided me with their presence alone was unmatched. To find that feeling in Ethan after Rashan's passing scared me. I was scared of myself around Ethan.

"I love you so much," he expressed, kissing me on my forehead.

FEBRUARY 19, 2013
NEW YORK CITY, NY

"Well, Malika aren't you going to sit down and eat something? You're always on the move, just sit and eat, it won't kill you," Ms. Sheema pleaded.

I looked down at my silver Audemars Piguet to check the time. It was only two in the afternoon; I had a meeting in mid-town at five in the evening so I was sure that I could spare a few moments. I sighed heavily before pulling out a chair at the dining room table. One thing about Ms. Sheema was that she was going to feed you.

"Ok, I have a few minutes but not too much time, I need to leave in an hour," I stated.

Ms. Sheema looked over at me from the stove, waving her hand to indicate that she was not paying me any mind. She then walked over to the round table with a plate of curry chicken and rice. Ms. Sheema still lived in the same cramped apartment in the Bronx. No matter how many times I offered to buy her a nice home or condo she refused it. This was all she knew and where she insisted on residing. There used to be a plethora of kids who lived here but since Ava, Noelle, and I, Ms. Sheema had retired from being a foster parent for any more incoming youth.

"Girl hush, shut up and eat this food. I didn't even tell you Kesha dirty ass been going around telling everybody about how you used to be friends back in the day and you used to borrow her clothes. I ran into her on White Plains the other day talking about, hey, Ms. Sheema. I looked her ass right up and down and said none of my girls ever had to borrow shit from you, don't hey me!" she gossiped, placing the plate before me.

My mouth instantly began to water, it all looked so good. One thing about Ms. Sheema, she loved to gossip.

"I used to wear her clothes? Kesha buggin, nobody was ever wearing them dingy clothes. I barely even ever spoke to that girl," I replied, looking up with my face contorted in disgust.

"Yes, little girl go on, everybody knows she always looked like Payless, nobody borrowing her damn clothes," Ms. Sheema insulted, handing me a water bottle from inside of the fridge.

As I picked up my fork to dig in my cell phone began to vibrate on the table.

323-555-3232 appeared on the caller ID. The number that appeared was a number that I was unfamiliar with, but something told me that I should answer. I placed my fork on the plate and proceeded to answer the phone.

"Hello?" I questioned.

"Hi, may I speak to Ms. Malika Tanners?" the lady on the phone requested.

"This is her; may I ask who is calling?" I quizzed.

"My name is Macy Weathers, and I am a nurse for Dr. Kutzmier. You came in for a routine checkup last week Thursday. I wanted to discuss some of your test results," the nurse informed me.

My heartbeat quickened as butterflies fluttered in my stomach. All of the air from my lungs seemed to dissipate as I held my breath. I had not been with anyone except for Christian in years and the last time I checked I was completely fine, so what could this be!

"One moment, please," I said, jumping up from my chair.

"Malika?" Ms. Sheema questioned; worry etched in her face.

I held up a finger and mouthed hold on before walking out of the kitchen and up the steps to the bathroom. I shut the door behind me before I continued.

"Ok, please continue," I replied to the nurse.

"Well, we performed a routine STD check, and it came back positive for Chlamydia, Trichomonas, and there were irregularities in your pap smear indicating the possibility of HPV," the nurse informed me.

Smack! My cell phone slipped out of my hand and crashed onto the floor.

The news came crashing down on me. I had been faithful so the only possible way for me to have any STDs was if Christian had not been. I had been checked periodically throughout our relationship and everything usually came back negative. Christian was responsible for not only one STD but two. I scrambled to pick up the phone from the floor. My screen was shattered but the woman was still on the phone.

"Hello, Ms. Tanners, are you still there?" the nurse questioned.

"Umm, Yes. Sorry about that. I think I misheard you, can you repeat that please," I questioned, hoping that I was hearing things.

"Your test results came back positive for both Chlamydia and Trichomoniasis. You also have an irregular pap smear that is an indication of HPV. The STDs can be cleared up with medication and antibiotics, I will send over the prescriptions to the pharmacy we have on file for you. You will need to come back into the office for additional tests to make sure that the HPV won't turn into cervical cancer. In most cases, it will clear itself up on its own, but we need to run additional tests to make sure that everything is okay," the nurse stated.

I heard the words over the phone, but I was unable to comprehend them. I understood what she was saying but it sounded like a foreign language to me.

"Ok, are you sure? Completely sure?" I questioned in disbelief.

"Yes, ma'am, we run all of our positive test results multiple times for accuracy. Would you like to schedule a date to come in for the tests?" Macy questioned.

"Tomorrow, I can be there tomorrow afternoon or Thursday," I responded.

I was keeping my composure but, on the inside, I felt a mixture of emotions.

"Ok, we will see you Thursday. The prescriptions will be sent over to your pharmacy within the next hour. Have a nice day," the nurse stated.

"Thank you, same to you," I said before hanging up the phone.

I bent over the sink, heaving, fighting so hard for air but I was unable to breathe. I needed air, and I needed it fast but somehow it felt like the space was shrinking. I bolted, rushing out of the bathroom, down the steps and out the door of the apartment. Hurriedly, I rushed to the elevator—pressing the down button repeatedly, wishing that it would come a little faster.

"Malika honey, what's wrong?! What happened?!" Ms. Sheema's voice boomed from behind me.

I pressed the elevator down button a few more times, jamming it so hard that my finger turned red. Ms. Sheema placed her hand on my shoulder.

“Come back in honey, please. What’s wrong?!” she questioned.

I turned to her, no words coming out. I just could not get anything out until I broke.

“I need . . .” I paused, trying to find air once again.

“I need to breathe, I can’t breathe,” I began, before a gut-wrenching cry burst out of me.

The cry took over my entire body, my entire being. My knees buckled and I fell to the floor. All of the energy had left my body.

“Ohhhhh! Get up, baby, get up. Come on, we’re going inside,” Ms. Sheema stated, bending down to lift me from the floor.

Ding! The elevator door opened but I had no strength to get up and enter it.

With the help of Ms. Sheema, I cobbled up from the floor and cried all the way back into the small apartment. I could not breathe. I fought so hard for air, but it felt like I still could not breathe. I was hyperventilating, having a panic attack. Ms. Sheema placed me on the couch and disappeared for a moment as I sat crying. I brought my knees to my chest and wrapped my arms around them. I sat, wailing for the next few moments.

“Water, drink some water, love,” Ms. Sheema said, handing me a glass of cold water.

I looked up at her, sorrow-filled eyes, shaking my head from side to side. My face contorted as the emotional pain ravaged through my body. The multiple STDs felt like a knife to the chest, but the most painful part was the revelation of the cheating. My intuition told me on numerous occasions that he was unfaithful, but I could never catch him, this revelation was all the proof that I needed. My heart felt like someone had ripped it out of my chest and cut a line directly through it. Where was the loyalty? How could the man that I lay next to every night think so little of me that he didn't bother to even protect himself? If not wearing protection for himself, then what about protecting me?

"You are having a panic attack; you need some water. Take a breath, you need to breathe," Ms. Sheema instructed, bringing the glass to my face.

Hesitantly, I drank it. The large gulps of water scraped the inside of my throat like shards of glass.

"Now, what is going on?" Ms. Sheema quizzed.

"He cheated . . ." I started but I was crying too hard to get anything else out.

"Ok, but that's not all, what else is it?" Ms. Sheema questioned.

"He gave me three STDs. Chlamydia, Trichomonas, and HPV," I admitted, crying even harder than I was before once the words escaped my mouth.

Ms. Sheema's eyes widened for a moment before she began shaking her head. She leaned in and placed a hand on my back, rubbing in circular motions.

"I dreaded the possibility of this day for any of you girls. Men and their wandering penises. It's going to be okay, baby; most women have been there," she offered.

"How could he do this to me. The least he could have done was use protection, how could he?" I questioned; disbelief registered in my tone.

Ms. Sheema paused for a moment before responding.

"Honey, that is the anatomy of men and I am sorry to tell you that the man you lay down with is rich and powerful with beautiful women at his disposal. You will get over this and thank God that it is all curable, except the HPV that could turn into cervical cancer but it most likely will take care of itself and fade into the background. What does not cost your life, does not cost anything. Just be grateful that the infections he gave you can be cured. Don't try to understand something that is not meant for women to understand. Even the best and most honorable men have stepped out—don't blame yourself. There's good men out there but even they have cheated, maybe not on every woman but in their lifetime, they stepped out before on someone. Shit, I have yet to find me a man that proved me wrong on that one," she stated.

"So that's it. I am just supposed to accept this because of who he is?" I questioned.

Looking up at her with bulging eyes as if she had lost her damn mind.

"No, who the hell said that!" She paused, pulling her head back and widening her eyes.

She placed her hands on her thigh before continuing.

"I am saying, don't try to understand it. As women, the first thing we do is try to make sense out of something that does not make sense. You blame yourself first then it's how could he do this to you, then it's maybe I didn't do this right or I'm not pretty enough. It's not you, it's not how could he, it's nothing you could have done differently. You make a decision if you want to stay with him and if you do, you make it very clear you will not deal with this shit or you can always cheat back; that always makes me feel a little bit better, but it doesn't take the pain away. I don't care much for that Christian, he seems nice, but I see right through him. In a perfect world, I'd tell you to leave and find a man who loves and respects you enough to at least use a condom. But I know you enough to know you won't leave, not yet; you love him too much to walk away right now but you will when you're ready. I can only tell you to be smart and to know that you will get through this because what does not cost you your life, does not cost you anything. So, moving forward, toughen up because if you choose to stay with a man like Christian, this is only the beginning. So, you go home and give his ass hell, let him know that he better not ever play with you again! Whoop his ass if you need to! Shit, I wouldn't even be sitting here crying right now, I would have found his ass already! Boop! Bop! And an extra little kick right in his balls! Yea, you better ask about me back in my day. My men knew what was coming if they ever played with me," Ms. Sheema counseled.

I chuckled a little through the tears, shaking my head and calming down some. I did not want to because absolutely nothing was funny, but Ms. Sheema never failed to amaze or amuse me.

Ms. Sheema was brutally honest. She was going to tell you what you needed to hear whether I wanted to hear it or not. I sat in silence, taking in the impact of her words. My cries continued, but it was now a silent cry. Her words, *if you choose to stay with a man like Christian, this is only the beginning*, played over and over in my head.

CHAPTER TEN

"Diamonds Are Forever . . ."

JUNE 17, 2015
BEVERLY HILLS, CALIFORNIA

"Ok, no bitch suck in more. I need a little arch; this is going on Insta! You know your five million followers are dying to get details about the wedding. Give energy, bitch! You're getting married! Stop looking all damn stiff!" Noelle coached.

I exhaled a deep breath.

"Bitch, hurry up. I'm over this!" I snapped before sucking in again.

What the hell I was sucking in anyways, I did not have a stomach. Noelle snapped a few more photos of me before pausing to critique them. She yelled once she found the one that she liked.

"Ok! Got the banger! This is the one, look!" Noelle beamed, rushing over to me.

"Yea, ok. Give it to Joel so he can post it," I instructed, waving her off.

Noelle handed a seated Joel, my assistant, the marketing phone.

"Well, what got into you, bridezilla? You are so unexcited

today! It's your wedding day, what's the problem?" Ava questioned, walking over from the makeup station.

"Can I get the room cleared, please. Everyone except Noelle and Ava, please. I need a few minutes of privacy," I requested.

Instantly, everyone except Taya stopped what they were doing and hurried out of the room. Noelle's brow dipped in confusion and she pulled her chair closer to me. Taya stood there ignoring my request.

"Taya, hello?" I questioned, confused.

Apparently, I was speaking in Espanol.

"Oh, you meant me too?" Taya replied, attitude laced in her tone.

"I mean, I said everyone except Noelle and Ava," I sassed, rolling my neck.

"Whatever, so over y'all little sister circle," Taya shot.

"Girl, go ahead, you been trying it all day," Ava interjected, rolling her eyes.

Ava was correct, Taya had been off all day. I could not put my finger on it, but something was different about her attitude.

"Anyways girl, what? You have not been happy all day?" Noelle confessed her observations.

"I just don't know, y'all. I love him, I do but we have been through some shit and I just don't know. Can I even trust this man? What if he cheats again? It's just too much," I expressed.

Noelle nor Ava knew of the STDs. The only people who knew were Ms. Sheema and Tamir. Noelle and Ava did know, however, that Christian was caught cheating, but I fed them a bullshit story about how I found out.

"Girl, before I married Mir, I was scared even though I never said anything, but I am so happy that I did not let that fear stop me. I get it, especially being married to someone famous but don't let your nerves stop you from being happy!" Noelle offered.

"Yes, y'all love each other! Don't think about that! Be

positive, you being negative! Think that the best will happen, and it will!" Ava offered, being optimistic.

A knock at the door interrupted my pending response. Ava, closest to the door, proceeded to open it. Tamir stood on the other side of the door.

"What you doing over here?" Noelle questioned.

"Joel texted me, he said something was wrong with Li," he informed everyone.

"Hmm, well, we had it under control," Noelle replied, sassily.

Noelle, sometimes, got jealous of the friendship Tamir and I shared. She knew that we were friends, but our closeness occasionally bothered her.

"Let me talk to her for a minute, y'all," Tamir requested.

Ava nodded, making her way to the door. Noelle rolled her eyes and followed suit. Tamir grabbed Noelle by the arm and kissed her on the cheek before she exited.

"Stop acting like that, Noe," he commanded, smacking her ass as she walked past.

Noelle melted at his kiss, then gave him a seductive look.

"Boy, after the wedding, ok!" Noelle snickered.

Tamir closed the door, then sat where Noelle was previously seated.

"Talk to me," he stated.

Tamir knew me well, by one look he knew when I was holding something in and needed to talk.

"I just don't know, Mir. I love him, I do but I'm scared. You know what he did in twenty thirteen. I just don't know if I should have stayed then and if I'm fooling myself now," I revealed.

Tamir leaned back in his seat, thinking before he spoke.

"I told you then and I'll tell you again now. A man is going to be a man. No excuse for it but it's the truth. It's up to him to decide that you worth it to not make those mistakes again. You want to be with him, you have to let that shit go. It's been over two years. You can't pretend to forgive somebody, be happy then pull that card when you want. I know he scared you, but you gave him another chance so judge him off of his actions beyond that point. You bringing up old stuff, it's time to move forward. We all here for y'all, to support y'all love. I know he spent a bag on this wedding, and you spent all your time planning how to spend his money, it's clear you love him so give it a chance. I know that shit hurt, I witnessed you firsthand and I never want to see you hurt that bad again, but you decided to stay, nobody forced you. Go be happy and leave that shit where it is, in the past. You ain't no fortune teller, just live in the moment, you don't know what's going to happen," Tamir counseled.

"Thank you," I said, emotion laced in my tone.

Tamir stood, opening his arms for me to hug him.

I stood, reciprocating his embrace.

"No thank you needed, pull it together and finish getting dolled up. You got a good man out there waiting to give you his last name. Don't sabotage this dwelling on your past and if anything, I'll fuck him up for you, sis," Tamir said, half-jokingly.

I exhaled sharply. Tamir was right. I decided to forgive Christian years ago, there was nothing left for me to do but let the past go and move forward. It was time to step into being a wife, Mrs. Christian Samuels.

"Do you Christian Samuels, take thee, Malika Tanners to be your lawfully wedded wife? To have and to hold from this day forward, for better, for worse, for richer, for poorer, in sickness and in health, to love and to cherish, till death do you part?" the officiant asked.

I sucked in air, awaiting Christian's response. Anxiety filled me and my nerves took over. I hoped that I would not grow to regret this decision. I loved Christian but we had our fair share of issues throughout our years of being together. *Can I really make a lifetime commitment?* I thought. My heart ached and so many different emotions filled me at the same time. Am I really getting married right now? No way this shit is really happening. *God please, if this is not right for me, I need a sign,* I thought. My eyes diverted away from Christian to take in the atmosphere of the ballroom. Everything was so beautiful. We were the center of attention, standing atop a spiral glass staircase located in the center of the venue elevated above the six hundred guests in attendance.

The theme of the wedding was Diamonds are Forever. Everything was white, including the guests' attire because white means purity. Purity meant a lot to me beginning this journey because our love was tainted with infidelity, disloyalty, distrust, and disrespect. This was meant to be a fresh start for us and not a continuation of the issues that we had before. The wedding was over the top and fabulous. Diamond chandeliers were hanging from the ceiling, white floral arrangements made of hydrangea and roses lined the walls, and Italian marble glass floors graced the venue. The total cost of the wedding was nine-hundred and fifty thousand dollars. There was no expense spared to complete my dream, this was the wedding of the current King of professional basketball and his Queen—we had no choice but to show out.

I wore a beautiful custom Vera Wang dress that was priced at fifty-two thousand dollars. The dress was a strapless and backless mermaid cut with a heart-shaped bustier made out of premium Italian lace accompanied with a twenty-foot diamond train made out of Swarovski crystals. My hair was simple in a low side part deep swoop ponytail. My makeup was flawless and simple with a nude lip and bronze glow. Five karat baguette diamond earrings dangled from my ear and a diamond crown veil sat atop of my head. I looked like money, a rich bitch indeed. My body looked amazing. I was snatched in my dress, my boobs sat up high, there was no waist in sight and my ass looked voluptuous. Your girl was serving. You wish I was your wife would be the caption for my fabulous social media photos later that evening. The entire event was gorgeous. Shit, after the bridezilla that I had become over the months leading up to my wedding there was no other option but for the Samuels wedding to be flawless.

Christian wore a handmade white suit with black lining made by a prestigious French designer. His hair was freshly cut, he had grown a shadowed beard and his waves were making everyone seasick. He looked and smelled so damn good. I could not wait until the wedding was over. I wanted to ride him all night, my God. Looking around the room, there was a strong urge to turn my head and look behind Christian.

Like a moth to a flame, Ethan's eyes found me. I froze. There was a sadness in his eyes, calling me to him, begging me not to go through with this marriage. His eyes told me that I was making a mistake marrying Christian. There was a yearning inside of me to run away, that Christian was not the man for me. I would never listen to that yearning. I loved Christian and years later I still did not know Ethan. Following the days that we had on the Amalfi Coast, Ethan and I avoided each other like the plague. In social settings, we avoided contact with each other by any means necessary. He had his assistant reach out to me as promised and she followed through connecting me with players from various sports teams that Ethan owned but that was it.

Christian's voice brought me out of the secret bubble Ethan and I were in and back to reality.

"I do!" Christian answered, smiling brightly.

Next, it was my turn so say the magic words. Christian looked into my eyes as the officiant began.

"Do you Malika Tanners, take thee, Christian Samuels to

be your lawfully wedded husband? To have and to hold from this day forward, for better, for worse, for richer, for poorer, in sickness and in health, to love and to cherish, till death do you part?" the officiant asked.

Here it was, this was my last chance to walk away if I wanted to. I was unsure if a man like Christian could be tamed, after years of partying and seeing different women, he would actually settle down and commit? I stalled for a minute, thinking. The weight of the burning eyes and stares around me was too much, causing the words to fly out of my mouth before I could stop myself.

"I do!" I screamed, anxiously.

I did not even feel my mouth moving when I said it, I only heard the words.

"Christian and Malika, you both have chosen to recite their own vows today. Christian, you may begin," the officiant offered.

Christian reached into the outer pocket of his suit jacket and pulled out a small sheet of paper. He opened the paper and made eye contact before reading.

"Bear with me, I am not the best at expressing my emotions. Malika, you are my everything. I never thought that I would ever decide to settle down and be a family man, but you changed that for me. Since the first night that we met, you have been my rock, my lover, my friend, and the best parts of my day. I promise to be the best husband that I can be, to love and uplift you at every step of the way. I know I'm not perfect and I make mistakes but thank you for loving me through it all. I question the intentions of most people in my life, but I never had to question your motives or intentions with me, it was always genuine love and for that, I owe you the world and that's what I plan to provide to you. I love you, forever my love," Christian read.

My heart fluttered hearing his words. It was now my turn and I had not written anything. I wanted to speak from the heart.

"Malika, it is now your turn to recite your vows," the officiant informed.

I took a deep breath, calming myself before I began.

"Christian, my love. I decided to speak from the heart today because that is all I ever need with you, my heart. I am so in love with you. You are my lover, friend, confidant, and support system. You push me to be better, consistently putting me in positions to elevate myself. My days are better because of you, our love is complicated, but I am willing to bet on us. This life with you has been a dream and I know that there is nowhere else I would rather be. You accept my flaws, insecurities, and up and down attitude. I know we were meant to cross paths and although this journey is crazy, it's our journey and our story. I am honored to be your wife and I vow to do everything in my power to love on you and make you happy. I love you," I spoke.

Christian squeezed my hand once I finished, his pearly white teeth shining through his bright smile.

"It is now time to exchange the rings," the officiant stated.

Both Christian and I turned to the side to retrieve the rings. I purchased Christian a custom brass silver Cartier Love Ring with C&M engraved on the inside.

"Christian, you may now place the ring on Malika's finger and repeat after me . . ." the officiant read.

"I give you this ring, wear it with love and joy. And this ring has no end, my love is forever," Christian repeated after the officiant, placing the ring on my finger.

The baguette diamond wedding band sparkled on my finger and complimented my pink twenty-four karat diamond engagement ring.

The officiant then turned to me and continued.

“Malika, you may now place the ring on Christian’s finger and repeat after me . . .” the officiant read.

“I give you this ring, wear it with love and joy. And this ring has no end, my love is forever,” I repeated after the officiant, placing the wedding band on Christian’s finger.

Nice! Christian mouthed to me, admiring the ring.

“By the power vested in me, before the state of California I now pronounce you Mr. and Mrs. Samuels!” the officiant happily affirmed.

“Woooooooooooooooo!” The guests all stood from their seats cheering and clapping at our union.

“Yessss!” Someone screamed.

“You may now kiss the bride!” the officiant yelled.

Holding one of my hands, Christian placed the other hand on the side of my cheek, pulling my face to his. He brought his lips to mine, kissing me with more love and passion than I experienced in our entire relationship. It felt different to kiss him, like I was kissing my husband and not my boyfriend or my fiancé. The feeling was surreal. I could have stood there kissing him forever, but everyone was watching. I attempted to pull away, but he held me to him, kissing me. Finally, we turned to face the guests who were all cheering and clapping.

Christian and I stepped down from the staircase into a sea of love. Noelle and Ava, who both shared the responsibility of being my matron of honor, rushed to us. They both looked fabulous yet simple. The entire wedding was so extra that we opted to keep the bridal party outfits simple. Noelle wore a strapless white gown with an open back that hugged her curves perfectly. Her long hair was curled and styled into a center part. Ava wore a dress similar to Noelle’s and her hair was styled in a side part with flowing loose curls. Their makeup was simple and flawless with a nude lip gloss. We all lived for a nude lip; the colorful lipstick was not our taste.

"Malika! You are married, girl! Married! You married Christian fucking Samuels! Girl, you are Mrs. Samuels! Yes, wife!" she cooed, hugging me.

Noelle was so happy; Noelle may have been happier than I was about this wedding. If I was at a ten Noelle was a twenty on the excitement scale. Noelle and Tamir were already married, the two got married the year after Tamir was drafted but she still acted like it was her special day.

"I cannot believe this! Bitch, you are really married! Wow! Congratulations!" Ava yelled, rushing to hug me.

I was not sure when but at some point, I began to cry because I could feel the tears running down my face. I was so happy; these were tears of joy. Christian noticed and wiped my tears away with his hand before leaning in and whispering in my ear.

"I know you won't forgive me if I let you mess up your makeup before we take our pictures. What's wrong?" he whispered.

"Nothing, I love you," I answered.

He leaned in and placed a kiss on the top of my forehead.

"Nope, no! Do not kiss her on her face! You're gonna mess up her makeup, no!" Noelle snapped.

Noelle's face contorted in disgust as she dabbed my forehead with her fingers.

Christian chuckled and shook his head.

"My wife. I can kiss her wherever I want to." He chuckled, winking at me.

Nasty ass! I thought, catching his side joke. Aww! I married the man that I loved despite my fears, and, in this moment, he was showing me exactly why I loved him. His caring nature did not help me to stop crying, it instead caused me to cry a little harder out of happiness. I was a cry baby, happy, sad, angry, frustrated, no matter the emotion your girl was going to bust out in tears.

"Lika! No, we are not crying today, no," Noelle said, rushing over to me with a handkerchief to catch the tears.

Christian took the handkerchief and turned to look at me.

"I got it; I got my wife," he stated, lovingly.

"Yea, bro! But don't mess it up!" Ava scolded, excitedly.

Taya, a bridesmaid, emerged from behind the staircase. She was wearing a white dress similar to Ava's and Noelle's. The dress was tightly fitted with a sweetheart neckline and off-the-shoulder straps. The only difference was that the bridesmaid dresses did not have an open back. Her hair was in a center part with long flowy curls and her makeup was flawless.

"Congratulations! I am so happy for the two of you!" Taya congratulated, leaning in to hug me.

I received her hug and proceeded to thank her.

"Thank you!" I replied as Christian pulled me to his chest.

Christian pulled me in front of him, wrapping his arms around my waist. There was an odd expression on Taya's face, an expression that I could not read. She looked uncomfortable and her smile seemed forced. *Maybe she's sad that she doesn't have a man,* I thought, knowing that weddings were difficult for some single people.

Tamir emerged from the crowd. He was a part of the grooms' party but went to socialize once everyone dispersed. Tamir and Christian grew to become friends while they both played in Miami. It was important to me that Tamir be at our wedding party so Christian obliged, making him a groomsman. He was wearing a white suit with black trim and black Tom Ford dress shoes, similar to Christian's attire. Tamir patted Christian on the back before leaning in to hug me.

"My boy! I'm proud of you, man. You finally locked my sis down!" Tamir beamed.

"Nigga, please, she was locked down since the day I met her," Christian countered.

I pursed my lips, rolling my eyes at him.

Christian shrugged his shoulders and held up his hands.

"Lil LiLi!" Tamir yelled, beaming.

"Or is it big LiLi Samuels now?" he asked, hugging me.

"I'm happy for you, sis! You're a wife now, I can't even believe it." He congratulated me.

Suddenly, I felt a tiny hand on my booty. I turned to find Armani standing behind me with Ms. Sheema and Christian's mother Ms. Netta on her heels. Armani was the flower girl. Her big brown doe eyes were staring up at me, excitedly. Armani's naturally curly hair was pressed straight for the occasion, she wore a flower headband and had the cutest little white ruffle dress.

"Aunty, you look so pretty!" she complimented, hugging me.

Armani was five years old.

"Thank you, princess! So do you, baby girl," I responded, bending down to reciprocate her hug.

"I want to be a pretty princess like you when I grow up!" Armani beamed.

Our relationship was special to me, I loved her like she was my own. I had suffered from so many missed carriages throughout the course of Christian and I's relationship that Armani gave me hope. I desperately wanted a child.

Tamir reached down, picking Armani up off of the floor once I was done hugging her.

"This little girl found her way over here as soon as she spotted her dad," Ms. Sheema said, approaching.

Ms. Sheema looked nice and graceful in a white silk halter gown with silver Christian Louboutin sandals. Her hair was styled in a jet-black short side part bob. Ms. Sheema was not to be played with; you could not tell her that she was not still young, killing shit.

“My new daughter! I am so happy for the two of you! I never thought I would live to see the day that my son decided to become an honest man and settle down. Start a family! Now, not to rush y’all or anything but I do see grandbabies in my future, my near future if you know what I mean,” Ms. Netta yelled.

Ms. Netta was an interesting character. She was loud and very outspoken. She was caring and rode for her son no matter what. Ms. Netta was tall, slim, and light-skinned. She was a fashionista. Her hair was mid-length, styled in a blunt-cut center part with brown and blonde highlights. She wore a strapless white bodycon Herve Leger dress with a handcrafted diamond blazer made with Swarovski crystals.

“Ahhh, ma, here you go with this,” Christian exclaimed, blowing out a sharp breath of air.

I chuckled before responding.

“Well, for one, everyone keeps saying they never thought he would settle down. Is it something I need to know? For two, let us get through the night but I might end up with a baby after tonight,” I answered, whispering the ending of my sentence.

Exasperated, Christian brought his hand down his face.

“Girl, please! I love my boy, but we all know that he is a hoe! Well, he was!” Ms. Netta stated, looking her son up and down.

She bawled her face up in disgust.

“Yea was, don’t come over here with all that negative energy speaking on my past. I am a married man now. You don’t have anything else to talk about?” Christian argued, smiling.

Christian and his mother had an interesting relationship, he was her only child. They loved each other to death and the two were so much alike which caused them to consistently go back and forth.

“Ok, ok, ok, Ms. Netta, stop harassing my husband,” I playfully interjected.

We all huddled around reveling in the joyous occasion and thanking guests for their congratulations.

Joel, Noelle, and I walked down the hallway to my dressing room. It was time for the reception, and I needed to change into my first reception dress. I had a total of three dresses for the evening, including my ceremony dress. I could feel his energy even though I could not see him. I had dog senses when it came to him, this shit was so weird. Ethan stood at the corridor, speaking to a man dressed in a cleaning uniform. Ethan looked clean and handsome like the groomsman himself. The all-white suit was perfectly fitted and tailored to his toned physique.

"Ok, sir!" the man stated before turning to walk away from Ethan.

Ethan looked up and our eyes connected. His brown eyes smiled once he saw me. Unexpectedly, he swaggered over to me.

"You look beautiful! Congratulations, gorgeous." He congratulated me.

His tone altered when he said congratulations.

"Thank you, ummm . . ." I began but my assistant cut me off.

"Sir, this is a private area, you are not supposed to be back here. Where is security when you need them?!" Joel interjected, reaching for the walkie-talkie that was attached to his waist.

Today must have been the day that I was invisible because as I went to check Joel Ethan cut me off.

"It's—" I started.

"I can be wherever I want to because my name is listed on the deed. Go ahead and call my security team, the only one who will be escorted out of here is you," Ethan chastised.

His smile had dissipated, and he was staring Joel down, daring Joel to challenge him. Noelle's eyes found mine as she searched for some explanation of who this man was. Shit, I wanted to know too. I never told anyone of the encounter between Ethan and me on the yacht years ago. I planned on taking that moment with me to my grave.

"You own this building?" I asked, confused.

How did he seem to appear everywhere that I was, what was happening?

"I own half the buildings, spaces, and event locations in this city. I own a few of the other locations you looked into to host your wedding," he confessed.

"Well, sir, I am so sorry," Joel started but Ethan cut him off.

"I'll let this slide because of her." He paused to nod his head at me.

"But you might want to know who you are speaking to before you speak in the future. A little tip, if I were not permitted back here, I would never have been able to get back here, to begin with," he scolded.

I stood there speechless. *Did this man just say he owned all of the locations I looked at to be my wedding venue, or am I hearing shit? Nah, he definitely said that shit,* I thought.

Ethan turned his attention back to me.

"Malika, I wanted to personally tell you that you look amazing. I hope that you have a wonderful evening and I wish you all the best. I'm heading out," he stated.

"The reception is underway, you should stay," I replied.

I was not sure why, but I wanted him to stay. I knew that I could not be with Ethan; he was the forbidden fruit that would end it all for me, but I was at peace when his energy was near.

"Nah, I have business to handle. I came for support and appearances. Besides, there's someone here that's best I stay away from, and it's best they stay away from me too," he revealed.

The juxtaposition in his words caused my heart rate to speed up. He was referring to me; it was best he stayed away from me and I stayed away from him. Ethan and I had avoided each other ever since the yacht trip a few years ago; this was the first time we had spoken in years.

"Well, thank you for coming. It was nice seeing you," I stated, sadness laced in my voice.

Joel's walkie-talkie went off snapping me out of the bubble that I was standing in with Ethan.

"Team B is looking for the bride, it is time to introduce the couple and Christian is changed and ready to go. Team A, are you here?" the man's voice blared through the device.

"Oh, yes, coming!" Joel yelled into the walkie-talkie.

Ethan nodded his head before walking away. Noelle gave me a knowing look; I would have to explain later. I shook my head and took off, damn near running to the dressing room.

CHAPTER ELEVEN

"It's Another One Coming . . ."

SEPTEMBER 23, 2016
LOS ANGELES, CALIFORNIA

"Damn, so none of y'all have been able to get into contact with her?" I asked Noelle, inquiring about Taya's whereabouts.

Three months passed following my wedding and the relationship that I once shared with Taya had changed dramatically. We went from speaking multiple times in a week to barely any communication. It did not help that Taya's brother was murdered in Philadelphia three weeks ago and no one had heard from her since. Noelle, Ava, and I all tried to reach out, but she had been giving us all the cold shoulder. Noelle spoke to her here and there, but she would not even answer my calls anymore. A part of me wanted to know what the issue was, the other part just wanted to be there for my grieving friend.

The sister circle was all together in Los Angeles for the week. Noelle lived in L.A. during the off-season, even though she still lived in Miami during the season. Ava was also in L.A. to spend time with Noelle and me.

"Girl, no, not since she came back from the funeral and that was about a week ago," Noelle responded from the passenger seat of my G-Wagon.

Noelle was the only person that seemed to be able to get a hold of Taya.

"Her house is close by; we might as well pull up and check to make sure that she's alright," I volunteered.

The three of us were leaving the spa in West Hollywood, California. Suddenly, a group of reports with cameras began to approach my truck. I rolled my tinted windows up to block out the Paparazzi that was beginning to crowd my vehicle, it was time for us to go.

"Yea, we should. She is probably going through a lot right now. Dang, I wish we planned this. I would have stopped to get some flowers or something," Ava replied.

"It's cool, the main point is that we stopped by to check on her, I'm sure she will still appreciate it," I spoke.

Taya lived in West Hollywood. She moved to Los Angeles after graduating from Syracuse University to chase her dreams of becoming an actress. We were about five minutes away from Taya's house and it made no sense to go out of the way just to pick up some flowers.

I pulled onto Taya's block anxious to make sure that she was ok. Noelle, Ava, and I had each reached out to her and were unsuccessful. She was evading our calls. Attempting to figure out why she was avoiding all of us, different scenarios played out in my head. Dealing with grief and the loss of a loved one can be difficult and I knew that Taya had a history of stress and extreme depression.

"Either Taya got a new car or she messing with a nigga with some real money that she neglected to inform us about." Noelle observed, admiring the matte black Lamborghini that was parked in the driveway.

I was ignorant of the existence of the Lamborghini until Noelle mentioned it. The license plate on the back read TML-CMS, which stood for To My Love Christian Marcus Samuels.

Instantly, my heart began to tighten as angst filled me. I knew that car! Shit, I ought to know it, I fucking bought it for his wedding gift! Why was my husband's car here? Why the fuck do I not know that my husband's car is at my friend's house? How, when Christian and Taya barely ever speak two words to each other whenever they are both in my presence? None of this shit was making any sense. My gut told me that something was not right, but I needed to see whatever this was with my own eyes to believe it. Was this the real reason Taya had been acting strange since Christian and I's wedding? Could my husband really be having an affair with my close friend right under my nose?

My worry for Taya went right out the window at the sight of Christian's car. I no longer gave a fuck about Taya's dead brother. If what my intuition was telling me was true, she would be joining his ass very soon.

"Hold the fuck up, that's Christian's car," I revealed.

Truth is, I was keeping my composure on the off chance that my gut reaction was incorrect. My heart wanted so desperately to believe that neither my husband nor my friend would betray me. I felt the knife hovering over my back, but I was going to have to feel the stab to believe that this was happening. I was a little embarrassed, even though these were my sisters, and I did not have to be. Something about a man doing you dirty in front of other people made the feeling ten times worse.

"Christian? Girl, what you mean?" Ava questioned; her eyebrows raised trying to make sense of my revelation.

"Yea, sis, I might need you to be a little clearer because I am confused. That can't be Christian's car," Noelle interjected.

Noelle's eyes were damn near popping out of her head as she turned to shift her body towards me. I pulled into the driveway directly behind his car. If some shit was going on in this house, he was not getting the fuck out of here until he answered to me.

"Bitch, you think I don't know my husband's car," I snapped before hopping out of the driver's seat.

I was so anxious that I left the engine running. I could not even think straight as I began to see red. Rage filled me just thinking of the possibilities of why he could be there. Noelle and Ava hopped out of the car almost as fast I did. I needed answers and I needed them the fuck now! Luckily for me, I was wearing yoga pants, a sports bra, and running sneakers. I reached Taya's door in half a second after hopping out of the car and began banging ferociously. My fists hit the front door so hard that I broke a nail, my adrenaline kept me from feeling the pain as I continued to pound on the door. I wanted so badly for the door to be Taya's face.

"Who the fuck is banging . . ." Taya screamed, snatching the door open.

Her mouth hung open and she quickly tried to shut it when she noticed that it was me, but I was quicker. A foot inside the crack of the door kept it open. Taya stood wearing Christian's Off-White tee shirt that he left the house with this morning. I looked her up and down, trying to piece this shit together.

"Fuck," Taya whispered under her breath.

"Baby, who the fuck is that?" Christian yelled from inside of the house.

A small smirk spread across Taya's face. This bitch was happy I found out; she would be happy for much longer.

"Baby!" I snapped, blacking out.

I saw red. Instantly, my fist connected with Taya's face. The unexpected blow sent her staggering backwards, tripping into the house. Taya attempted to fight back but she was no match for my rage. I dragged her inside like a rag doll, throwing her body to the floor. I jumped on top of her and started punching. My fists connecting with both sides of Taya's face, over and over. Floyd Mayweather had nothing on me, your girl was whooping her ass.

"Yea, hoe, take that ass whooping! It's another one coming!" Noelle hollered, kicking Taya from the sidelines.

"Raggedy ass bitch, I never fucking liked you!" Ava spat; disgust laced in her tone.

"Bitch! I had you in my fucking wedding and you fucking my nigga!" I barked, continuing to punch on her.

Taya was trying to fight back but my heavy blows were relentless. I could not stop hitting her even if I tried to. Christian hobbled his way down the stairs wearing only his Ethika boxers to see what all of the commotion was about and bolted, running back up the steps, once his eyes landed on me.

"Oh shit!" he yelled, doing the one-hundred-meter dash back up the stairs.

Christian's voice brought me out of my trance. I was not done with Taya yet, but I had to get on his ass. Fuck her. Taya owed me loyalty as a friend, but Christian, the man that I laid with almost every night for six years, the man that I married owed me more than loyalty. I could not believe this shit. Men cheat but to stoop this low and cheat with a supposed friend, a bitch that was in our wedding was low, real low. How long had this shit been happening behind my back? I needed real answers. I hopped off of Taya and took off in Christian's direction. I panted, trying to catch my breath.

"I'm not done with you, bitch!" I said, looking down at her in disgust.

I worked my jaws trying to gather a spitball from my mouth.

"Phewww!" The spit flew out of my mouth and landed directly on Taya's eye.

"I should send you right up there with your fucking brother. Matter of fact, count your fucking days, bitch!" I yelled, running up the steps.

I'm not sure if it was the comment about Taya's dead

brother or me spitting in Taya's eye but something set her off. Taya attempted to jump up from the floor before being knocked back down.

"No, bitch! Where you think you going?" Ava snapped, punching Taya in the face sending her back to the ground.

Noelle followed up and the two began to tag team Taya, whooping her ass. I smirked, catching my breath before continuing to run up the stairs. My bitch ass husband was somewhere up there trying to figure out how he was going to get out of this shit.

"Christian! You lying no good dirty dick ass bitch! Get the fuck out here now!" I yelled, banging on Taya's bedroom door.

A few seconds passed and the door did not open so I began to kick. I kicked and kicked for a good five minutes yet he refused to open the door. Suddenly, the rage began to dissipate, and the hurt began to settle in. How was it that I caught my man cheating on me and he was not even man enough to come out and offer an apology, an excuse, nothing? He hid in the room like a coward. I stopped kicking the door and rested my back against it. The tears were uncontrollable, no matter how hard I tried to hold them in I just could not. No way this was happening, I felt like I was in a bad dream. The hollers that came out of me, came from another depth of me. I had not felt a pain this bad since the day I found out about the STDs. No, actually this was worse. This pain was different, there was no explanation for this level of betrayal. Cheating was bad but with my friend, a bitch that I lived with for years! I gripped my stomach cradling my belly. To make matters worse, I was pregnant. I found out what was supposed to be the good news earlier this week and I was waiting on the right time to tell Christian, but that time never came. This was all a mess. The thought of my baby alone made me cry even harder.

"Malika babe, I think we should go," I heard Noelle's voice, but I could not see her through the lake that formed in my eyes.

Noelle walked over to me and grabbed me by my arm, attempting to pull me up. I was dead weight; I had no energy to get up off of the floor. No energy to move, no energy to breathe, no energy to even be. I was so heartbroken, hurt, betrayed, so many different emotions and feelings at once. I knew that Christian was no good, but I tried so hard to put the past behind me and move forward. I was a fool, he showed me who he was a long time ago and I refused to believe him.

"I know, Li, I know," Noelle consoled with sorrow-filled eyes, picking me up.

"We have to leave, babe," she said as my body fell into her. I was crying so hard that the words were barely audible coming out of my mouth.

"He won't even come out and talk to me," I babbled, it sounded more like jumble than plain English.

Noelle used all of her strength to carry me down the stairs and out of the house. Noelle, Ava, and I beat Taya's ass so bad that she laid on the floor unable to move. She was fucked up, to say the least, but not dead. Taya laid there naked and exposed, the tee shirt that she was wearing had been ripped off of her. She had cuts and bruises all over her face, two swollen eyes, a bloody mouth and nose. She earned that ass whooping and so much more.

SEPTEMBER 24, 2016

LOS ANGELES, CALIFORNIA

"I don't even want to do this, and my makeup looks terrible! I look tired, how the hell are my bags so bad that they are still visible under the makeup?!" I barked.

I was in a mood and shooting a magazine cover was the last thing that I wanted to do. Oh, and I forgot the worst part. The shoot was with Christian, it was supposed to be a visual display of our love. Our love? Ha! Our love! That is hilarious! I tried my utmost best to cancel the shoot, but my publicist was not having it so here I was, pretending. I had not seen, spoken to, or heard from my husband since finding him at Taya's house. Even now at the shoot, he was hiding from me, refusing to come out until it was time to get on set. This nigga was a bitch, a coward. Desperately, I wanted to make a scene, yell, scream, fight, cuss his ass out but I could not. One wrong move and I would be the scandal for all of the blogs and gossip sites. My pride would not allow me to be the butt of the joke or ruin my reputation despite how much my heart ached. I was a prisoner in my own life.

Joel exhaled a sharp breath as the makeup artist rushed back over to me.

"I can add more powder, we usually don't have this issue," she offered.

Instantly, I felt bad. The lady looked confused and scared. It was not her fault. I could not get a hold of my husband to let my anger out on him, so I had been taking it out on everyone else. The bags were a result of no sleep because I was up crying all night.

"It's fine. It's not you. I'm sorry, everyone. I have a lot going on today. Please, excuse my attitude," I offered.

"Girl, we know, you are usually a doll to work with unless someone done pissed you off. So, who did it?" Joel inquired.

"Nothing, it's nothing. Just call me when it's time to shoot. I'm ready to get this over with," I stated, hopping up from the makeup chair.

On cue, the shoot director appeared at the dressing room door, halting me.

"Malika, we are ready for you on set!" the shoot director informed us from the door.

I exhaled a sharp breath. I was not in the mood for pretending. I was used to the facade, making it believable that we were happily in love even when we were not on good terms. This shit had become an art form over the years. I wanted to be a regular person, sad and crying at home. I needed a day to process my emotions, but I could not get that. It was time to deliver an Oscar-winning performance and serve on the front of the magazine.

"Let's get some bronzer on her and apply the final touches to her look. Malika gets hot quickly, so we need to have someone cool her down periodically," Joel instructed like I was an object.

This was the reality of my life; I was here but everyone else ran the show.

"I'm going out," I informed Joel.

"Taylor, please escort Malika to set. Don't forget the shoes and the props. We need outfit two and three to be steamed and put out! Let's get this together, people. We have a tight schedule, and she has an appearance right after this shoot for a hosting!" Joel commanded.

I exited the room, ready to get this shoot over with. Anxiety lived in the pit of my stomach. Christian stood in the center of the backdrop, waiting. My eyes stalked him down like prey, but he refused to look at me. The tension in the room was so thick you could cut it with a knife. Everything in me wanted to take off running, swinging at him, throwing shit but I couldn't. I had to stand there and keep my composure, hold it all together because eyes were watching.

"Malika, for the first scene we were thinking you could sit in Christian's lap. We want to capture the essence of your affection and admiration for each other," the director informed, escorting me to the backdrop.

Affection and admiration for each other? Ha! Fuming, I followed the director's instructions. Christian looked up at me as I approached, still refusing to look me in my eyes. My nostrils flared in anger at the sight of him. I was uncomfortable, to say the least. Slowly and reluctantly, I lowered myself into

Christian's lap. The hairs on my body stood up at his touch. Disgust, his fingers felt like bugs crawling up my skin.

"Christian, we need more intimacy! Malika, turn and face him. Look passionately into his eyes!" the director instructed.

Christian placed his hand on my waist, pulling me closer to him. I faced him; our bodies so close I could feel the rhythm of his heartbeat. He leaned into me, still fighting to not make eye contact until he did. Guilt lived in the soul of his eyes, they pleaded with me saying I'm sorry. My heart wanted to give in, but my mind said nigga fuck you! I cut my eyes at him and composed myself. It took everything in me not to spit on him.

"Yes, perfect. Malika, bring your hand to his cheek and lean in some more," the director continued.

I obliged the director's request, leaning in so they could get the shot.

Christian and I continued on with the shoot for over an hour before I reached my boiling point. Everything about this man repulsed me. I couldn't do it anymore. Suddenly, I pulled back, hopping up from his lap.

"We have a lot more to get through, Malika. Where are you going?" production questioned.

"Yea, and I'm done. I don't feel good. You have enough shots, get something from one of those," I stated, walking off of the set.

I was done with the shoot; I had no more fake in me for the day.

SEPTEMBER 29, 2016

CALABASAS, CALIFORNIA

The days following the revelation of Christian and Taya's betrayal were filled with misery and heartache. My chest burned, it felt like someone was stabbing me over and over with a knife in my heart. The pain was unbearable and unlike anything I have ever felt before. That feeling of betrayal ran so deep. How could I not see this happening right in front of my face? How long had this been happening? Why did he choose Taya . . . fucking Taya of all people in the world? This nigga could not be fucking serious. Oh, but he was serious, he was unbelievably serious. To make matters worse, I had not seen or spoken to Christian since the shoot. My husband was too much of a bitch ass coward to come home and face me. One-hundred and forty-four hours and twenty-eight thousand eight hundred seconds passed . . . and still nothing. I was livid, angry. I could not believe this shit was real, my life had to be a joke. How much of a bitch ass nigga do you have to be to not come home and talk to your wife after you get caught having an affair with one of her friends? For all I knew Christian was still over there with that bitch.

Taya seemed to miss the part where she was wrong. That snake had the nerve to text my phone and tell me that I was lucky she was not pressing charges because of Christian but she would be suing me for everything I had. I wanted to beat the bitch ass all over again. What the fuck did she mean by because of Christian? Was that trifling nigga still in contact with her but could not even come home and speak to me?

I was on a roller coaster of emotions. One minute I was crying, bawling actually as the cries seemed to come from another depth of me. A cry so gut-wrenching your stomach hallowed. I felt like I was on an airplane that was falling from the sky. You know that butterfly feeling that stirs inside of your stomach when you hit the peak of the ride just before the big drop, when your stomach aches and fear paralyzes you; that was the feeling. The next minute I was in a blind rage. Bleaching, cutting, and breaking all of Christian's things. All of his favorite possessions were completely ruined. His favorite cars? I cut the seats up, broke the windows, and threw paint on them. His jewelry? Oh, I had a field day with that shit. His diamond Patek Philippe?

I smashed all of the diamonds and broke the face. His diamond chains? I sold them. His one-of-a-kind artifacts? I fucked them up. I was ruining shit. Like a wrecking ball, I came down crashing. Christian was going to feel my wrath.

I did not know if I wanted to be angry or cry. I guess I wanted to be both. Most importantly I wanted, no fuck what I wanted . . . I expected the man that I married to come home and explain himself to me! I expected that man to not do no shit like this to me. I pegged Christian to be a lot of things but never just a bitch like this, he was so guilty that he could not even face me. How could he not care enough to explain? Was it me? Am I the problem? So many thoughts swirled around in my head. Truth be told I had no idea what I was even going to do following this? Do I leave? Do I stay?

CHAPTER TWELVE

"You Are Not Leaving Me . . ."

SEPTEMBER 29, 2016

CALABASAS, CALIFORNIA

Ding! The sound of the elevator inside of my master bedroom echoed throughout the room.

I jumped up out of my sleep and looked over at my phone to check the time, it was two-fifty-six in the morning. My heart stilled in anticipation. The elevator was predominantly used by Christian and me. It was too late for staff to be coming up here so that had to be Christian. *Is this him, is this bitch finally home?* I thought, sitting up in the bed.

Tiptoeing, Christian walked into the bedroom. This nigga was not serious? After almost seven fucking days this bitch was trying to creep into the house. Yea, he had me fucked up.

Quickly, my feet carried me out of the bed, moving before my brain could register what was happening.

"Where the fuck have you been?!" I barked, meeting him at the elevator.

The elevator was located towards the rear of the room, attached to my three-story walk-in closet.

Christian looked down at me, attempting to avert my death stare. He stared blankly at me, his eyes connecting to every part of my body except my eyes.

"Bitch, you hear me!" I screamed, stabbing him in his forehead with my pointer finger.

Christian's head flew backwards.

"Yo chill, I thought you would have calmed down by now. Can we do this shit tomorrow?" he dismissed, attempting to step past me.

"Do this shit tomorrow?!" I yelled.

"I know you did not just fucking come in here talking about calmed down! Yea, that bitch must have crack in her pussy because what the fuck are you even talking about! Are you on drugs?! Calm down! I got your fucking calm down," I screamed, flying past him.

Aggressively, I pushed him in his chest and out of my way.

Exhaling a deep breath, Christian swiped his hand down his face. I was inside of his closet before I could stop myself. The closet was already a mess with all of the ruin that I did over the past few days. I grabbed a suitcase from the top of the luggage case and threw it in front of the clothes that I had not gotten around to tarnishing. I grabbed everything in my sight and threw them into the suitcase.

"Get the fuck out! Out you dumb ass, cheating ass, lying ass, dirty dick ass bitch! I hate you! Get the fuck out before I kill your stupid ass! Go back to that raggedy bitch house!" I barked, pulling clothing off of the hangers.

I was so loud that I could have woken up the entire neighborhood if we were not secluded on acres of land. Christian waltzed into the closet with distress written all over his face. He shook his head, bringing his elbows to the side of his face as he took in the damage that I had done.

"Malika, what the fuck are you doing! I wasn't even with that hoe!" he pleaded.

"Nigga, fuck you! I don't give a fuck where you was at! Get the fuck out! I'm done! Sign them papers!" I yelled, hauling a Maison Margiela sneaker at his head.

He ducked the sneaker before stalking over to me. Grabbing me roughly by my wrists, he pulled me over to the corner of the room. Throwing me up against the wall, he pinned both of my wrists above my head. Panting heavily, I turned my head to the side. I refused to look at him. I wanted him out of my face.

"Get the fuck off of me!" I commanded, squirming.

I attempted to wiggle my body out of his tight grip, but my efforts were in vain.

"Calm down! I'm letting you get your shit off because I'm dead wrong and I know I hurt you but you getting beside yourself. I'm not leaving this, my house, that I paid for with my money," he asserted, raining spit particles down on me.

I scoffed, looking at him with squinted eyes. My mouth hung open as I tried to find the words to react because he could not be serious. No way, this was a real moment. This nigga had a fucking nerve. What's the word again? Audacity, noun, a willingness to take bold risks, or also known as rude or disrespectful behavior, imprudence. Yea, this nigga had a lot of that shit.

"That you paid for with your money? Last I checked my name was on the deed too so what you saying? What's mine is yours, right bitch? I want you gone. Get the fuck out!" I yelled.

Angrily, the spit flew right out of my mouth and on the side of his face. Christian stilled, looking up at me as if he saw a ghost. Anger reflected in his eyes, but he did not react. He took in a deep breath and lifted my wrists from the wall before slamming them back down.

"Yea, that I fucking paid for. Your name is on the deed because I put it there, bitch. How much does this house cost? Matter of fact you couldn't afford the shit if you fucking tried.

Calm down! I'll let that slick shit you just tried go but this is your last warning," he stated arrogantly through gritted teeth.

My mouth opened in disbelief, who the fuck was he talking to? What part of the script was this? You cheat on me with my friend, don't come home or answer the phone for days, walk in during the hours of the morning and I am supposed to calm down?

"Yea, you lost your mind," I stated, bursting into laughter.

I felt like Ashton Kutcher was going to appear any minute because I had to be getting *Punk'd*, this had to be a joke.

He let my wrists go and shoved me to the wall before turning to walk away. He took three steps forward before turning and speaking.

"This mess was cute but you and I both know this shit cost me nothing. I'm not going anywhere, we can talk about this shit tomorrow; I'm going to sleep, and I expect you to join me," he stated, looking around the closet.

You could not buy the type of arrogance that Christian possessed. I must have been in a twilight zone because this was some bull shit. My blood boiled as I reacted without a second thought. I came up off of the wall in the corner running, I pushed Christian roughly before making my way out of the closet.

"Yea, I don't know who you think you are! Since you not leaving, I'm fucking leaving! I'm done! This shit is over, and I want a divorce! It's nothing to talk about! You didn't want to talk, remember! You ran and hid like a little bitch," I yelled, rushing to my closet.

Christian was right on my heels.

"Yo, sit down and chill the fuck out! You're not going anywhere. Where are you going to go? You are not leaving me? I'm not letting you leave so all of this shit is irrelevant. You had days to calm down and you still going, you want to argue or fix this shit cause either way we're together," he commanded, stopping at the entrance of my closet and leaning his head on the wall.

I rolled my eyes at him, scoffing.

"Where were you?" I asked stopping in the middle of the closet to look at him.

I placed both of my hands on my hip and cocked my head to the side.

"I'm not talking to you until you chill out. Go sit your ass down because you're not going anywhere," he asserted, pulling his hands down his face in distress.

"Yea, ok, we're going to see," I stated, stalking over to the glass luggage case.

Smiling sinisterly, I pulled my vintage Louis Vuitton luggage case out of the glass case.

"It's nothing to see, Lik, you not leaving me because I'm not done," he dismissed, waving his hand at me.

"You should have thought about that when you were fucking that dirty whore. My friend really? You would go that low? Wow," I sassed, rolling my eyes.

I threw the clothing into my luggage aggressively. Each item hit the bottom of the luggage like darts hitting a board.

Christian scoffed.

"I'm not going to hear the end of this shit," he complained.

"Yea, you're not you cheater. Not until we're even and I'm fucking one of your teammates so good that I make his toes curl. I wonder how you would feel if I sat on Andre's dick? Or actually, if I let Kareem taste this pussy like I know he wants to because he's always staring. Hmm, I bet you he would love the tight wetness of my pussy, huh? Hmm, what you think, should I pack my sexy lingerie just in case?" I said, smirking.

Christian's entire body stiffened at my words. He glared at me, like a pit bull before he attacked his prey. He stalked me with his eyes. *Checkmate bitch, you want to play let's play then.*

It's playtime, I thought. He was livid at the thought of me and another man. I reached for the lingerie and all hell broke loose in the closet. Before I could protest, Christian lunged at me, tightly wrapping both of his fingers around my neck and lifting my body into the air. A flashback of my last day in my father's house played before my eyes as he hoisted me into the air. The feeling of my lungs begging for air was all too familiar to me. His grip around my neck was extremely tight. The look that I saw in his eyes scared the life out of me. His irises were black, like he was lost in there. I clawed at his hands, fighting for air.

Christian! Please! Were the words that I was trying to say out loud but there was no air to speak. Suddenly, he pulled one hand from my neck and loosened the other one. He was still choking me but now I was able to breathe. Desperately, I gasped for air trying to catch my breath. He brought his hand back as far back as it would go before hitting me.

Smackkkkkkkkkk! The sound of his hand connecting with my face vibrated through the room. A loud vibration wrung off in my ear. The smack was so hard that my head went flying backwards banging against the wall that he had me pinned to. My lip burst as the side of my lip connected with my teeth.

"Christian! Please! Stop!" I hollered, tears erupting from my eyes.

I was balling because the pain was excruciating.

"You better not ever let me hear you even mention another man fucking name out your mouth! Ever!" he barked, mushing me in my forehead.

My head flew backwards once more, banging into the wall. A vein appeared on his forehead, as his eyes damn near popped out of his head. He released his hand from around my neck causing me to drop to the floor. He spun on his heels to walk out of the closet.

"And clean this shit up! In here fucking up my damn house when you and I both know you not going nowhere!" he yelled.

Somehow, he flipped a switch and went back to normal. Running off of adrenaline, I hopped up from the floor and jumped to my feet. I charged at Christian, pushing him in his back, swinging with everything in me.

"Don' ever in your life put your fucking hands on me!" I screamed, punching him relentlessly.

Quickly, he spun on his heels, backhanding me so hard that I flew backwards into the glass luggage case.

Crack! The sound of glass shattering echoed throughout the room.

I gasped for air as the shards of glass pierced into my skin like little needles. The pain was too great to process. Blood appeared from all over my body. Suddenly, a sharp pain erupted within my uterus, crippling me. The moisture that I felt between my legs caused me to look down, bringing my hand to my thighs. The crimson red blood covered my hands.

"The baby!" I screamed, barely able to formulate the words.

For days I had been so angry at Christian that through all of this bullshit I forgot all about the baby. The small, fragile, eight-week-old baby that was growing inside of me. At my revelation, Christian's eyes bulged out of his head.

"Baby?!" he shrieked, running over to me in a panic.

Blood spewed from between my legs like a faucet. Despite my adamant protests for him to not touch me, Christian lifted me from the ground.

"Get off of . . . Ahhhhhhhhhhh!" I cried as the pain became unbearable.

I held on to my stomach for dear life, clenching. Christian carried me over to the love seat that was located on the other end of the closet. He laid me down and bolted out of the closet.

"Ahhhhhhhhhhhh!" I cried.

My screams of horror transformed into a gut-hollowing cry. Physically, I was in so much pain, but I was crying because I knew what the blood meant. I was losing my baby; it did not take a doctor to tell me what I already knew. A woman's intuition is rarely wrong, and my intuition told me that my little ray of sunshine was no longer with me. Cell phone in hand, Christian rushed back into the room. Hurriedly, he called our private doctor. A concoction of worry, regret, sadness, and panic resonated in his facial expression. I sucked in a sharp breath. The room was spinning, and I was overwhelmed. An indescribably heavy feeling came over me.

"Hello! Yes! My wife she, she's bleeding from between her legs and she's pregnant. I need you over here now!" he spoke into the phone.

Christian hung the phone up and brought his hands to my stomach. His touch felt foreign to me. I did not know this man.

"A baby. Our baby," he stated; guilt dancing in his eyes.

I recoiled at his touch, it felt like the devil's touch. I did not know this man and the last thing that I wanted was his hands on my body. Crying, I pushed his hand off of me. I was distraught and in so much pain. I wanted Christian away from me, a part of me was petrified at his touch. This was his fault. I was not sure what more he was capable of doing to me. We sat in silence waiting for the doctor to arrive.

"I'm sorry but you had a miscarriage," Dr. Harris confirmed, looking at me sincerely.

My stomach hallowed at the confirmation. I knew that I lost the baby before he told us but hearing the words made the feeling more real. Christian, sitting on the bed beside me, squeezed my hand and lowered his head in shame. I recoiled, pulling my hand away from his. Everything about him made my skin crawl, he disgusted me. Why the hell was he here still. He did this! Now he wants to act fake concerned. A pitiful excuse for a man.

The doctor proceeded to pack his items into a small black leather duffle bag before continuing.

"I know this can be a difficult and painful time for you all. Here are some prescriptions for pain medication and antibiotics to prevent an infection. Please call to schedule a follow-up within the next five days," he stated, handing Christian the paperwork.

Dr. Harris gave me a reassuring look before turning to exit the room.

"Take care of her, and Mrs. Samuels, be sure to take care of yourself. This would be a great time to seek a therapist, I know some great ones if either of you need a referral," Dr. Samuels offered.

"Thank you so much," Christian thanked, standing to shake the doctor's hand.

Christian led the way for Dr. Harris, escorting him out of the manor. I, however, had no words, no thank you, no ok, nothing. I was empty, nothing was left. I was inside of my body but mentally I was not there. I wanted to escape. A lone tear ran down my cheek as I laid in the bed, staring blankly out the full-length windows. I had nothing tangible left. In the last week, my life had completely been turned upside down; my husband beat my ass, resulting in the loss of my unborn child. I felt alone, back to square one. I did not know this man; he was a complete stranger to me. He was a lying, cheating, woman-beating, possessive, disrespectful coward.

Christian entered the room, bringing me out of my trance. Seeing his face made me angry, his smell, everything about him repulsed me. My stomach turned as he approached our bed and sat on the edge. He looked at me and I turned my head to the side, not wanting to see his face.

"I—" he started but I interrupted.

"Just stop," I stated.

"I'm sorry. I'm sorry for all of this. I'm sorry for cheating on you, I'm sorry that it was with Taya and I'm sorry I—" He apologized.

His voice was filled with sorrow, regret, and sadness but it made no difference to me. I could see the turmoil ripping through him as he fought an internal battle with himself to take accountability for his actions. There was nothing that he could say to me to fix this, there was no coming back from this.

"Why didn't you tell me about the baby?" he asked.

My head whipped to the other side so that I could make eye contact with him. Christian previously expressed his desire to start our family, we had been trying for months and months for me to get pregnant prior to this incident so the news of the baby hit him hard.

"Fuck you. Why didn't I tell you about my baby that you just killed?" I shot.

Injury lived in the pit of his eyes as he recoiled at my words. He and I both knew the truth that this was his fault, yet somehow hearing me say the words caused him great injury. The tears that erupted from me were so heavy. Hysterically, I cried.

Slowly, Christian got up from the edge of the bed and approached me, attempting to wrap me into an embrace. I fought him, throwing my hands at him in protest.

"Get away from me! This is on you! You killed our baby! You killed our baby! You killed my baby! How could you do this!" I wailed before succumbing to his embrace.

I was exhausted, broken, and hurt. I was so damn hurt. This pain of losing the life growing inside of me was too great. This was the heaviest burden that I ever had to carry. He held me to his body, holding on to me for dear life. I clung to him, I hated him, but I needed him to get through this. This was my loss, but it was his loss too. I needed him to go through this emotion with me, I needed someone to be there even if the only person available was both the problem and the solution. I balled into his chest, releasing the pain. I needed to deal with the whirlwind of emotions that were sweeping through me.

Silently, Christian cried as well. He was not a man that cried, this was the first time in our six years of being together that I ever saw him cry. He always kept up a tough exterior. His tears let me know that he felt the loss. He may have even felt it a little deeper than I did because he was guilty. I was unsure if he was sad because of the loss of our child, guilt, or a mixture of both. We sat there holding each other, no real answers to the current state of our marriage. We mourned the loss of what could have been, our unborn child that we would never be able to meet.

PART II

CHAPTER THIRTEEN

"Destined to Be . . ."

FEBRUARY 22, 2017
PHILADELPHIA, PENNSYLVANIA

MALIKA

The months that followed my miscarriage were extremely difficult. Whew! The depression! I went through extreme highs and extreme lows in an attempt to balance my emotions. One day I would feel normal and the next I desperately wanted to escape my world. Weed and alcohol became my best friends. The emotions that I could not process haunted me. I buried myself in my career, focusing on everything besides the current state of my marriage. My main priority was my bag. I grossed a total of two-point-seven million over the past few months. I devoted myself to my business; money became my motivation and the only thing that mattered in my life.

Christian and I barely spoke yet we lived in the same home. Thankfully, we were in the middle of the basketball season, so he was extremely busy. Basketball was the only thing that could get him to lay off of me. I could not stand the sight of him, but he refused to leave. I wanted space but instead, I was being smothered. His ass followed me all around the manor and if I left to get a hotel, he found me. He became my stalker, desperately wanting to know my every move.

Following the incident, there had not been sexual intercourse between Christian and me, he repulsed me. I cringed whenever he was near. Subsequently, his infidelity increased, and his care decreased. Christian was a dog ass nigga. He answered phone calls in front of me, made miscellaneous purchases for other females from our joint accounts, and on a few occasions had obvious passion marks on different parts of his body. I ignored the cheating because I no longer cared, the hoes could have him. The truth was something inside of me changed that night I miscarried. I loved him but I was no longer in love. I saw Christian in a different light. He could go ahead and do whatever with whomever because I no longer gave a fuck.

I filed for divorce, but Christian refused to sign the papers. I felt trapped but relieved at his refusal. There was a part of me that was scared to leave him because I feared being alone. Over the course of our relationship, I had gotten used to Christian. As much as I hated him, I was unsure if I would be better off without him. It became more difficult by the day to pretend we were happy. Together we attended social events, charity galas, TV appearances, basketball games, business meetings, and so much more. The façade never stopped. I would hold his hand and smile for the cameras, pretending—all the while I was dying inside. If I was not already pretending enough, my new podcast was centered around women and how to build a successful relationship. Here I was telling women how to deal with their relationships yet mine was in shambles. I was a fraud.

To make matters worse, I learned that Christian and Taya had been sleeping together for two years. Yes, you heard me correctly, two years! The affair began the night of Christian and I's engagement party. Leading up to our wedding, Christian attempted to end the affair but by that time Taya was deeply in love and threatening to tell me if he stopped seeing her. That whore pretended, for years, to be my friend. I had that bitch in my wedding party while she continued to have sex with my husband. Jealousy was dangerous. Unfortunately for Taya, money talks and I had a lot of it. I personally saw to it that Taya was exiled from the acting world of Hollywood. Taya could not get booked by any agents, called in for any auditions, or booked for any jobs—not even a role as an extra. She was being blackballed. She fell off so bad that she was forced to return to Philadelphia, good riddance bitch!

Taya pitched her story of getting jumped by my girls and me to any blog that would listen, but Christian paid good money to make sure that the story never aired. A few blogs posted about it in underground chats but for the most part, the story stayed under wraps. When all else failed, Taya sued Noelle, Ava and me for assault and sued Christian for intentional infliction of emotional distress, claiming that Christian purposefully placed her in a situation that he knew would cause her severe emotional disturbance. We were in a very heated and very expensive legal battle because the bitch was a snake. The claim she had against Christian was unsubstantiated, she would never win that one or see a dime. The claim that Taya had against Noelle, Ava, and me, however, was a little different; if we lost, she would be a rich bitch. Taya's ass whooping could potentially cost me a lot of fucking money.

ETHAN

I sat at the head of the conference room table at the Philadelphia 76'ers headquarters. Recently, I purchased the majority stake in the professional basketball team. I wore an all-black custom-tailored Ermenegildo Zegna suit. I looked like money. Actually, I always looked like money because I was the epitome of money. I exemplified wealth and excellence in every stride that I took. I come from wealth and power; this has always been my lifestyle. Have you ever heard of the Rockefellers? Well,

I was a Jacob, and the Jacobs were more powerful than the Rockefellers.

I owned properties, corporations, oil refineries, sports teams, publishing companies, tech companies, pharmaceutical companies, major stock portfolios, streaming services and restaurants. I took the wealth of my family and quadrupled it. I was the boss above the boss, the real power player that people rarely even saw or knew existed. I never had to do too much; I was always in control of everything because I owned everything. My family ties come with a lot of shit, legal and illegal.

As a Jacob, homicide, drugs, racketeering, extortion, bribery and anything organized crime was always a part of our life. I, on the other hand, had an affinity for the underground world and I took our empire a step farther than my family ever did. I ran a global organized crime family with both legal and illegal drugs in six of seven continents.

On the outside, I appeared to be cool, calm and collected. On the inside, I was unable to calm the butterflies that were flying around in my stomach. What was it about this woman? She had me stuck, open. I wanted her. I was not sure why, maybe it was the chase. Here we were years later and since two thousand and twelve, I had not been able to stop my attraction to her. At first glance, something told me there was more to our story, but I could never figure it out.

I was single, previously married for eleven years but my wife passed away in a car accident. Following the tragic death of my wife, I dated women, had flings and consistent sexual encounters but I never felt anything for any of them beyond the surface of sexual pleasure. I could not let my guard down; I had no interest. They bored me. Everything changed for me the day I met Malika. I wanted her, more than I ever wanted any woman but she was the only thing I could not have.

I could not understand what it was about Malika, she had me stuck on stupid. She was beautiful but I have had and seen the most beautiful women, however, her beauty did not move me. It was something about her that I could not wrap my mind around. I did not even feel this strong of a desire for my late wife. I was so used to being the one in control, the power player, I could have any woman I wanted but I wanted her. Little did she know, she could have anything that she wanted from me, but she was married to my fucking employee. I wrote this nigga checks and he had the woman I wanted; shit threw me for a loop.

Malika was a little different than my usual type. She had a ruggedness to her. I was used to dating the pageant queens. The woman that looked pretty and sat tight. Malika was different. My research on her revealed that she was no angel. She was loyal, she would kill for you, rob for you, lie for you. Her ruggedness made her even more enticing to me, I had to have her. Over the years, I kept close tabs on her. Secretly sending clients to her, making business deals on her behalf, I even got her a podcast deal with a company that I owned a significant percentage of. I went above and beyond to make sure that she was able to establish a life of her own, so that she never felt that she needed anyone for financial stability. I had been her blessing in disguise . . . and she had no idea.

I felt her presence before I could actually see her. I was ignited whenever she was in the same vicinity as me. *What is this feeling that I get with this* girl*?* I thought, exasperated by my unyielding attraction. I sat, nervously, in anticipation as she walked through the glass doors. *So fucking gorgeous!* I thought, taking in her exceptional beauty.

MALIKA

Bing! The elevator chimed as the doors slid open.

Anxiously, I placed one Tom Ford heel on the black marble tile, exiting the elevator. Goosebumps appeared on my forearm as I felt his presence. His energy was so damn alluring. I was in

Philadelphia to meet with the man himself, Ethan Jacobs. I had no business meeting with him, ever, but Ethan brought a lot of clients my way and money was the motive. Since acquiring Christian's team, Ethan had gone on to purchase three additional professional basketball teams, one of those teams being the Philadelphia 76'ers. I was here for a potential offer that could result in at least five of Ethan's players signing with my firm. I needed all of the money that I could make on my own. Eventually, I would be leaving my husband and starting over with only what I had to my name. I was unable to provide myself with the nine-figure lifestyle that I had become accustomed to then so be it. I needed money and Ethan had lots of it, a few hundred billion to be exact; he was the man that I needed to see.

Nervously, I strutted into the conference room. I felt his presence the moment I stepped into the building but being in here with him, was too damn much. Secretly, I had been awaiting this meeting since I reached out.

Ethan sat at the head of the table looking like a model straight out of a GQ magazine. Everything about his demeanor screamed boss. He carried himself with elegance, opulence, and grace. His presence felt like a dream. His stare was intense as our eyes connected; it was something special about him that I could not put my finger on. Damn, everything about this man was enticing. He was fine! Lust filled me as I took in every part of him.

"Hello, Ethan," I greeted.

God, why does he look so damn good? I thought.

"Hello, Malika," he returned, staring me down.

I strutted over to the opposite end of the conference table and began pulling out a seat before he interrupted me.

"It will only be the two of us, you can sit over here," he offered, standing to pull out the seat next to him.

I nodded, walking to the other end to sit in the seat that he requested. A gentleman he was.

"I hope that I did not have you waiting, I know you are a very busy man," I provided, sitting down.

Internally, I was going crazy, but I would never show it. Being this close to him felt wrong, like I was cheating. Not that I cared at this point if I cheated on my piece of shit husband, but damn just his energy made me feel like I was already being inappropriate.

"Don't worry about that, everyone else on my schedule can wait. They work for me, they're on my time," he asserted, leaning back.

He was turning me on. He flipped the imaginary switch and lit the spark between my legs.

"So, tell me, what do you need?" he asked, getting straight to the point.

"Well, I am looking to expand my company. I have about two agents that I am looking to hire, but I need to sign some more clients before bringing those agents onto my team and that is where I was hoping that you could come in," I informed him.

"How many clients would you be looking to sign?" he questioned.

"I am thinking of signing at least three clients, but I would be open to signing more if that was an option," I replied.

"How many clients do you need to make your business goals? If you need ten, I will get you ten, whatever the number is I will make it happen. What do you need?" he asked, a smile playing at the corner of his lips.

"Well, in that case, I need ten new clients," I stated, calling his bluff.

Devilishly, I smirked. Ethan squinted his eyes at me intensely before reaching across the table and picking up one of his cell phones. He was silent for a moment as the phone rang, then Ethan placed the phone on speaker before speaking, all the while staring me directly in my eyes.

"Mr. Jacobs, sir what can I do for you?" a man with a deep raspy voice said through the phone.

"Richard, I need you to get ten players from any of my teams that would be open to signing with a new agent. I know players have long-standing relationships with their agents, you can let all of them know that their contracts will be renegotiated with a salary increase between two—five million each if they choose to switch agents. The bigger the star, the more you should offer them," he asserted.

"Right away, Mr. Jacobs, I will get a list of potential players and shoot it over to you for approval. You are recruiting clients for the M.T.S. Agency, correct?" the man inquired, catching Ethan off guard.

My eyes bulged at the mention of my agency. *Did he just say M.T.S.?* I thought. Ethan paused, taking a moment to check my reaction before speaking.

"Hello, Ethan?" the man questioned when he did not receive an answer.

"Yes, I am here. Correct, for the M.T.S. Agency," he replied, jumping back into the conversation.

"Ok, sir, it is done. Is there anything else that you need from me?" the man asked.

"No, that will be all for now. Thank you." He thanked Richard before hanging up the call.

I looked at him questioningly; I needed answers.

"M.T.S. Agency? How did he know the name of my business?" I asked, my eyebrows dipped in confusion.

I moved my hands as I spoke.

"Yes, M.T.S.," Ethan answered, casually.

"How does he know the name of my business to ask you that? I'm not understanding," I pressed.

"He knows the name of your business because I have done

this before in the past," he stated, passively like it was nothing to him.

"In the past?" I questioned.

"Yes, that was the guy that I first called years ago when I offered you my help . . ." He paused, but I waited before speaking, prompting him to continue.

"I have, on occasion, made some phone calls to send clients your way," he revealed.

"So, you just pay people millions of dollars . . . to sign . . . with me? Why would you keep doing that, for me of all people?" I asked.

I was not sure if this was a sweet gesture or a little creepy.

"I knew you were new to this business so whenever an opportunity presents itself, I make it a point to help as best as I can," he said, vaguely, not really answering my question.

I could tell that there was more to this than he was letting on. I had so many questions, but the most pressing question was why, and I wanted an honest answer.

"That is all appreciated, but you still have not answered my question. Why all of this for me? You barely even know me," I pressed.

ETHAN

"You, it's something about you. Since the moment that we met, there has been something that I could not shake. I am a giving man when I want to be. I knew that we could not be much more than acquaintances because of your situation so I did the only thing that I could, help from a distance," I replied.

Malika had me in a corner. I could lie to her and not tell her the truth, but that was not in my character. I was a straight shooter. Typical woman shit, of all that I said the only part that was relevant to her was why her when I barely knew her. I could not provide her much more than I did because the truth was, I did not know myself. I asked myself what it was about her on so many occasions.

My response was honest and from her reaction, a shocking revelation to her. Malika's eyes widened slightly just before she caught herself, masking her shock.

"Well, what gave you the impression that I needed help? I take great care of myself," she sassed, cocking her head to the side.

I chuckled before I spoke.

"No, I never thought you needed my help. I just wanted to help. Truth be told, helping made me feel like I was a part of something that you were. I have thought about you on many occasions since the day that we met and helping you from behind the scenes was the only way that I could leave you be. I am a man that always gets what I want, and what I want is you, but you already have someone so out of respect for you, I leave it alone," I said, my tone altering from playful to serious.

She was silent. Her cheeks flushed crimson as she fought to turn her head to the side, breaking the intensity of my stare.

"Oh, I—" was the only thing that she managed to say before silence again.

Her facial expression told me that she was in deep thought. Suddenly, like a light switch, her eyes lit up and she had more questions for me.

"So, all of the clients I sign come from you?" she quizzed, prompting me to provide her with more information.

"No, not all just some. You do an amazing job, your work speaks for itself, people come to you because they want to. You close deals," I offered.

I did what I did for her because I wanted to not because she needed me. I had the utmost confidence that even without me she would have grown her firm to become the success that it was.

Malika was quiet, her face screwed in deep contemplation.

I looked at her questioningly, my forehead scrunched. I was desperate to know what she was thinking. A smile crept across her face as she began giggling. She was silly.

"Thank you, that means a lot to me. I'm flattered," she said laughing, bringing her hands to her chest.

She was adorable, she had a fun-loving spirit about her that was captivating. I smiled, breaking down the barrier to my intensity. I was always so serious around her, feeling like I had to uphold a sense of professionalism because I was not sure how far I would take it if I allowed her into my world. Laughing and smiling with her felt good, it felt right, like we were supposed to be here together. I always knew there was a vibe between the two of us, but I always thought that maybe I was the only person that felt the energy.

Her next question caught me off guard.

"Are you busy after this?" she asked, anticipation lingering in her green eyes. "I mean I am kind of hungry if you want to get something to eat."

CHAPTER FOURTEEN

"Our Story Was Already Written . . ."

FEBRUARY 22, 2017
PHILADELPHIA, PENNSYLVANIA

MALIKA

My breath stilled as anxiety filled me. I bit down on the inside of my lip, awaiting a reply. I was so damn nervous, awaiting his reply. I was not sure what made me ask the question, to begin with, but here we were. I know I had no business asking the boss of my no-good ass husband if he wanted to get food with me, intimately, only the two of us. Why did I do that? The words came out before I could process the thought. *What the fuck are you doing, Lika! This is a bad idea and what the fuck you gonna do if he says no?* I thought.

"Yes, I can eat . . ." he answered finally, his perfectly straight white teeth sparkling in the light.

I was speechless, a bitch was stuck on stupid. Am I hearing him correctly, did this fine ass, rich ass billionaire just say yes? This was all too much for me. I was overwhelmed at the thought that he wanted me. Of all the women in the world, me, little old me, LiLi? I must have been too caught up in my own thoughts because he continued before I had the opportunity to respond.

"I can have any restaurant you'd like to open up a private area for us, secluded or I can have a chef cater for us? Whatever you'd like better. I know you're married to my player; I would not want to make it complicated for you," he offered, looking at me sincerely.

The look of genuine concern reflected in his eyes; he was thinking of me before I was even thinking of myself. I was touched, he had a warmth and a caring nature to him that I did not expect.

"The chef can cater for us," I replied.

Without speaking, Ethan picked up his cell phone and dialed, placing the phone on speaker as it rang. Ethan acted, he never spoke on what he was going to do or how he was going to do it, he just did it. The phone rang only once before a Hispanic lady answered.

"Mr. Ethan, shall I have security come up to escort you to the car?" the Hispanic woman greeted in a heavy accent.

"Yes, Paula, thank you. Also, please call Dianne and have her cook for a three-course dinner. Actually, one moment." He paused, placing the phone on mute before looking up at me.

"What do you want her to make?" he asked me.

I went to answer his question when we both spoke at the same time.

"I can do sea bass," I spoke.

"We can do sea bass," he said, at the same exact time as me.

We looked at each other in disbelief, this shit was weird. Did we just say the same exact thing and at the same exact time? I chuckled; this was beginning to get creepy. We were in sync with each other seemingly all of the time.

"I guess we both want sea bass tonight," he joked, chuckling as he took the phone off of mute and continued speaking.

"Yes, Paula?" he questioned.

"Yes, sir, I am here," Paula replied.

"Please, have Dianne make a three-course meal for two, and the entree of the night is pan-seared garlic sea bass," he instructed.

"Oh, and Paula, have the car prepped for two, my guest will be joining me," he continued, his eyes never leaving mine.

"Right away, sir," Paula spoke before hanging up the call.

He was just so damn hmmm. I did not have the words. His demeanor, it was so damn sexy. He spoke with so much authority, but not in a controlling way.

Four men dressed in all-black suits appeared at the door. Ethan rose from his chair, reaching for my hand to help me out of my seat. I did not need his help to stand but I damn sure took advantage of the opportunity to touch him. I placed my hand inside of his and the intensity of the touch left me yearning for him. I desperately wanted him to touch me in other places. This moment felt so right yet so wrong, as if we were destined to be here and this part of our story was already written.

AUGUST 29, 2017
CALABASAS, CALIFORNIA

MALIKA

Over the past few months, the relationship between Ethan and I grew quickly. Our relationship began as lighthearted fun. He understood me and I understood him. Our upbringing was so different, yet we had so much in common. We were two peas in a pod, developing a genuine friendship. We would talk for hours on end. I could talk to him about any and everything, business ventures, TV shows, books, music, movies, religion, spirituality, travel locations, literally everything. We never did anything sexual, we never kissed, we just enjoyed each other's company and took our time getting to know each other. We were in sync with each other. I had never met anyone who understood me the way that he did. The only other person that I ever shared such a deep connection with was Rashan. The connection that Ethan and I shared made me question if we met previously, how could I be this connected to a complete stranger? The crazier part about Ethan and me was that our personalities were so much alike. Ethan kept up this tough exterior because he had to but deep down inside, he was a completely different person. He was caring, appreciative, observant, protective, supportive, and assertive.

Ethan was everything that I ever wanted in a man and so much more. When I met Christian, I was young, and he exposed me to a life that I had never experienced. Christian was aggressive, attentive, the sex was amazing, and most importantly he was rich. Christian's riches allowed him to open me up to a completely different way of life, I was just a regular girl from the Bronx living a regular life. It was easy then for me to be blinded by the money, the sex, the attention, the lifestyle. I loved Christian and despite his negative ways he always made sure that I was taken care of. Ethan made me feel like what Christian provided was no longer enough. Christian did not possess any loyalty, there was nothing sacred about our union. What he gave to me he consistently gave to other women.

I needed a man who understood me, made my spirit smile, respected me, and most importantly, was gentle with my heart. I needed Ethan whether I knew it or not. I was having an emotional affair with my husband's boss and it ate me up inside. I felt scandalous. Despite the fact that Christian was an abusive cheater, something inside of me still felt the need to be loyal to him. I could not bring myself to hurt him the same way that he hurt me. Ethan and I spent so much time together that I was actually hurt that Christian did not notice. I spent approximately ninety-five percent of my time with Ethan, yet my husband did not notice because he was too busy slanging dick. Here I was, feeling bad about being in love with another man when my husband was still doing me dirty. I was a fool, a delusional fool that was holding on to the fantasy of what I wished my marriage was. I was not sure of this thing that I had with Ethan, however; it felt good being with him, but the guilt was weighing on me.

Ethan sat across from me on his private jet. He was dressed down today, black Balmain jeans, a black Balmain tee shirt with Balmain written on the front in black writing, a black Louis Vuitton leather jacket, a black Chanel belt, and black Gucci shoes. He was a simple guy, simple and clean, a silver Audemars Piguet watch was his only accessory. Only those who actually knew Ethan were able to see him this way, usually he was dressed up in his signature look, a business suit. I admired his seriousness while he was engulfed in reading *Mastery* by Robert Greene, who was the author of the famous book *The 48 Laws of Power*. That was something that I loved about him, his craving for intellect. He was a nerd, he loved to read. He would read all types of shit, the classic urban novels by infamous authors like Celsi-Leigh, intellectual books, and self-help books. Ethan peeled his eyes away from the book and brought them up to me, per usual he could feel my eyes on him.

"What's wrong?" he asked, his forehead bent in concern.

One thing about Ethan, he always thought there was something that he needed to fix. He thought there was nothing he was unable to do or nowhere on this earth that his money could not reach, in hindsight he was right. He was a powerful man.

"Nothing, just admiring the view," I complimented, smiling.

He smiled before responding.

"You can admire it a lot better from over here," he said, smiling.

He tapped his leg motioning for me to come over and sit on his lap. I obliged, rising from my seat so that I could go to him.

Ethan and I's relationship was complicated, to say the least. We maintained a close level of intimacy without actually doing anything sexual or too intimate, but God did I want to feel that man's penis inside of me. I craved sexual intimacy from him, but we both knew that the moment we crossed that line there was no going back. We would both want to be all the way in. Some days, I found myself going home and fucking the shit out of my husband just so that I could imagine it was Ethan. That was the only time that Christian got to have sex with me these days. I barely spoke to Christian, much less let him touch me.

"Yea, you're right, the view is so much better from over here," I agreed, sitting down in his lap.

He winked at me as I wrapped my hands around his neck.

"How many times are you going to read this book? I've seen you read this book at least three times already," I stated, pulling back to look down at the book.

Ethan had a tendency to reread specific books over and over.

"Well, until I master it. Some books have so much knowledge and information that it takes a few reads to really understand it all. It also teaches me patience, it takes a lot of patience to sit and reread a book multiple times, you read slower, you have to make sure that you are reading to understand and not just finishing the pages," he said, schooling me.

I sat quietly taking in his words. Ethan was an educator, no matter what he did he always tried to make sure that he dropped little gems. He wanted me equipped with as much knowledge and information as possible. Ignorance was a choice was his mantra, the information was out there so it was up to you to find it no matter how easy your access may have been to the information.

"You never cease to amaze me," I responded.

God only knew how this man became more and more amazing every single day that I spent with him.

"It would actually amaze me if you ate all of your food for once," he stated, eyeing my plate.

A half-eaten salmon burger and sweet potato fries sat abandoned.

Ethan and I went through this back and forth at least once a day. I never finished my food, and he went from my man to my dad, informing me of the importance of three balanced meals throughout the day, blah, blah, blah.

"E, don't start this. I'm full." I lied; the truth was I could never finish my food in one sitting.

"Didn't I tell you to stop trying to lie to me? I know when you're lying to me. I see right through you," he said, using this hand to caress the side of my cheek.

I rolled my eyes playfully, trying to fight a smile that I was unable to hide. He was right about that, I am not sure if this man had a sixth sense, was psychic or some shit but he saw right through me. He would know what I was going to say sometimes before the thought came to me, shit was scary. He began to tickle me, like a little kid.

"Who are you rolling your eyes at?" he questioned, playfully tickling me on my abdomen.

I was wearing a cropped shirt, giving him easy access to my stomach. Ethan was very playful and silly. He was really a character, he was funny and played a lot, making jokes. He had a very dry and sarcastic sense of humor, just like your girl. Most people never saw this side of him, but he was so easygoing with me.

"Stop, E!" I hollered, unable to contain my laughter.

I was giggling like a schoolgirl. He brought out the little girl in me, I was light and free whenever we were together. Our relationship was easy despite the fact that nothing in our lives was easy, nothing else mattered when we were together. He stopped tickling me before bringing his forehead to mine. He stared into my eyes intensely . . . passion, care, love were all of the emotions that I saw within them. Then, before I could stop myself, I brought my face to his and kissed his full lips. The kiss was slow and passionate, so much emotion wrapped into one exchange. I wanted to do that for the past four months. The connection was unlike anything I had ever felt. The kiss was filled with so much love, unexplainable love.

Suddenly, I was sitting on a rock. Ethan's manhood had risen to the occasion. Abruptly, Ethan stopped our kiss, pulling away from me and turning his head to the side. He tapped my ass, requesting that I get up. I obliged, returning to my seat across from him.

"Malika, I can't go there with you," he said, shaking his head.

I was taken aback. I knew we had a connection; I felt this amazing vibe. *Did I misread things?* I thought. Picking up on my swirling thoughts, Ethan grabbed my hands, bringing them to his lips as he explained further.

"I want to, but I can't do it. I'm in love with you and until you decide what you're doing at home I can't go there. If I go there, this shit is over for that marriage, it's done and it's no questions about it. I don't trust myself to take it there sexually with you because if I do, that's it, you're mine after that and I don't share. So, before we take it there, you need to figure out what you want this to be," he said, seriously.

He was now staring me down and I felt uncomfortable under his microscope. I was taken aback by his words. So many pieces that I needed to decipher, the fact that he was in love with me being the first and the only thing that I could bring myself to respond to.

"You love me?" I asked, my voice shaking as I asked the question.

"That's what I said, right?" he said, looking at me sincerely.

"Yes," I answered.

He was silent, but his silence spoke volumes.

"I'm in love with you too," I finally replied.

Those were the only words that I was able to get out. I was in shock that this man, Ethan, even loved me, this perfect, God-sent man, loved me.

"We need a break after today. You need to go home and figure out what you want without me around to cloud your judgment. I can't have half of you. I didn't think I could even feel after my wife passed but you brought something out of me, and I want you to be sure before we take it any further," he asserted.

I nodded my head in understanding and turned to the side, breaking his stare. I stared out the window, taking in the scenery outside of the plane. The clear sky was beautiful, not a cloud in sight. I had some thinking to do, my heart wanted Ethan, but my mind was screaming that I was a married woman, and this was wrong.

CHAPTER FIFTEEN

"No More Second Chances . . ."

DECEMBER 26, 2018

CALABASAS, CALIFORNIA

"Morning, baby," Christian whispered into my ear.

He placed his head between the nape of my neck before wrapping his arms around me.

"Good morning," I whimpered.

Christian and I had a long night filled with family, fun, laughter, alcohol, weed, karaoke, spades, basketball, and sex. The holidays this year were a fun time. For the first time in almost two years, my life felt like it was back to normal. Good or bad I made a commitment through thick and thin to be a wife, a life partner. I owed it to myself and my marriage to give Christian another try, to give my family another try. This would be Christian's last chance. Christian did a lot of damage to me emotionally and physically His infidelity even did damage to all of us financially. Noelle, Ava and I settled our lawsuit with Taya for six point four million dollars. Christian paid the entire settlement as it was his fault. I had a tendency to give people chances until I was completely burned out. My only hope was that this decision did not come back to bite me in my ass.

I ended my relationship with Ethan to give my marriage another chance. Ethan and I kept our distance from each other. He was still helping me with my business behind the scenes, but I had to stay away from him. It was better that way. I loved Ethan; I was still in love with Ethan, but I had a husband before he came along. The truth was, I partially went back to Christian out of guilt. My affair with Ethan felt wrong, like I was a cheater no better than Christian was and the guilt ate me up inside. I missed Ethan dearly, I missed everything about him. There was so much of my day-to-day life that I wanted to share with him. Some days I wished I could be around him, but I could not. According to the streets, he was casually dating a princess of an East African country, but she was not me so whatever.

"How are my two favorite girls doing?" Christian asked, bringing his hand to my bulging stomach.

Christian brought his face to my belly, placing soft kisses. Then, he began to talk to the little person inside of my belly. He was so excited. I had never seen Christian this happy about anything; not money, basketball, me, family, or even an orgasm. He was elated, our baby girl brought him so much joy.

Yes! You heard me correctly. I did say my bulging stomach and our baby girl. Angel Serena Samuels was the name of my unborn princess. I was six months pregnant. This pregnancy was extremely high risk for me, so I was taking it easy, laying low. My doctor was very adamant that I needed to remain stress-free throughout this pregnancy. Every day was a gamble for my nugget, but I was blessed and highly favored, so I tried not to worry. She would be my angel baby after the one that I previously lost, my God-sent princess. She was my rainbow at the end of a storm.

"Well, mommy is ok; the little princess has been very active this morning," I said, my eyebrows dipped in concern.

I brought my hand to my stomach, touching the spots that Christian kissed with his lips.

"I can't believe this shit!" a voice boomed throughout the house.

"Hmmmm, what time is it? They're down there arguing, I don't feel like this," I stated, hearing all of the commotion that was happening downstairs.

Noelle, Ava, Ms. Sheema, Ms. Netta, Tamir, Armani, and Dasani (Ava's newborn daughter) were all downstairs raising hell. Our master suite was located on the left side of the manor, so they had to be extremely loud for us to hear them all the way up here. They were all spending the holidays with us this year. With our family finally being in a good space, and my high-risk pregnancy it was only right that we hosted this year.

"Eleven-thirty-three. Let's go downstairs and see what the hell is happening," he said, checking the time on the digital clock.

Christian's phone began to vibrate once more from under the pillow, the phone had been going off for the past twenty minutes. He ignored every call, as he usually did in the mornings. He did not check his phone until he was up and out of the bed.

"Damn. They've been going off for a minute, you sure you don't want to get that. Hmmm, where are my phones?" I questioned, observing that they were not in the bed with me.

I could not have been that tired last night, I thought as I rose from the bed.

"Nah, you know the routine. I'm not starting my day with that shit, they never stop calling, that's nothing," he stated, rising from the bed.

We were both walking to the bathroom when the commotion from downstairs grew even louder, something was up.

"Nah! This shit right here is fucked up!" someone hollered.

Confused, Christian and I looked, faces contorted because we did not know what was happening.

"Hold up, it sounds like they're arguing. What now?" I asked, alarmed looking over at Christian.

The question was more rhetorical than anything because I did not actually care to know the reason why.

"Let's go find out," he offered, exhaling a deep breath.

Christian and I entered the dining area, attempting to find out what was going on.

"Your raggedy ass community dick ass son done lost his fucking mind!" Ms. Sheema barked at Ms. Netta.

"You old washed-up ass bitch, don't talk about my son. You don't even know if that shit true," Ms. Netta countered, pointing her fingers in Ms. Sheema's face.

Noelle and Ava quickly jumped in the way, grabbing Ms. Sheema before all hell broke loose. Ms. Sheema was about to light her ass up for having that finger in her face.

"Somebody better get her! Ya'll better fucking get her! That finger gon end up her ass in a minute!" Ms. Sheema threatened as Noelle pulled her backwards.

"Ma, chill!" Noelle yelled.

"She ain't gon do shit, let her go!" Ms. Netta egged her on.

Christian and I looked at each other puzzled, what the fuck was going on? I brought my hand to my forehead in distress! Something in my gut told me that I did not want to know.

"Woah! Woah! Woah! What's going on here?" Christian yelled, alerting everyone of our presence.

"This nigga," Noelle mumbled under her breath.

Christian went to respond to Noelle but Ms. Sheema's words halted him.

“Oh, you know what the fuck is going on, but I’ll show you,” Ms. Sheema said with an attitude, rolling her eyes.

My heart began to race at her words. Suddenly, I was burning up. I fanned myself as I prepared for whatever bullshit this was about to be. Ms. Sheema and Christian had been on bad terms ever since I lost the first baby due to Christian. Ms. Sheema picked up the television remote and pressed the rewind button.

The headline at the bottom of the screen for the news channel The Gossip Network read:

BREAKING NEWS: THE GOSSIP NETWORK EXCLUSIVE, THE SECRET BABY MOTHER OF CHRISTIAN SAMUELS COMES FORWARD.

The headline alone caused me to brace myself, I rushed to sit in one of the chairs. Christian was on my heels, his eyes popping out of his head. I was not sure what was happening, but Christian was in a panic. He brought his hand down his face in exasperation. Ms. Sheema pressed play.

“We are here with famous social media model Taylor Kelly, also known as @thelifeoftayke on all her social media platforms. She had over one million followers and subscribers. Now Taylor, you came to my team with a shocking and heartbreaking story. We here at The Gossip Network want to give you a platform to tell your truth,” the host, Lisa Williams said.

I hated Lisa Williams. For years, she had been yearning to spill a story about Christian and me but we always got wind of the story before it aired. I was not sure how this made it to national TV without me knowing.

“So, I have taken a lot of shit over the past three years with people insinuating that I don’t know the father of my child when I was just trying to protect him. The father of my son is

Christian Samuels, which is why my son's name is Christopher. I am also currently three months pregnant with my second child by Christian. I am tired of all of this. I just can't continue to live my life like this," Taylor said, sadness written all over her face.

"Wow, so star NBA player Christian Samuels is the father of both of your children. I have a few questions about this shocking revelation. My first being, it is very public that Christian is married to Malika Samuels, his agent, and she is also pregnant at this time. Why did you have an affair with a married man and why come forward now?" Lisa asked.

"You know, I was prepared for this question. I want to first and foremost say that none of this was to hurt Malika. I actually think she is a great woman but Christian he . . . you know all of this started before they were married, and I was pregnant during their wedding. Our baby was born while he was away on their honeymoon and I had to do it all alone. I fell in love with him. He has told me time and time again that he was leaving her, their marriage was a business marriage because she's his agent for all types of things. Then recently, I found out she was pregnant, and this is obviously not a business marriage. That is his wife. You know, yesterday my son cried all day because he could not understand why his father could not spend Christmas with him, or why he was only allowed to see him for a few minutes after the game. I don't have the answers to provide to my son and I can't go through another pregnancy alone, not again. Christian comes around and he swears up and down that he wants his family but then treats us like we are nothing. I want my son to meet his family, to not be a secret. I refuse to raise two children in secret any longer. I am tired of hiding my son from the world because he looks exactly like his dad," Taylor said.

She was crying now making this shit real believable. This bitch just said my name like we're friends or something. My gut hallowed at the revelations coming out before me. I bent over, placing my hand on my knees because this was too much! To no surprise, Christian cheated again, but this time was worse how the fuck does my husband have two kids that I know nothing about. How the fuck was I pregnant at the same time as a side bitch who happens to be his baby's mother.

"Can we bring up the image of your son?" Lisa asked, placing her hand on Taylor's arm.

"Yes . . ." The image appeared.

"This is our beautiful baby boy, Christopher," Taylor said, smiling at the image that appeared on the screen.

"Wow, he looks exactly like Christian Samuels. Also, what do you have to say to the fans that say you should have gone directly to his wife, why bring this here?" Lisa said as they pulled a side-by-side image of Christian and the young boy to the screen.

I took in the image of the child; he did look exactly like Christian. They had the same nose, eyes, face really. The little boy looked exactly like Christian did when he was a baby. I knew then that it was true, I did not need to hear anything else. I was calm though, becoming irate would endanger the baby so I sat and listened, processing the news as it was delivered to me. Everyone in the room was silent. Christian ducked off in the corner. I looked back at him and he refused to look at me, just like the coward he was he could not bring his eyes to mine.

"Yea, he does. I put up with a lot of shit from everyone and was called all types of whores and people said that my child was ugly because I refused to show him. I wanted to tell my story today. I can no longer be this man's punching bag. I have tried to find a way to get in contact with her and I have been unsuccessful, he does a great job at keeping me secluded. He has threatened me with money and my career when I mentioned speaking with her. I need more, I need a man who loves me and my children. I am sorry to his wife, I never meant for any of this or to hurt anyone. I just fell in love with a dishonest and controlling man. I wish his wife the best during her pregnancy. I hope that she knows we are not enemies but two women who are victims," she said, laying it on thick.

Taylor brought her hand to her face, wiping away her forced tears. This bitch had some fucking nerve.

There was more but Ms. Sheema pressed the power button, turning the TV off. I looked up from the TV with a straight face, no reaction present because I did not know how to react. Everyone was silent, including me. I had no words. I had never felt this level of embarrassment. I was not surprised by the baby or the girl because let's face it, I knew the devil I dealt with, but the world was watching. Even now, in my own home, eyes were watching, they were family but still. Eyes were always fucking watching. The devastation that I felt was beyond measure, I had never in my life been so humiliated by anything. I felt raw, open, violated, uncomfortable. I could not understand how another woman had given my husband a child before I could. I could feel the anger rising inside of me as I tried to keep calm. I knew the risk of this pregnancy and I could not allow Christian to cause me to lose this child, not again. I had to keep calm.

Christian was a sad excuse for a man, he really was. I did not have the same energy that I once did, the care that I once had I no longer did. I was more humiliated than anything, humiliated that I even allowed myself to be in this situation, humiliated that millions of people tuned in to listen to my failed marriage. How the fuck did the world find out my business before I did?

"So, you just going to stand there looking stupid and not have anything to say?" Ms. Sheema asked Christian.

"Mind your business, this had nothing to do with you," Ms. Netta replied.

"It's the world's business now," Ms. Sheema answered, clapping her hands together.

Christian appeared next to me. He softly placed his hand on my elbow, attempting to pull me up from my seat.

"Get off of me," I said calmly, barely audible.

"Malika, can we go talk," he replied, tugging at my arm.

"No, get off of me," I responded again through clenched teeth.

I turned my head in his direction, looking down at his hand on my elbow in disgust. I had one thought to spit on him. I jerked my arm forward, removing my elbow from his grip. He grabbed my elbow once more and pulled, a little harder this time.

"Malika, can we not do this in front of everybody?" he questioned, aggravation dancing in his tone.

"Yo, I think she asked you to get off of her more than once now," Tamir interjected from his seat at the other end of the dining table.

"What?" Christian replied, frowning at Tamir.

"Nigga, I ain't stutter. She said get off of her," Tamir replied, calmly staring intensely at Christian.

There was a challenge in Tamir's stare. Tamir rarely inserted himself in anyone else's drama but today, he had enough.

"This my bitch, my wife actually, since you so fucking concerned. You can't tell me how to handle nothing when it comes to her," Christian replied, cockily.

Tamir stood from his seat, still calm at this point.

"I tried to mind my business when it comes to ya'll shit but at this point you got her fucked up, and me on the strength of her," Tamir stated, letting his position on the situation be known.

"Nigga, I don't give a fuck about none of that shit. This my bitch, like I said," Christian repeated.

He grabbed my arm aggressively in an attempt to make a point. Tamir flew across the room so fast that no one saw him coming.

Punch! Tamir's fist connected with the side of Christian's jaw. Christian staggered backwards, but quickly recovered throwing a jab back at Tamir. Christian missed and Tamir hit him in the side of the jaw again. As the two began to throw punches, I rushed out of my seat and out of the way. Christian was holding his own but Tamir was getting the best of him, whooping his ass.

"Stop!" Ms. Netta yelled.

She was jumping up and down screaming.

"Fuck his ass up!" Noelle screamed, cheering on the fight between the two men.

"Security! I need security!" Ms. Netta yelled at the top of her lungs.

I got up from my chair and bolted from the room. This was all too much for me. The news of Christian and his illegitimate kids, Tamir and Christian fighting, me being pregnant; all of it bundled together was extremely draining. I was suffocating. Unable to breathe, I needed to escape. What is this life that I decided to return to? I had the perfect out, a man that wanted to be with me, that respected me and cherished me, and I chose to come back to this. I felt dumb, stupid, a fool.

As J. Cole once said, "Fool me one time shame on you, Fool me twice, can't put the blame on you, Fool me three times fuck the peace signs, Load the chopper, let it rain on you."

I was a fool. I was unable to blame Christian at this point, I should have known better. I was not even surprised by the cheating, I expected it, but a baby! A fucking baby! This man has had a child for the past three years and I had no idea! How is that even possible? How is this bitch pregnant at the same time as me? This bitch was pregnant while this man said I do to me. This man continued to cheat on me while I was pregnant and got another woman pregnant . . . who the fuck does that? If he was having raw unprotected sex with this woman for years, how many other women has he been with?

I made it to the backyard of the manor before I stopped running. I could finally breathe. I stopped at the fountain and bent down towards the water. Gripped the side of the fountain, I used the other hand to cradle my stomach.

Shit! I don't have my phone. I thought, feeling inside the pockets of my robe.

It was probably a good thing that I did not have my phone. I was sure that there were hundreds of messages, comments, phone calls, emails, everything, you name it. I was not sure what to do or where to go from here. One thing I knew for certain was that this relationship was officially over. Everything thus far that I have gone through with Christian, I was able to go through in private. This was completely different; my entire world was turned upside down and everyone was watching. They were waiting to see what I would do, already judging me before I even knew what I would do. The thought alone gave me anxiety. I could not be here. I needed to escape. I needed a way out of this madness, just my Angel and me.

CHAPTER SIXTEEN

"I Moved On . . ."

DECEMBER 26, 2018
ATLANTA, GEORGIA

ETHAN

Bzzzzz! Bzzzzz! Bzzzzz! Dazed, I awakened to the sound of my cell phone vibrating underneath my pillow. Groggily, I reached under the pillow to retrieve my phone. The bright light was blinding as I checked to see who was calling. It was six in the morning the day after a holiday and I was, supposed to be, on vacation from all business activities. It was too early for this, I had only gotten about two hours following my sexual escapades with Aamina, the Princess of an East African nation.

Larry, my lieutenant, had called five times. *What the fuck happened now,* I thought, rolling onto my back. Larry had been instructed to only call me in the event of an emergency.

Bzzzzz! Bzzzzz! Bzzzzz! My phone began to vibrate once more. Half asleep, I answered.

"This better be an emergency," I groaned.

"I'm afraid it is, sir. Lisa Williams is set to air a scandalous story about one of your star players in a few hours, I anticipate this may be bad for business," Larry informed.

He was speaking at a million miles a minute.

"Which player?" I questioned, blowing out a sharp breath.

"Uhmmm, Christian Samuels sir, it is alleged that he had an illegitimate child with a woman who is currently pregnant at this time. This is especially troubling because his wife is pregnant now too. Christian has always been able to uphold the family image which is an asset to his star power. With this news, the team stands to lose endorsements and a list of other potential benefits. There are talks about possibly withdrawing the offer for the team to host the annual Charity Gala if this story airs," Larry explained.

I was silent for a moment, thinking. This news story was indeed bad for business. The truth was, I knew about Christian and his out-of-wedlock child for years. I knew before the baby was born and while the woman was pregnant. This is not the first time this story has come up; my team has been able to keep it under wraps for years. I knew about everything, while it was happening and after it happened. There was very little information that I did not have access to.

"So, Larry, what is the point of this call? Do damage control early, reach out to our business partners and assure them that this is not a reflection of our team. Trade Christian if you have to, but we do not want this reflecting badly on our team," I stated.

"Sir, Lisa Williams' team wants to know if you have any grievances with the story being aired? She has hinted at being open to taking a payout to not run the story. There is also another matter at hand. A former friend of Malika's, a woman by the name of Taya is shopping around the story that she was violently beaten and assaulted by Malika. A major cable network is set to do a docu series on this allegation. Such a story could ruin her career and be bad business of all players that are represented by Malika's agency," Larry informed.

I brought my hand to my head, placing a fist to my forehead.

It was too early in the morning to be dealing with someone else's problems. I was silent for a moment as I considered my options.

"No, I will not be paying. Alert Christian's PR team and if they want to pay to stop it then they should do so. I have spent more than enough covering up shit. As for the story about Malika assaulting the girl, kill it, whatever is needed," I replied.

The story about Malika assaulting a woman was damaging to her business and by default, damaging to my invested interest.

"Well, sir, Lisa's team stated that the offer is only extended to you out of courtesy. Christian's team will not be able to stop the story," Larry revealed.

"Let me know how much the backlash is going to cost me and if we are trading Christian, we need another star player," I stated, pulling the phone from my ear.

"Have a nice day then, sir," Larry said, prepared to hang up the phone.

"Oh, and before I forget, have a jet on standby. She will be calling at some point today, I'm sure of it," I instructed.

"Ok, sir, I will do that right away," Larry stated, before hanging up.

Once I ended the call with Larry, I made another call, this time to my private investigator, Adam. I looked over to make sure that Aamina was still asleep. She laid soundly asleep, her voluptuous ass sitting high in the air. Aamina was a dark-skinned beauty with long hair who was thick in all of the right places.

The phone rang once before it was answered.

"Hello, Mr. Jacob," Adam answered.

"How has she been?" I asked, desperate for an answer.

"She seems to be doing ok, sir. She has been a little happier these days. Her family is in town and she has been smiling more and more," he revealed.

I exhaled a sigh of relief before responding.

"Ok, thank you. Nothing further," I responded before hanging up the phone.

I placed the phone on the bedside table before laying back, staring up at the twenty-four-carat gold ceiling. I felt bad for Malika, but I could not save a woman who did not want to save herself.

"What are you doing up, baby?" Aamina whimpered, awaking from her sleep.

She stirred in the bed, bringing her soft hands to my chest.

"Nothing, just up," I replied, scooping her naked ass in the palm of my hand.

I pulled her body closer to me as she ran her hand down my abdomen until she reached my manhood.

"Hmmm, he's up too." She flirted, while stroking my growing erection.

Slowly, Aamina slid her head down, stopping at my penis. I sucked in air as she took the head of my penis into her mouth. The suction of her jaws combined with the wetness of her mouth and stroke of her tongue drove me crazy.

"Mhhhhh!" I grunted.

I grabbed a fistful of her hair and began to thrust into her mouth. Aamina was a professional at all things oral pleasure, she did not need any assistance but something about the visual turned me on.

Aamina looked up at me. Staring me directly in the eyes, she toyed with me, swirling her tongue around the head while using both hands to perform a two-hand twist. Slowly, she ejected my penis from her mouth, a long spit trail connecting from my dick to her mouth. Continuing to massage me with both of her hands, she released a glob of spit onto my dick before placing it back inside of her mouth. She used no hands this time, bringing my dick to the back of her throat.

"Mhhhhhh! Shit!" I grunted, a little louder this time as I neared my climax.

I tightened my grip on her hair, adjusting my body so that I could thrust a little harder. I pushed her head down further, causing her to gag as my dick plunged into her esophagus.

Damn! I thought as I reached my climax, releasing my semen into her mouth. Devilishly, Aamina looked up at me. I released her hair, and she came up for air. She licked her lips, then used her fingers to wipe the corners of her mouth.

MALIKA

The waterfall of tears was never-ending as I crouched over the fountain attempting to gather myself. I was crying so hard it had become a hassle to breathe. The feeling of disappointment was all too familiar to me. The feeling of embarrassment, however, was a new beast that I had yet to conquer. It was one thing to go through my husband's infidelities alone but, this was the big-league baby, and everyone was watching. *Just breath, take a deep breath,* I thought.

"Li?" Tamir stated, approaching me from the direction of the manor.

Startled, I turned to find my best friend standing right behind me. Tamir gave me a knowing look; a look that said I know, let it out. I turned to him, attempting to speak the words that did not seem to make sense.

"I. I'm. So. Fucking. Dumb," I wailed into his chest.

"Calm down, Li, the baby. Think about the baby, you can't let no nigga get you like this," he counseled, pulling me into a bear hug.

I stood there, crying into his chest for a few more minutes before pulling myself away. Tamir handed me a napkin before sitting on the edge of the fountain. I cleaned my face then proceeded to sit next to Tamir.

"You want to talk about it?" he asked, concern written all across his face.

Tamir was the only person who knew everything, shit he knew more than my sisters did. I trusted and confided in Tamir with every aspect of my relationship because I knew it would never leave his lips. I have trusted Tamir with my deepest darkest secrets for years, my secrets were safe with him. Usually, he remained objective, providing a man's take on the issues that Christian and I encountered. Tamir kept me grounded, gave great advice, checked me if I was wrong, and let me know when I deserved better. Tamir and Christian were once good friends but following the incident that led to my first miscarriage, their relationship took a turn for the worse.

"I knew that nigga wasn't shit! I knew! I could be somewhere with a man that loves me, and I chose to come back to this shit! I'm not even surprised at the cheating but a baby! A fucking baby, bro! I can't make peace with him having a child on, two at that! The bitch is pregnant while I am!" I exclaimed; my face contorted.

"That nigga don't deserve you, sis. I don't get why you went back after he beat your baby out of you. I don't get it, shit never made sense to me. You're better than this," he scolded, shaking his head.

"Tamir, you think I don't know that shit! I don't want to hear that right now!" I barked, rolling my eyes.

Tamir was not the type to take it easy on anyone, he was going to tell you the truth whether you wanted to hear it or not.

"Nah, you buggin you need to hear this shit! You need to leave him alone! This what you want? To be cheated on, beat up, abused, and disrespected. This can't be the Malika I know. The Malika that doesn't put up with nobody shit yet you put up with this! What do you want me to tell you? Until you leave him this is the reality. I don't know what you don't see. I'm an athlete just like him, I know what comes with this shit, the power we have to hurt our women. Even if I ever did any dirt, not saying it's right, but I would never be that disrespectful. That girl in there can never say that any woman, ever, came to her or came out and said nothing about me. I cheated once or twice . . ." he explained, pausing to gauge my reaction to his revelation.

My facial expression was unmoved. There was never any proof to Tamir's infidelity, but Noelle was always suspicious, nothing that she could ever prove. My theory was: all men cheated, at least once, maybe not in every relationship, but all men will cheat at least once. Besides, I knew Tamir, I witnessed him do his dirt so many times before he and Noelle decided to be together.

"But you would never know that I did. It's not right, I'm wrong as men we all dead ass wrong but the temptation is a lot. It's beautiful women throwing themselves at us, sometimes we get caught up. I say that to say, it's how you do shit. Wifey doesn't know because I care enough to make sure that she would never know. You don't give these bitches amo to fuck up your home. You don't give them access to you in certain ways. He sloppy, he don't give a fuck, and worst of all he don't care. He thinks you won't leave because you allow him to get away with this shit, he's comfortable. I try to mind my business, but you make me feel like I'm a part of this shit now. I can't keep watching somebody dog you out. You're my family. This shit has gone too far, you need to go," Tamir advised.

I stared at Tamir, taking in his counsel. He was right. There were no excuses for Christian's actions, but I did make him feel comfortable. I turned a blind eye to his dog ways for years. I needed to take my power back. I needed to leave Christian and be done with this marriage. There was no coming back from the revelation of a baby mother and two children. This was the final straw, it had to be.

Bzzzzzz! Bzzzzzz! Bzzzzzzz! A cell phone began to vibrate.

I could hear the vibration, but I was unable to see anything. Tamir reached into the pocket of his black Off-White hoodie and pulled out my phone.

"I forgot I brought this," he stated, handing me the phone.

The call ended by the time I received it. There were fifty-seven missed calls, two hundred and nineteen text messages, and over three hundred thousand social media notifications. I exhaled a deep breath and ignored all of the notifications. There was only one person that I wanted to, actually, needed to talk to.

ETHAN

"Ethan baby, what's wrong? You have not been yourself all day," Aamina whimpered, sitting down on my lap.

Aamina was needy, she needed money, time, attention (lots of attention), and sex. My mind had been in a daze ever since this morning. I tried to distance myself from Malika and her drama, but I could not shake the feeling. I was uneasy worrying about her.

"Nothing, I'm good. Don't worry about me." I lied.

I grabbed Aamina's hand, bringing it to my lips, I kissed her softly. Before Aamina could respond we were interrupted by an incoming call.

Bzzzzz! My phone vibrated. Aamina and I both looked down to see who was calling. Observing the name on the screen, Aamina raised an eyebrow and looked up at me.

Malika displayed on the caller ID. Instantly, I tapped Aamina on her lower back, prompting her to stand up from my lap. I stood, stepping to the side before answering the phone. She was silent on the other end then I heard her voice.

"E—Ethan." she whispered, barely audible.

I could hear the pain in her voice. She sounded like she was crying.

"The jet is on standby; I'm sending a car to pick you up and Larry will meet you once you land," I instructed, not waiting to hear another word.

"Ok," she replied, unreservedly.

Silently, I breathed a sigh of relief at her willingness.

This is it. If you go back after this, I'm done," I affirmed.

She took a deep breath before replying.

"There is no going back." She paused.

"I should not have gone back the first time. I wish I would've stayed with you," she continued.

I brought my hand to my head, bringing down my face in frustration.

"I'll see you when you get here. I have to go," I said, hanging up before she could respond.

I stood there, thinking. Aamina would be all over me once I went back to my seat, so I needed a moment of peace. Malika was the only woman that ever had me this open. Never in my life have I allowed a woman to come and go as she pleases. I did not go back and forth. I was always in control of the situation and my emotions with women, but it was something about Malika. I could not shake the way I felt for her. No matter how many times she called, I would always come no matter how hard I tried not to. A year later and I still was in love with her. I was stumped. I could not understand my love, attraction, or vulnerability with this woman. This woman was married, bad for business, pregnant with another man's child, and a potential publicity nightmare yet I still could not shake her. I had it bad, really bad.

I walked back to the table. Aamina sat pouting, arms crossed over her chest, in the seat that once belonged to me.

"Who is Malika?" Aamina questioned.

Confused, I looked up from my phone. She lost her mind asking me any questions.

“Don’t question me. I don’t answer to you or no one else. Especially ones you don’t want the answer to,” I answered, calmly.

She scoffed, rising from her seat.

“Maybe you’re unaware of who I am,” she proclaimed, placing her hand on her hip.

I laughed, sitting down in my seat. This shit was a joke, Aamina was getting beside herself.

“Mhhmmmm, I guess not,” I exclaimed, shaking my head.

I did not give a fuck who she was, she was not Malika. I did not owe her any explanations; we were not together.

MALIKA

The flight to Atlanta allowed me some time to clear my head. The tranquility of the plane ride gave me a much-needed break from my reality. I opted for silence, enjoying as much of the scenery as I could. Following the call with Ethan, I packed my luggage and I left. My life was a shit show. My marriage was a trending topic on social media, and dozens of paparazzi crowded outside of my home. I needed an escape.

Christian, as expected, left the house following the altercation with Tamir. My husband was the definition of a coward. Per usual, he ran away so he would not have to deal with his problems. Unlucky for him, I was running too and this time we had nothing to discuss. Pregnant and all, Christian would not be hearing from me. I was done, fed the fuck up, officially over this marriage. This was a shit show, not a sacred union. I had no intentions of speaking to Christian again, the lawyers would handle every shred of our breakup.

“Ms. Malika, how are you?” Larry greeted me as I descended the steps of the plane.

“Hi Larry, I am doing well. How are you?” I responded, lying.

“Good, good,” he announced while smiling.

Larry extended his hand to me, leading me to the black Range Rover that awaited my arrival. The driver exited the car and retrieved my luggage from the baggage handler before placing me inside.

"Ms. Malika, Ethan has instructed me to bring you to his loft in Buckhead," Larry informed me once I was inside of the truck.

"Is Ethan there?" I questioned, scrunching my face.

"No, ma'am," Larry responded.

"Well, where is he?" I pressed.

I was annoyed. Why was he trying to send me to his loft if he was not there? Ethan and I were attached at the hip during the months that we spent together, why did he not want me around?

"He is at the estate, ma'am," Larry confessed.

Without responding to Larry, I dialed Ethan. I needed to be wherever he was.

The phone rang twice before he answered.

"Hello," Ethan greeted.

"I am not going to the loft; I am coming there with you," I asserted, not offering a greeting.

Ethan was trying my patience by attempting to send me to the loft.

"That's not a good idea right now," he protested.

"And why not?" I quizzed.

"Malika, let's not play this game," he replied.

"No, I'm coming there. Tell whoever is there that it's their time to go," I said, firmly.

He chuckled before offering a condescending response.

"This shit doesn't work like that. You left . . . remember? You went back to your life, you're pregnant. I'm not on standby for you. It's been a year, I moved on. You can't come and go as you please," he asserted, irritation present in his tone.

The words "I moved on" hit me like a ton of bricks. It hit me more than finding out the news about my husband cheating on me. Silently, I pondered his words. He had never spoken to me that way. I wanted to come up with a smart remark, something, anything, but nothing. There was no smart remark, he was right. I made my choice now I'd have to live with it.

"You told me to go. I would have never gone back if you didn't tell me to go," I expressed, holding back the tears that threatened to fall.

He sighed before responding.

"I told you to go because you were unsure. I needed you to be committed to me all the way and like I thought, you weren't. If this is where you wanted to be you wouldn't have thought twice." He challenged me.

"It's not that simple! Ethan, everything is not as black and white like the perfect fucking world that you live in! I felt guilty! Like I was doing the same thing to him that he put me through! You know what, fuck it. Don't worry about me! I'm done, you won't be hearing from me again!" I yelled, hanging up before he could get another word in.

I was seething, how dare he move on! Who the hell was this bitch anyways? She was not me! There was no way that they shared the connection that we did! I knew that I had no right to be angry because he was right, I did choose, and I chose the wrong man. The green-eyed monster that sat on my shoulder could not accept the fact that another woman was now in his life. Did he love her? Did he not love me anymore? I lowered my head, sadness taking over. Silently, I allowed the tears to fall.

Bzzzzz! Bzzzzz! Bzzzzz! Larry's phone rang from the driver's seat of the car.

"Hello, Ethan, sir?" Larry answered.

Larry was silent, listening to Ethan on the other end.

"Ok sir, I understand. Goodbye now," he stated, hanging up the phone.

"Ms. Malika?" Larry called out, turning to face me.

"Yes," I responded, looking up.

"The boss has instructed me to bring you to his estate, where he is," he informed me before pulling off.

CHAPTER SEVENTEEN

"Sticky Situation . . ."

DECEMBER 26, 2018

ATLANTA, GEORGIA

ETHAN

Malika, Malika, Ma. Fucking. Lika. This woman drove me crazy, crazy in both a good and a bad way. The audacity of her to think that she can come and go as she pleases. How is it possible to be mad at me for moving on when she was a married woman? This shit was mind-boggling. What was even more mind-boggling was the fact that I could not help my affinity for her. If Malika was any other woman, she would not be able to get away with this shit. I tolerated her shit because I loved her. She made me feel like a sucker. She had me open, feeling emotions, and experiencing shit that I had not experienced for years following my wife's death. Shit, some of this shit I never experienced with my wife. Malika had me, all she had to do was pull a string and I would let her back in. I could not help it. No matter how hard I tried to turn off my feelings for her, all I had to do was see her face or hear her voice and I was back in.

I had no idea what I was going to tell Aamina about why Malika was there. It was disrespectful to bring Malika there while Aamina was there too. Despite the fact that I knew this would not end well and I was jeopardizing my current situation, I could not tell Malika no. I liked Aamina, she was beautiful, fun, full of personality, and the sex was great. I wished that I could be happy and settle with Aamina. The two of us had done this dance for years, every time I led her on a little more than I did in our previous exchange, but I did not love her. I tried time and time again to force a feeling for Aamina, but my attempts were unsuccessful. I cared deeply for Aamina as a person; I had love for her, and I would always look out for her, but I was not in love with her. Aamina was someone to pass the time with. I would choose Malika every time over anyone, but this time had to be the last time.

This situation with Malika was bad for business. Malika's husband was my employee, the potential backlash for me, if this got out, was implosive. I could potentially lose millions of dollars if this went wrong. This entire situation had me out of character, I was risking it all and I hoped that Malika was worth it.

I sat at the edge of the fifty-five-thousand-dollar loveseat in my living room awaiting the arrival of Larry and Malika. I buried my head into my hands, thinking of how I would maneuver through this sticky situation. I loved Malika, but the relationship between the two of us was rocky. Then there was Aamina, I was not ready to give her up. Not until I was certain that Malika was here for good. Life was simple with Aamina, easy. Aamina was single and she wanted to be with me, there was no one else. I was not sure how I was about to pull this off.

With any other woman this would be easy, but I cared about both of them in different ways. Malika was not going to take Aamina's presence here lightly and Aamina, for sure, was not going to be okay with Malika being here. This was drama and I did not do drama. In an attempt to buy myself some time, I sent Aamina out with my personal shopper. Initially, I sent Aamina away so that I could meet Malika at my loft but now that Malika was coming here, I had some thinking to do. I had to make a choice between two women. My heart wanted Malika, but my head told me that Aamina was the better woman. I was unsure of what to do. Was this the feeling that Malika referred to earlier? The feeling of being tied to two different people in two different ways. I was confused and I needed time to think this through before the two women collided.

The sound of approaching footsteps pulled me from my trance, causing me to lift my head from my hands. David, the head of security for my manor, stood dressed in an all-black suit, the security team's typical uniform.

"You have two visitors at the gate, sir. Larry and Malika, should I let them inside?" David questioned.

"Yes," I replied, exhaling a deep breath.

I'm not sure how I am going to explain this one, I thought while running my hands down my face.

MALIKA

Lost in my thoughts, I gazed out of the tinted window of the Range Rover. An eerie feeling filled me the entire way to the estate. I was nervous, anxious. I missed him. I missed him so damn much! The entire year with Christian, I forced myself to pretend that I was happy, that my family was what I wanted, and Christian was the man that I wanted. Sitting in the back seat of this car, knowing that I was on my way to see Ethan sent chills through me. The very thought of that man left me pining, needing him. I avoided Ethan for months so that I would not have to experience this feeling, but the closer I got to him the more uneasy I was.

I wished that I was able to see Ethan under better circumstances. The fact at hand was that this visit was not a happy one. I was here due to circumstances. The last thing that I wanted was for Ethan to think that he was a last resort for me.

Ethan and I both knew when we began our emotional affair that the situation was complicated. Here I was in the back seat of Ethan's car, pregnant by another man, still married to another man, and I had the audacity to have an attitude about Ethan having a complication himself. I was selfish. It was selfish of me to put him in this position. I wanted to have my cake and eat it too. I mean, what good is cake if you could not eat it anyways?

I was so lost in my trance that I did not hear Larry speaking to me at first.

"Ms. Malika?" Larry questioned.

He turned around in the driver's seat, facing me.

"Huh, sorry, yes!" I said, coming back to reality.

"Security requires your ID, ma'am," Larry informed me.

Ethan was a very thorough man. The security at Ethan's estate was extreme, but for good reason. No one was allowed inside without proof of who they were unless they were personally accompanied by Ethan. I reached inside of my black Crocodile Birkin bag and pulled my ID out, handing it to Larry.

"Here you are, Ms. Malika," he stated, handing back my ID card.

"Thank you," I replied, taking the ID.

The drive through the gates and up to the manor felt like an eternity. Literally, no exaggeration they were the longest few minutes of my life. I was so nervous. What would Ethan say when he physically saw my belly? How would he feel? Was this a bad idea? Leaving an impossible situation to put another person that I loved in an impossible situation did not seem like the right thing to do. Prior to becoming pregnant for the second time, if I had left Christian and ended up with Ethan it would have been complicated but simple. Now? This entire thing was a shit show.

Larry pulled around the circular fountain and stopped at the bottom of the stairs. I looked up to see Ethan standing at the double door entrance atop of the steps of his manor. He looked so damn good. He was wearing grey sweatpants, no shirt, and Fendi slides. His beautiful eleven-inch print bulged out of his pants. Hmmm, this is how I got pregnant in the first place, that was the last thing I should even be noticing, let alone thinking about. I admired his physique, his perfectly sculpted six-pack glistened in the night light.

Larry opened my door, helping me out of the car before he spoke.

"Have a nice day, ma'am, and congratulations again," he said, motioning to my stomach.

Out of habit, I brought my hand to my belly, rubbing it before I spoke.

"Thank you," I beamed, smiling.

I was smiling on the outside, but sadness lived in my eyes because I was having a baby by the wrong man. Ethan descended the stairs, greeting Larry before he turned to me.

"Thanks, Larry, you can put the bags in the foyer, someone will be down to get them," he greeted, shaking Larry's hand.

Ethan reached down and grabbed my hand. His touch sent a jolt of energy through me; it felt so good to be in his presence. I looped my perfectly manicured fingers through his as he escorted me up the stairs and into the foyer of the house. He stood there, averting his gaze away from my protruding belly. He fought so hard not to look down, waging a personal war with himself before he did the unthinkable. Ethan reached down and caressed my belly with his hand, staring intensely at me the entire time. I lowered my eyes to see him touching my belly.

"Ahhh!" I hollered as the baby kicked in response to his touch.

Even my little angel could feel the intensity of our connection.

"This was supposed to be our baby," he whispered, barely audible.

I stilled at his words. There was sadness lingering in his tone. He was right, this was supposed to be his baby, our baby. If only I would have chosen differently.

"I know," I whispered as a tear escaped from my eyes.

Ethan used his other hand to wipe my tear away while keeping his other hand on my stomach. My rainbow baby was going crazy in there. She had been kicking since he touched my stomach.

Clank! Clank! Clank! The sound of stiletto heels strutting on the ceramic tile popped the bubble that Ethan and I were in. The balloon popped and reality hit me in the face as the dark-skinned beauty entered the foyer. She strutted in, and as much as I wanted to hate on the bitch, I could not lie she was gorgeous. Now, do not get it fucked up, she was definitely not LiLi, but she was cute. A fitted black body con dress with thigh-high Yves Saint Laurent feather heels graced her feet. Her hair was pulled up into a high ponytail and silver Chanel earrings graced her ears. She was cute or whatever, I guess. Was this what he wanted? Was she prettier than I was? Was her body better? What was it about this woman that he called his girlfriend?

"Babe?" she questioned, entering the foyer.

She was speaking to Ethan, but her eyes never left mine. She took me in, looking me up and down. Her eyes stopped when she reached my protruding belly. The glare that I received from her was deadly, but not as deadly as the one that I gave to her. Ethan pulled his hand away from my stomach before turning to respond to her.

"Yes," he responded calmly, tucking his hands in his sweatpants.

"Who is this and what is going on here?" she asked, softly.

She was calm but I could tell from her demeanor that she was fighting to keep her composure. Before I could stop myself, I responded.

"Malika, and you are?" I said, smiling.

The smile on my face did not match the ill intent that lived in the soul of my eyes. The revelation of my name was like a punch to her gut. I could tell from her demeanor that she either knew exactly who I was to Ethan or heard my name before.

"This is my friend Malika, Malika this is my girlfriend Aamina," Ethan interjected.

The word girlfriend hit me like a ton of bricks. *Girlfriend? Did he just say girlfriend?* I thought. I had to be hearing things. Girlfriend! He claims this girl as his girlfriend, wow. I was speechless, attempting to hold my composure because another woman would never have the privilege of seeing me sweat or hurt about her presence. I held it together but, on the inside, it felt as though someone stabbed me in the heart for the second time today. Actually, looking at the girl standing here made it even worse, this time the knife was being turned while inside of my chest.

"Malika is going to be staying here while she figures a few things out," he continued, informing Aaminah.

"So, you didn't think that this is something that we should have discussed privately at any point before you brought her here?" she said, now with an obvious attitude.

She brought her hand to her hip and glared at Ethan.

"Brought me . . ." I began but was quickly cut off by Ethan.

"Malika, give me a minute. I'll have housekeeping set you up in one of the guest bedrooms. I'll come check on you sometime later or tomorrow," he stated before turning his attention back to Aamina.

"Let's go talk," he said to Aamina.

He walked towards her, grabbed her hand and led her to the direction of his private office. Aamina looked back at me once more, then snatched her hand from his grip before walking off.

The two disappeared and I could not breathe. I was going to be sick. Suddenly, I ran out of the house. I needed an outlet. I needed fresh air. Somehow, the only thing I managed to do for the entire day was run. I ran from my home in Calabasas and here I was running out again. I just needed a minute. How was it possible for two different men to crush your heart in one day? The aching that I felt inside tore through me as I gasped for air. I rushed to the steps to lean over the banister. I gripped the rail for support with one hand, using the other to grip my belly. I was unable to contain the tears that flowed from my eyes. I wanted to come here knowing there may be someone else. I left him; I went back to my no-good ass husband. I had brought all of this on myself. I felt like I was having a heart attack, but there was no heart attack, only heartache and heartbreak.

I reached inside of my Birkin, retrieving my cell phone. I could not be alone, I needed to talk to someone. Frantically, I dialed Ava, the voice of reason.

"Lika, where are you?" Ava answered.

Ava was back in Calabasas at my home. Earlier, I did not inform anyone of where I was going. I left and told them that I needed to get away.

"Ethan's house in Atlanta. He has a girlfriend, she's here," I cried.

Ava exhaled a deep breath before speaking.

"I don't want to say this while you're going through so much but Sash what did you expect? Realistically, you could not have expected that man to wait around for you to figure your marriage out. You come and go in his life whenever you want to. You had to know that this was a possibility," she reasoned.

I was silent, listening because she was correct. I did know that this was a possibility but seeing the truth was difficult to handle.

"I know. I just—I don't know what I thought," I answered.

"Lika, he let you come there while that woman is there, correct?" Ava asked.

"Yea, he did," I answered.

"Yea, so he fucks with you, that's clear. He fucks with you so much that he is willing to blow up his own situation. Not to mention you are pregnant bitch, pregnant! You need to figure out if this is what you really want. You can't walk in and out of someone's life and expect them to wait on you. Your marriage is going through a lot, but do you really want to be with Ethan or are you running from situation to situation to fill a void?" she continued.

I was quiet, contemplating as her questions provoked deep thought. Do I want to be with Ethan? Am I ready for a relationship of this magnitude? Is this all to fill a void?

"No, it's not to fill a void," I started.

Needing to sit down, I lowered myself onto the steps of the entrance before continuing.

"I want to be with Ethan but being honest, I don't know that this is the right time. I don't know if there will be a right time and I fear losing him to someone else," I confessed.

"I can't tell you the right thing to do. You have to decide what's best for you but keep in mind you are wrapping someone else in your problems. It's not fair to no one to have them cut their situation off if you aren't sure what you want. Figure it out, don't be selfish and string him along. That's a good man," she advised.

Suddenly, the approaching footsteps behind me gave me pause. I turned to find Larry exiting the manor.

"Ma'am, Ethan has requested that you come inside. There is a designated outside area if you would like to sit," Larry informed me.

I nodded my head, signaling that I would be on my way. Larry stood, waiting on me to leave with him. It was clear that I could not hide from Ethan anywhere around here.

"Girl, I have to call you back but thank you! Love you!" I responded to Ava, jumping back into the conversation.

"Try not to let Christian stress you out, I'll call to check on you later, love you too!" Ava replied before hanging up.

I stood from my seat on the step, turning to Larry. I had some thinking to do. Ava was right, I needed to figure out what I want.

CHAPTER EIGHTEEN

"Whenever It's Convenient . . ."

DECEMBER 26, 2018
ATLANTA, GEORGIA

ETHAN

"You brought another woman here while I am here? Have you lost your fucking mind?!" Aamina quizzed, slamming the door to my private office.

She was pacing the space between the door and my desk. I was silent as she continued her rant. I was wrong so I opted to let Aamina get her shit off.

"The same woman who you told me earlier was none of my concern, that I could not ask you any questions about! A pregnant woman at that! Is she pregnant with your child?!" Aamina barked.

I blew out a deep breath, releasing my frustration. I knew when I decided to have Malika come to the manor that confrontation between Aaminah and me was inevitable. I walked to the front of my desk, standing in front, I leaned backwards, placing my hands in my pocket.

"You need to calm down," I replied.

I needed to diffuse the situation; I could not take too much more of the yelling.

"Calm down! Calm down! How am I supposed to calm down when you brought your pregnant ex here? What the fuck is wrong with you?!" she yelled; this time angrier than before.

Aamina took a step closer to me, pointing her finger in my face as she continued to verbally spar with me.

"What the fuck is going on, Ethan?!" she pressed, jamming her finger into my face.

I moved my head to the side, avoiding her finger. Aamina was taking this too far now, choosing violence.

"Sit down. I'm not talking to you like this. You can be mad but calm down. I don't do this, this is extra, sit down," I commanded, motioning my hands towards the accent chair for her to take a seat.

Reluctantly, Aamina walked over to the chair and took a seat. She took a deep breath, folding her arms before speaking.

"What the fuck is going on, Ethan?" she asked, calmly this time.

"That's my friend. She's going through a difficult situation and she needed somewhere to go. She's pregnant but not by me," I confessed, only the partial truth.

I only told Aamina what she needed to know. Malika was in fact my friend going through a difficult situation. Technically, I never had any sexual relations with Malika, so we were friends.

"Ethan, I am far from stupid; you could not possibly expect that I would believe the two of you are just friends," she scoffed, rolling her eyes.

I pulled my hand down my face. This was proving to be much more complicated than I anticipated. I liked Aamina, but I did not care if I lost her.

"She's my friend. I have feelings for her, yes, but we are only friends. We have never had any sexual relations or anything. I care for her but it's just a friendship," I responded, honestly.

Though I would maybe never love Aamina, she was a good girl. I owed her the truth to some extent. She glared at me, sadness lingering in her eyes. She was silent for a few moments before asking her next question.

"Do you love her?" she quizzed, her eyes connecting with mine.

The question caught me off guard and I was not sure if I should answer it.

"Yes," I admitted.

"More than you love me? Do you even love me?" she whispered her response; it was so low that I barely heard her.

She seemed ashamed to be asking the question. She turned her head to the side, avoiding my gaze as she awaited my answer. I did not want to answer this question. I knew that the answer would hurt her feelings and that was the last thing that I wanted to do.

"Come on, Aamina. What does that have to do with anything that's irrelevant," I said, in an attempt to evade the question.

"No, Ethan, I'm serious because what are we even doing anymore if this girl can come in and it's fuck me or how I feel? I need an answer. What is she to you, I need to hear you say it?" Aamina pleaded, her eyes begging, searching for answers.

I stalled for a moment, aware that my answer would potentially mess up everything that we had going on, but she wanted to hear the truth. I looked down, breaking our stare. I had been in a carousel with Aamina for years. For years, she has loved me, coming in and out of my life, waiting for me to pick her. The truth was, I would never pick her. I did not love her in that way.

"Yes, I love her more than you, more than anyone. I have

love for you as a person, but I don't love you in that way. I'm not sure I'll ever be able to give you what you want or really love you for that matter. I'm not in love with you," I answered, honestly.

Aamina recoiled at my words, injury was present in her facial expression as she turned her head to the side, attempting to hide the tear that crept down her cheek.

"Come here," I said softly.

Guilt gnawed at me. I led this girl on for years. I knew how much she cared for me and loved me, but I did not feel that way for her. In hindsight, I had been doing to her what Malika was doing to me. Aamina shook her head, trying to hold back her falling tears. I grabbed a cloth napkin from my desk and brought it to her. I handed her the napkin and knelt beside her.

"This doesn't have to change anything, but I get it if it does," I spoke.

She looked up at me, chuckling.

"You're selfish and entitled. I could be with anybody I want, and I pick you. I give you everything you could possibly want and yet you love a woman who belongs to another man. This is a joke. This changes everything. I'm done with this and I'm done with you. Don't call me when you realize that this was the biggest mistake you ever made," Aamina proclaimed, rolling her hands.

She stood from her seat, wiped the tear under her eye and walked towards the door.

"Bye, Ethan, have the staff send my stuff over to me. Good luck with another man's family," she said while leaning on the office door.

I was silent as she walked out of the room and shut the door. Once again, Malika came in and ruined shit. Her drama was never-ending. I wondered if she was even worth it. I loved her but love was not enough. This was her last opportunity to get it together or there would be no coming back, no more saving her, no more being indecisive. The options were clear, she either left her husband for good this time or I was done with this situation.

DECEMBER 27, 2018
ATLANTA, GEORGIA

MALIKA

"Hmmmmm . . ." I groaned, rolling over in bed.

I was met with a splitting headache as I woke up from my few hours of sleep. It was seven-fifty-two in the morning, and I was not able to fall asleep until five in the morning. It was needless to say that I was sleep-deprived. I stayed up all night thinking, thinking of what to do and what was next for me. I placed my hand at the top of my head, applying pressure to the origin of the pain. I needed to take something and fast. I reached over and pressed the intercom button located above the end table.

"Ms. Malika, good morning, ma'am," a female voice boomed through the intercom.

"Good morning, can someone bring up some pain medication please?" I croaked.

"Yes, I will send that up right away," the staff responded.

"Thank you," I groaned before rolling back over in the bed.

Moments later, a knock at the door brought me out of the bed. When I opened the door, I expected to see the staff with my pain medication but instead, I was greeted by an angry Ethan.

"Oh, I wasn't expecting you," I admitted, surprised.

I looked a terrible mess, my eyes were puffy from all of my crying, my hair was in a messy bun at the top of my head, and I had sleep crusted in my eyes. Ethan was the last person that I wanted to see while I was in this state.

"We need to talk," he said, letting himself into the guest room.

"Can we talk later, please?" I whimpered, heading back towards the bed.

"No. We need to talk now," he exclaimed with a deep sense of urgency.

He was uneasy, bothered, irritable, something was troubling him. He stepped into the room, closed the door and made his way to the bed. He sat on the edge of the bed before he began speaking.

"Is this a game to you? You think you can just come and go? Come in and fuck my life up whenever it's convenient for you. Why did you insist on coming here? Everything was cool, why the fuck are you here?" he hissed at me.

I was taken aback by his words. Scared even, I was so used to being in an abusive relationship that Ethan's anger scared me. I scooted back in my seat. In all of my days knowing Ethan he had never once spoken to me this way; he never even raised his voice at me. What was happening here?

"Excuse me? What you mean? You told me to get on the PJ!" I yelled, confused.

I gripped the blanket pulling it to myself.

"Cut the shit, Malika. You know that when you call, I come, I'm always there for you in any situation. This shit here I'm done with. You fucking up my money, my head, and now my relationship. I'm not doing this shit with you no more. I can give you everything you want; I give you everything you want but you don't want to be here, but you pop up and do this whenever you feel like," he barked.

"Wow!" I scoffed before proceeding to yell. "Your relationship! Relationship! Fuck that bitch and fuck that relationship!" I yelled.

Suddenly, I had a burst of energy and I was heated. I flew from the bed, pacing. Everything that he said was right but somehow, I was stuck on the word relationship. He had some nerve really giving a fuck about that bitch. A relationship of all things. I could not believe it.

"You got some fucking nerve," he said, chuckling.

He paused, shaking his head.

"You don't know who you want to be with or what you want but you think you can dictate what I do. Yes, relationship! Just like you're married, I have a situation, or I had one, a good one until you came back in. You don't dictate shit over here. I'm not sitting around waiting on you to come back, this ain't that," he said, exasperated.

"You think you fucking know! You don't get it! I didn't want to be there with that nigga! What was I supposed to say, Oh, Christian, I'm leaving you for your boss?! Your fucking boss! Did you ever think of the situation I was in? What the fuck did you want me to do?! I was in an impossible situation before, and I am in an even more impossible situation now!" I screamed.

My screams turned into uncontrollable sobbing as I looked down at my stomach. The hormones of my pregnancy mixed with the stress of this situation sent me into an emotional frenzy. I stopped pacing and stood there, staring down at him. An ugly cry escaped me. I was lost and confused. This was all fucked up and I was the one fucking everything up.

Ethan rose from his seat on the edge of the bed and walked over to me. He pulled me into his body and hugged me tightly. Carrying me over to the bed, I sat crying, hysterically. I was unable to contain the tears or the screaming that erupted from my lips. So much pain that needed to be released.

"I'm sorry," I whimpered, attempting to wipe my tears.

"It's ok, love. A man can't really help who he loves. I'm to blame too," he said softly.

Ethan reached over and brushed my hair out of my face. He looked at me sincerely. His eyes filled with passion and love. He exhaled before speaking again.

"Is this what you want, Malika? Be real with me. If this is where you want to be, I'm happy to have you but I can't keep playing this game with you. This is it Lika," he said looking at me sincerely.

I nodded my head in understanding as I attempted to gather myself.

"This is where I want to be. This is the only place that I ever really wanted to be," I said solemnly while looking into his eyes.

The intensity of the energy that lingered between us was strong. An energy so strong that it pulled me to him. He pinched my chin between his fingers, pulling my face to his before placing a soft kiss on my forehead. I swooned, igniting at his gentle touch. This man was a stone wall to everyone, everyone except for me. He melted before me. The way that he let his guard down with me and was so vulnerable, caring, and open was beautiful to witness. He was a gangster but with me he was childlike.

I placed my head in his chest, sitting still I could hear the rhythm of his heartbeat beating to the same rhythm that mine was. I was not sure why, but I wanted him inside of me right now. I needed him inside of me. The circumstances were fucked up but fuck it, he was exactly what the doctor ordered. I looked up at him. He was staring down at me. The intensity of his eyes let me know that he was having similar thoughts. I reached my hand up, caressing the side of his face with the palm of my hand. I pulled my face to his, and his lips met mine. The passion of the kiss told a story of longing; a story of desire; a story of two people who urgently needed to feel each other.

He scooped me in his arms, picking me up and repositioning me on the bed. Gently, he laid me down. I was wearing an oversized tee shirt with black panties underneath. I laid on my back and stared up at him as he took his time admiring my body. He reached down and pulled the tee shirt over the top of my head before standing. Silently, he stood looking down, his eyes trailing down my breasts and finally down to my stomach. The look in his eyes was pained. I could see the hurt resonating through him as he processed the sight of my bulging belly. He was conflicted. Gently, Ethan reached down and placed his hand on my stomach.

"This is still our baby," he said under his breath.

Hearing those words sent a flutter of emotion through me. *How did I get so lucky?* I thought. Ethan pulled my panties down and around my ankles. He was gentle, taking his time. He lowered himself to his knees before me, pulled my body to him and then . . . bliss. I sucked in air as his mouth found my clitoris.

"Hmmmmmm!" I moaned while clawing at the sheets of the bed.

He sucked and licked on the lips of my vagina like he was eating a peach. It felt amazing. He was taking his time, making sure that I felt his passion in every touch. While keeping his mouth buried in my juices, he entered me with his fingers.

"Ethan!" I gasped, sucking in air.

He used two fingers to enter my vaginal walls and placed his thumb inside of my ass. My mouth fell open in pleasure and my mouth contorted into an ugly scowl as I threw my head forward to observe the mess that he was making between my legs. I was soaking in my own juices. He worked his fingers inside of both of my holes at the same time, while sucking on my clitoris. Momentarily, he came up for air and smirked at me. A trail of my stickiness followed him, connecting to the hairs on his chin. He looked up at me taking in my reactions as he worked his fingers inside of me. Making eye contact, he spit inside of me before diving back in with his tongue. Oh, this nigga was nasty, just how I liked it.

"Ethan! Fuck! E!" I screamed, unable to contain my pleasure.

I came all over his face and even then, he still would not

stop. He was in heat and I needed a release. He licked and licked until he was sure that he had sopped everything up like a biscuit. Slowly, he pulled his fingers out of me and pulled his mouth away before standing to his feet. I jumped up, eager. I needed to make him feel how I did. I tugged at his sweatpants, attempting to release his erection. I wanted him inside of my mouth, now. As I reached down to grab his dick, he stopped me.

"No, I want to feel you. I don't want that right now. I want this," he said, placing one of his moist fingers inside of my mouth as he pushed me back on the bed.

I licked my juices off of his fingers, submitting to his wishes. Swiftly, Ethan pulled his girth out and mounted me. I was not prepared for this.

"Hmmmmmm!" I hollered as he entered me.

I clawed at his back, digging my nails into the depths of his skin. His curved penis filled me up perfectly. My God, he was hitting spots inside of me that I didn't even know existed.

"Damn! I knew this shit was going to be good but shit!" he grunted, stroking me slowly before speeding up.

He brought his mouth to mine, kissing me passionately, while using his other hand to caress my full breasts. He twirled my nipples between his thumb and index finger before trailing kisses down my neck and over my breasts. He took one breast at a time into his mouth.

"Oops!" I chuckled as a droplet of milk, accidentally, made its way into his mouth.

Unfazed, Ethan continued. Trailing kisses down to my protruding belly, all the while continuing to stroke me.

"Ethan baby!" I moaned.

How was it possible for sex to be this good? I had great sex in my day but this, this shit was next level. I was floating on a high. A high from dick so good that you never wanted to come down, I'm talking have you speaking in tongues type of high.

I could just lay here and take this dick all day and night, God damn! This was worth the wait. The passion, love, and emotion made everything feel so much better.

"Why are you so fucking wet!" he barked through clenched teeth hovering over top of me.

"I'll kill you if you ever fuck somebody like this besides me!" I screamed because the dick was so good, I was choosing violence, every time!

Ethan smirked, leaning in to kiss me once more.

"Hmmmm, I'm coming!" I screamed unable to contain my pleasure.

I exploded all over his dick while screaming. This man had managed to make me orgasm twice in a matter of minutes. If I knew the sex was this bomb, I would have left my husband a long time ago.

"Me too!" he whispered in my ear, biting the bottom of my ear lobe.

He collapsed on top of me before rolling to the side. He pulled my body into his arms and wrapped himself around me. He brought his hands to my stomach and began rubbing my belly. We laid there in silence, reveling in the moment. After years of back and forth, unspoken energy and wasted time we were finally here, together.

"I love you," I whispered.

"I love you more, LiLi," he responded.

CHAPTER NINETEEN

"A Thin Line between Love and Hate . . ."

JANUARY 19, 2019
ATLANTA, GEORGIA

MALIKA

"Oh, I wasn't hungry, you can eat all of my food," Ethan said sarcastically, shaking his head.

A Cajun lobster po'boy sandwich paired with fresh-cut steak fries was on the menu for today. Before Ethan could get to the rest of his food, I stuffed his remaining steak fries into my mouth. Ethan shook his head in dry amusement, fighting a smile. For the past few weeks, I somehow managed to eat all of my meals and most of his as well. This baby loved to eat! Well, maybe it was me that loved to eat but you get the picture. Playfully, I threw my middle finger up at Ethan while rolling my eyes. I had eaten his food every day for the past three weeks and somehow, he still managed to complain, he should be used to my gluttony by now.

"Shut up, I left you some," I countered, rolling my eyes.

When I said some, I meant exactly some because I ate most of his lunch.

“By some, you mean no fries and a half a sandwich?” he questioned, raising an eyebrow.

“Yes, that is exactly what I mean! How much more food do you need?” I stated, looking at him in disbelief.

Ethan pulled his head back, staring at me with a raised eyebrow. The two of us stared at each other in silence, attempting to hold in our laughter and keep a straight face. It was the battle of the fittest, who would break their stare and burst into laughter first. Similar to the infamous stare down between Sean ‘Diddy’ Combs and Elijah Connor on the talent contest *The Four*, neither Ethan nor I were letting up.

“Ok! I’m serious! Stop playing!” I hollered, conceding before bursting into laughter.

“That’s the problem.” He chuckled, shaking his head.

“I don’t know where you put all the food, the baby can’t possibly be that hungry,” he stated.

“Well! I’m hungry, damn! Didn’t anybody ever tell you not to question a pregnant woman!” I scolded, rolling my eyes and taking a gulp of my ginger ale.

Ethan raised both his hands in surrender.

“I don’t want no smoke,” he yielded.

“Yea, like I thought,” I boasted, rolling my neck with an attitude like only a black girl from the Bronx could.

This has been the dynamic between Ethan and me for the past few weeks. The two of us played all day. It was so easy and light with Ethan. Our vibe and connection were unmatched, we understood each other on a different level. I could talk to Ethan about anything. The two of us were attached at the hip. We went to his office together, the gym, private doctors’ visits, morning meditation sessions; we did almost everything together. The only things I did not attend with Ethan were his private business meetings. We were inseparable. The sex between us was mind-blowing as well. We waited years to indulge in each other and it was worth the wait. My only regret was that we did not do it sooner because God damn! Sex should not be allowed to be that good! Ethan was a pleaser. He took his time with my body, quickly learning the depths of my sex. He was not satisfied until I was satisfied. He did not even allow himself to orgasm until he gave me one. He was sensual yet aggressive, passionate yet raunchy. He made me feel in places of my vagina that I did not know even existed. His sex was different. He left you craving for him, yearning for more. We fucked like wild rabbits and my raging hormones made the sex all the better.

To my utmost surprise, Ethan was so accepting and loving towards the idea of my baby girl. He took on the role of father so naturally, he was better than Christian. He was attentive to my every need. He set me up with a private OBGYN, the best in the country. Initially, I was unsure of how Ethan would handle my pregnancy, but I could not have been happier with his acceptance. I never expected anything less from Ethan but being able to witness his actions firsthand was heartwarming. Ethan's love for me was unconditional. His acceptance of my child with another man showed me that there were no limits to his affinity for me. I wished Ethan were the biological father of my child. Ethan was a real man, biological father or not, he made it clear to me through words and actions that he had every intention of taking care of the baby as if she were his own.

Christian, on the other hand, was going crazy. I had him blocked on every device I owned. He spent every single day stalking anyone that may have been able to get in contact with me. He stalked my office, my assistant, and anyone in my immediate circle that he was able to get in contact with. Christian had gone as far as filing a missing person's report. When the police contacted me, I told them that I was not missing and instead choosing to stay away from my husband. I was provided the option of filing a restraining order against him for harassment, but I decided against it. Christian could kiss my ass, I wanted nothing to do with him.

I was done with Christian, there was no longer anything to discuss or to be worked out. Our attorneys could hash out the logistics for custody of our unborn child. I filed for divorce once again. I had not heard anything back about the paper. He did manage, however, to leave threatening voicemails and send nasty emails, he was livid. One minute Christian was begging for a chance to explain, the next he was threatening me and letting me know that I was not going anywhere. He was delusional and narcissistic. I could not understand for the life of me what I ever saw in his bitch ass. I desperately regretted the day I met him. The biggest mistake that I ever made was marrying Christian Samuels.

Bzzzzzzzz! Bzzzzzzzz! Bzzzzzzzzz! The loud vibrations of my cell phone commanded my attention.

Joel My Bell displayed on the phone screen. Joel was my assistant. I picked up the phone from the dining table and answered the call.

"Damn, I forgot that I had to look over some numbers for a potential team transfer. Joel is about to yell! I know Courtenay has been on his ass!" I exclaimed, believing that Joel was calling to remind me about business.

Courtenay was my attorney, whenever she could not get in contact with me, she reached out to Joel.

"Hey . . ." I started before Joel cut me off.

"Lika! You need to go on Instagram and get on Christian's live right now!" he yelled through the speaker.

Simultaneously, both Ethan's business and personal cell phone rang. Questioningly, Ethan looked up at me. *Bzzzzzzzz! Ring! Bzzzzzzz! Ring! Bzzzzzzz! Ring!* Whatever Christian was up to must have been major. Ethan looked up at me, his eyebrows bent in confusion.

"Joel, I told you . . ." I started again.

"Malika, no this is serious! Get on the live!" he hollered.

"Yea?" Ethan answered one of his phones at the same time.

It was all too much commotion at once. Joel was in my ear yelling and Ethan's phones were going off. It was a bit much.

"Ok," I conceded.

Joel hung up the phone in a haste. I took a deep sigh. *Why does this man spend his every waking moment attempting to make my life a living fucking hell?* I thought, exhaling sharply.

"Get it shut down!" Ethan stated.

I was confused, why did we need to shut anything down.

"Well, get the fucking company owner on the phone then! Shut it down! This shit is not negotiable!" he barked into the phone before hanging up.

Ethan looked up at me, stress etched all over his face.

"What is it?!" I questioned, anxiety creeping up on me.

Usually, Ethan was not shaken by any of Christian's antics so this had to be next level.

"Malika, I don't think you need to see this," he offered; in true Ethan fashion, he was trying to protect me.

This was my life; however, he could not keep me in the dark.

"Ethan," I said, sternly.

My eyes pleaded with him, almost begging him to tell me what was happening. He sighed before picking up his business phone. He unlocked the phone and went to the social media application. He clicked on Christian Samuel's profile and pressed play on the live button.

"I have not seen my wife in weeks! Fucking weeks! I have no idea where she is! The police won't help me! Her fake best friend who she's been fucking for years, Tamir Rawlins, won't help me! Where the fuck is my wife?" Christian's voice boomed through the speakers.

"Ya'll need to shut the fuck up saying I was cheating on her why do I care! Ya'll believe any fucking thing! I never cheated on her! I've had an open marriage for years. Ya'll don't know shit! She pulls this disappearing shit all the time! She's pulled it so many times before with other people!" Christian lied, responding to fan comments.

Christian was a sick individual. His ability to lie so easily was a disgrace to watch.

"I have someone really important here who is worried sick about her," Christian said, pausing to pass the phone to another individual.

The sight before me sent me into an immediate panic attack. This could not be real, no way this nigga would stoop this fucking low or so I thought. No low was too low for Christian Samuels.

Trevor Tanners sat before the camera, looking old and dirty as ever. His ugly crater face seemed to get uglier as he aged. His skin was saggy and there was hyperpigmentation all over. He seemed to be even uglier than I remembered.

"We are looking for my daughter Malika. My sweet Lika, it was always her and me after her mother passed during her birth. Malika was troubled as a child, running away at the age of thirteen. She has been troubled for a while. We are begging you all, if anyone has any information of my daughter's whereabouts, please . . ." Suddenly, the live feed was interrupted.

LIVE FEED DISABLED, displayed on the phone screen.

I looked up at Ethan, disbelief written all over my face. I was unable to find the words to express my disgust. Ethan knew the story of my father. I did not speak on him much, but Ethan knew the abuse and trauma that he brought to me as a child. Shit, anyone that was close to me knew of my disdain for my sperm donor. Christian knew the pain that my father caused me, he knew everything. I never thought in a million years that Christian would stoop to this level. He was a narcissistic, manipulative, controlling, sick son of a bitch. How demented could he fucking be? He not only did the unthinkable and brought forward the one person on this earth that I would not piss on in a fire, but he also spread nasty lies that I was fucking my best friend and sisters's baby dad. This was some bullshit! In that moment it dawned on me how much I hated Christian. It's a thin line between love and hate. Officially, I crossed the line of hate.

"How could—" I began.

"It's nothing to say. Don't even worry about it, I'll handle it," Ethan asserted, calmly rising from his seat.

Ethan walked away from the table and out of the dining room.

ETHAN

"Yes sir, the live feed was shut down, sir," Larry greeted, answering the phone on the first ring.

"Get Bill Russel on the phone and every fucking body from that social media company! Now!" I barked angrily into the speaker.

I stood in my office, pacing back and forth. I was livid and unable to sit still. I allowed this shit to continue for long enough, it was time to put a stop to Christian Samuels and his bullshit.

"Right away. I will get on that immediately," Larry conceded.

"And set up a private meeting, tonight," I ordered.

I did not need to say much more for Larry to know exactly who and what I was speaking of.

"Ok, sir," he answered before I hung up the phone.

In a matter of seconds, my business phone was ringing with just the man that I needed to speak with, Bill Russel.

"Hello, Mr. Jacobs," Bill greeted.

"Hello, Bill, thank you for finding the time to speak with me so urgently," I replied.

"Of course, Ethan, we have done a lot of business together.

I will always make time to speak with a businessman such as yourself. What can I do for you?" he stated.

"Christian Samuels, I need his account suspended and all videos and clips from his live today removed," I informed him.

I had no time to waste. We needed to get to the point of this conversation, I wanted this handled. Bill paused for a moment.

"I can have his account suspended immediately, no problem but the removal of all videos and clips will be a difficult task. That may also lead to issues for our legal team," Bill explained.

"I am equipped to make a sizable financial donation to make sure that this happens. I will pay the legal fees if needed but I need this done, today," I responded.

Bill exhaled a sharp breath.

"Ok, let me see what we can do here. The account will be suspended no later than the next hour, but I may need a little more time for the video removals. I anticipate that even if I am able to get some of the videos removed, I may not be able to get all of them but for you, I will do my best," he stated.

"Some are better than none, do what you can. Thank you, my friend," I declared.

"Nice speaking with you Ethan and please, do not hesitate to reach out if there is anything else that you need done. We must go golfing sometime," he replied.

I chuckled before responding. Bill has been trying for years to get me to go golfing with him.

"I don't know, Bill, I'm not much of a golfer but I might take you up on your offer someday. Take care," I said right before hanging up the phone.

Like clockwork, my personal phone began to ring. *Bzzzzzzz! Bzzzzzzzz! Bzzzzzzzz!*

The phones never stopped ringing; it was one thing after a-fucking-nother. I answered, noticing that it was Larry calling.

"Tonight, at the warehouse at nine, sir," Larry informed.

"Ok. Thanks." I thanked him, hanging up.

I was done waiting around for the right moment. The moment was now, and I needed Christian handled and out of the picture.

MALIKA

The sight of my father brought back so many painful memories. I was not mad at Christian for his actions, Christian was Christian. I expected nothing from him, especially not anything good. Trevor fucking Tanners, the devil himself, had resurrected from the dead. I knew that him coming around meant one thing. He wanted something. He had an end game for that little show that he helped Christian put on, I was not sure what the end game was. There was a possibility that his only motivation to help Christian was to help fuck me over, but I was sure that Christian paid him. Money or no money, you know how the saying goes: A friend of my enemy is a friend of me. I was both of their enemies.

Bzzzzzzz! Bzzzzzzz! Bzzzzzzz! Bzzzzzzz! Bzzzzzzz! Bzzzzzzz! Bzzzzzzz! Bzzzzzzz!

The vibration of both of my cellphones brought me out of my thoughts and into reality. My phones were blowing up and my social media was on fire. I was sure there was a mix of love and hate happening at this exact moment. I sat, elbows on my knees, with my head buried in both hands. I was trying so hard to stay calm for the baby, but I was failing.

Bzzzzzzz! Bzzzzzzz! Bzzzzzzz! Bzzzzzzz! Bzzzzzzz! Bzzzzzzz! Bzzzzzzz! Bzzzzzzz! Bzzzzzzz! Bzzzzzzz! Bzzzzzzz! Bzzzzzzz! Bzzzzzzz! Bzzzzzzz! Bzzzzzzz! Bzzzzzzz!

The nonstop vibrations were sending me into an emotional spiral. Against my better judgment, I unlocked my phone and went to check my social media notifications. My notifications were flooded with nasty comments. I scrolled down my feed reading the vile comments that were left on my page.

1sexylex: I always knew you was fucking Tamir! SMH!

Mosthatednae: SMH bitch you crazy!

Fineasslisa: You a snake you fucking your sister baby daddy wow! That's low! This is exactly why I don't trust bitches. SMMFH!

Christiansamfanpage: Dirty slut! I never liked that bitch from back home! She was in my group home thinking she better than somebody!

Welovemalikasamuels: Hold your head Queen! This too shall pass! No one believes the lies! We saw what he did to you!

ChrisandMalika: You are breaking Christian's heart, just go home to your husband!

Joethehustler: SMH bitch! This is why I don't trust bitches! Is that even my man Chris baby? SMH! Triflin hoe!

Kiannakeys: Girl fuck that nigga! I don't believe shit he saying! We all know he lied and he cheated on you and had babies by that girl!

I took in the disgusting comments. I was sick to my stomach. These people really believed this shit! Christian acted the scene out so well that his fans were wrapped around his finger. If all else fails and his basketball career ever comes to an end, he damn sure had the talent to become an actor.

Bzzzzzzz!

The notification of yet another comment popped up at the top of my screen. This time it was a comment under a blog site from Tamir.

Traw7: I could say a lot of shit today but all I can really come up with is WOW. I cannot believe a grown ass fucking man,

I mean bitch, would get on the fucking internet and tell a lie as nasty as this one. @malikassamuels is my fucking sister! Never touched her! Never the fuck would I touch her! EVER! The difference between me and you is I respect mine. I would never in my life even have those types of thoughts about my wife's sister yet alone to even do that. Tell them people the truth, that you really mad I almost knocked your teeth out in your own house. Tell them people how you do my sister in real life. You sitting there playing victim like you some good guy. For you to bring her father up here is crazy too. Her father! Nigga you know that relationship! You a different breed. You a clown. She deserves better. Fucking clown. Imma see you, it's nothing to talk about. TO THE WORLD: NO, I NEVER FUCKED MY SISTER. NO, I NEVER FUCKED THE BEST FRIEND AND SISTER TO MY WIFE. FUCK IS WRONG WITH YALL NIGGAS!!!!

I read Tamir's comment and locked my phone. I did not want to talk to anyone or hear anything else. I had enough.

Bzzzzzzz! Bzzzzzzz! Bzzzzzzz! Bzzzzzzz! Bzzzzzzz! Bzzzzzzz! Bzzzzzzz! Bzzzzzzz!

My phone continued to vibrate as more notifications came pouring in. Then it began to ring. The name Noe-Noe appeared on the screen and my heart sank. Why should I have to explain to my best friend that this shit was not true? This situation was fucked up and I had no energy to deal with any of it. I hit the red circle, declining the video call before placing the phone back down on the table. I needed it to stop, all of it! No matter where I went, how far I ran, how much I did not see or speak to Christian, he still found a way to consistently make my life a living fucking hell. I grabbed one of my cell phones from the table and threw it across the room.

Crackkkkkkkk! The sound of glass breaking echoed throughout the dining room.

"Fuck!" I hollered, as glass shattered all over the floor.

Bzzzzzzz! Bzzzzzzz! Bzzzzzzz! Bzzzzzzz! Bzzzzzzz! Bzzzzzzz! Bzzzzzzz! Bzzzzzzz! My other phone began to vibrate on the table. I jumped from my seat, swiping my hand across the table, knocking everything to the floor. In a blind rage, I grabbed the phone and began banging into the wall. I was losing my mind, to say the least. I needed all of this shit to stop! I needed everything to stop right at this exact fucking moment!

Bang! Bang! Bang! I slammed the phone into the wall, smashing the glass on the phone screen.

"Fuck! Fuck! Fuck!" I screamed, banging the phone on the wall.

The screams had turned into a holler. I was balling. I placed my back on the wall and slid down it, buckling at my ankles because I could no longer hold myself up. Suddenly, the baby began to kick. It was as if she could feel my distress. I forgot all about my little baby until that moment. I was so caught up in my own emotions that I completely forgot about the most important person in this world to me. I cradled my stomach as she kicked and kicked on the inside. She was bothered because I was bothered.

I was crying so hard that I did not hear anyone enter the room until they had entered.

"Ms. Malika, are you ok, ma'am?" a familiar voice called out to me.

It sounded like Jordan, a member of Ethan's security team. I was crying so hard that I could not see past the pool that formed within my eyes. I attempted to catch my breath so that I could respond to him, but I could not. I was hyperventilating. I was trying hard to breathe but the air was not filling my lungs fast enough. Suddenly, I felt lightheaded and a pain that I knew all too well erupted inside of my uterus.

"Ma'am! You're bleeding, ma'am!" the voice boomed.

Those words were the last thing that I heard before everything went black.

ETHAN

"Mr. Jacobs! Come quickly to the dining room, it's an emergency!" Jordan screamed through the intercom system.

My heart plummeted and without a second thought, I bolted out of my office. *What! Emergency!* I thought, running through the door. I was running so fast that I damn near flew down the steps to get to the other section of the manor. I was not sure what was wrong but the only thing that I could think of was Malika. I left Malika in the dining room.

"What's wrong?!" I yelled before reaching the inside of the dining room.

"I . . . I . . . I . . . don't know. I called the medics; they should be rushing in from the other side of the estate!" Jacob yelled.

Jacob was towering over her, attempting to shake her but she was unconscious. The blood puddle that formed between her legs sent me into a panic. Though her baby was not mine biologically, she was mine and anything that belonged to her was sacred to me. I rushed over to Malika, moving Jordan out of the way and jumping into action.

"Get me a towel, now!" I instructed Jordan.

I picked Malika up from the floor and placed her bloody body in my lap.

"And water!" I called out, placing my hand on her wrist to check her pulse.

She was breathing.

"Maria! I need Maria!" I called out to Jordan.

I was calm, as calm as any person could be in this situation, but on the inside, my stomach was in knots. My heart raced as I held her in my arms. I needed her to come to. I needed the baby to be ok.

“Mr. Jacobs!” I heard a familiar voice call out from the hall.

“In here! The dining room!” I responded.

A team of medical personnel burst into the dining room wheeling in a stretcher and emergency medical equipment. Daniel was the in-house physician for my estate, Daniel was present anytime I was at the estate in the event of an urgent situation such as this one. They rushed over to me, kneeling down to check her vitals.

“Get her on the stretcher!” Daniel instructed a member of his team after he finished checking her out.

I stood, holding my elbow out to block his medical team from taking her from me. I placed her on the stretcher and placed her hand in the palm of mine.

“I’m not leaving her,” I stated, sternly.

“Sir, I feel we need to get her to a hospital now,” he informed me.

“Ok, get it done and get her up. I need her to be conscious. I’m coming with you,” I explained, my voice filled with urgency.

My gut hollowed as we wheeled her out of the manor and into the back of the ambulance. I could not lose the love of my life, not today. I already lost one wife; I could not lose the other half of my heart.

CHAPTER TWENTY

"I Would Rather Be Dead . . ."

JANUARY 19, 2019
ATLANTA, GEORGIA

ETHAN

"Sir! Sir, you cannot come back here!" the nurse yelled at me, extending her arm to block me from entering the double doors.

I heard the words she was saying but they did not register in my brain. I was determined, committed, hell-bent on getting behind those doors. I looked down at her extended arm like it was a disease before I stalked towards the double doors, completely disregarding her. It had been hours since we arrived, and they were not telling me anything. I needed to know what was happening back there and why would they not allow me to be with her.

"Security! We have a code yellow!" she screamed, calling for assistance.

I disregarded her call for security, continuing to walk through the double doors. What the fuck was security going to do to me, besides nothing?

"Ethan, Sir! Maybe we should wait a moment. Let them

go back once and get this all situated. It will be much simpler," Larry stated, halting me with his hand on my shoulder.

My head whipped to the side faster than I could think. My eyes bulged as I looked down at Larry's hand. He knew better than to ever touch me.

"Get the fuck off me! I'm going back there!" I barked, snatching my shoulder from Larry's grip.

If looks could kill Larry would have been dead because the glare that I gave to him was deadly.

"Ethan, every moment that they spend out here fighting with you, care is being taken away from her! Is that what you want?" a familiar female voice emerged from behind me.

I stilled. Startled, because I had not heard that voice in years. My eyes bulged as I quickly spun on my feet. I was sure that I was hearing things because no fucking way could that be who I thought it was.

Charlotte Jacobs stood before me in a fur chinchilla coat that swept the floor. I had not seen or spoken to her in years, to say that her visit was shocking news to me was an understatement.

"What are you doing here?" I asked dryly, confusion sprawled across my face.

The sight of my estranged mother sent chills down my spine. I was a gangster, but she was the O.G.

"Oh, don't be so happy to see me, dear," she replied sarcastically, rolling her eyes.

"Cut it," I scoffed.

"Well, I thought it was time for a visit. I mean, if the things I have been hearing are true I should have made my way here a year ago when you took up with that woman," she stated.

"Larry, would you be a dear and take this coat off of me. I am burning up in this place," she asked Larry.

Larry approached her from behind. Charlotte extended her arms, allowing Larry to pull the coat off of her arms. She peeled out of her fur. My mother was the only woman that I knew that would wear a fur coat in any weather or at any event.

"I don't have time for this, what do you want?" I asked, sternly bringing my hand down my face.

"I want to know why my son is embarrassing the family name. Taking up with a married woman who happens to be the wife of one of your players? Are you absolutely fucking crazy? Have you gone mad!" she quizzed; eyebrows bent.

"I'm a grown man. I can take up with whoever I want! Not to mention, I haven't seen or spoken to you since Layla," I responded; my agitation was now on full display.

"I do not understand why you insist on being bothered with these women that bring disgrace to our name! Layla was a sick woman! A woman who was the family of our enemies! I could have killed you for the disgrace you brought upon us for that marriage. Now this! A married woman of one of your employees who is pregnant with another man's baby! Have you gone completely fucking crazy, son? I know I raised you with at least some sense!" she screamed, shaking her head.

I was happy that the waiting area had been cleared of all other guests because I was sure that everyone within the vicinity heard her.

"I'm not doing this shit with you. Matter of fact, don't even speak Layla's name to me, ever. The woman I love is on a fucking surgery table and this is the shit you pull! Please leave!" I barked, turning my back to her.

I was livid. My mother and I did not have a mother and son relationship, we had no relationship at all. She was always much more of a dictator than a mother to me.

"Please leave! How can I leave when I have received endless phone calls all day about you and your fucking bullshit! What is it with you Jacobs men! You can never seem to control the sewage that you put your dick in!" she yelled.

"The sewage?" I questioned, chuckling.

She wanted a reaction out of me, and I refused to give her one. I had bigger issues and my crazy ass mother was not one that I wanted to be bothered with today.

"Yes, sewage! The trash! The garbage! The nasty, no name, whore, enemy bitches that you Jacob men seem to love! The sewage!" she yelled.

I stilled at the mention of the word enemy. My mother knew how to get a rise out of me. I did not tolerate any mention of Layla in a derogatory way, from anyone, especially not a lady who was never a real mother to me.

"Just remember that Daddy found you in the sewage as you like to call it," I said, turning to face her.

Her hand connected with the side of my face before I was able to see it coming.

"I am still your fucking mother! Check yourself before you ever, in your fucking life, that I gave your ungrateful ass, ever disrespect me!" she screamed, stomping as she spoke.

I grabbed the side of my face with my free hand. Everything in me wanted to react to her but I turned and walked away. This was why she came here, the only reason she ever came anywhere I was, to raise hell.

"Larry, get her away from me," I commanded, walking away from her.

I was done with this conversation; my mother could stand there and talk to herself. I did not really understand the purpose of her visit.

Before Larry could even take a step in Charlotte's direction, her words halted him.

"Don't even think about coming near me unless you want that to be the last step you ever take," Charlotte warned.

Charlotte's goons emerged behind her toting CZ 75 pistols. One of the men had his gun drawn on me and the other on Larry. I was itching to reach for my gun, but I knew that one wrong move and I would end up a dead man.

I was so distracted by the current situation with Malika that I did not see the two men dressed in all black that escorted my mother into the waiting area until they walked over from next to the door. I should have known when she arrived that she had some sort of security. Charlotte did not go anywhere without her goons, ever. Charlotte was not the typical sixty-seven-year-old woman, she was a gangster, a cold murderer who did not give a fuck about anyone but herself. Charlotte did not even care about her own kids; our family was nothing but a business to her.

"Like I said, the last step you ever take. Now, son, have a seat and we can have a civilized conversation. I would hate to have to explain to your father what happened to his firstborn," she said arrogantly, motioning for me to sit down.

I gritted my teeth and looked around the room. I did not have time for this shit yet here I was. I raised my head to Larry, jaw clenched. I nodded my head telling him to comply. I sat down in the chair, placing both of my elbows on the handles.

"You want to talk, talk," I said, looking up at my mother.

Charlotte raised her hand, motioning for the men to lower their weapons. The men did as they were told. Charlotte sat in the chair across from me.

"It is so sad that I always have to threaten you with violence just to have a simple conversation with me," she said, calmly.

"Cut the shit. What do you want? I keep saying the same thing yet you're still not getting to the point," I exclaimed, exhaling sharply.

Charlotte loved to hear herself talk; this was not the time for that.

"Well, we have a situation, and I am not speaking of your married girlfriend. The family needs you to put a stop to your extra business activities. We have been compromised and until we are able to figure out the source of that compromise, shut it down," she ordered.

“What do you mean compromised?” I questioned.

“Compromised. I don’t know much at the moment to tell but the FBI has been asking questions,” she informed me.

I nodded in understanding. The nurse that I was fighting with appeared at the double doors. Her expression was alarming as she spoke.

“Mr. Jacobs?” the lady said aloud, bringing my attention to her.

“Understood, now have to go!” I informed Charlotte, standing.

“Yes!” I responded, turning in the direction of the nurse.

“She is awake, in emergency labor, and asking for you!” the nurse shouted as I walked towards her.

“Sewage! Don’t forget to take out the trash!” Charlotte yelled behind me.

“Take me to her right now!” I commanded the nurse, paying my mother no mind.

The dark-skinned woman turned and walked towards the double doors with me on her heels. I could not begin to process the information that my mother just dropped on me. The only thing that was on my mind was Malika and Angel.

MALIKA

“Ok, ma’am, I need you to keep pushing for me!” the doctor yelled from between my legs.

Push! Keep pushing! Nothing is happening! I don’t even have any energy for this! I thought, as I took a deep breath.

“I—I can’t,” I whimpered, exasperated.

I had no energy for this. I was not sure how exactly they expected me to keep doing this. I had been at this for hours, nine to be exact. I did not know how much longer I could continue.

“Yes, you can,” Ethan called out.

I could hear him, but I could not see him. *All these drugs they gave me, I must be hearing shit,* I thought. As if he was reading my mind, he appeared inside of the room.

"I'm right here Li! I'm right here, baby," he said rushing over to me.

He leaned down to kiss the top of my forehead, pushing my sweat-filled hair strands out of my face and behind my ear.

"Ms, we are going to need you to push for me," the doctor called out from between my legs.

"Ethan, I can't!" I cried out, clinging to his arm.

"Yes, you can, baby girl, you got this," he said, comforting me.

I looked up at him as he nodded his head at me reassuringly. His nod was the reassurance that I needed to continue trying despite the pain. I was already too far into labor and unconscious when they brought me to the hospital to receive an epidural. I was thugging this labor shit out and the pain was excruciating. Little by little I could feel my vagina ripping with every push. I could never have imagined pain this intense.

"Ahhhhhhhhhhh!" I screamed, my chest heaving up and down dramatically, as I pushed as hard as I could.

Still nothing so I continued to push.

"Ahhhhhhhhhhh!" I continued, putting a little more effort into the second push than the first.

"That's it! Keep going!" the doctor called out below.

Ethan leaned down and placed a soft kiss to the top of my forehead. The love in his kiss gave me the motivation to keep going. With Ethan's support, I could do anything no matter how difficult.

"You got it," he whispered, squeezing my hand.

"Ahhhhhhhhhhhhhhhhhhhhh! Ahhhhhhhhhhh!" I pushed relentlessly, hollering.

"Almost there, I can see the top of her head," the doctor screamed.

I was all prepared to continue pushing but the commotion coming from the hallway caused me to stop dead in my tracks.

“That’s my wife and my baby! I’m going in there!” Christian hollered.

“Sir, please stand back!” the man yelled.

“What fucking room is she in? Do you know who I am nigga?” Christian barked.

Security!” the man screamed.

Alarm filled me as I looked up at Ethan, my eyes pleading with him to get rid of Christian.

“Ethan, please, no! No! Get him out of here now! I don’t want him near me or our baby,” I begged.

I did not mean to say our to Ethan but that is how I felt. I did not care who the father was biologically; she was our daughter, Ethan and I’s baby. She was ours and Christian would never ever get the opportunity to be a dad to her. I did not know that man or what he was capable of. I did not want him at the hospital or anywhere near my child. Call me bitter but I hated him.

“Consider him gone,” he stated, squeezing my hand once more before departing out of the room.

ETHAN

I swiped my hand down my head in frustration before pulling my phone out of my pocket to dial Larry, who was inside of the waiting room. Today has officially become the longest day ever. I thought Charlotte was the last person I wanted to see but apparently, it was Christian fucking Samuels. I blew out a sharp breath as I dialed Larry.

“Sir,” Larry greeted.

“Larry, what the fuck do I pay you for? How did Christian fucking Samuels walk right past you and into the maternity ward?” I asked, gritting my teeth in irritation.

“Sir, I apologize, he did not come this way,” Larry proclaimed.

“Get the fuck in here now and handle this shit,” I commanded before handing up the phone.

My patience was thin today and besides what I knew to be my better judgment, I walked into the hallway to handle this shit myself.

"Where is my wife! Somebody, tell me where the fuck my wife is!" Christian rambled, smashing his fist onto the nurse's desk.

"Sir, we have to ask you to leave," security pleaded, extending their hand to hold him back.

"Nigga, get the fuck out my face! Two-dollar ass nigga! You ain't no fucking cop! Topflight security ass mother fucker!" Christian barked, smacking the security guard's hand away from him.

"It's time to go, Christian," I said, calmly approaching him from behind.

I could tell by the stillness in his body before he turned that I was the last voice he thought he would hear inside of this hospital. Surprise, surprise, Malika was my bitch now, excuse me, my woman.

Cautiously, Christian turned around slowly like he was in disbelief that it was me. His eyes bulged out of his head when he finally saw me.

"Nigga, what the fuck you are doing here!" he snapped, balling his fists at his side.

I placed my hands inside of my pocket before speaking.

"The question is, why are you here? It's time to go. Malika is no longer your concern, and she does not want nor need you here. It's time to go and I'm not asking," I stated, arrogance laced in my tone.

Christian's temples throbbed at the revelation. I could see the wheels turning in his head as it finally registered in his brain the real reason why he was unable to find Malika for weeks no matter how much money he spent looking for her. Christian raised his fist ready to leap at me but was stopped dead in his tracks with a pistol to the side of his head. Checkmate. Larry had arrived.

I approached Christian, leaning in so that I could talk quietly.

"See if I were you, I would turn and walk the fuck out of here. You in here disturbing all these fucking people, making a scene. It's time to go and as I said, I'm not fucking asking," I stated, a confident smirk spread across my lips.

I walked over to Larry and took the gun from out of his hands. I placed the gun under Christian's chin as I leaned in and spoke.

"You see. If I kill you right here, right now, like I fucking want to for all the times you put your fucking hands on her and that time you beat the baby out of her, that'll be too easy. You're gonna suffer, I'll make sure your death is nice and slow. You gonna feel every, single, fucking thing, you ever put her through. Oh, and before I forget, that's my daughter now." I threatened him, chuckling.

I was damn near whispering, but there was no doubt in my mind that he heard me. Christian looked up at me through the corner of his eyes. He was seething, angry, livid, blood rushing, but most importantly, he was scared. Christian knew me and he knew my power. He knew that my words were not idle threats but instead, promises.

Christian did not say a word. He knew he had no moves, I played chess, not checkers. Christian knew he was at war with the devil. I would not hesitate to blow his head off. If he were a smart man, he would turn and walk out that door quietly, like the bitch he was.

"Now, I'm going in there with my bitch and my child and you're gonna head home and hope you still have a basketball contract tomorrow. Maybe go to your other baby mama and start a life with her, this shit is over for you. That's my wife now.

You're gonna be cool about this. Civilized. You are not going on social media anymore. You are not spreading lies on her name or speaking bad about her. Matter of fact, don't speak on her at all. You're gonna sign divorce papers, with no objections raised to anything she wants, and last but most importantly your gonna give her full custody with supervised visitation," I stated, calmly, pushing the pistol deeper into Christian's chin.

"Yea, ok," Christian scoffed.

"See I was hoping you would say some shit like that so I could say this. If you act like you hard of fucking hearing everybody you ever knew is going to end up in a fucking body bag. I might start with uhm Taylor Kelly or maybe Ms. Netta or depending on what mood I'm in I might save them the trouble and start with you," I avowed.

I removed the gun from Christian's chin before turning to Larry and handing him the gun. Christian stood there, stuck, frozen.

"Get the fuck out here," I shot at him, disgusted.

"Have a nice night! You got training in the morning, go make my wife, my baby and me some fucking money," I stated, tapping Christian on the chest before turning to Larry.

"Get him the fuck out of here and get them fucking cameras. My lady is delivering a baby, I don't want any more surprise visits. Do your fucking job!" I ordered Larry, before turning and walking away.

I headed down the hall, Malika needed me.

MALIKA

"Is he gone?!" I cried out as soon as Ethan re-entered the delivery room.

I sat up the bed, panic written all over my face. I refused to push while Ethan was speaking to Christian. Ethan nodded his head in confirmation before rushing over to my side and grabbing my hand.

"Don't worry about that, you got your hands full here," he said, bringing my hand to his lips.

The feeling of his touch was so comforting, and the sound of his deep baritone voice was soothing. I needed him.

"Ok, now we can resume pushing, Malika! Would you believe that she refused to push without you!" the doctor stated, the second sentence directed to Ethan and not me.

Ethan chuckled slightly, not saying anything in response to the doctor. I needed to find out what happened in that hallway, but this was not the time for that. I needed to stay focused on my baby girl who was two and a half months too early.

"Ok, give me a big push! I only need a few more; I can see her head!" the doctor ordered.

"Ahhhhhhhhhhhhhhhhhhhhhhhh! Ahhhhhhhhhhhhhhhhhh!" I pushed with all of my energy.

This had to hurry up!

"Her head is out! I need another one!" the doctor yelled; panic laced in her tone.

I was so distracted by the pushing I had to do that it did not register right away that the baby was not crying or screaming.

"Ahhhhhhhhhhhhhhhhhhhhhhh! Ahhhhhhhhhhh! Ahhhhhhhhhhhhhhhhhhhhh!" I hollered, delivering the final push.

She was out, my angel was finally out!

"Is she out!" I screamed.

Physically, it felt like she was out, but she was not screaming.

"I need a respirator here! Now! Call a specialist and prepare the NICU!" the doctor screamed, looking back at the nurses.

I looked up at Ethan in panic, his facial expression told me that he was as alarmed as I was. He let go of my hand and rushed over to the doctor.

"Why isn't she crying! What's wrong! What is happening!" I cried out in panic.

I attempted to raise my body to leap from the bed but that was to no avail, I was unable to move. My lower body felt pinned to the bed even though no one was physically holding me down.

"Why is she not breathing! Tell us something!" Ethan pleaded with the doctor.

"Sir, please, I am trying to do everything that I can. I need you to back up. Give us some space so we can work!" she informed me, extending her hand to Ethan.

Ethan brought his hands to his head in despair. He placed bald fists to the top of his head and began walking in circles.

"Ethan!" I called out.

He refused to look at me. I could see the distress and torment coursing through him as he fought with himself to turn my direction, yet he was unable to.

"Bring me my daughter! She isn't breathing! Please! Please! Tell me something! What is happening!" I yelled.

A team of doctors burst into the room with all types of fancy medical equipment. They placed my daughter into an incubator and onto a high-frequency ventilator.

"Get her to the NICU stat!" the doctor ordered.

The doctors rushed Angel, inside of the incubator, out of the room.

"Somebody, please, tell me what's going on!" I called out.

I was in a panic, tears streaming down my face at record pace. I could not do this again; under no circumstance could I lose another child. Not the child I carried for seven months and delivered. I needed her more than she needed me. I needed her because she was the only sunshine I had. She made me keep going!

"Ma'am, your daughter is having difficulty breathing and we are doing everything we possibly can to help her. I want to be honest with you, this does not look good," the woman said, sadly.

Ethan appeared at my side, gripping my hand. Anxiety filled me, there was a sinking feeling on the inside of my stomach. I would rather die than live without her. There was no possible way that I could have delivered a stillborn child, this must be a bad nightmare! I needed to wake up!

"What do you need? Are there any specialists that we can call, medical procedures we can do, anything, whatever it is it's already paid for no matter the price? Please do something," Ethan pleaded.

"Sir, we have the best specialists' money can buy up there with her now doing everything that we can. This was a high-risk pregnancy given your wife's history and she has suffered a lot of trauma. It may have been too much. I am so sorry but only time can help now, we have to wait and see. They took her into emergency surgery so hopefully, something positive comes out of that. I am not sure what your religious affiliation is or if you believe in a higher power but now is a good time for prayer," the doctor informed, empathetically.

I could not find any words. The tears were overflowing at this point. I needed to breathe.

"Can we see her?" Ethan asked.

"After surgery, yes, you may. I must warn you; it will be painful to see her like this," the doctor stated.

"Thank you, doctor, please keep us informed," Ethan responded.

The doctor turned and walked away. Everyone left the room except Ethan. He climbed into the bed with me and pulled my body to his chest. I cried so hard, bawled even. I had never felt a pain like this in my life. This was worse than any feeling I had ever felt.

"We are going to be patient, wait, and pray for the best. I got you, baby, just let it out," he whispered into my ear, wrapping both of his arms around me, holding me, pressing my body to his.

The past few hours awaiting more information were excruciating.

"Ma'am," the doctor greeted as she walked into the dark room.

The doctor cut the lights on before she continued to speak. Ethan pulled me into his arms even tighter. It was as if he knew what she was going to say before she spoke.

"Yes," I responded, bracing myself for the impact of whatever she was about to say.

"I am so sorry to inform you that the surgery was unsuccessful. She is unable to breathe on her own and even with the ventilators, she is not developed enough to sustain life. She has a maximum of twenty-four to seventy-two hours to live. I must also inform you that every moment she fights to breathe causes excruciating pain for her. You can see her now if you would like," she informed me.

I heard the words coming out of the doctor's mouth, but I could not register them. Every word felt like a knife to the heart and a kick to the gut. If this was life, I was not sure if it was worth living.

"Yes, we would like to see her," Ethan said, breaking the deadly silence that fell after the doctor's words.

"Ok, I will take you right up. I'll be outside the door to give you two a moment," the doctor said, exiting the room.

Ethan attempted to pull me up from the bed, but I was dead weight pulling myself back down.

"Babe, I don't want to see her like that. I can't do it," I whispered.

I was on the verge of a mental breakdown trying to hold myself together. I was not sure I could handle seeing my baby on the brink of death, fighting for her life. Just the thought sent chills down my spine.

"You will never forgive yourself if you don't, love. I got you, you won't ever have to go through this alone," he stressed, extending his hand to me.

Reluctantly, I took his hand. I was not sure that I was ready for this, but Ethan was right. I would never forgive myself if I did not see my daughter, hold her, and love on her, at least a little bit, before I sent her back to the angels.

CHAPTER TWENTY-ONE

"Seventy-Two Hours . . ."

JANUARY 20, 2019
ATLANTA, GEORGIA

MALIKA

Deafening silence lingered between Ethan, Dr. Williams and me as we rode the elevator to the NICU. We were all wrapped in our own thoughts and emotions. A palpable sense of loss and sadness was among us. We were in mourning, mourning the loss of a beautiful soul that would never get the opportunity to grace this earth.

On so many occasions, I blamed myself for the death of my mother but now I realized what a mother's love was. A mother would not hesitate to trade their life for their child. I understood now that Mallory Hines would not have had it any other way. I was not the blame for the passing of my mother. It was Mallory's love for me, her child, that allowed her to continue on with a high-risk pregnancy that she knew could potentially end her life. The unconditional love of a mother was unmatched. I wished I had the opportunity to choose between saving my life or Angel's, without hesitation, I would choose Angel. How could I be expected to walk in here and walk out without the love of my life? I spent seven months growing this life inside of me for it to be taken away in a matter of seconds.

Ding! The elevator door opened, bringing me out of my thoughts and into reality.

Dr. Williams was first off of the elevator then Ethan. I, on the other hand, could not move. My brain was saying step off, but my legs could not find their way. I stood there, fingers playing with the fabric of my hospital gown, staring down at my feet. Timidly, Ethan grabbed my hand, pulling me forward off of the elevator and into his body. I was so lost in my trance that I did not even know I was crying until I began screaming into his chest.

"I can't do this!" I hollered.

The screams that were erupting from my vocal cords were nothing I ever heard before. A cry so gut-wrenching that everyone in the vicinity felt my pain without even knowing the cause. I threw myself into Ethan's body so that he could hold me up. My legs were giving out beneath me as I tried to stand but I was no longer able to. Knowing that I was only inches away from Angel made the pain even more palpable. This shit became more real than it was before I got off of the elevator and I was not sure that I was strong enough to handle the overwhelming emotion.

"It's ok. Let it out," he counseled, holding me tighter.

Ethan caressed the back of my head, while simultaneously rubbing my back in circles. He became my legs and my strength because I could not hold myself together.

"I brought her a wheelchair; she might need to take a seat," Dr. Williams said, speaking to Ethan.

Dr. Williams rolled the wheelchair to Ethan.

"Yes, thank you." Ethan thanked her.

"Whenever you are ready, I will be at the entrance of the NICU to escort you inside," Dr. Williams offered before turning to walk away.

Ethan stood with him, holding me up. I needed to let this one out. I had no strength left in me; I was breaking. I was being tested; God was testing me. Was this my karma for stabbing my father, killing Tay, and robbing folks back then? Was this some sort of sick test that I was being put through? What kind of evil have I brought into this world that I deserved so much pain? Every time I got pregnant by Christian Samuels somehow my child ended up not surviving. I was not sure who to blame; myself for going back to him; Christian for all the stress that contributed to issues carrying a pregnancy to term; God for allowing this to happen not once but twice. I was not sure who was at fault or why this was happening. Maybe there was no one to blame, maybe this was just the circumstances of my life that I needed to accept.

"Li, let me sit you down," Ethan suggested, lowering me into the wheelchair.

I obliged. Ethan placed me into the chair and kneeled down before me. He used his fingers to wipe the tears from my face before pinching my chin to tilt my face upwards. He stared at me solemnly, our eyes connecting.

"I don't know the pain that you feel but you aren't alone. I will be with you every step of the way. This hurts me because to love you means loving her too. I don't like seeing you like this, but I got you. You have me, whatever you need from me to get you through this, I'm going to give. I love you and that little girl in there loves you. Let's go in there and make the best out of the moments that you have with her. This is painful, I don't even understand how painful but you're a fighter and it's nothing you can't handle. I love you," he counseled, placing a kiss to the top of my forehead.

Ethan had become my rock through this entire situation. I was not sure how I would have made it without him. Silently, I looked up at him. There was an understanding between the two of us that needed no words, he could feel my appreciation and unconditional love for him. For Ethan Jacobs, I'd go to war, start a war, and risk it all because I loved him. His unwavering affection for me and another man's baby was something that you had to respect. His love for me had no limits and I felt the same for him.

I brought one hand to my eyes and wiped the tears away before sucking in a gulp of air.

"Let's go," I whispered, hesitantly.

I was scared out of my mind, but I had to put my big girl pants on. In life we only get to experience people, we do not get to possess them. Well, here I was, going into the NICU to experience one of my greatest loves for only a few short moments in a lifetime.

Ethan wheeled me down the hallway and to the entrance of the NICU where Dr. Williams was standing, awaiting our arrival. I extended my arms, blocking Ethan from pushing me into the NICU. This was all happening too fast, I needed everything to slow down. Ethan paused, looking down at me.

"You don't want to go in?" Ethan asked.

"No, let's go," I answered, removing my arms.

"Are you two ready?" she asked empathetically, noticing the exchange between Ethan and me.

I nodded, unable to speak the word yes. Dr. Williams opened the doors of the NICU, leading us inside. The babies were all so beautiful that it was heartbreaking. They were so tiny, fragile, some had tubes inserted into their nostrils and were hooked up to so many machines. Babies were the most precious blessing in this world, seeing them in so much pain was agonizing. They deserved the world, so innocent and pure, yet all they received was pain.

Arriving at the incubator, Ethan stopped pushing. My beautiful princess laid beneath me. She was so tiny, so small, so fragile. She had the most beautiful round green eyes, like mine. Her face was round, and her full pink lips poked out. She was gorgeous. She looked exactly like me, my twin. There were tubes attached to her nose and heart monitors attached to her chest. She looked like she was in pain, my poor baby. Seeing her in such a fragile state tore me apart. I was staring at a human version of my heart outside of my body. How was it possible to love a little person the way I did when I just met her? This was motherhood. This was the feeling of carrying a person inside of you for months, loving them and caring for them. This was a feeling that not even words could describe, it was indescribable.

"I'll give you two some time. You can stay here as long as you'd like. If you decide to remove the breathing machine today, please alert a member of our team. Take as much time as you need, and we have a psychiatrist that would like to speak with you as well," the doctor offered before turning and disappearing.

Dr. Williams leaned in, offering me a hug.

"Thank you, doctor," Ethan responded.

I did not hear much of anything that she said, I was too busy staring at my Angel. Ethan began rubbing my shoulders. I reached my hand inside of the incubator hole to touch her mini fingers. Instinctively, Angel wrapped her small fingers around my index finger. Feeling her touch, my heart skipped a beat. A smile erupted from the corner of her lips as she fought to smile at me. The connection that we both shared for those few seconds was exhilarating. Somehow, she knew I was her mommy. I wanted to cry but I could not. I felt her there with me and she brought me strength. Her presence brought me peace.

"I'm going to step out and give you some time with her alone. I'll come back in a little bit to check on you," Ethan said, leaning down and placing his chin on the top of my head.

"Wait, can you get someone. I want to hold her," I whispered without taking a moment to look away from Angel's beauty.

"Yes," Ethan replied behind me.

I got lost in the escape of her eyes. She was so beautiful and pure. She was innocent. Maybe, just maybe, this was a good thing. God knew the evils of this world, maybe my rainbow baby was too good for this dark place. She deserved better than this, so much better. I was brought out of my escape by a male nurse, electing to take her out of the incubator for me to hold her.

"Ms., would you like to hold her?" he asked compassionately.

"Yes, please," I replied.

The small white man moved to the right of me, opening the incubator and taking Angel into his arms.

"You may want to remove the gown, skin to skin contact helps to form a special connection. I know you don't have a lot of time with her, but it would help the two of you bond," he provided.

"Yes, ummm . . . do you have a blanket or something so that I can cover myself?" I asked.

He turned and picked up a blanket from the shelf behind. Slowly, I partially removed my gown exposing the skin on half of my body. The nurse bent down, placing Angel in my arms. He leaned in, bringing her small frame into my arms. I was in love, in love with everything about her. Her scent, the softness of her skin, her aura. Angel Serena Samuels was peaceful. The calm that came over me with her in my arms made me feel, for the moment, like it would be ok. She gave me hope. She used her tiny fingers to claw at my chest. It was like she knew I was who carried her inside of me for those months. She managed to smile up at me once more, this time the smile was a little wider than before. I used my hand to brush her soft hair, placing small kisses on the top of her head.

"Can I hold her?" Ethan asked, emerging from behind me.

I was so lost in Angel's essence that I did not hear or see him come back inside of the room until he spoke.

"Of course, take your shirt off," I commanded him.

His eyebrows dipped in confusion as he looked at me questioningly, so I explained further.

"The skin-to-skin contact will help her to bond with you," I explained, clarifying his confusion.

He nodded, doing as he was told before sitting in the seat next to me. Gently, I handed Angel to him. At his touch, the biggest smile spread across her face, a smile greater than when I held her. She wrapped her small fingers around his large finger, pulling him to her. My baby was as smitten with Ethan as I was. He was just as mesmerized by her as she was with him. The look in his eyes was one of awe, like he had never been more in love with anyone. Their connection was effortless.

"She is perfect," he cooed, admiring her beauty.

"Isn't she? I can't even believe she came from me. She is literally an angel," I agreed, nodding my head.

I leaned into the two of them, brushing her soft hair out of her face as I looked up at him. He was too busy; lost in Angel's eyes to see how I was looking at him. I had officially gained another level of respect for Ethan.

"Thank you," I began before pausing.

I took in a deep breath before continuing.

"Thank you for being here and never leaving my side. Thank you for loving her like you do me, thank you for being the man that you are," I expressed, gripping his arm.

I felt emotionally heavy. Lost in pain yet I was grateful to experience her for even a short period of time. Experiencing her for even the shortest period of time made the pain all worth it. I was thankful, thankful to him and thankful to God for making this all possible. Watching Ethan and Angel was bittersweet because I wished that Angel was his biological child.

"No, thank you," he corrected me.

Confused, I looked at him.

"Why are you thanking me?" I asked, confused.

"Thank you for letting me experience her," he continued.

His words warmed my heart. Ethan and I got lost in that moment. Lost in her beauty, her magnetic essence, her innocence, her purity, and our love for her. She was perfect, her little features, everything about her brought tears to my eyes. How could something so beautiful come out of such a fucked-up union, the marriage between Christian and I? If we did not do anything else right throughout our marriage, we created a gorgeous little Angel, my Angel.

Sitting there, we both fell in love with Angel. Despite the fact that she could not stay with us here on earth, she would live in both of our hearts forever. Angel brought us closer; if we could even be brought closer. We had both experienced a love that was so potent yet that only existed amongst the three of us. For the next few hours, we sat there basking in bliss. I was so in love with my creation that I was able to block out the lingering heartache. Those moments with Angel placed a band-aid over my aching heart, nothing else mattered. I was so caught up in love that the hours flew by. The doctor returned a short time later and now it was time for me to make a choice.

"Malika, have you reached a decision yet?" Dr. Williams asked, interrupting our time with Angel.

"Can we talk outside for a minute?" I said solemnly.

"Yes, of course," Dr. Williams replied.

I passed Angel back to Ethan before standing to go into the hallway.

"Are you ok to speak with her alone?" Ethan worried.

"Yes, my love," I stated.

The past few hours that I spent with Angel calmed me. I was so appreciative of God for granting me this short time with her that I was able to pull myself together, slightly. Dr. Williams stood by the nurse's desk reviewing paperwork from the chart of a patient, potentially Angel's.

"Hi, Dr. Williams," I greeted, approaching her.

"Yes," she responded, looking up from her paperwork.

"Can you explain the pros and cons to pulling her off of the ventilator? I need more information before I make an impossible decision," I asked.

"Yes. Your daughter's internal organs are underdeveloped so much that she is not able to breathe on her own without the aid of a ventilator and her heart has irregular palpitations. Her organs are not strong enough to survive. She is also not developed enough to receive a transplant. She would need a transplant for multiple organs. It is my medical opinion that she can only survive for up to seventy-two hours, even with the assistance of the ventilator. You can wait the entire seventy-two hours and let nature take its course, but those hours will be extremely painful for her and it is very unlikely that she will see them through. Everything inside of her body is struggling to function. I leave the decision with you but I do want to present all of the information so you can make the best choice for you and your family," Dr. Williams explained.

"You say that it is very unlikely, is there any chance or possibility that she could survive despite her current condition?" I quizzed further.

"Technically speaking, yes, there is a small possibility, approximately a ten percent chance that she could survive the seventy-two hours but even then, that does not guarantee that she will survive. She needs a heart transplant, and she will have to stay on the ventilator for an extended period of time until her lungs are able to function on their own. Getting her to the point of a heart transplant will be extremely difficult, no medical professional will clear her for a transplant in her current condition," Dr. Williams provided.

"Doctor, do you have any kids?" I pried.

"No, ma'am, I do not," Dr. Williams responded, contouring her face to display her confusion at my question.

"I am asking because if you had children, you would know

the experience of growing a person inside of you for months and you would already know my answer. If God chooses to call her home, then so be it, but I cannot in good conscience take her off of the ventilator. Despite the pain, I know she is a fighter, and she can pull through this. We will be waiting the seventy-two hours out. Whether she survives or not will be God's will, not mine, yours, or any medical professional. I also would ask that you please stop speaking death over my daughter, just let it happen how it is meant to, there is power in the words we speak," I stated.

I refused to give up on my child, no matter what the circumstances were we would keep fighting. It was not over yet, I believed that. I prayed that if I kept my faith that she would see this through. Angel was too young to believe in herself and fight for herself, so I would do the fighting for her.

"Ok, ma'am. We will wait the next seventy-two hours out," Dr. Williams conceded.

"Oh, and before I forget to inform you, I will be having a neonatal specialist that specializes in premature children brought in. Then when she makes it past the seventy-two hours, I will be moving her to a private location with her own team of doctors. Thank you so much for your help, but we will take it from here," I asserted.

I spoke confidently that Angel would make it past those seventy-two hours because that is all that I had. The belief that there was hope kept me going.

"Ma'am, you may do whatever you please, but I assure you our hospital staff provides exceptional care. We are some of the bests in the country, there is no need to move her or bring in a specialist," she argued.

"See, about my child I need the best, not some of the best, the best that money can buy. I need a doctor who has hope, who sees the upside of things. You have spoken to me over and over about the possibility of her not making it but not the possibility of her making it. You have already counted her out as far as I am concerned," I countered, shaking her head.

"Ma'am, I can assure you that is not the case, I have always provided my very best medical prognosis. However, I do respect your opinions and choices. We will wait and monitor her condition for the next seventy-two hours," Dr. Williams responded, bringing her hand to her chest in defense.

"Now if you'll excuse me, I have to get back to my child," I stated.

I nodded my head in confirmation and turned in the direction of the NICU. The next seventy-two hours would play a crucial role in my life, the only thing left to do was wait, pray, and ultimately, be patient.

JANUARY 23, 2019
ATLANTA, GEORGIA

"I cannot say with certainty that she is out of the woods yet, but she has survived a lot longer than we anticipated so that is a positive sign. She still has a long way to go and will need a heart transplant but her strength to stay alive is remarkable," Dr. Kelar stated, looking up from his clipboard.

Dr. Kelar was a neonatal specialist that Ethan flew in from Beverly Hills to provide a second opinion. There was no doubt in my mind that some of his recommendations attributed to my daughter surviving her unlikely three days. The past seventy-two hours were filled with excruciating agony. I sat by Angel's side for every minute of every day. She was not alone, and I needed her to feel that. Ethan was God-sent, only ever leaving my side for important business matters. He may have been more in love with her than I was. It was something special about their connection since the moment he touched my stomach. She clung to him more than she clung to me. Whenever he was in her presence, she smiled the entire time. I fell more in love with him just watching his care for her. How was it possible that a man could be so caring of a child that was not biologically his?

"Thank you so much," I said in awe, a tear rolling down my cheek.

Ethan wrapped his arms around my waist, pulling my body to his before placing his chin on the top of my head.

"She is stable enough to have her moved to another facility," Dr. Kelar confirmed, looking over at Angel.

"Yes, can we set up a facility in the manor or will we be taking her to a private location?" Ethan questioned.

"It will be very expensive to—" Dr. Kelar began before Ethan interjected.

"The cost does not matter, we'll pay whatever," Ethan offered.

"Well, in that case, we will have all necessary medication and equipment moved to the estate. We can move her once that has been completed," Dr. Kelar informed us.

"Thank you, my staff will assist you with anything that you need. Consider it done," Ethan responded, pulling out his cell phone to send a text.

We were not out of the doghouse yet; Angel's life was still hanging in the ballots but there was hope. I had not informed anyone that I had the baby, no one knew besides Ethan. Well, Christian somehow knew that I was brought into early labor, but he had no idea if the baby was born or not. I thought about having my assistant call Christian because after all, this was his child as well, yet I could not bring myself to do that. Call me bitter but I could not do it. This was the second child that I almost lost as a result of Christian and his bullshit. My daughter's life was hanging in the balance due to all of the stress that Christian caused me. I was not sure Christian was fit to be a father; besides, Angel had a new daddy, we both did.

CHAPTER TWENTY-TWO

*"He's Not the Only N***a with Money . . ."*

AUGUST 20, 2019
CALABASAS, CALIFORNIA

MALIKA

"Look at mommy's pwetty baby! Yes, she is! Fat mommas! Look at that chunky baby!" I cooed at Angel.

I leaned in, placing soft kisses on Angel's belly.

"Hahahahahaha!" Angel erupted into uncontrollable giggles.

Her laughter warmed my heart. I leaned into Angel's beautiful face, lightly pinching her chunky cheeks. Oh, excuse me. I forgot to tell the good news! Angel is officially seven months and doing well. Yes! My baby is a fighter, she fought with everything she had to stay alive. The medical experts that Ethan and I hired saved our daughter's life. She underwent a heart transplant at six weeks old and her condition improved, drastically. The first three months following her procedure were challenging for Angel, and all of us, but she has made significant improvements since then. My baby was a survivor, she was determined to stay here.

Contrary to what I wanted; I knew that it was not right to keep Christian away from his child, so I informed him of her birth once she was in a stable condition. The past few months have been exhausting dealing with Christian. He was permitted supervised visitation with Angel once a week. I had full custody and it burned him up knowing that his daughter lived in a house with me and another man. I was in the middle of a nasty divorce, actually fuck nasty, grimy, spiteful, vile, and distasteful were much better adjectives to describe this mess I was in. We always hear of a woman scorned but never about the men. Christian was bitter and had taken the word hell to another level. He made every single thing he could a miserable experience for me. He had some fucking nerve. After ten years of emotional and physical abuse, this nigga had the audacity to act as if I wronged him.

Christian was stuck on my relationship with Ethan, borderline obsessed. He fought to get out of his contract with Ethan's team, but Ethan refused to let him out of the contract or trade him to another team. Ethan did not really want to deal with Christian but Christian's elicit disrespect caused Ethan to keep him on the team. Ethan wanted to make the point to Christian that he ran shit. Ethan technically owned him, at least in the context of basketball, and until Christian found a way out of that contract he was staying on the team just to spite him. Ethan was the boss, and no moves were made unless he approved them. The two men hated each other, despised each other. It ate Christian up that Ethan had more money than him and was the boss. The fact that Ethan was a billionaire damn near had Christian ready to kill himself. He would tell anyone that would listen about my affair with his boss and according to him, I was a gold digger that was for the streets. He was attempting to make me look immoral but all everyone said was checkmate. I leveled up there was no denying that. It was so sad to watch Christian; he was living in his karma and karma was a bitch.

Christian and I had no communication at all, we did

everything through our attorneys. Despite the lack of communication and contact, he found ways to be disrespectful. He went as far as telling the social worker that I was a dirty whore. His exact words were, I needed to kill myself and flush my head down the toilet. He was crazy and as a result, we were getting nowhere in mediation. He refused to be civil in any way. I requested an even split of all finances, joint business, and properties. Christian contested everything. He refused to give me anything, saying that, and I quote, I was a nasty dirty whore who had an affair with his boss who happened to be a billionaire and I deserved nothing. He even told the courts that my motive for marrying him was financial and there was no love. He was sick. Some days I thought about walking away and leaving him with it all, I did not need it, I had my own money. My net worth was officially nine million and with Ethan in my corner, I never spent a dime. My businesses were running themselves without me having to lift a finger. I could not let Christian win, however; it was not about the money, my pride would not allow me to let him have the satisfaction. Christian put me through too much throughout the course of our relationship. I was determined to make him pay one way or another.

Ethan strutted into the bedroom looking like a model. He was so damn fine; it was a shame. He was dressed in business attire today, like most days. He was wearing an all-black Tom Ford suit with black YSL dress shoes. The plain-faced silver Patek Philippe sitting on his wrist, emulated luxury.

"Look at Daddy's princess!" Ethan said, walking over to the bed where I was getting Angel dressed.

Ethan leaned in down and planted a kiss on Angel's forehead before kissing me on the lips. This had been the dynamic between us ever since Angel was born, they loved each other more than me. Angel came alive every time he walked in. I often watched in awe as they interacted with each other. I hit the jackpot. Ethan wholeheartedly accepted Angel, loved her, and wanted the best for her. He spoiled her rotten, at seven months she got everything she wanted. If she made a sound, he came running. Surprisingly, he began cutting his business trips short and working from home more to be with us. I was blessed.

Angel brought the corners of her mouth into a smile as she extended her arms reaching for him.

"Baba!" she cried out for him to pick her up.

Angel was attempting to say Dada, but she was not yet that advanced, her Ds sounded more like a B. I could not believe that she said Dada before Mama. It was clear that I was the third wheel.

"Not right now, princess, Daddy's running late and you're going to slobber all over my suit," he cooed at her before turning his attention to me.

"You know she's going to cry as soon as I hit the door. Pick her up! Don't start with that she's too spoiled shit," he instructed.

I rolled my eyes at him because I was not sure who he thought he was.

"Bye, Ethan. Have a nice day," I said sarcastically, purposely ignoring his instructions.

"I'm serious, stop letting her cry to teach her a lesson. What y'all got planned today anyways?" he questioned.

"I think I'll leave her with Isabella for a little bit, maybe only about three to four hours. I'm going to swing by Noelle and Tamir's to catch up with them then do a little shopping maybe with my girl." I partially lied.

I did plan on going to Noelle and Tamir's house, but I neglected to tell Ethan the part about me going to the home that Christian and I once shared. The only heirlooms from my mother were at his house, a picture of her pregnant with me and a gold necklace with a heart pendant. I left them at the house when I left abruptly, and Christian refused to have the staff return my things. Christian could keep everything else that I left there, all of the material items had been replaced by now anyways, but those items were priceless and irreplaceable. I was going to get them by any means necessary, they were my only connection to the mother I never met. Now that I had Angel, I felt a special connection to Mallory; I needed those items. Ethan would have a fit if he found out I was going there. He did not trust Christian or want me anywhere in the same vicinity as Christian. He feared that Christian may try something when he was not around. I had set up a small window of time today with a member of the security team, allowing me to get in and out of the house while Christian was away on a basketball conference. I hated lying to Ethan, but I knew he would not understand my logic.

"Well, take security. I'll be home later tonight. I have to fly to Seattle to take care of a few things. I'll be back probably around eight so we can still have dinner, a little later than usual," Ethan exclaimed.

Ethan, Angel, and I made it a point to have either dinner or breakfast together as a family every day that we could. Ethan was big on family time. I could tell that this life is what he always desired.

"I am. Walter is returning from leave today, I'll take him and give him a chance to get back on the schedule." I partially lied again.

Walter had been my security guard for years and his loyalty was to me. Walter had suffered an injury a few months back and had been on disability ever since so it was not all a lie. I was giving him a chance to get back on the schedule. The truth was, however, I could trust that Walter would not tell Ethan or his staff that we went to Christian's estate. The other security guards feared Ethan and would tell in a heartbeat if I even asked them to take me to Christian's home, much less went to his estate.

"Walter? He's been out of commission for a while, you

sure you want to use him?" Ethan questioned, looking at me suspiciously.

"Yea, he's a good guy and he's been with me for a while, so you know," I replied, attempting to evade his glare.

Ethan could always tell when I was not being completely honest, I hoped that he did not think too much about this because he would see right through me.

Bzzzzzzz! Bzzzzzzzz! Bzzzzzzz! Ethan's business phone began to vibrate in his hand. Whew! Saved by the bell! He looked down at his phone to see who was calling before silencing it. With Christian, I would have been alarmed at the silencing of the cell phone, but I had no concerns with Ethan; he was all business all of the time.

"I got to go, I'm late and running later! Tell me about your day later, love you, Li and I love you, Daddy's princess!" he said, leaning in to kiss me once more and tickling Angel on the bottom of her feet.

Angel erupted into laughter as Ethan headed out of the bedroom.

"Oh, sis, I like that! Let me see!" I gagged at the exclusive Louis Vuitton custom leather bag.

"Yes, girl! They don't got this! This is one of one honey!" Noelle bragged, holding up her exclusive luxury pocketbook.

"T, you keeping my sis laced I see!" I yelled.

Tamir was in the closet and I was sure he was not paying either one of us any mind.

Noelle placed the pocketbook inside of the Louis Vuitton dust bag before placing it in the luxury suitcase. Noelle and Tamir were headed on a family vacation to Dubai.

"Girl, he can't hear you, he be deaf as hell in that closet. But yes, my man keeps me laced as you can see!" Noe exclaimed, pouting her lips for extra emphasis.

"Oh, so bitch, what you needed to talk to us about?" Noelle inquired, getting to the real reason for my visit.

I needed to talk, I needed advice, and I needed it both from my sister and my best friend.

"Well, you know my necklace that I always had from my mom, the one with the heart pendant?" I asked Noelle.

"Girl, spit it out. This ain't a mystery show," Noelle replied sarcastically, rolling her eyes.

"Well, it's at the house, Christian's house and I'm going to get it today, he's not there," I confessed.

I needed to tell somebody I was going, I needed to hear that this was not as bad of an idea as I knew it to be.

Noelle stopped folding the clothes that she was packing inside of the suitcase to look up at me. She raised her eyebrows in confusion and scrunched her face.

"Bitch, no! Hell, the fuck no! I must not be hearing you right," Noelle yelled, placing her hand on her hip.

"Girl! It is ok, y'all are so dramatic. I will be in and out and I'm bringing security," I explained, exhaling sharply.

Deep down inside, I knew this idea sounded a little crazy, but I was hoping that it would work out.

"No! I say fuck no! That nigga is throwed off ok, you never know when he's gonna pop up. I swear it's like he got special powers or something when it comes to you. I don't know what kind a special shit you got in your pussy, but he seems to find your ass anywhere these days. I vote no! Matter of fact, fuck no! Sit the hell down!" Noelle reasoned, bouncing from leg to leg.

Noelle could not stand still when something bothered her.

"Actually, I'm telling on your ass! Mir!" Noelle shouted, turning towards the closet.

Noelle placed the items she was packing down on the bed before taking off towards the closet.

"Tamir!" she yelled, like an older sibling telling your parents.

Noelle was a tattletale childish.

"Noe! Don't get him started, please!" I pleaded, rolling my eyes.

I was not in the mood for a speech from Tamir, he swore he was my dad or something. He was always scolding and giving advice that no one asked him for. I loved and hated him for this at the same time.

"What's all the commotion?" Tamir questioned, swaggering into the room behind Noelle.

Tamir came in dripped out and stylish, per usual. He was in the house, but he was always dressed. He wore light-colored distressed Amiri jeans, a white Chrome Hearts shirt, and a diamond Audemars Piguet graced his wrist. My brother was fly, always.

"Go ahead, tell him your stupid ass plan. Shit bout dumb as hell because you know better!" Noelle chastised me, shaking her head.

I stared up at Noelle, rolling my eyes at her.

"So, long story short I need to go get my priceless heirlooms." I paused to look up at Noelle, rolling my eyes one more time for the dramatic effect.

"Out of Christian's house while he's not there," I exclaimed, evading the glare of Tamir at the mention of the name Christian.

"No," Tamir said coldly, not wanting to hear anything else.

He did not react or anything, just a simple no.

"I'm going," I shot.

"You're not," he said simply.

"Nigga, you not my dad, I'm going," I argued.

"This idea dumb as hell and you know it. What Ethan got to say about all this?" Tamir questioned, eyeing me.

Tamir was trying to be funny because he and I both knew that there was no way Ethan knew about this. I would not have even been able to make it this far in my plan if he did know about it.

"He doesn't . . ." I began but Tamir interjected before I could finish.

"Yea, like I thought. He doesn't know and you hid it from him because you know he not having that shit. I know how important that necklace is to you but Malika, this is your ex-husband we talking about. That nigga retarded. I'm not worried about Christian and I guarantee Ethan isn't either, but he is not to be trusted with you. I'm sure Ethan or even us can figure out a better way to get that back for you but this is dumb as shit and you know it," Tamir reasoned, shaking his head.

Tamir had to turn everything into advice column hour. He really should have been a therapist or some kind of advisor because he swore, he knew everything.

"Exactly what I told her," Noelle chimed in, rolling her neck and cutting her eyes at me.

"Girl, shut up." I paused, waving my hand at her.

"I appreciate the concern, guys but I am going, and I will be fine. I have security, it will be quick, just in and out, grab that and maybe a few other things and I will be out of there. He will never even know I was there," I stated.

"This shit stupid but do you. Be safe and keep your guard up man. I don't feel right about this but I'm out," Tamir said dismissively, waving his hand at us as he went back into the three-story closet.

Tamir had a tendency to remove himself when he was annoyed about something. If he did not agree with your choices, he did not even want to discuss it.

"Why does everybody fucking think I can't handle my ex-husband! I was with that man for nearly ten years, he does not fucking scare me," I barked; I was officially annoyed.

Noelle and Tamir had blown this thing way out of proportion.

"You can handle him? Oh, my bad! I didn't know you were handling him when he was beating your ass, or calling you all types of bitches, or constantly disrespecting you, or cheating recklessly with these bitches! You can't handle shit! You keep fucking around with that crazy ass nigga you gone end up dead or some shit! It's like you can't fucking leave him alone! When it's not priceless heirlooms it'll be something else. I understand the not having a mother thing, we both come from the same, so I know how important that is to you, but damn you gotta be smarter than this. I don't trust Christian or anybody that works for him. I don't care how good of a relationship you think you have with anyone in his staff, he is not to be trusted. He's doing this shit on purpose. He's not stupid, he knows eventually you coming to get that necklace," Noelle snapped.

I wanted to argue and to get mad at her. I felt like she was throwing my past in my face, but I knew that was not her intention. Noelle, like so many of the other people in my life that loved me, was tired of seeing me go through this roller coaster. I was done with Christian this time for good, however, so she was wrong. I strictly wanted my items. I needed them.

"Noe-Noe, I get it. I really do but I promise you, myself, and my fucking daughter that almost died because of him again, I am done with him. Not to mention I am so happy and in love where I am, I would never go back. I just need these things, not want but need. I never knew her or had anything from her. This is all I have as a connection and I need it," I pleaded.

Noelle looked up at me from her suitcase before getting up and sitting next to me on the bed. She held out her hand for me to take it. I did, placing my hand inside of hers.

"You my girl, my sister and I love you. I don't agree with this. I think it's risky, but I get it. I really do, I know how much that relationship or not having it affects you. Be safe and call me the entire time. I need a text before you go in and when you come out," Noelle conceded.

I rested my head on her shoulder before speaking.

"I love you too and I'll be fine. I'll let you know when I

get in and get out of there," I responded, in compliance with Noelle's terms.

I understood Noelle and Tamir's fear, but I had to go get my things.

AUGUST 20, 2019

SEATTLE, WASHINGTON

ETHAN

"It's been months, Dan! Almost eight fucking months later and we still have no idea who the informant is. This shit doesn't add up," I expressed, exposing my frustration.

I was fed the fuck up and I needed answers.

"The shit is way over my head! Way over! This shit runs so deep the investigation is from another agency, brother, I don't know who it is, but it is for a fact not the FBI. I think it's the CIA or Homeland that's the only possible answer. I tried every resource I had, everything and I was unable to find any information," Dan Collier stated.

Dan Collier was the head of the Drug Enforcement Administration for the FBI. He had been a valued asset to my organization for the past fifteen years, even before I took over for my father. We kept him on the payroll to avoid instances such as this one. Dan kept my family informed on everything. We knew about every raid, every time we came across the FBI radar, every informant, and every single agent who decided to look into our family. Dan had never been unable to find out information until now.

I began combing through my beard with my fingers, thinking. This shit made no sense at all. Despite all of my contacts and connections, I could not find out any information.

"Why the fuck would the CIA be conducting an investigation that shit doesn't even make any sense?" I argued.

I brought my hand down my face in frustration. This shit

was bad for business. I had still been able to move product despite the pending investigation, but I had not been able to move nearly as much as I was before news of this investigation broke.

"Are you shitting me! I'm the fucking leader of the DEA for Christ's sake, if they found out I'm involved that is every reason for the CIA to be involved. Those cocksuckers have hated me for years. Not to fucking mention my guy, the amount of drugs you have brought into this country in the past few years. You wanted to expand but did you think about how much fucking heat that was bringing! You were selling thousands of kilos of cocaine all over the fucking world! Are you shitting me right now! This shit is bigger than the fucking FBI!" Dan debated.

"Oh, and I almost fucking forget the craziest part! You are legally and illegally supplying your fucking Oxycontin and Percocet pills all over the fucking world, not the fucking country, the fucking world across continents! You wanted this shit, E! You had enough money! Fuck you have more money than a person can spend in one fucking lifetime and you can never stop! You wanted to expand. I told you that this was next level and now we're knee-deep in shit!" Dan continued.

"I don't know what the fuck you talking about. Shit sounds like new information to me," I barked, eyeing Dan suspiciously.

I was paranoid, looking at everyone as if they were the informant. Dan speaking so much on my involvement did not sit well with me.

"I'm just saying, man. We need to really figure this shit out. It could be any fucking body. It's probably a person who has been undercover for years now!" Dan stated.

"We can't figure shit out because we don't know what the fuck they know, Dan! This is your fucking job! This why I pay you what the fuck I do! You keep coming in here telling me you don't know shit Imma start thinking it's you!" I yelled.

I was so angry that I flew off of the hood of the car and was in Dan's face before I could stop myself. Before I could think, I had my pistol pointed in Dan's face.

"I mean it makes fucking sense! You know everything right! You worked your entire career for this shit, maybe they found out and you needed to save yourself," I snapped, curling my finger around the trigger.

Dan held up his arms in surrender.

"Woah! Take it easy, brother! Come on, E, I would never do that shit to you or your family! Your father, you, your mother, you're all like family to me. You put me in a position to get this job! Not to mention, I know what you all would do to me, my kids, my family, my wife. I'd rather go to jail for life than to fuck with you guys. You're crazy as fuck but your mother, I'd blow my own fucking head off before I do something to have her coming for me," Dan pleaded, shaking his head.

I stood silent for a moment, contemplating, thinking. I needed to sort my thoughts out and calm myself. The only sound was the echoing water droplets in the empty underground garage.

I looked at Dan searching for an ounce of disloyalty but found nothing. Dan had always been straight up with me and my entire family. Dan was so deep in this shit he was like family. I was letting my anger cloud my judgment. I lowered my gun, taking a step back out of Dan's face before I spoke.

"Figure this shit out! If it's CIA I need to know who the fuck it is. I need answers, Dan, it's been almost a year, figure it the fuck out!" I commanded, tucking my gun back into my waist.

"I got you, brother; I'm trying. I'm telling you this shit is big, the entire family file is sealed and the more questions I ask the more eyes are drawn to me. I'll get to the bottom of it though. That's my word, E," Dan said, extending his hand in good faith.

I looked down at Dan's hand for a moment. My face

contorted into a scowl, looking down at Dan's hand as if it was covered in shit. I pondered on the handshake for a moment before shaking his hand.

"If you can't figure out who the fuck is running this shit and what they know, plan your funeral. You have four weeks starting today. That's my word, Dan," I said calmly, walking towards the SUV.

"Don't worry, I got you brother!" Dan stated, reassuringly.

Dan kept his composure, but I could tell he was scared shitless. His pale white skin had become paler, he was turning blue. There was no doubt in my mind that Dan knew I was serious. He would be digging the grave that I buried him in if he did not have the information that I wanted to hear in the next four weeks.

CHAPTER TWENTY-THREE

*"You Are The F*** Home . . ."*

AUGUST 20, 2019

CALABASAS, CALIFORNIA

MALIKA

Shaking, I entered the foyer of the home that Christian and I once shared. I was nervous and on edge. I needed to get in and get out. How could a place I once called home only a few months ago feel so foreign to me?

"You only have a few minutes, Mrs. Malika. I do not want Mr. Christian to find out you are here. You were good to me, so I did this for you," Rosea said in a thick Mexican accent.

She was flustered, hell she ought to be, risking her job by allowing me to enter the property much less the home. Christian had informed all of his staff that I was not permitted on the premises.

"No problem, Rosea. Thank you so much, I will be in and out," I replied.

"And be quiet, if one of the other staff hears you, they might tell Mr. C," Rosea pleaded.

I nodded at her before pulling out my phone and found

Noelle's name. My fingers moved a mile a minute across the screen. I texted Noelle to alert her that I made it inside, as she requested.

Instantly, she replied.

The text read: *Five minutes! In and Out! No funny shit or I'm calling Ethan! Seriously Lika, this is not a game!*

I rolled my eyes at her response and tucked the phone into the back pocket of my sweatpants.

Quietly, I hustled into the home and to the direction of the kitchen. I knew that walking up the main stairs could potentially get me noticed by one of the other staff members, so I opted for the entrance next to what used to be my multi-story closet. Everything inside of the closet was as I left it, like Christian left it there in the hopes of me returning.

Swiftly, I maneuvered the sliding mirror out of the way to gain access to the safe that I had built into the wall. I was the only one who knew the password, so I was sure that the contents had to still be inside. I hurriedly typed the six-digit code into the safe. The code to the safe was the due date for the child that I lost years ago, June fourth.

Beep! Beep! Beep! The safe rang out as the red light dinged.

I was typing so damn fast that my nails accidentally hit the wrong number.

"Fuck," I cursed quietly under my breath.

I took a deep breath before I tried again, I was so anxious that I missed the fact that my hands were shaking. I tried again once more and with ease, the safe unlocked. The green light on the side lit up and the door opened. My heart sank once I looked inside. I expected to find my necklace and the folder that I left sitting on the shelf but to my surprise the safe was empty. I threw my hands around the inside of the safe frantically, trying to find the imaginary contents.

"Looking for this?" Christian said calmly from behind me.

My entire body stilled at the sound of his voice. *He was not supposed to be here! Shit, Shit, Shit!* I thought.

"You can turn around, I'm right here, you not hearing shit," he stated.

Christian was calm, almost too calm and that was not like Christian. I turned to find my mother's necklace dangling from his fingers and the folder on the table beside him.

"What . . . What are you doing here?" The words fell out of my mouth without even a second thought.

Shit, those were the only words that I could get out. I was startled at his presence, fear gluing my feet to the spot I stood in. This was his house, not mine. He should be the one asking me that.

"No, the question is what are you doing here. You think old Ethan the only rich one huh, he not the only nigga with money, baby. Don't ever forget that. I put you on to this lifestyle remember. You can't trust anybody; you have no idea what people do for money. Little ole Rosea sold you out for a bonus and some paid time off. Actually, I sent all of my staff home for the day. It's just me and you now," Christian said smugly.

I took a deep breath, because I should have known better. I should have listened to Noelle and Tamir. I only hoped it was not too late.

Bzzzzzz! Bzzzzzzzz! Bzzzzzzz! Bzzzzzzz! My cell phone vibrated in my back pocket. I knew that it was Noelle calling to check in to see what was taking me so long. I was sure that I had been inside for way more than five minutes by this point. I reached into my back pocket and pulled the phone out. The caller ID read: *Noe-Noe.* I placed the phone on the self that sat on the wall next to the hanging mirror.

"Go ahead and answer and tell ole boy you are not coming back. Tell him you back home, where you belong, and tell that nigga bring my fucking daughter. I can't believe you. You're predictable. Our dead baby's due date wasn't hard to figure out,

I know you Malika, I know you like the back of my fucking hand," Christian boasted, taking a step closer to me.

I was silent, attempting to keep my composure. Christian was like a pit bull, they could smell when their prey was in fear.

"Christian, I have to leave, please. Security is out front; he'll be in here any moment not to mention we both know . . ." Christian cut off in an angry outburst.

"If you don't get home what? You are the fuck home! I'm tired of playing this game with you. My boss, bitch! My fucking boss, you whore! Tell that nigga ya'll done playing house! That shit is over! All the shit I did for you! Bitch, when I met you, you were nothing. Just another pretty face. I should've fucked you and passed you around. Instead, I changed your fucking life. You didn't know money until I came along! I guess millions wasn't enough, you wanted billions right bitch!" Christian ranted.

He took a step towards me and I took a step backwards. Lucky for me, I had brought insurance in the event that he was here and tried to pull some bullshit. I reached into my back and pulled out a .22 caliber handgun. Ethan had been paranoid over the last few months and made sure to get me my own gun. I pulled the hammer back releasing a bullet into the chamber.

I raised it in the air, pointing it upwards directly at Christian.

"Now, you're going to put the necklace down on top of the folder and let me walk out of here," I ordered, attempting to regain control.

Christian chuckled.

"I'm not taking too kindly to these fucking guns being pointed in my face," he stated, raising an eyebrow.

"Back up!" I barked, still pointing the gun in his direction.

"You won't shoot me, Malika," he replied, shrugging.

I moved the aim of my gun slightly to the right, letting off a warning shot to signal that I was not playing. Christian ducked just in time. The bullet wisped right past where Christian's head was prior. A few centimeters over and it would have been over for him.

"Put my necklace down and move!" I yelled.

"You have lost your fucking mind!" Christian stated, bursting into laughter.

"Yea and I'm crazy enough to shoot you, bitch! Put it down!" I cautioned.

Christian smirked devilishly before lowering the necklace onto the table, placing it on top of the folder. I took one step towards him, never taking my eyes off of him or lowering my weapon. Christian eyed me like a hawk stalking his prey. I removed one hand from the gun and reached down for the items.

Bzzzzzzz! Bzzzzzzzz! Bzzzzzzzzz! Noelle called again. Instinctively, I looked to the shelf where my phone was located.

Smackkkkk! The sound of Christian's hand connecting with my cheek echoed throughout the large closet.

It all happened so fast that I did not see it coming. Christian backhanded me, sending me backwards into the tufted chair. Consequently, the gun flew out of my hands and skated across the floor.

I did not know what it was about this damn closet, but it was always some shit in here. I jumped to my feet. My eyes searching the floor frantically for the gun as Christian stalked over to me. He reached down, grabbing me roughly by my hair before lifting me into the air. I could feel the strands of my hair ripping out of my scalp.

"Christian, please!" I cried out in pain, my hands tugging at his tight grip.

"Nah, we just get started, wife!" He taunted me, throwing me down onto the floor.

"Ahhhhhhhhhh!" I screamed.

"Shut the fuck up!" he shot, waving his hand.

I was wounded but adrenaline kept me going. I grabbed

anything that I could find and began throwing them in his direction. The first thing that I saw was a glass vase on the table above me. I grabbed the vase and hauled it at him.

Crackkkkkkk! The sound of glass cracking as it connected with the wall behind Christian rang throughout the room.

Christian ducked the vase. That managed to give me a few seconds to escape him. Next, I threw a Christian Louboutin heel at him.

This time, I hit my target. The heel connected with the side of Christian's face.

"Ahhh, imma fuck you up!" Christian hollered.

I climbed to my feet. The pain in my hips was excruciating but it was do or die. I needed to get out! Once again, my eyes hunted for the missing gun. Bingo! I found it. I took off running to the other side of the room where the gun was.

Christian's injury bought me a few seconds but not enough because Christian was on my ass. Christian kicked the gun towards him, out of my reach.

"Boom!" Christian pistol-whipped me.

Blood rushed from both my nose and my mouth. Shrieking, I grabbed the side of my face in horror. The adrenaline was wearing off and I was now feeling all of the damage Christian had done. Christian was not letting up however, he was just beginning.

"Get up!" he ordered.

"Fuck you!" I shot.

I could barely get the words out, but he heard me clearly.

"Fuck you, huh? You know what, that's a good idea. Open your mouth you dick-sucking bitch! You went from me to my fucking boss!" Christian barked.

He stalked over to me, towering over my body. I was attempting to stand but to no avail, I was knocked back down.

"Nah, stay on your knees! Open your mouth!" he barked.

I pinned my lips shut, refusing to open my mouth. Christian pulled his sweatpants down, exposing grey Calvin Klein briefs. Roughly, he grabbed me by my hair, pulling my head back.

"Open your fucking mouth, Malika!" he instructed.

I shook my head to the side as best as I could to say no. I was too scared to open my mouth for fear of what he might do. Christian brought my .22 to my forehead.

"Open your mouth before I put some hot shit in it!" he threatened.

A part of me would have rather died than to give him the satisfaction of watching me perform oral sex on him but then Angel flashed before me. My daughter needed her mother.

AUGUST 20, 2019

SEATTLE, WASHINGTON

ETHAN

I headed back to the black Rolls Royce truck that was waiting at the other end of the garage. My meeting with Dan Collier proved to be pointless, turning up no valuable information. The threat of a federal investigation had been lingering over my head for months. I needed answers and Dan was unable to provide any.

Bzzzzzzz! Bzzzzzzzz! Bzzzzzzz! My phone vibrated. I reached inside of my pocket, retrieving the cell phone to see who was calling. I hoped that it was Malika, I had been so consumed with my day that I did not get a chance to check in with her. Instead, it was an unknown Calabasas number. My brow bent as I declined the call, unsure of who it was. There were very few people that had my personal phone number, but I did not take unknown calls. I placed my phone back inside of my pocket and proceeded to open the Rolls Royce door.

Emanuel Jacobs sat in the back seat of the black Rolls Royce.

He looked up as the door opened, a lit cigar pinched between his fingers. He sucked in the smoke, exhaling before he spoke.

"You lost control back there, we don't ever lose control," Emanuel scolded.

"Yea, I know," I replied, hoping inside of the truck.

"You know, you can always take my advice and shut everything down. A wise man would take heed to my warning," he continued.

"Pop, we've been over this. It's not that simple. It's complicated," I protested.

"Complicated? Please. Nothing is ever complicated for a Jacob man," Emmanuel boasted, turning to face me.

"Yea, Pop, I know," I groaned, shaking my head.

My father was a proud man, there was nothing better than a Jacob man in his eyes. *Bzzzzzzz! Bzzzzzzzz! Bzzzzzzz!* My phone began to vibrate once again. Exasperated, I blew out a sharp breath before pulling my phone out of my pocket. The same unknown Calabasas number appeared on the caller ID as before.

"Who the hell is this?" I questioned under my breath.

I stared for a moment, pondering if I should decline the call again.

"Are we ready to go, sir?" Larry questioned from the driver's seat.

"Uhm, yea," I replied, distracted by my phone.

Who could this be? I thought as the car pulled out of the parking garage and onto the main road. I decided to answer. Before I could get a word in, a loud female voice boomed through the phone.

"Ethan! Malika's at Christian's house and something is wrong!" the woman yelled.

"Slow down! What happened? And who is this?" I questioned, leaning forward.

"It's Noelle, we haven't officially met but I am sure you've heard of me. Malika's sister! She went by Christian's house to get some important things; he wasn't supposed to be there, he should be at a basketball retreat, but she went inside and told me she made it in and hasn't answered any of my calls since then!" she rambled.

I took a deep breath, pinching the bridge of my nose in frustration. Leave it to Malika to get herself into some bullshit. She lied to me earlier today, telling me that she was going to her friend's house only to sneak off.

"How long has she been in there? And where is Angel?" I questioned.

"About twenty minutes. She was only supposed to be in there for five minutes. She has security with her, but I don't have his number. Angel is with Isabella," Noelle replied.

"I'll handle it. Thanks for the call," I replied, ready to hang up.

"Please hurry up, I'm scared!" Noelle pleaded.

"Ok," I stated, hanging up the phone.

I looked up, speaking to Larry.

"Change of plans, take me to the airport and get the plane on standby. I have to go back home. I also need Walter from the security team on the phone, now," I instructed Larry.

"Right away, sir, give me one moment," Larry stated.

Larry pulled to the side of the road. He was unable to look through his phone and drive at the same time, so he opted for the safer option of pulling the car to the side. Awaiting Walter's number, I texted my assistant instructing her to cancel all of my meetings.

"Everything ok, son?" my father questioned.

"Not really, it's a personal emergency. Something with Malika," I responded.

"I stay out of your business as you are a grown man, but that girl is proving to be more trouble than she is worth. I would be careful with this situation if I were you," he cautioned.

"Pop, please, this is not the time," I protested.

Larry chimed in before Emmanuel continued, providing a much-needed interruption.

"Sir, Walter is on the line for you," Larry stated, passing the phone to the back seat.

I took the phone from Larry, nodding my head to thank him.

"Hello, sir?" Walter questioned.

"Why the fuck would you bring her to that house when I made the rules clear! Get in there! She's been in there too long and something is wrong!" I barked, angrily.

The more I thought about this entire situation, the more annoyed I became. This was all becoming much more drama than I was willing to deal with.

"My apologies, sir! I will get in there right away! She told me that it would be ok with you," Walter explained.

"Get in the house!" I yelled, hanging the phone up.

As my mind mulled over the revelations of today and Malika's sneaky ways another thought came to me. Christian was not enlisted in any basketball conferences. Matter fact, no player on any of my teams was scheduled to attend this week's basketball conference. I shook my head, frustrated. Malika, unknowingly, walked right into a setup.

AUGUST 20, 2019

CALABASAS, CALIFORNIA

MALIKA

"I guess you think I'm fucking playing with you!" Christian screamed at me.

He lifted the gun from the center of my forehead and raised it above my head.

Bang! A bullet hit into the glass case that held my pocketbooks.

Crackkk! The sound of the shattering glass erupted throughout the room.

I jumped at the sound of the gunshot. Christian looked down at me sinisterly.

"The next one goes in your head! Now, open your mouth!" he barked, bringing the gun back down to my temple.

The gunshot seemed to do the trick. I was scared shitless, shaking. I wanted to protest, kick, yell and scream but I could not. He had the upper hand, and I now had another life to think about.

Reluctantly, I complied with his wishes, opening my mouth. Christian began easing his penis inside of my mouth. Disgusted was an understatement. He kept his eyes glued to me.

"Don't act like you don't know what you doing. Get to it!" he snarled, biting his bottom lip, pushing the gun deeper into my skin.

I rolled my eyes in disgust, this man belonged in a mental hospital. I tightened my jaws, accepting his penis inside of my mouth.

Christian threw his head back, gripping my hair tighter. I had a move in mind, but first I needed him to lower the gun from my head. I watched him closely, waiting.

"That's it," he moaned, pushing my head further and further down onto his girth.

He closed his eyes and lifted his head to the ceiling. Christian lowered the gun from my head, dropping his hand by his side. Bingo, he was comfortable, exactly what I needed. *Bastard, I got something for you,* I thought.

I bit down as hard as I could on his penis.

"Ahhhhhhhhhhh!" Christian screamed in pain, dubbing over.

Instantly, he released both my hair and the gun, causing the gun to fall to the floor. Christian reached down with both of his hands and coddled his penis. I was not sure how intense the pain was, but he was bleeding.

"I hope I bit that shit off!" I yelled, rushing to my feet.

"Come here, bitch!" Christian yelled, toppling to his feet.

My first thought was to try to get the gun off of the floor, but I did not have much time; I desperately needed to get out of there. I took off running towards the nearest exit.

Bang! Bang! Bang! Christian fired shot after shot behind me.

"Ahhhhhhhhhh!" I screamed, ducking.

I made it out of the room and to the top of the back steps that led to the kitchen. I had to make it down the steps. Luckily, he could not aim for shit.

"Malika! Malika are you here?!" Walter called out from downstairs of the manor.

Finally, some help! I thought.

Bang! Bang! Christian fired again.

"Up, Ahhhhhhhhhh!" I called out in pain.

I felt the bullet hit the side of my thigh and a burst of pain shot through me. I was injured but adrenaline provided me the fuel I needed to keep going. Christian was on my heels, my gunshot wound providing him the leverage he needed to catch up to me. As fast as I could with my injury, I hobbled down the steps.

"You ain't going nowhere!" Christian yelled behind me.

"Malika!" Walter said, finally finding me.

Christian came running into the kitchen, he was so dead set on me that he skipped over Walter. Christian lunged at me and was met with a pistol to the side of his face. Walter slammed the handle of his gun into Christian's head.

"Christian, no!" I yelled as Christian brought the gun to Walter's face and pulled the trigger.

I gasped, bringing my hands to my face in distress. I was waiting to hear the sound of the gun going off but nothing.

Christian pulled the trigger over and over in a panic but there was nothing. The clip was empty, he had no bullets left. Walter followed up with another blow to Christian's face with the handle of his gun. Christian put up a fight in the beginning, but he was no match for the skilled fighter that Walter was. Walter delivered blow after blow, this time with only his fist. He beat Christian unconscious. I felt a sense of vindication watching Walter whoop Christian's ass. He deserved this ass whooping and then some.

"Malika, it's time to go!" Walter yelled at me.

I turned towards the entrance of the home, prepared to follow instructions when I realized that I did not get what I came here for.

"I need to get what I came for!" I yelled, hobbling back towards the kitchen stairs.

I was in so much pain, I could barely walk but I was not leaving without my mother's heirlooms.

"You can barely walk. What is it that you need? I'll get it, then we are getting the fuck out of here!" Walter yelled.

"It's in the closet on one of the end tables. It's a folder with a necklace on it and grab my phone!" I instructed.

Walter nodded before taking off up the stairs. He returned a few moments later with the items in his hand.

"Got it! Let's go!" he said, entering the room.

Walter walked over, handed me the items then picked me up, scooping me up off the floor.

"This needs immediate medical attention. I should have never let you talk me into bringing you here! The boss is very upset about this," he exclaimed, shaking his head.

I could see distress written all over Walter's face as he carried me out of the house. *What the fuck did I do?* I thought. Ethan was going to lose his shit and Walter would for sure be on the receiving end of Ethan's anger.

CHAPTER TWENTY-FOUR

"I Can't Help You . . ."

AUGUST 21, 2019

CALABASAS, CALIFORNIA

ETHAN

Beep! Beep! Beep! The sound of the vital sign monitor echoed throughout the patient room.

I sat at the foot of Malika's bed with my elbows pressed to my knees. Forehead pinched, I sat in deep contemplation of the events that took place.

Knock! Knock! A light knock on the door brought me out of my trance.

I looked up to find Malika's private surgeon Dr. Fredricks standing at the door. Dr. Fredricks was a short, chubby, Caucasian man with a bald head. He wore oversized glasses that sat on the bridge of his nose.

"Hello, Ethan," Dr. Fredricks greeted.

Dr. Fredricks stepped inside of the room holding a clipboard.

"Hello," I replied, looking up at him.

"I wanted to drop in. I haven't had a moment to come by and speak with you since I completed her surgery. Malika is a very lucky woman. Although this was a thigh wound, a centimeter to the left and it would have nicked her femoral artery. I think we both know the complications of that. She will be fine with proper rest and care. I have prescribed a series of pain medication and antibiotics to see her through recovery. I know you have an in-house nurse and doctor that will be taking care of her but please do not hesitate to reach out if she needs anything," Dr. Fredricks explained.

I stood up from my seat, placing my hands inside of my pocket before speaking.

"Thank you for your help and discretion. I will be sure to reach out if she needs anything. Will she be able to walk or move around?" I inquired.

"Not really, she can walk on it physically but the less pressure the better. It is best that she refrains from placing excess pressure on it. She will need a little bit of physical therapy, but she should be perfectly fine, up and running in no time," Dr. Fredricks assured.

I exhaled a sigh of relief at the facts presented by Dr. Fredricks. I pulled both of my hands out of my pocket and extended my right hand to him for a handshake. Dr. Fredricks shook my hand.

"You will be properly compensated for your emergency services. I can't thank you enough." I thanked him.

"It is my pleasure, Ethan; it is always a pleasure to do business with you and your family," Dr. Fredricks stressed.

I nodded my head at Dr. Fredricks before he turned and exited the room. Now that I knew that Malika was going to be ok, I had business to take care of.

I walked to the door of the patient room. There were three men dressed in black suits on both sides of the door. They stood with their hands folded in front of them. Two of the men were for Malika and the third was my personal guard and driver, Larry. The private facility that I owned was used as a surgery center for high-class plastic surgeons. There was very little chance that anyone would try to harm Malika, but I was not taking any chances. There would be armed security until she was able to return home.

I approached Elliot, one of the security guards, before making my exit. I stood, adjusting the collar to my jacket.

"I'm stepping out. I will be back later on tonight. No one is allowed in or out of this room except her nurse and only her nurse. Call me if there are any issues," I instructed.

"Of course, sir," Elliot responded, nodding.

I turned to Larry, before nodding in his direction. He knew the head nod meant that it was time to leave. I walked out of the facility and to the Rolls Royce truck that sat in the front of the valet.

"Hello, Mr. Jacobs," the valet greeted, opening the back door of my car for me.

"Hello," I greeted.

I reached inside of my pocket and pulled out my Hermes wallet. I peeled off ten one-hundred-dollar bills and handed them to the valet before stepping into the car.

"Thank you, Mr. Jacobs, you are always so kind!" the valet beamed.

I brought the corners of my lips into a stiffened smile before climbing into the truck. The moment that the truck pulled off from in front of the facility I got right down to business.

"Is that done?" I asked Larry.

"Yes, sir. He is waiting. Would you like to go there now?" Larry replied.

"Yes, directly there. Was my extra suit delivered?" I questioned.

"Yes, sir, in the back," Larry informed.

"Thanks, Larry," I stated.

The thirty-minute drive to the abandoned warehouse in a desolate section of Inglewood seemed to take forever. I was jittery, itching for revenge. The news of Malika being shot and sexually violated left a bad taste in my mouth. Everyone involved needed to be handled. I needed to see blood. Somebody had to answer for this and until I was able to get my hands on Christian, Walter, the security guard would have to do.

We pulled inside of the empty warehouse. I placed black leather gloves on and turned off all of my devices before exiting the truck. Three men dressed in black toting military-grade M16 rifles stood at the back of the warehouse, in front of the bulletproof door.

"E. Larry," the men greeted in unison as Larry and I approached.

I nodded my head at the men as they stepped to the side to let me enter.

"Second door on the left," one of the armed men informed me.

"Good look," I said calmly, stepping past them.

Drip! Drip! Drip! Drip! The sound of water falling from the ceiling echoed.

Inside the warehouse, it was dark, muggy, and cold. I strolled down the hallway until I located the second door on the left. I turned the knob before entering the room. Walter stood with his hands on his head, pacing. His face was balled up in distress as he walked back and forth. He looked up at me, finally noticing my presence.

"Please. I only took her there because she begged me! Please, man! I have a family! I have kids! I promise this will never happen again. I am begging you, please!" Walter whined.

My dark and cold eyes pierced into Walter.

"Put the silencer on," I instructed Larry, ignoring Walter's begging.

Without responding, Larry retrieved the gun from his waist

and placed the silencer on. Next, he extended the gun to me. I took the weapon without breaking my stare.

"Please, man! Please! I'm fucking begging, please!" Walter pleaded, begging for his life.

"Kneel down," I instructed, this time talking to Walter.

"No! No! No! Please!" Walter protested, walking backwards towards the back wall.

I breathed a sigh of frustration, clenching my jaws in annoyance. Walter wanted to make the last few moments of his life more difficult than it needed to be. I looked from Walter to Larry, nodding my head at Larry. A look that told Larry exactly what to do. Larry leaned down to pick up a steel pipe that laid on the floor before walking over to a pleading Walter.

Walter attempted to use his hands to block the blow that followed but he did not stand a chance. Larry brought the steel pipe down onto Walter's face time and time again.

"Ahhhhhhhhhhh!" Walter cried.

Walter cried out in agony as he fell to the floor with blood gushing from the side of his head.

Larry gripped Walter roughly by the collar of his shirt and dragged him to his knees.

"Please, man, I was just trying to help her," Walter pleaded, sobbing.

I walked over to a sobbing Walter who was somehow still pleading for his life. I hovered over him, placing the gun to the temple of his forehead.

"Save your explanation, I can't help you," I stated, before I pulled the trigger.

Walters's lifeless body fell to the floor, blood and brain matter spewing everywhere. I walked down a little further, standing overtop of Walter's body. I pulled the trigger until there were no bullets left. I was so fucking angry that I could bring Walter back to life to kill him all over again. Walter defied a direct order that resulted in Malika getting shot. He had to be taken care of. He placed her life in danger, but Walter was not the real person that I wanted dead. Christian was next on my list.

MALIKA

"Excuse you! That's my sister, I am going in there!" Noelle's voice boomed from outside of my patient room.

Uncomfortably, I shifted in the bed, attempting to sit up. I could hear Noelle at my door arguing with someone, my security guard I was sure because knowing Ethan he had this place on lockdown.

"Ma'am, please step back before I have to forcibly remove you. We have direct orders, no one is allowed in or out of this room except medical personnel," the man replied to Noelle.

"I'd like to see you touch me. Come on remove me, I dare you because all hell will break loose in here!" Noelle challenged.

I knew that Noelle was not one to make threats, she was making a promise. I needed to get up and to the security guard before Noelle had time to start her bullshit. I grabbed the rail for support as I tried to stand up from the bed. An excruciating pain shot through my leg. Quickly, I sat back down. It was clear that I was not getting up and walking anywhere without assistance.

"She can come in!" I yelled, hoping that my raspy voice was loud enough.

"Ma'am. Please, this is the last time I will ask you nicely," the man informed Noelle.

"And this is the last fucking time I am going to tell your goofy ass that my sister is in there!" Noelle barked.

It was clear to me that they could not hear me due to their arguing. Frantically, I began searching for my phone. I needed to hurry up and diffuse this mess before it went any further. My security team did not play any games and they would, without hesitation, remove Noelle.

“Found it!” I whispered as I discovered my cell phone underneath the pillow.

“Let go of me! Watch when I get in there, y’all asses getting fired!” Noelle carried on; her voice was now trailing off down the hallway.

It was safe to assume that she had been escorted out.

I dialed Ethan. He answered on the first ring.

“Malika,” Ethan answered dryly.

“Can you tell security to let Noelle in, please,” I requested.

“That’s it?” he questioned.

“Yes,” I responded.

“E—” I began but I was too late, he hung up the phone the moment that I said yes.

I could feel his anger. He was livid. I knew that I had some explaining and apologizing to do. I pursed my lips and bent my forehead in confusion. I was unsure of what to do to fix the mess that I caused. I was consistently putting him in fucked up situations, dragging him into my drama. I needed to get my shit together fast before he realized that he deserved better.

Moments later, I heard Noelle’s voice again outside of my room.

“Told y’all dippy asses that’s my sister! I’ll be sure to file a complaint, stupid asses!” she yelled before storming into my room.

Noelle burst into the room wearing a black Off-White sweatsuit and Nike running sneakers. Her hair was pulled up into a natural ponytail and she was wearing minimal makeup. She was flustered and her facial expression gave away how annoyed she really was. Noelle threw her large Go Yard tote onto the chair.

“Hype ass security! Anyways, sis! Are you ok?! I was worried sick!” Noelle exclaimed, rolling her neck in the direction of the door.

Noelle made sure that she was loud enough for both guards

to hear. She rushed over to me and wrapped her arms around me. Her hug was so tight, I could feel the intensity of her worry.

"Yes, boo, thank you! You saved my life; I don't know what would have happened if you did not call Ethan!" I expressed.

I was filled with so many emotions. The first emotion that I felt was gratefulness. I was lucky to have Noelle in my corner. The tears that followed were an innate reaction. I was so overwhelmed with emotion that I could not contain it.

"I was scared. He forced me to suck his dick and everything, girl, it was terrible. I thought he was going to rape me," I wailed.

"It's ok, love, let it out," Noelle consoled.

Noelle wrapped her arms around me tighter, rubbing circles in my back to comfort me.

"I can't understand how someone I loved for so many years does the things that he does. That man has broken me down to nothing in every way possible. I hate him. I wish I never met him; he was the worst thing to ever happen to my life," I rambled.

"Well, I heard you bit his dick! I wish you bit that shit off! Dirty ass nigga!" Noelle insulted.

Her words brought an unexpected chuckle out of me. Leave it to Noelle to make a bad situation a joke.

"I did bite it. You should've seen him, little bitch!" I chuckled, sucking up tears.

"Girl, I know, I wish I did. That shit probably better than a Beyonce concert and you know I love me some Bey! I would pay good money to see that shit!" Noelle joked, shaking her head.

"On another note. My man is livid. He won't even speak to me unless I need something. I don't know where to begin even explaining myself. This is our first real issue as a couple," I confessed.

"Well, girl, you did lie to him and then go and get yourself shot. This wasn't a quick fight; you could have died. He'll probably be upset for a little minute, but he'll get over it. You might have to get on your knees to make a few things right though and I don't know about all that since you all cripple, but you'll need some tricks, girl," Noelle said, pulling out of our embrace to look down at me with a raised eyebrow.

"Girl! Sex does not fix everything!" I said, hollering.

"Shit! This pussy got power over in the Rawlins house, ok! T is a sucker for this kitty and don't get me started on what this mouth do!" Noelle teased.

"Girl! Shit, the mouth probably can't fix my problems," I stated, smiling while shaking my head to the side.

Suddenly, a turn of the doorknob halted Noelle and I's conversation. The room door opened, revealing Ethan who was standing at the opening. My man was a sight for sore eyes. He was wearing a suit today, not his usual black, he opted for a light blue jacket instead of his traditional look. It had only been a day since I had seen him, but the recent events made me all the more grateful.

"Thank you, boss." The man presented on the other side of the door.

Ethan nodded his head in acknowledgment before shutting the door and entering the room. Ethan paused to look at me, then turned his attention to Noelle before walking over to the armchair.

"Hi, I'm Ethan and you?" Ethan greeted Noelle from across the room.

"Noelle, I'm the one that called you. Nice to meet you," Noelle replied.

"Oh, thank you for that. That was stand up of you to do, probably saved her life," Ethan thanked, nodding his head.

"No need to thank me. This is my girl, always and forever, I got her," Noelle replied leaning in to hug me tighter.

"I didn't think you were coming here," I inserted.

Ethan looked up at me, annoyance dancing in his eyes.

"Where else would I be?" He paused.

"I'm here for everything else. Why wouldn't I be here if you're hurt?" he continued, annoyed.

He clearly had an attitude.

"I'm going to get going. I just came by to check on you, boo," Noelle said before I could respond to him.

Noelle leaned forward and gave me a hug before walking to the other end of the room to retrieve her bag.

"Girl, don't forget to call me as soon as you get home! Nice to meet you, Ethan. Oh, and before I forget topflight out there was hype as shit earlier old rent a cop ass security," Noelle cussed on her way out the door.

Ethan chuckled and shook his head. Noelle knew damn well that those were anything but topflight security guards, those were the real deal. They were trained and certified to kill. Once the door was closed, I turned my attention back to Ethan who was now looking down at his phone.

"How long are we going to do this?" I asked.

"Do what, Malika," Ethan said, exhaling a deep sigh.

He did not even give me the courtesy of looking up from his phone.

"This! You being mad. I just went through more than enough. I don't need to beef with you too," I said, my frustration apparent.

"That's your problem. You're selfish. Everything revolves around you, always. You lied to my face and got yourself in some bullshit once again. You always find the need to go back there. I'm tired of this shit. I don't even know what the fuck to make of this. Did you think of me? Your daughter? Anyone but yourself when you made the choice you did? No. You never do because in your world the world revolves around you and only you. My world is bigger than just you, sorry to tell you but this shit has to stop," Ethan scolded.

"Baby, I'm sorry. I didn't think. I know I fucked up. I had

a legit reason for going there but I didn't think of the reality of what I was doing. The last thing I want you to think is that I lie to you. I was wrong and I apologize," I conceded.

"Yea, well, apology or not I don't trust you. We're going to have to build that trust back," he stated.

"Come here, please," I pleaded.

He was silent for a moment just looking at me, pondering. Reluctantly, he stood and walked over to me. He stood in front of me looking down at me. I wrapped my arms around him and pulled his body close to mine. He was stiff, not as comfortable as he usually was. I placed my chin on his stomach and looked up at him with sad eyes. He turned his head away, not wanting to look into my eyes. We both knew that no matter how mad he was that his anger would melt.

"I'm sorry. I love you," I whispered, solemnly.

Like ice, I could feel him melting before me. Hesitantly, he turned his head and looked down at me. His demeanor softened and he returned my embrace, wrapping me tightly in his arms.

"I love you more. Don't lie to me again especially about no dumb shit that can get you killed," he said, softly.

Ethan and I had some work to do to get our relationship back on track, but I was ready and willing to do whatever to make our relationship work. He was everything to me and I refused to lose him.

CHAPTER TWENTY-FIVE

"I'll Let You Do the Honors . . ."

AUGUST 25, 2019
CALABASAS, CALIFORNIA

MALIKA

"That's mommy's big girl! Yes, she is! Good job, my rainbow," I cooed at Angel who was sitting up on her own.

Angel earned the nickname rainbow from being my rainbow baby, my first child after losing my previous baby. Angel threw her hands up in excitement and bounced on the hospital bed. She was smiling from ear to ear, laughing as I tickled her stomach.

"Yes, mamas! Yes! That's a big girl!" I encouraged Angel, clapping my hands in front of my face in excitement.

Angel brought me so much joy. Watching her grow has been heartwarming, a true love that I never knew I was missing until the day I was blessed with my baby girl.

"Look at Daddy's baby!" Ethan's voice boomed as he entered the room.

Angel turned her head in his direction and lost it at the sight of him. She went off crying and bouncing for him to come get her. I was always in awe of the relationship between the two. Whenever Ethan was around, no one else existed to Angel.

"Wahhhhhhhh!" Angel wailed, reaching for Ethan.

Ethan placed the duffle bag down on the armchair and walked over to the bed. He was dressed down today, in an all-black Nike sweatsuit and black sneakers. He leaned down and picked Angel up. Immediately, she stopped crying.

"It's ok. Daddy's here, you don't have to cry," Ethan whispered to sniffling Angel.

Angel had her head placed on his shoulder and her arm wrapped around his neck. Ethan brought his hand to Angel's face, using his fingers to wipe the tears from her face. She was spoiled and knew how to get whatever she wanted out of him.

"Are you ready? I brought the bag with a change of clothes for you to shower and get dressed. Isabella is on her way to pick Angel back up," Ethan informed me.

"Yea, I'll go get ready. I'm ready to go home. Where are we going? Why is Isabella coming to get her?" I inquired.

I attempted to stand up from the bed on my own. I was able to walk but I did need the assistance of crutches until my wound healed. Ethan rushed over to me, still holding onto Angel with one hand, he extended his hand to help me down from the bed. A multitasker, that is exactly what he was because he always found a way to do everything.

I took his hand, standing before reaching for my crutches that were leaning on the wall.

"Yea, we're going home but we have to make a stop first just the two of us," Ethan answered.

"A stop?" I repeated, looking back at Ethan with a raised eyebrow.

I was confused, I had no knowledge of anything that we had to stop and do.

"Where are we going?" I questioned.

"Just chill, don't ask too many questions, you'll see when we get there," Ethan answered.

I was even more confused by his answer, but I decided not to press it. Ethan was a man of many tricks and surprises.

"You and these surprises all the time, ooooohhhh mysterious," I joked.

Ethan shook his head, the corners of his lips beginning to form into a smile. He walked back and forth, rocking Angel on his shoulders to calm her down.

"Just hurry up and get yourself together," he commanded.

"Alright, ok, I'm going," I said playfully before disappearing into the bathroom.

I showered quickly. I only needed to get in and out and make sure I was clean. I was dying to get back home and take a proper bath with all of my herbal products. I stepped out of the bathroom, with my crutch, to find Ethan sitting on the bed with a sleeping Angel in his arms. I knew he did not put her down because he did not want to wake her. I was so fixed on Ethan and Angel that I did not see Isabella standing at the door, she spoke when I looked in her direction.

"Hi, Ms. Malika, how are you feeling?" Isabella whispered, rushing over to me.

Isabella was a middle-aged Spanish woman. She was petite, with long brown hair that she opted to wear in its natural curly state. Isabella threw her arms around me, her embrace filled me with so much happiness. I was grateful to have someone like Isabella as a part of my team. She was a member of the family. She handled Angel with so much care that I never had to question her intentions with my daughter.

"I'm okay, thank you for asking and thank you for taking wonderful care of my baby." I thanked her, pulling away from her embrace.

"I am relieved to know that you are ok, I was so scared. Angel is wonderful. I love her like my own, no need to thank me," Isabella replied.

"She seems to have that effect on people," I said, chuckling.

"Do you need help, are you okay walking?" she continued.

"No, no, I'm ok. I have this with me," I insisted, pointing to the crutch that I was holding.

"You know I am always here for you. You guys are my family, you have always been kind to me, please do not hesitate to ask if you need anything, my dear," Isabella offered.

"Of course, now let's get out of here," I suggested.

"Oh, let me get the princess," Isabella stated.

Princess was the nickname that Isabella gave to Angel. Isabella turned to retrieve the car seat from the outside of the door. Ethan stood from the bed, while still holding Angel in his arms, he carried her over to the custom car seat and gently he placed her inside. She fussed a little when he set her down, but she did not wake. Ethan leaned down, kissed the tips of his fingers and placed his fingers on her cheek. My heart melted at the sight. I hopped over to where Isabella, Ethan, and Angel gathered. I wanted to be a part of her essence as well. I began to lean down, Ethan grabbed me by my elbow to provide support, then I placed a soft kiss on Angel's cheek.

"Well, I will get going now. See you two back at the house," Isabella stated, bending to pick up the car seat before turning to the door with Angel.

"It's extra security on everyone, one of the guards at the door will be accompanying you. You will have two guards moving forward," Ethan informed her.

"Ok, Mr. Jacobs. Thank you," Isabella provided before walking out.

Ethan then focused his attention on me.

"You ready?" he questioned.

"Yes, babe," I offered.

Ethan grabbed the duffle bag and placed all of my belongings inside. He then walked over to me and extended his hand.

"I can walk, you know?" I asked, sarcastically.

Ethan was in the business of treating me like a baby whenever I needed anything when I wanted to be self-sufficient. He tilted his head to the side and looked at me blankly, a look that said take my hand before I grabbed yours. I retreated, placing my hand inside of his so he could escort me out.

"Only Larry will be needed. You can go back to the house. Contact Daniel for instructions on your schedule," Ethan said to the remaining security guard.

"Ok, sir, thank you," the man replied to Ethan, nodding.

Ethan's instructions to the security guard left me with questions. Ethan usually only took Larry when he had private business to handle or some sort of secret operation. Larry was Ethan's go to guy; he knew where all the secrets were kept. I was not sure where we were going but something was up. If we were headed to an outing, we would need both guards. *Where the hell were we going? Oh well, I trust him,* I thought.

Ethan led me out of the facility and to the black Range Rover that sat in the valet.

The ride with Ethan was long and quiet. Ethan did not say anything, and I was too caught up in my thoughts trying to figure out where we were going. The only sound that existed the entire car ride was the new Rick Ross album, Port of Miami 2. We pulled into an abandoned warehouse in a deserted part of Inglewood. I was confused. Where were we and why the fuck were we here? Alarm filled me, I needed answers. I trusted Ethan but this was some scary shit; not to mention that it had become dark. Yea, I was not feeling this at all. This looked exactly like one of those scenes in a movie where the Caucasian woman runs in and gets killed first, oh no, get me the hell out of here.

“What is this?” I asked, my voice filled with alarm as I turned to Ethan.

“I told you to relax, right?” he asserted; eyes glued to his phone.

“No, tell me what the fuck is going on? Where are we? I don’t like this shit, it’s getting scary,” I admitted, losing my cool.

“Li, when have I ever put you in any situation to be scared? What are you scared of? You should know I would never hurt you,” he stated, calmly shaking his head.

He was calm but there was injury in his words. Injury in the fact that I would insinuate that he would hurt me. His feelings were hurt, but he would never admit it. I placed my hand on top of his reassuringly.

“I don’t think you’d hurt me, I just been through some fucked up shit and I don’t like surprises like this,” I admitted, squeezing his hand.

“I get that, but I am not your ex or any of those men who hurt you. I have a surprise for you, that’s why you are here. No one is going to hurt you, just relax and follow me. No phones, turn them off,” he reassured me.

I nodded my head and sat back in my seat. I pulled out my cell phones and powered them off. Larry pulled the car inside of the warehouse. It was dark, the only light coming from the back. Ethan and Larry climbed out of the car first, then Ethan walked over and helped me out of the truck. I climbed down and followed Ethan and Larry to a back door. There were three armed men standing at the door, all toting high-grade military weapons, M16s to be exact.

“What kind of surprise is this?” I murmured under my breath.

Both men paid me no mind, ignoring me as they continued walking.

“E. Larry. Ms.,” the men greeted in unison as we approached them.

Ethan nodded his head at the men as they stepped to the side to let us enter.

"Hello," I responded.

I was the only one who spoke out of Larry, Ethan, and me. Nonverbal cues were the only recognition they gave.

"In the back room like you requested," one of the armed men informed Ethan.

"Got it," Larry said as we entered.

Inside the warehouse, it was cold and dark. The only light came from the flashlight that Larry was holding, leading us to the back. Larry touched the knob to enter the room but was halted when Ethan placed a hand on his shoulder.

"You go in, let me talk to her real fast then we'll come in," Ethan commanded Larry.

Larry nodded his head before Ethan took my hand and turned me to the other direction, away from the room.

"Before we go in there, I need to let you know a few things," Ethan stated.

A knot formed inside of my stomach at his words because where was he going with this. This was creepy.

"If this is too much for you just let me know at any moment if you want to leave, say something. Everyone has a price to pay for their actions and some shit can't be left unanswered for," Ethan provided.

Shit, I was ready to leave right now, what the fuck was going on! Unsure of what was happening I nodded my head. Ethan was talking to me in codes but somehow, I was starting to understand what this was. I needed the confirmation though, I needed to see with my own eyes exactly what or who was in that room.

Ethan took my hand and turned me in the direction of the room. He opened the door and led me inside. My eyes could see the truth, but my brain needed a moment to register what was happening. Christian Samuels, my soon-to-be ex-husband stood in the back of the warehouse. He hung from the ceiling; his hands tied above his head to a metal bar with steel chains. Ethan took a seat in one of the folded black chairs that sat on the other side of the room.

Christian laughed, while shaking his head from side to side.

"This shit is hilarious. The couple of the fucking hour! I hoped I killed the bitch, guess not," Christian sneered.

I lost it; I could barely walk on my damn legs but somehow, I hopped at lightning speed over to where he was.

"Pew!" A glob of spit flew out of my mouth and right into Christian's face.

Smackkkkkkkk! The sound of my hand connecting with his face echoed throughout the room.

I followed up with a smack to the side of his face. Christian began chuckling.

"That's it! That's all you got. I don't know why y'all brought her here, she can't kill me. This bitch loves me too much to ever kill me, this my bitch, remember that! Matter fact! Ya'll all acting like you don't know who the fuck I am! How the fuck you think you can do this to Christian Samuels?!" Christian spat, his rage now turned to Ethan.

Ethan sat calm, stoic. He did not give Christian any response, his facial expression did not change, he held stern, unmoved by Christian's words. There was a darkness in Ethan's eyes. It was like I was staring at a completely different person. I had never seen Ethan in this way before.

I turned to refocus my attention on Christian who was still smirking at me. He puckered his lips, blowing a kiss at me. All hell broke loose after that moment because I went bat-shit crazy. I hauled over to Christian, throwing punches left and right, blow after blow my fist connected with his face. With every punch I threw, a different memory flashed before me. I was in a blind rage. I zoned out so much that I was unaware that both Christian's face, lip, and my knuckles were bleeding until I snapped out of it. I was so angry, emotionally I was on a high of payback. I spun on my heels, almost losing my balance.

Larry, who was the closest, rushed to me, lending me a hand to keep my balance.

"Relax, don't hurt yourself," Ethan chimed in from his seat.

"A knife, I want a knife!" I said to Larry.

Larry looked down at me and then over at Ethan. Ethan did not say anything, he just nodded his head. Larry turned and walked over to a black book bag that sat in the corner. He emptied the contents of the bag on the floor. The contents were as follows: combat knives, tasers, an array of pistols, silencers, duct tape, and zip ties. Larry extended his hand, pointing downward at the objects. I was taken aback by the preparation, I pondered for a moment before choosing my instrument. I leaned down and grabbed one of the knives, a military-grade Kershaw Secret Agent Boot knife was my weapon of choice. Instantly, before the thought of what I was about to do registered, I grabbed the knife and rushed over to Christian. I rammed the knife into his ball sack so quickly that he did not register what happened until the pain set in.

"Ahhhhhhhhhhh!" Christian hollered, attempting to bend but the chains held him up.

"Suck it huh, bitch? That's what you told me, right! Nobody is ever sucking shit again!" I barked, as I pulled the knife out and jammed it right back in.

This time I took my time turning it while I held it inside of him.

"Ahhhhhhhhhhhhhhhhhhhhhhh! You whore ass bitch!" Christian screamed; this time louder than before.

I went to pull it out and place it back in when I felt Ethan's hand on the back of my shoulder.

"Take it easy for a second, have a seat, you're putting too much pressure on your wound," Ethan stated.

His words were more of a command than a suggestion. I

complied, dropping the knife on the floor then turning in the direction of the chair.

"Silencer," Ethan stated, talking to Larry.

Ethan stared coldly at Christian; this was personal. Larry turned and picked up a silencer from the floor. He then handed it to Ethan who pulled a pistol out of his waist. He screwed the silencer onto the gun and without a second thought turned the gun on Christian. Ethan did not flinch, react, or blink an eye as he pulled the trigger.

"Pew. Pew." The muffled sounds of the gunfire emerged as Ethan shot one bullet into each of Christian's thighs.

"Ahhhhhhhhhh! Fuck!" Christian screamed, his legs giving out.

"Fuck! Fuck! Fuck!" Christian continued to cry in agony.

Christian began panting, his injuries getting the best of him.

"You had a better chance of killing yourself than ever fucking shooting her and living," Ethan proclaimed.

Ethan walked over to me, who was sitting in the folded chair in the corner.

"I'll let you do the honors," he said, extending the gun to me.

I knew exactly what he meant, he wanted me to be the one to kill Christian. I stared down at the gun, thinking for a minute, pondering, could I really do this? Ethan began to pull his hand back when I placed my hand on his, halting him.

"No, I want to do it. I have to," I said, honestly.

The truth was Christian deserved to die but I was not sure if I would ever forgive Ethan for killing him. I needed to be the one to do this, I needed to be the one left with any remorse or guilt if any ever came. I did not want to put this on Ethan because I may end up resenting him. This was my burden to carry. Hesitantly, I took the gun from Ethan, who sat back in the seat. My stomach tightened. Suddenly, it was extremely hot in there. My heart ached and my stomach clenched. I hated this man so much but something in me loved him at the same time. Either way, he earned his fate, I knew that there was no turning back.

I hopped over to Christian, using one of my crutches for assistance. I could not look at him, my eyes were fixed on the gun that hung from my right hand. I was shaking, standing there thinking, this was it, the moment of truth that I could never take back. Then Christian lit a rage in me like never before with his words.

"I wouldn't do that if I were you. You might want to find out where Angel is, you kill me, you never see her again," Christian taunted, panting as he was running out of breath.

Instantly, his words sent a flame through me. At the thought of my daughter, I lost it.

"Wa—" Ethan began.

I raised the gun to Christian's chest and pulled the trigger repeatedly, I shot nine times until the entire clip was empty. Christian's body jerked uncontrollably as it hung, lifeless, from the steel pipe. That was it, the thorn in my side was finally dead. I was brought out of my rage by Ethan's panic.

"Malika! It's no more bullets! Did you hear what he said! You shot him before we could confirm! Fuck! A phone Larry! Get me the burner, now!" Ethan roared.

I was so angry and so emotional that I did not think. At the mention of harm to my child, I reacted! I shot first and asked questions later. *What the fuck did I do?!* I thought, panic setting in. Larry rushed to the spot where he emptied the contents of the bag. He quickly found a flip phone among the pile. He tossed the phone to Ethan who made one phone call.

"Get Isabella's security team on the line now!" Ethan yelled into the phone.

Ethan was quiet, pacing as he awaited the connection. I

stood, my stomach in knots. I rushed over to Ethan, I needed answers just as much as he did, maybe more.

"What the fuck do you mean you can't get in touch with them! They left the facility hours ago; they are supposed to be at the estate!" he barked.

"They never made it to the estate?!" Ethan asked; panic filled his tone.

"I need all fucking resources, now! Find my fucking daughter! Find her, now! I'm on my way!" Ethan hollered.

My heart dropped hearing his words.

"We need to go!" Ethan said, more to Larry than to me.

"Get the cleaning crew in here now. All guns disposed and I want no trace of a body, he goes in the barrel. Burn the weapons, wipe everything in here down from top to bottom. No traces. This is high profile; everyone will be looking for him. No fuck ups," Ethan ordered.

Ethan grabbed my arm and turned to rush us out of the room. I pulled back, aggressively causing my body to jerk away from his. I needed answers, something, he needed to tell me something.

"What happened?! Where is she?!" I yelled at him.

He turned to me; anger and sorrow filled his eyes.

"I don't know. She is missing, someone took her," he confirmed.

My entire being stiffened as the world stopped, where was my daughter and who took her! Did I just kill the only person who knew where to find my baby girl?

THE END OF UNVEILED: BOOK ONE

Letter to my younger self . . .

There are no words to express how proud I am of you for completing this dream. This has been your dream since age ten when you first picked up a fiction novel and began writing on forum blogs. You finally did it! We did it! I did it!

Oftentimes, you doubt yourself and tell yourself that you are not good enough, but you are. You are resilient, beautiful, smart, creative, and you can do anything you put your mind to. This novel serves as physical proof that there is nothing you cannot do. Keep going, we are just getting started. Novel after novel we will inspire young girls and authors the same way you were once inspired. Always remember, hold your head up, your crown is tilting Queen!

This is our journey Celsi-Leigh and we are just getting started.